Marriage Law Defence Union

Tracts

Volume 1

Marriage Law Defence Union

Tracts
Volume 1

ISBN/EAN: 9783337399405

Printed in Europe, USA, Canada, Australia, Japan

Cover: Foto ©Andreas Hilbeck / pixelio.de

More available books at **www.hansebooks.com**

TRACTS

ISSUED BY THE

MARRIAGE LAW DEFENCE UNION.

Vol. I.—SCRIPTURAL.

PUBLISHED AT THE OFFICE OF
THE MARRIAGE LAW DEFENCE UNION,
1 KING STREET, WESTMINSTER, LONDON.

PRICE TWO SHILLINGS.

1889.

TO meet the convenience of those who wish
to have the Religious grounds for opposing
the legalisation of Marriage with a Deceased
Wife's Sister, and those of a Social and Political
nature, more handily arranged for separate
reference, these two Volumes are now issued.

As, frequently, in one Tract all the various
reasons for resisting the change have been set
forth it was not possible to make either volume
treat solely of its own topic, but it is hoped
that no argument on the one ground has been
given solely in the other volume.

In the Table of Contents is specified what
each Tract contains and the page where it
begins. An Index at the end of each volume
gives assistance in finding where and by whom
the various arguments are stated.

To those who desire further to study particular points, we commend the various works
of which a list will be found at the end of either
volume.

CONTENTS—VOL. I.

Marriage Law Defence Union Tracts.
No. I.

OFFICE: 1 KING STREET, WESTMINSTER, S.W.

What the Bishop of Lincoln says;

*As addressed to the Clergy and Laity of his Diocese at
his Triennial Visitation, Oct. 1882.*

THE question of *Marriage with a Deceased Wife's Sister* is
one which ought now to be carefully considered by everyone who holds any position of influence in society, and
especially by those who are appointed to declare God's will,
and to preach His Word, and to watch over immortal souls,
of which they will be required to give an account at the
Great Day.

It is not possible to overrate the importance of this
question for its own sake, and also because the determination of it affects the whole 'Table of Prohibited Degrees of
Kindred and Affinity' which now regulates marriage, on
which the happiness of English homes depends. No one is
able to foresee what changes may not be made in that
table if one of its prohibitions (viz., to marry a wife's
sister) is abrogated. We know that in other countries, such
as Germany, the change *has been* followed by others, and
none can tell where these changes will stop.

The urgency of considering this question is also evident
from the fact that, whereas in the year 1880 the number of
votes in the House of Lords for removing the restriction
was 90, in this year it amounted to 128, and was less only
by four than the number of the votes for maintaining the

prohibition. And there can be little doubt that if the Bill for abolishing the restriction had not been negatived by this narrow majority in the House of Lords, it would have been carried in the other House of Parliament.

We must therefore be prepared for a renewal of the struggle in a short time.

I do not underrate the argument against this measure from *social considerations*, and I have often dwelt on it formerly.* But this argument has little weight with those whose interests and passions are in favour of the proposed change; and every succeeding year diminishes—not the force of the argument—but the chance of its success.

The appeal made to men's feelings on behalf of the large and increasing number of innocent children, the issue of these marriages, who are now under a ban of illegitimacy, has great power to move their tender compassion. They are swayed also by the fact that one after another the Legislative bodies of our English Colonies, and our English and Scotch Municipal Corporations—which were formerly opposed to the change, and can hardly be said to ignore 'social considerations'—have pronounced in favour of the relaxation of the law. Germany and America have done the same.

The appeal also to 'natural instincts' will be equally fruitless. This is evident from the practice of the most civilised nations of antiquity. Among the Greeks and Romans their principal deity, Jupiter, was said by them to have married his own sister. Ptolemy Philadelphus, the celebrated King of Egypt, did the same. The Persians did not scruple to marry their own daughters, mothers, and sisters.

If also it be objected—as it is justly—that there is *no*

* Diocesan Addresses, 1873, 1876, 1878; Address to Diocesan Conference, 1880; Occasional Sermons in Westminster Abbey, No. 55, preached in 1859.

principle in the present proposal which would allow a man to marry his wife's sister, and that it will be followed by other relaxations in the law, the objector may be fairly challenged to substitute some other principle of his own. And when pressed to do so, what will he do? He will fall back on the 'Table of Degrees.' But he will find it impossible to maintain that table on the basis of 'social considerations,' or of 'natural instincts,' or even of long prescription.

To speak plainly, the only sound basis on which that table can be maintained is that on which its own framers placed it, namely, *Holy Scripture*. Look at its title. It calls itself 'A Table of Kindred and Affinity wherein whosoever are related are forbidden in *Scripture* and our *Laws* to marry together.' And in our Canons of 1603, Canon 99, which refers to that table, the Church of England thus speaks : 'No persons shall marry within the degrees prohibited by the *Laws of God*, and expressed in a Table set forth by Authority in the year of our Lord God 1563 ; and all marriages so made and contracted shall be adjudged incestuous and unlawful.'

Let me therefore ask this question—Are we wiser than the Church of England? Or shall we be guilty of the inconsistency of going to the Church of England for her 'Table of Degrees,' and yet abandon the basis (that of Scripture) on which that table is grounded by the Church? Such a course as that would not be found to do much good to us, or to our cause.

I will not do you the injustice to suppose that you need to be reminded that the eighteenth chapter of the Book of Leviticus, from which that table is derived (either by express transcription, or by logical inference) is *no part of the Levitical Law as such*, but is a Marriage Code promulgated to *all nations* by God Himself, Who exterminated the Canaanites (who knew nothing of the Levitical Law) for violating that Code.

Nor need I take up much of your time in proving that the framers of that 'Table of Degrees' were quite right in declaring that marriage with a deceased wife's sister is prohibited, not in a single verse, but in the general framework of the Code in that chapter.

That Code expressly forbids a man to marry certain near *kinswomen of his wife.* It forbids him to marry his *wife's daughter* and his *wife's grand-daughter.* And why? Because they are his wife's near kinswomen (Levit. xviii. 17). And surely her *sister* is also her 'near kinswoman.' Indeed a *sister* is expressly called a 'near *kinswoman*' of her brother and her sister in verses 12 and 13. And therefore it is perfectly clear that this Code forbids a man to marry his wife's sister. Accordingly our Church has declared in her 'Table of Degrees' that a man many not marry his wife's sister ; and she pronounces, on the authority of God's Word, such a marriage to be unlawful and incestuous.

Nor is this all. Not only the Church of England, but the Church Universal, to which Christ promised His presence (Matt. xxviii. 20) and the gift of the Holy Spirit 'to teach her, and to guide her into all truth' (John xiv. 26 ; xvi. 13), condemned these marriages. Not a single authority in favour of marriage with a wife's sister can be adduced for fourteen hundred years after Christ.

Yet further. Christ Himself has plainly condemned such marriages. He says that by marriage man and woman become one flesh (Matt. xix. 5 ; Mark x. 7). Consequently a man's wife's sister is as his own sister ; and he might as well marry his own sister as his wife's sister.

This saying of Christ has by some been·regarded as

superseding the Code promulgated in the Old Testament in the eighteenth chapter of Leviticus. But this is a mistake. It does indeed strongly confirm that Code ; but it is to be construed with it. For if we were to dispense with *that Code*, we should not know *where to stop* in the series of prohibitions of marriage, either by reason of consanguinity or of affinity. One of the speakers who supported the Bill (in the recent debate in the House of Lords) said that while he could not bring himself to vote against the marriage relations by *affinity*, such as that of man with his wife's sister, he condemned all marriages of *blood-relations*, such as *first cousins*.

Another objector may say, since according to Christ's words man and wife are one flesh, how can you justify a marriage of a man with *any* relative of his wife? Where are you to stop?

What is the answer to these objections? None can be given by those who abandon or disparage the eighteenth chapter of Leviticus. And why? Because that chapter *defines the limit* of prohibitions. No prohibition in it is extended *beyond* the *third degree* of relationship, either by consanguinity—such as cousins who are related in the *fourth* degree*—or affinity. This is what gives a special value to that Code, which no other document in the world possesses. And our '*Table of Degrees*' being rightly grounded on that Code, and not *going beyond it*, nor *falling short of it*, is,† in fact, as its title indicates, a declaration of God's Law on Marriage.

* The degrees in this case are counted by ascending from one cousin to the common ancestor (the grandfather or grandmother), and then by descending from that ancestor to the other cousin. And so the degrees are *four* on marriage of cousins. See Hooker, iii.–ix. 2.

† This is clearly pointed out by the late Lord Chancellor Hatherley in his excellent letter to the present Archbishop of Dublin, then Dean

6

To sum up what has been said. If we disparage the Scriptural argument, and abandon the foundation on which our wise and religious forefathers based our Marriage Code as expressed in our Table of Prohibited Degrees, then we shall be hastening on the change in the law which has been made by other nations, and is now urgently demanded by many powerful advocates among ourselves. We shall be giving a force to that demand which nothing will be able to resist.

But if we hold fast to that Scriptural foundation, we shall not fail of success; or if we fail, we shall fail gloriously. We shall not have been accomplices in a bad cause, but martyrs in a good one.

True it is that Germany has made the change which is now demanded of many in England. True it is that America has made it. But is the social and domestic condition of Germany or America one that England can envy or desire for herself? In those countries, incestuous marriages,* conjugal unfaithfulness, and facility of divorce are

---

of Westminster. London, 1869. In page 37 he lays down the following propositions :

I. 'The Code of prohibited unions contained in the eighteenth chapter of Leviticus is *binding on all men.*

II. 'The general guiding rule is laid down in verse 6 of that chapter, which prohibits approaching to anyone that is near of kin.

III. 'Nearness of kin is there explained by several examples, *none of which go beyond the third degree*; and such examples include relationship by *affinity and by consanguinity* without *distinction.* The marriage of a cousin is *beyond* the third degree.'

A cheap Tract on the subject has been written by the Rev. Thomas Vincent (No. 16 of this series; price one penny), which may be recommended for general distribution.

* For example, in Germany a man may marry his sister-in-law; and a woman may marry her brother-in-law; and a man may marry his niece, and a woman may marry her nephew. In the State of New

now rife, and are producing consequences which we may well shrink from describing, and even from contemplating. True it is also, that many of our Municipal Corporations in England and Scotland ask for the change. But the question is not what men desire, but what God commands. The question is not what is pleasing to the nations of this world, but what is right and true in the sight of Him Who is the Arbiter of the destinies of nations, and in Whose sight 'the nations are but as a drop in a bucket, and as small dust in the balance, and Who taketh up the isles as a very little thing' (Isaiah xl. 15), and before Whose judgment seat all nations will be gathered (Matt. xxv. 32).

Hitherto the Truth in this vital matter, having been banished from many other countries, and even from many of our own English Colonies, has found a shelter in England. Hitherto, thank God, it has found refuge in the House of Lords. And if the House of Lords had done no other service to our country in this age, it would be entitled to our great gratitude for this benefit. Will England forfeit this glorious privilege, and noble prerogative? Will she surrender her own Law, which is God's Law, and sit down as a learner at the feet of those which have made havoc with the Divine Code of Marriage, and are now reaping a miserable harvest of their own sin? Will she sacrifice that Divine Law, which, when duly observed, has hitherto preserved our domestic purity and happiness, and made England to be the land of pure and happy homes? Is our own national condition such, that we should now venture to pro-

York a man may marry his father's or mother's sister, or his brother's or sister's daughter. A father and son may have the same wife in succession. See the work of H. W. J. Thiersch, *das Verbot der Ehe* (Nördlingen, 1869) ; and Mr. Bach's evidence before the Royal Commissioners on Marriage.

voke God's indignation against us by violations of that Law of Marriage, which He has set before us in His Holy Word, together with terrible denunciations of His fierce wrath against those nations of Canaan who had been guilty of breaking it, and with solemn warnings to us of similar and worse chastisements, if we, who have so much clearer knowledge than they had, imitate their example by violating it?

And you, my reverend brethren, remember this, I entreat you. To each one of you God says, 'I have set thee a watchman; therefore thou shalt hear the word at My mouth, and warn others from Me. When I say unto the wicked, O wicked man, thou shalt surely die; if thou dost not speak to warn the wicked from his way, that wicked man shall die in his iniquity; *but his blood will I require at thy hand.'* (Ezekiel xxxiii. 7, 8.) If you do not warn your people against contracting these marriages, which God forbids, you will be accountable to Him for them. But if you bear your testimony faithfully and courageously against them, then, whatever change may be made in the law by the temporal power, you will have delivered your own soul (Ezekiel xxxiii. 9), and you may save their souls from the sin and misery of contracting them, and you will not be accountable for the sore distress and anguish of mind which all faithful Priests will feel when persons who have contracted these marriages present themselves for Holy Communion. You will not be responsible for the contradiction between the law of the Church and that of the State; and for the conflict, and perhaps the disruption, which may then ensue between the temporal and spiritual powers. And you will have the inexpressible comfort of having done your duty to men and to God, and will receive your reward hereafter at the Great Day.

To be had also of E. W. ALLEN, 4 *Ave Maria Lane, E.C.*
Price One Halfpenny.

Spottiswoode & Co., Printers, New-street Square, London.

Marriage Law Defence Union Tracts.

No. II.

OFFICE : 1 KING STREET, WESTMINSTER, S.W.

What the Bishop of Exeter says

At his Diocesan Conference.

I SHOULD like to say a few words with regard to my own opinion on this matter. Of course, I have been compelled to form an opinion, and I have formed that opinion very slowly, and not without, I confess, very considerable reluctance, because I have always felt, with very great sense of its weight and importance, the argument which Lord Fortescue has pressed upon us. This argument, it seems to me, cannot be set aside without the most serious consideration, and the setting of it aside can only be justified by full and formed convictions ; and while for many years I have looked a good deal into this matter, and studied it to the best of my ability, I have held back from forming any opinion at all, because I wished to be quite sure of myself. I think it is a subject on which any man who is to take part in leading in any degree the public opinion, either of Christians or of others, ought to ascertain his own convictions, and the ground of those convictions, before he expresses himself in public at all. There have been two occasions on which I have been present when the matter was debated in the House of Lords I did not on either occasion have an opportunity of saying anything on this matter. On the first occasion, indeed, I was very glad to be relieved from saying anything about it. On the last occasion I wished very much to speak, and I certainly should have spoken if an opening had been given. But the division was taken rather unexpectedly, and I had not, therefore, the opportunity then which I desire to use now—in some small degree, because there is not time for a long speech on the subject—of giving an account of the reasons which had convinced myself. I do not mean that my reasons are different from those which actuate a very large number of persons, but the effect of them on my mind was exceedingly slow. Before I say anything further, may I ask you to do me one kindness, and that is, that, suppose I say anything you agree with, you will accept it with silence and not with applause. I find myself, then, driven to the conclusion that it would be wrong to alter the law. I am very unwilling to come to that conclusion, because I feel so strongly how very serious a matter it is to interfere with the liberty of all Christian men and women in matters of this kind. I feel this most deeply, but it seems to me that in all these cases the one consideration must be the good of the Christian community ; and the great guide in judging what is best for a Christian community must be found in the best application you can make of the directions given in God's Word. I cannot escape from the conclusion that it was intended by God's Word to put a man and his wife in these respects precisely on the same footing. I cannot

3

escape from the conclusion that this was included in what our Lord meant ; and I look upon the law of Leviticus as not, indeed, laying this down, but as so distinctly and plainly corroborating it that, when the two are taken together, there is no other way of interpreting God's Word that can be made consistent with itself. We are taught in the New Testament, as plainly as we are taught anything, as it seems to me, that in the Old Law we should look, not indeed for the immediate and precise directions for the rule of our conduct, but for the principle and spirit which is to govern us ; and that when we find these old directions before us, we should ask ourselves, what is the spirit in which these are written, and how do they bear on us? What, then, do I find is the very fundamental idea, as I may say, of these prohibitions of marriage? It seems to me unmistakable that the purpose and object of them always has been to protect the purity of the family. It is, as a mere matter of fact, quite certain that there is nothing which so surely protects the purity of the domestic circle, as the impossibility of marriage within it ; that the impossibility of a marriage with a sister by blood is the real bar which, in cases of temptation, protects the family from impurity absolutely without restraint, and that anything which would interfere with the prohibition of the marriage of those who are nearly related by blood would very seriously affect the purity of the home and the morality of all Christian people. And it seems to me further that, in the prohibitions of marriage within near degrees of affinity, the case is precisely the same. It is intended to throw over the wife's family precisely the same shield as that which is thrown over the man's own family. For, precisely as this bars a man from possible wrong as between himself and his own family, so, too, there should be some bar to prevent all possibility of wrong between him and the members of his wife's family And it is impossible in this matter to confine ourselves to the question as to what is to happen after a wife is dead. The wife is still living—shall it be possible that a man should be allowed to entertain those feelings towards her sister which may end in marriage afterwards ? and yet, if marriage be then allowed, such feelings, such temptations, such natural impulses of the flesh are absolutely impossible to prevent. I know of no other way by which they can be restrained than by the law of the Church as it now stands. Of course this is only one particular instance, and it is proposed to relax the law only in one particular case, but we all know in matters of this sort that changes always come by degrees. There are very many men who now advocate this marriage who would be shocked at the idea of a man marrying his step-daughter, and who would feel at once that if you allow such a thing as a man to marry his step-daughter after her mother's death, you might be putting a terrible temptation in the man's way during the mother's life. There would soon be no horror in some men's minds to prevent wrong feelings from rising and growing within. If a man does allow such feelings to grow up within him, because he may look forward in some future time to gratify those feelings, the consequence is, this step-daughter, necessarily under his authority and necessarily brought into close familiarity, is robbed of her natural protection. And the sense of this is strong enough at present to make the great majority of us feel that there is something horrible in allowing a marriage, first with the woman and then with her daughter. But if you begin by altering the law in this particular, how long will this horror last? You may depend upon it that by-and-by a great many men will begin to question each restraint in its turn. Soon a large number will feel that they have no principle to guide them at all, and that this is a mere question of expediency; and inasmuch as it is a mere question of expediency, we have no right to impose restraint on one another. At the present, no doubt, there is a strong natural instinct against the marriage of a man with his own mother. It is awful to think of. The marriage of a man with his own blood sister is fearful. But this instinctive protection of our domestic purity, how far does it go if we begin to pare the edges off? Why, there have been such things as marriages between uncles and nieces by blood. Are we to sanction this? They have been allowed by dispensations in the Roman Catholic system; and, of course, if such marriages are to be possible on this condition, where are they to stop? You allow such marriages—we don't allow them now, thank God—but you allow them, and then comes a doubt about other marriages. It seems to me that it is imperative to require that, before you make any change in the law of marriage, you should provide that the change shall be made, not in detail, but by a definite rule, a definite principle, which will show precisely where you stop; because otherwise it is inevitably certain that these things creep on and on, and we know that in these matters the moral sense of people, left without any kind of restraint, cannot be trusted long, even in Christian countries where we should expect that purity would be maintained on Christian grounds. I do not mean that the passing of this law would immediately be followed by great impurity, but I do mean to say this, that the passing of this law would tend to introduce the possibility and the probability of many impurities, seductions, and adulteries of a new and peculiar kind, such as adultery with the wife's nearest relations. Is it not awful to think of the added guilt of such adultery? I know if we could we would prevent adultery altogether, but surely we ought to endeavour to prevent the possibility of a new kind of adultery like this, which, of course, from the nature of it is far more terrible to the wife that is sinned against than any ordinary adultery can be. I cannot help feeling that the maintenance of the present law is required if we desire to maintain the sanctity of the marriage tie ; and, much as I feel the force of what has been said on the other side, I cannot bring myself to any other conclusion. I do not think that I have come to that conclusion from any desire whatever to agree with other people who have already come to the same conclusion. I do not think it is a mere professional feeling in the slightest degree. I do not think I have been moved by finding the great majority of my brethren on that side. I do not feel that I should flinch, if I had come to the opposite conclusion, from saying so fearlessly here. But I have been compelled to it by the course of my own study and consideration of the subject ; and although I cannot but admit a great deal of force in what Lord Fortescue has so ably said in regard to marriage, considered simply as a civil institution

and without any reference to the law of God, I cannot consent to a change of the law which from the nature of the
case must touch it as a religious institution also.   Even considering marriage as a civil institution, yet, viewing the
present law, as I do, as necessary for the defence of domestic
purity, even then I say that the liberty of the individual
ought to be restrained for the general good.   It is quite true
that this is a matter which concerns us in our own individual and personal relations, but we cannot leave out
of sight the effect of legislation upon general morals, and
I do believe, as I believe anything, that it is impossible to
prevent mischief coming out of such relaxation as this.
Now I have said what I have said because I thought it a
duty, and I am grateful to you for having heard me in
silence, because it is a subject which I do not like to have
handled with either applause or disapprobation.   It seems
to me too deeply and too nearly to touch the most vital
of all questions that Christians can handle—the purity of
the body.   I do not hesitate to acknowledge that there are
men who take the other view—men who are really good,
really high-minded, high-principled men, and I feel strongly
the pain of differing from them, but it is not a matter upon
which hesitation appears to me to be possible when conviction has been attained.   Most deeply do I mourn over
the mischief which has been done by the Roman Catholic
Church in this matter—for the mischief began there.   When
the integrity of the law was broken down by dispensations,
of course it necessarily followed that there would be those
who would be ready to grant themselves dispensations ; nor
can I see how it is possible to maintain that in matters of

8

this kind, if dispensations are to be granted at all, it would not be most in accordance with sound Christian principles to leave to every man's own conscience the granting of the dispensation. The mischief has been done—and I mourn over it as a mischief which is most serious in its character—and has had consequences which certainly were never intended by those who began it. Of course, as things are it may be the case that the law may be passed, and the rule hitherto governing our marriages will, in that case, be relaxed. What will be the result is in God's hands, but those who feel how serious the matter is ought, I think, to do their best to impress their convictions upon public opinion generally, and, if possible, prevent all that seems to be so immediately threatened. Perhaps, if we had been somewhat more careful to explain the doctrine of the Church as soon as ever it was first questioned ; perhaps, if the clergy had earlier taken it in hand—we might have done much to make people understand better than they seem to do now what is the ground on which the present law is maintained. Even yet I think we may do something. At any rate it seems to me that we ought to do what we can. I will now put the question, and may I ask you, simply as a matter of feeling, to vote without any further demonstration of opinion ?

To be had also of E W. ALLEN, 4 *Ave Maria Lane*, E.C.
Price One Halfpenny.

Spottiswoode & Co., Printers, New-street Square, London.

Marriage Law Defence Union Tracts.
No. III.

OFFICE : 1 KING STREET, WESTMINSTER, S.W.

What the Archdeacon of Middlesex says.

' A Scripture Argument against permitting Marriage with a Wife's Sister, in " A Clergyman's Letter to a Friend," addressed by Dr. Hessey to that Friend in 1849.' Revised 1883.

MY DEAR FRIEND,

A QUESTION has been mooted lately upon which we have not been happy enough to think alike. It is a very important one in every point of view, religious, social, and personal. Were it not so I should have been content to differ from you and to retain my own opinion without endeavouring to influence that of another. You will at once perceive that I allude to the question (alas ! that it should have become such), 'Whether a man may marry his wife's sister or no ? ' Your own feelings, you confessed to me, are, that you would not think of entering upon such a connexion yourself—that you felt something more than a dislike to it. But, at the same time, with your characteristic regard for the wishes of others, and with an impression that the law of God says nothing upon the subject, and that the Table appended to our Prayer Book is merely an ecclesiastical institution, you do not like to stand in the way of the happiness of persons who might desire the law to be changed.

It is impossible not to estimate highly an amiable unwillingness to give pain. But there are occasions on which a higher principle does and ought to step in. And this is the case here. The law of God does take notice of the subject ; and, therefore, as personally we should part with whatever is most dear to us—'an eye' or 'a right hand'—rather than break its enactments, so we should be anxious to use our influence with others to prevent even the least violation of it. Let us therefore calmly and quietly consider the subject together.

The Table which the Church has put into our hands is headed thus : 'A Table of Kindred and Affinity, wherein whosoever are related are forbidden by Scripture and our laws to marry together.' The marriage of a man with his wife's sister is prohibited in this Table. And the Table professes to be founded upon Scripture. If it is founded upon Scripture its prohibitions must be part of the Moral law which is binding upon Christians still, although the Political enactments given from God by Moses are not binding upon us. And if it is part of the Moral law we must neither break it ourselves nor, as far as in us lieth, allow it to be transgressed by others.

Where then is the chapter to be discovered upon which the Table is founded? It is the 18th chapter of *Leviticus*, for although the same degrees are interdicted in the 20th chapter, they occur there in connexion, not with the simple announcement, 'It is wickedness,' but with punishments peculiar to the Jewish constitution annexed to them. I think I shall be able to prove to you, *first*, that *Leviticus* xviii. contains an enunciation of precepts of the Moral law, not merely of precepts relating to the Jewish nation, and, *secondly*, that the prohibition of marriage with a wife's

3

sister fairly comes within the range of the precepts given in that chapter.

I begin by asserting that—*Leviticus* xviii. *contains an enunciation of precepts of the Moral law, not merely of precepts relating to the Jewish nation,* for—

1*stly.* The Israelites, whom we may suppose to represent the spiritual Israel, are warned at the commencement of the chapter against practising the abominations of the Egyptians, and of the Canaanites ; and the warning is repeated even more solemnly, so far as the Canaanites are concerned, at the conclusion of the chapter. Now neither of these nations could have transgressed the Jewish Political law. It had not yet been laid down ; and if it had, they had possessed no opportunities of becoming acquainted with it. Of course, therefore, they could not have been condemned or punished for transgressing it. Still they are condemned for trans-gressing the precepts mentioned in the chapter. Those precepts, then, must be a re-enactment of the principles of God's Moral law, which those nations might have known, and which they could and did transgress.

2*ndly.* If the chapter relates to the Jewish Political law at all, it must relate to it entirely. No distinction is dis-coverable in it by which the Moral and Political precepts can be separated. If some of them be Political, all must be Political, and therefore all must be abrogated, which no one will venture to affirm. If some of them be Moral, all must be Moral, and therefore all must be still binding upon Christians.

3*rdly.* Until the fifteenth century, the Church held the precepts of this chapter, which relate to marriage, to be Moral, and, therefore, not to be tampered with or reversed. And the most ancient Table of prohibited degrees founded upon the chapter was virtually the same as our own. I may add, that the first recorded instance of this degree being dispensed with took place in that

4

century * (Since that time the Church of Rome has held very close kindred or affinity to be no bar to the issuing of dispensations. But with such a monstrous assumption we have nothing to do.) It is true, that from the sixth to the fifteenth century the Table of forbidden degrees was much extended ; and it is true, also, that the degrees thus added beyond Scripture were frequently dispensed with. But they were dispensed with on the ground that they were merely ecclesiastical, not Scriptural, prohibitions ; whilst the degrees in our Table were never dispensed with, on the very ground that they were Moral precepts, and part of the unalterable Divine law.

I conclude, therefore, that *Leviticus* xviii. is part of the Moral law, and therefore binding upon Christians. Here is an analysis of its contents, as I believe they should be understood :—

Verses 1—5 contain general warnings against such transgressions of God's Moral law as were committed by the Egyptians and Canaanites.

Verses 6—17 contain a republication of the principles of God's Moral law, so far as marriages of persons connected already by consanguinity or affinity are concerned.

Verse 18 contains a republication of God's Moral law against polygamy. (It has nothing to do with the forbidden degrees, but *vide infra*, pp. 12 and 13.)

---

* The first pope who issued a ' licentia ducendae sororis prioris conjugis ' was, as Mr. Knight Watson has recently shown from Thomassinus and Baronius, Martin V. (1417-1431), with a view to settling difficulties as to the succession of Navarre. Alexander VI. (Borgia, 1492-1503) followed his example by granting a dispensation for the union of Emmanuel, King of Portugal, with his wife's sister, and afterwards to Ferdinand, King of Sicily, for a union with his aunt. Julius II. (1503-1513) issued a dispensation for the union of Henry VIII. with Catherine of Aragon, his deceased brother's wife. [*Note* 1883.]

5

Verse 20 contains a republication of God's Moral law against adultery.

Verse 21 forbids the burning of children to Moloch. Here idolatry is condemned ; and with it want of affection to offspring.

Verses 19, 22, 23, forbid certain grievous offences against nature, upon which we need not dwell.

The remainder of the chapter is a denunciation of God's wrath against those who had transgressed, or who should hereafter transgress, His Moral law in the things forbidden from verses 6 to 23 inclusive.

But it is time to enter upon our second question, ' *Is the marriage of a man with his wife's sister fairly included in the enactments of this chapter ?*'

I believe it is so included, and that it is to be found between verses 6—17.

1stly. Because the whole Church, till the fifteenth century, and our own Church for 350 years more, have thus understood the chapter.   And—

2ndly. Because a critical examination of the chapter from the 6th to the 17th verse leads me to the conclusion, that not merely the degree in question, but every degree in our Table is so contained, either expressly or by implication —*i.e.*, either in so many words, or by the laws of converse and analogy.   For instance, a nephew is forbidden in so many words to marry his aunt.   By the law of converse, an aunt may not marry her nephew.   By the law of analogy, as the relationship of uncle and niece is analogous to that of aunt and nephew, an uncle may not marry his niece.

On the first ground of belief, the Church's understanding of Scripture, I will not enter at present.   You will find it treated of at length in larger works ; but I will endeavour to explain to you, as briefly as I can, my second ground of belief.

The words of the chapter, *Leviticus* xviii. 6—17, are as follows :—

'6. None of you shall approach to any that is near of kin to him, to uncover their nakedness : I am the Lord. 7. The nakedness of thy father, or the nakedness of thy mother, shalt thou not uncover ; she is thy mother ; thou shalt not uncover her nakedness. 8. The nakedness of thy father's wife shalt thou not uncover ; it is thy father's nakedness. 9. The nakedness of thy sister, the daughter of thy father, or daughter of thy mother, whether she be born at home, or born abroad, even their nakedness thou shalt not uncover. 10. The nakedness of thy son's daughter, or of thy daughter's daughter, even their nakedness thou shalt not uncover ; for theirs is thine own nakedness. 11. The nakedness of thy father's wife's daughter, begotten of thy father, she is thy sister, thou shalt not uncover her nakedness. 12. Thou shalt not uncover the nakedness of thy father's sister ; she is thy father's near kinswoman. 13. Thou shalt not uncover the nakedness of thy mother's sister ; for she is thy mother's near kinswoman. 14. Thou shalt not uncover the nakedness of thy father's brother, thou shalt not approach to his wife : she is thine aunt. 15. Thou shalt not uncover the nakedness of thy daughter-in-law ; she is thy son's wife ; thou shalt not uncover her nakedness. 16. Thou shalt not uncover the nakedness of thy brother's wife : it is thy brother's nakedness. 17. Thou shalt not uncover the nakedness of a woman and her daughter, neither shalt thou take her son's daughter, or her daughter's daughter, to uncover her nakedness ; for they are her near kinswomen : it is wickedness.'

And here is the Table. I have quoted after each forbidden degree, the verse in which it is forbidden, in one of the ways which I have mentioned.

A Man may not marry his—

1. *Grandmother*	Verse 10 forbids a man to marry his grand-daughter ; therefore conversely a woman may not marry her grandfather ; therefore, analogously, a man may not marry his grandmother.
2. *Grandfather's Wife* ... .. } 3. *Wife's Grandmother* ... ...}	Both of these are considered to be grandmothers. Why? By analogy; because, in verse 8 a father's wife is looked upon as a mother ; and in verse 17 a wife's mother is not to be married.

7

A Man may not marry his—

4. *Father's Sister*	... ...	Verse 12 forbids this connexion in so many words.
5. *Mother's Sister*	... ...	Verse 13 forbids this connexion in so many words.
6. *Father's Brother's Wife* ...	...	Verse 14 forbids this connexion in so many words, and alludes generally to the connexion of a man with his aunt as an unlawful one.
7. *Mother's Brother's Wife* ... 8. *Wife's Father's Sister* ... 9. *Wife's Mother's Sister* ...	...⎫ ...⎬ ...⎭	Verse 14 forbids these connexions in the comprehensive terms 'she is thine aunt.'
10. *Mother*	...	Verse 7 forbids this connexion in so many words.
11. *Step-Mother*	...	Verse 8 forbids this connexion in so many words.
12. *Wife's Mother*	...	Verse 17 forbids this connexion in so many words—'No one is to marry a woman and her daughter.'
13. *Daughter*	...	Verse 7 forbids a man to marry his mother ; therefore, analogously, a woman may not marry her father ; and, therefore conversely, a man may not marry his daughter. Again, verse 10 forbids marriage with a daughter's daughter ; *à fortiori*, therefore, a man may not marry his daughter. Again, verse 17 forbids marriage with a wife's daughter ; *à fortiori*, therefore a man may not marry his own daughter.
14. *Wife's Daughter*	...	Verse 17 forbids this connexion in so many words—'No one is to marry a woman and her daughter.'
15. *Son's Wife*	...	Verse 15 forbids this connexion in so many words.
16. *Sister*	...	Verses 9 and 11 forbid this connexion in so many words.
17. *Wife's Sister*	...	Verse 16 forbids this by the law of analogy. It is said there that a man may not marry his brother's wife, *i.e.*, that a woman may not marry two brothers; analogously, a man may not marry two sisters, *i.e.*, he may not marry his wife's sister.

A Man may not marry his—

18. *Brother's Wife*	Verse 16 forbids this connexion in so many words.
19. *Son's Daughter*	Verse 10 forbids this connexion in so many words.
20. *Daughter's Daughter*	Verse 10 forbids this connexion in so many words.
21. *Son's Son's Wife* ... ... 22. *Daughter's Son's Wife*	Verse 10 forbids these connexions by implication, for these are considered grand-daughters; and if, in verse 8, a father's wife is looked upon as a mother, by analogy a son's son's wife, or a daughter's son's wife, should be looked upon as a grand-daughter.
23. *Wife's Son's Daughter* ... ... 24. *Wife's Daughter's Daughter* ...	Verse 17 forbids these connexions in so many words.
25. *Brother's Daughter* ... ... 26. *Sister's Daughter* ... ... 27. *Brother's Son's Wife* ... ... 28. *Sister's Son's Wife* ... ... 29. *Wife's Brother's Daughter* ... 30. *Wife's Sister's Daughter* ...	Verse 14 forbids these connexions by implication; for there it is said that a man may not marry his aunt; conversely, therefore a woman may not marry her nephew; and, therefore, by analogy, a man may not marry his niece.

A Woman may not marry with her—

1. *Grandfather*	Verse 10 forbids this connexion by implication. It is there said, that a man may not marry his grand-daughter; therefore, conversely, a woman may not marry her grandfather.
2. *Grandmother's Husband* ... ... 3. *Husband's Grandfather*	Both of these are to be considered as grandfathers. These cases are analogous to those of grandfather's wife and wife's grandmother.
4. *Father's Brother* ... ... 5. *Mother's Brother* ... ... 6. *Father's Sister's Husband* ... 7. *Mother's Sister's Husband* ... 8. *Husband's Father's Brother* ... 9. *Husband's Mother's Brother* ...	Verse 14 forbids a man to marry his aunt; therefore, by analogy, a woman may not marry her uncle.
10. *Father*	Verse 7 forbids a man to marry his mother; therefore, by analogy, a woman may not marry her father.

9

A Woman may not marry with her—

11. *Step-Father*	Verse 8 forbids a man to marry his step-mother ; therefore, by analogy, a woman may not marry her step-father.
12. *Husband's Father*	Verse 17 forbids a man to marry a woman and her daughter, *i.e.*, to marry his wife's mother ; therefore, by analogy, a woman may not marry her husband's father.
13. *Son*	Verse 7 forbids a man to marry his mother ; conversely, therefore, a woman may not marry her son.
14. *Husband's Son*	Verse 17 forbids a man to marry a woman and her daughter ; *i.e.*, to marry his wife's daughter ; therefore, by analogy, a woman may not marry her husband's son.
15. *Daughter's Husband*	Verse 15 forbids a man to marry his son's wife ; therefore, by analogy, a woman may not marry her daughter's husband.
16. *Brother*	Verses 9 and 11 forbid a man to marry his sister or half-sister ; therefore, by analogy, a woman may not marry her brother or half-brother.
17. *Husband's Brother*	Verse 16 forbids a man to marry his brother's wife ; in other words, two brothers may not marry the same woman ; conversely, a woman may not marry two brothers, *i.e.*, her husband's brother.
18. *Sister's Husband*	Verse 16 forbids this connexion by the law of analogy. It is said there that a woman may not marry two brothers ; by analogy, therefore, a man may not marry two sisters ; or, conversely, that two sisters may not marry the same man, *i.e.*, that a woman may not marry her sister's husband.
19. *Son's Son* ... ... 20. *Daughter's Son*	Verse 10 forbids a man to marry his grand-daughter ; by the law of analogy, therefore, a woman may not marry her grandson.

A Woman may not marry with her—

21.	*Son's Daughter's Husband*	...	Forbidden on the same grounds on which a man is forbidden to marry those who are considered his grand-daughters.
22.	*Daughter's Daughter's Husband*		

23.	*Husband's Son's Son*	... ...	Verse 17 forbids these connexions by analogy. A man may not marry his wife's son's daughter, or his wife's daughter's daughter; therefore, by analogy, a woman may not marry her husband's son's son, or her husband's daughter's son.
24.	*Husband's Daughter's Son*	... ...	

25.	*Brother's Son*	...	Verse 14 forbids these connexions by implication ; for if a man may not marry his aunt, conversely, an aunt may not marry her nephew.
26.	*Sister's Son*	...	
27.	*Brother's Daughter's Husband*	...	
28.	*Sister's Daughter's Husband*	...	
29.	*Husband's Brother's Son* ...	...	
30.	*Husband's Sister's Son* ...	...	

It appears from this examination, that every degree forbidden in the Table provided by the Church of England is forbidden either expressly, or by implication and fair inference in Scripture.

Some persons, however, boldly object to any inference whatever being allowed. They will have nothing forbidden unless it is set down in so many words. Now, let us see to what this will lead them.

1*stly*. It is not *said* that a father may not marry his daughter. *We infer* that to be unlawful thus : it is said that a son may not marry his mother ; conversely, *we infer* that a mother may not marry her son; and then, by analogy, *we infer* that a father may not marry his daughter. But this is a prohibition by inference ; it is not found in so many words.

2*ndly*. It is not *said* that an uncle may not marry his niece. *We infer* that to be unlawful thus : it is said that a nephew may not marry his aunt ; conversely, *we infer* that an aunt may not marry her nephew; and then, by analogy, *we infer* that an uncle may not marry his niece.

3*rdly*. In the same way, *it is inferred* that the marriage of a man with his wife's sister is unlawful. It is said that a man may not marry his brother's wife, *i.e.*, that a woman may not marry her husband's brother, *i.e.*, two men who are brothers ; and this case is exactly analogous to the prohibition of a man's marriage to his wife's sister, *i.e.*, two women who are sisters.

Those, therefore, who will admit nothing but what is set down in so many words to be Scripture, are brought to this ; they must either allow all these inferences, or none of them ; *i.e.*, if they allow a man to marry his wife's sister, they must allow an uncle to marry his niece, and even a father to marry his daughter.

There is another strong reason for the admission of inferences. The prohibitions on the woman's side of the Table are all of them of this character. The restrictions upon marriage in the chapter of *Leviticus* are addressed to men. *We infer* the woman's side from what *is said* to men. But, after all, the introductory words of verse 7 may be received as comprehending the whole matter. ‘ None of you shall approach to any that is near of kin to him,’ are the words of our translation. The original means literally ‘ flesh of his flesh,’ which is a very strong expression : let us consider its purport. It includes, as is evident from the instances supplied, connexions by consanguinity, that is, relationships radiating from father or mother ; and connexions of affinity, that is, relationships radiating from husband or wife. Indeed, husband and wife are emphatically designated in Scripture* ‘ one flesh ’ ; nay, so mysteriously are they one, that their union is even to supersede that of blood, and is selected by our Lord to be an emblem of His union with His Church. One would think, therefore, that the sister of his wife is quite as nearly connected with a man as his own sister or half-sister ; or, at any rate, that if the brother of the husband is forbidden to the wife as a lawful

* *Gen.* ii. 23. And Adam said, This is now bone of my bones, and flesh of my flesh. 24. Therefore shall a man leave his father and his mother, and shall cleave unto his wife : and they shall be one flesh.

alliance, the sister of the wife is equally forbidden to the husband.

The result, therefore, of a close examination of *Lev.* xviii. 6–17, both inclusive, is this : that any relaxation on the part of the Church of the rule by which marriage with a wife's sister is prohibited would be a contravention of Scripture—and that, not merely of Scripture as interpreted by all Christendom till the fifteenth century, and by our own Church for 350 years more, but of Scripture as interpreted by the ordinary laws of criticism and common sense. I need not insist on the arguments, that it would break up families— produce jealousies and heartburnings—and limit that affectionate intercourse which at present exists without suspicion ; nor need I refute the falsehood which has been imposed upon the world, that such a relaxation is loudly called for in England. These topics are beside my purpose. I set out by endeavouring to warn you, my dear friend, against partaking in other men's sins, and other men's dangers ; for surely it is a sin to break God's law ; and surely it is dangerous to expose oneself to the penalties denounced on those who transgress it.

But here you will perhaps remind me that you have heard the 18th verse of *Lev.* xviii. adduced more than once as an argument for the lawfulness of marriage with a wife's sister. For my own part, I conceive that this verse has nothing to do with the matter, especially if the case in question has been, as I suppose it to have been, already decided in the earlier part of the chapter. The words of verse 18 are as follows— ' Neither shalt thou take a wife to her sister to vex her, to uncover her nakedness, beside the other in her life-time.' It is assumed by some persons, that this verse is correctly translated, and that its meaning is, that a wife's sister may not be married during a wife's life, but that she may be married after a wife's death. But this interpretation, to say the least of it, is not very easily gained from the text. It seems strange to find the marriage of a man with his wife's sister during the lifetime of his wife, forbidden, not directly and by itself, but in a precept permitting that connexion at some future time. I have little doubt, therefore, that the margin of our Bibles which gives ‘one wife to another,’ supplies at once the true translation of the words represented by ‘a wife to her sister,’ and a key to the true meaning of the passage. The verse will then stand thus—‘ Neither shalt thou take one wife to another,* to vex her, to uncover her nakedness, beside the other in her lifetime’—and thus too it will furnish, as we supposed, a prohibition of polygamy—a practice which prevailed to as great an extent as marriage within the forbidden degrees, or adultery, or the unnatural offences also mentioned in the chapter, amongst the Egyptians and Canaanites.

With this interpretation of verse 18, which I may tell you has been sanctioned not merely by the translators of the Bible but by other Hebrew scholars of considerable eminence, you will, I hope, be satisfied. You mentioned another objection when we last met, to which I replied at once. It is almost too absurd to repeat ; but I know that in matters like the present, objections start up again when the answer is out of reach. You told me that some have urged that the prohibitions from verse 6 to verse 17, relate not to the marriage of one person with two successively, but to illicit intercourse of one person with another. To this I

* The words which are to be translated according to the margin of our authorised version, ‘One wife to another,’ appear to have been a proverbial expression among the Hebrews to denote ‘one thing to another of the same kind.’ In *Ezek.* iii. 13 they are translated ‘one another.’ ‘The wings of the living creatures that touched (or kissed) *one another.*’ In *Exod.*. xxvi. 3, 5, 6, 17, they occur five times in reference to the coupling of the curtains of the tabernacle, ‘*one to another.*’ In *Ezek.* i. 9 and 23, they are again used of the joining of the wings of the cherubim, ‘*one to another,*’ or, ‘*the one toward another.*’

replied, and reply again, that if only illicit intercourse of near relatives is intended to be forbidden, the chapter admits by implication that marriage between those same relatives, father and daughter, aunt and nephew, would be lawful, which would be too revolting to be thought of.

I come now to an objection which has assumed a very specious form, and has probably perplexed you as it has perplexed others.

It has been said, Surely the prohibition against marriage with a wife's sister cannot be part of the Moral law, cannot be irreversible ; for we find that marriage with a husband's brother was, under certain circumstances, not only permitted but even enjoined by God. It is then asked, May we not suppose that the law against marrying a wife's sister admits of similar relaxation ? A little consideration will clear up the difficulty. In the first place, the passage referred to (*Deut.* xxv. 5) is a special provision of the Jewish Political law, which had reference to the Jewish law of inheritance. In case an elder brother died childless, his next brother had liberty, and some kind of obligation lying upon him, to take his brother's wife, and raise up seed to his brother. God, in this instance, but in no other, dispensing, by a particular enactment, with His general Moral law against marrying a brother's wife. The Author of all law had surely a right to do this. In the same way He dispensed, on other occasions, with the observance of other Moral precepts ; the prohibition of killing, for instance. But none of His creatures may so dispense with His precepts. Nor does a particular exception, granted under particular circumstances, at all impair the authority of the general law. Besides, the circumstances which rendered the exception necessary have passed away ; and with them have passed away also the peculiar enactment permitting or enjoining the marriage of a man to his brother's wife, and, indeed, the whole of the Jewish Political law.

15

In the second place. Let it be granted for a moment that a man may still marry his brother's wife, in case his brother has died childless, and that the Moral law is capable of being thus far still dispensed with, one does not see that this will help persons very much in their design of dispensing with the Moral law in reference to marrying a sister's husband. Analogy would only go so far as to sanction such an alliance when the sister died childless. This will scarcely meet their case, who urge that a widower, *not childless*, but *with children*, requires a mother's care for his offspring— that a wife's sister is the best person to fill the deceased mother's place, and that she cannot do so without becoming a wife also.

In reference, therefore, to this objection, I conclude that the particular exception permitted to the Jews for a season does in no way invalidate the eternal and general Moral law of God against marrying a brother's wife, much less the analogous general Moral law against marrying a sister's husband.

I now conclude. Pray think upon what I have written. We both of us agree, that *if* the precept prohibiting marriage with a wife's sister is part of God's Moral law, it is most stringently binding upon us. I have endeavoured to show by various considerations that it *is* such. It would be no real kindness to any one to give him licence to commit sin. It would in the end be cruelty to him, and also to ourselves. That we may be delivered from 'contempt of God's word and commandment' is the prayer of

My dear Friend,

Yours most sincerely,

J. A. HESSEY.

London,

    March 28th, 1849.

    [*February 1st*, 1883.]

P.S.—The foregoing Letter was suggested by an esteemed friend saying, 'I think that the Scripture argument against marriage with a wife's sister fails. I am opposed to a relaxation of the present law, on personal and social grounds ; but I am not sure that I am justified in insisting on a prohibition which does not clearly appear in Scripture.' The writer believes that the Scripture argument does *not* fail ; and he has endeavoured to state it with all possible clearness. If anything, he has dwelt too much on points which may seem to some minds self-evident. But he can fairly say, that he has found even the most simple points relating to the subject full of difficulties to those with whom he has from time to time come in contact. Persons who are not accustomed to consider such topics, will read even verse 16 of *Leviticus* xviii., which prohibits the marriage of a man with his brother's wife, over and over again, without perceiving that its drift is that a woman may not marry two husbands who are brothers ; and hence they fancy that the exception in case of a brother dying childless, under which the instance mentioned in the New Testament comes, is the only mention made of that sort of alliance. No wonder then that they are slow in discovering the analogous prohibition of a man's marrying two women who are sisters. This will justify the introduction of the Table

Spottiswoode & Co., Printers, New-street Square, London.

Marriage Law Defence Union Tracts.
No. IV.
OFFICE: 1 KING STREET, WESTMINSTER, S.W.

What Scotchmen say

On the Law of Marriage.

IT is again suggested that the Legislature should alter the Marriage Law of this country. The first step proposed is to legalise marriage with a deceased wife's sister.

Now, what is the nature of our existing marriage law?

Every one will see that in this important matter one would expect clear, simple principles : one would expect to find a plain, strong line, easily discerned and easily applied, fencing what is lawful from what is not lawful. If some marriages are to be allowed and some forbidden, men have a right to claim that there shall be a plain rule, grounded on a plain reason, separating the forbidden from the allowed.

1. The existing law, founded on Scripture,* forbids, first of all, marriage between *certain blood relations*. We are accustomed to count these up as so many different relations in which marriage is forbidden,—as, for instance (to take only the practical cases), that a man may not marry his mother, daughter, sister, aunt, niece, &c. ; nor a woman her father, son, brother, uncle, nephew, &c. But all the cases are shut up in one short rule, viz., No marriage is lawful in which the man is marrying a descendant of

---

* For example, on the Divine Law of incest in Lev. xviii., which cannot have been designed for the Jews only, since the nations which preceded them are expressly condemned for the violation of it, and declared to be subject to Divine judgment.

his own father or mother, or the woman is marrying a descendant of her own father or mother.*

That is a plain principle ; it draws a clear line ; it suggests a convincing reason.

Nobody maintains that the Bible states the principle in these words. But it names cases enough to show us that this is the principle intended.

The Bible does not expressly name *all* the cases. The law in Leviticus, for instance, does not expressly forbid a father to marry his own daughter. But it names cases enough to let us see the principle, and then we can apply the principle to every case.

Accordingly, *as yet*, all parties *in this country* profess to agree that the principle of the law as to marriage between blood relations is Scriptural and right. This agreement, however, will probably not continue if change once begins in other portions of the law.

2. Prohibitions of marriage are not confined to the case of *blood relations*. Some *relations by marriage*, or, as it is commonly called, by affinity, are also forbidden. Out of thirteen cases specified in the leading passage of Scripture in which marriage is forbidden, six are cases of blood relations, and seven are cases of relations by marriage or affinity. Prohibitions in cases of the latter kind rest of course upon the principle that man and wife are one flesh. Such prohibitions are authorised applications of *that principle*. And it is to be remembered that our Lord has plainly told us that that principle was not so strictly enforced during the Jewish dispensation as in its own nature it ought to be,— not so strictly as it was to be among His followers.

But the question is, In *what* relations by affinity is marriage forbidden?

The existing law is, that a man may not marry of his wife's kindred *nearer in blood* than he may of his own, nor a wife of her husband's nearer in blood than she may of her own. To put it in other words, though not in plainer, a man may not marry *those* blood relations of his deceased wife, whom he might not marry if they were his own ; and,

---

* In the case, for instance, of marriage with an uncle or aunt, the uncle is marrying a descendant of his own parent—and so of the aunt.

3

in like manner, a woman may not marry those blood relations of her deceased husband, whom she might not marry if they were her own.

Here, again, is a plain rule that instantly marks out all the cases. And it goes upon a plain principle. It goes on the principle that when a man unites himself to a woman in marriage, he accepts a relation to *her* blood-kindred in the forbidden degrees, which is to put marriage between him and them henceforth out of the question ; and so a woman uniting herself in marriage to a man accepts a corresponding relation to *his* blood-kindred in the same degrees.

Now, this is not only a plain rule, *but there is no other rule.* If you are not to go by this rule, you must either allow all persons related in affinity to marry as they please, or, if you still forbid some, you must do it *on no principle at all*.

The Scripture cases support the rule laid down, because they cannot be brought under any other rule.

In this instance, just as in the instance of blood relations, the Bible does not set down the principle in words such as those used above. But it names cases enough to show us that this is the principle intended.

The Bible may not expressly prohibit marriage with a deceased wife's sister, though it prohibits cases precisely parallel. But it names cases enough to let us see the principle, and then we can apply the principle to every case that falls within it, as this does.

Candid men among the supporters of the proposed change acknowledge that it cannot stop with legalising marriage to a sister-in-law. People will not be restrained from other marriages now forbidden when once that is admitted, because then you can no longer point them to a plain rule founded on a plain reason. The legalising of other marriages now forbidden will be demanded, and in due time the principle applicable to blood relatives themselves may be attacked in like manner. This is the process which has taken place in countries where the marriage has been legalised, which is now proposed to be legalised with us.

Were these changes to take place, a certain number of

4

people in all classes would be encouraged to form marriages recognised as marriages by law, but which conscientious Christians and conscientious Churches could not recognise as such. It is easy to see the social difficulties, confusions, and temptations thus arising.

Were these changes to take place, the family relationships, the innocence of which is at present sheltered by law, would be placed in a suspicious and ambiguous position. A sister-in-law could not then any longer feel as a sister, or be treated as a sister, without finding herself exposed to suspicion and misconstruction.

It is earnestly represented to you—

1. That the proposed alteration of the law is unscriptural and wrong.
2. That unless you make a stand now by united representations to Parliament, you will see the nation involved in a growing course of declension, and will find yourselves at the greatest disadvantage for making a stand at any future points in the progress of it.

THOS. J. CRAWFORD, D.D.,
Professor of Divinity in the University of Edinburgh.

CHAS. J. BROWN, D.D.,
New North Free Church, Edinburgh.

ANDREW THOMSON, D.D.,
Broughton Place United Presbyterian Church, Edinburgh.

D. F. SANDFORD,
St. John's Episcopal Church, Edinburgh.

W. H. GOOLD, D.D.,
Reformed Presbyterian Church, Edinburgh.

A. CAMPBELL SWINTON, of Kimmerghame.

JAMES PEDDIE, Writer to the Signet.

D. DAVIDSON, Lt.-Col.

Those who may desire a fuller statement of the facts and arguments bearing on this important subject are referred to No. 8 of this Series, 'What the Presbyterians say; or The Relationships which Bar Marriage, considered Scripturally and Socially: being a respectful Address to the Nonconformist Ministers of England by Ministers of the Presbyterian Churches of Scotland.'

To be had also of E. W. ALLEN, 4 *Ave Maria Lane,* E.C.

Price One Halfpenny.

Spottiswoode & Co., Printers, New-street Square, London.

Marriage Law Defence Union Tracts.
No. VI.

OFFICE: 1 KING STREET, WESTMINSTER, S.W.

What does the Table of Kindred and Affinity say

WHEN COMPARED WITH LEVITICUS?

MANY persons may have noticed, still existing in parish churches, a framed board, and on it either painted or printed

Table of Kindred and Affinity,
Wherein whosoever are related are forbidden in Scripture and our laws to marry together.

The same TABLE will also be found in most Prayer-Books, printed a few years back, on the last page : but it is no part of the Prayer-Book, since it did not appear in the sealed copies which represent the book as it was sanctioned by Convocation in 1602 : it belongs to the Canons of 1604, which Canons are still in force and refer directly to it.

The 'Table of Kindred' was drawn up in its present form and issued by the Archbishop of Canterbury early in Queen Elizabeth's reign ; it represents faithfully the teaching of the BIBLE, and of the ancient laws of the Church, which, in this matter, of course, are based upon the Bible; for it will be observed that the second title speaks of the relations which are forbidden in 'Scripture and our laws' to marry together.

In the two chapters of the Book of Leviticus the law of God as to marriage amongst relations is very clearly expressed to all who will try and understand. But there are those who will not do so, and will argue that only just what is expressed *in so many words* is forbidden, and nothing else.

Now, the office of the Church is not only to guard and make known God's Word, but also to explain it, and make it clear when, at first sight, it may not be so clear. And in drawing up this Table the Church of England has exercised her office in this respect. And if these two chapters are considered carefully, it will be seen that the rules which the Church has laid down in this Table are partly to be ' read ' in the Scriptures, and partly may be ' proved thereby.'

The first point which will strike the attentive observer in summing up the contents of the two chapters in question is, that fifteen relatives are distinctly stated which a man may not marry, but none are distinctly stated which a woman may not marry. It is distinctly stated, for instance, that a man may not marry his sister, but it is not stated that a woman may not marry her brother. It will no doubt be said that the latter is obvious, because the crime, in the case of an incestuous marriage, is shared by both parties alike ; and, having said that the brother should not marry the sister, it would be unnecessary to say that the sister should not marry the brother. When, however, we come to consider the prohibition for a man to marry his granddaughter, which is definitely stated, what are we to say to a woman marrying her grandson? This would not be a repetition like the other. Yet would any one for one moment doubt that the second is forbidden as much as the first? Surely it was not necessary to state the second in so many words, having stated the first ; and so no one could honestly say that the omission to forbid the second actually allowed it.

In the same way, neither is a man forbidden to marry his grandmother, nor is a woman forbidden to marry her grandfather ; but since a man is, in so many words, forbidden to marry his granddaughter, and by direct analogy a woman, as we have said, to marry her grandson, so it follows that 'the granddaughter cannot marry her grandfather, nor the grandson his grandmother.

Just so is it the case when we come to the wife of the brother and husband of the sister. Twice over, namely, in Lev. xviii. 16, and in xx. 21, a man is forbidden to marry his [deceased] brother's wife. It follows by analogy that a woman is forbidden to marry her [deceased] sister's husband. These and other similar analogies rest upon the same ground. It would be an absurd argument to use that the granddaughter *may not* marry her grandfather because *it is forbidden in so many words* for the grandfather to marry the granddaughter, but that the grandson *may* marry his grandmother, because it is *not forbidden in so many words* for the grandmother to marry the grandson. The grandfather and grandmother must be to the granddaughter and grandson respectively of the same relationship in every way. And this being admitted, it would be equally absurd to say that though a man may not marry his [deceased] brother's wife (which in words is forbidden), yet a woman may marry her [deceased] sister's husband (because in words it is not forbidden), for each stands respectively in the same relation to the man and the woman. But then, how can the woman marry her [deceased] sister's husband without the man marrying his [deceased] wife's sister ? People forget this, though it is so plain. They would admit that the one was forbidden in the Bible, and not the other, overlooking that they are the same thing.

A TABLE OF KINDRED AND AFFINITY, &c.

A. *A man may not marry his*	*Reason.*	B. *A woman may not marry with her*	*Reason.*
1. Grandmother.	*Anal. of* B. 1.	1. Grandfather.	*Conv. of* A. 19, 20.
2. Grandfather's Wife.	*Anal. of* B. 2.	2. Grandmother's Husband.	*Conv. of* A. 23, 24.
3. Wife's Grandmother.		3. Husband's Grandfather.	
4. Father's Sister.	*Lev.* xviii. 12, xx. 19.	4. Father's Brother.	*Anal. of* A. 4.
5. Mother's Sister.	*Lev.* xviii. 13, xx. 19.	5. Mother's Brother.	*Anal. of* A. 5.
6. Father's Brother's Wife.	*Lev.* xviii. 14, xx. 20.	6. Father's Sister's Husband.	*Anal. of* A. 6.
7. Mother's Brother's Wife.	*Lev.* xx. 20.	7. Mother's Sister's Husband.	*Anal. of* A. 7.
8. Wife's Father's Sister.		8. Husband's Father's Brother.	
9. Wife's Mother's Sister.		9. Husband's Mother's Brother.	
10. Mother.	*Lev.* xviii. 7.	10. Father.	*Anal. of* A. 10.
11. Step Mother.	*Lev.* xviii. 8, xx. 11.	11. Step Father.	*Conv. of* A. 14.
12. Wife's Mother.	*Lev.* xviii. 17, xx. 14.	12. Husband's Father.	*Conv. of* A. 15.
13. Daughter.	*Anal. of* B. 13.	13. Son.	*Conv. of* A. 10.
14. Wife's Daughter.	*Lev.* xviii. 17, xx. 14.	14. Husband's Son.	*Conv. of* A. 11.
15. Son's Wife.	*Lev.* xviii. 15, xx. 12.	15. Daughter's Husband.	*Conv. of* A. 12.
16. Sister.	*Lev.* xviii. 9, xx. 17.	16. Brother.	*Conv. of* A. 16.
17. Wife's Sister.	*Anal. of* B. 17.	17. Husband's Brother.	*Conv. of* A. 18.
18. Brother's Wife.	*Lev.* xviii. 16, xx. 21.	18. Sister's Husband.	*Anal. of* A. 18.
19. Son's Daughter.	*Lev.* xviii. 10.	19. Son's Son.	*Anal. of* A. 19.
20. Daughter's Daughter.	*Lev.* xviii. 10.	20. Daughter's Son.	*Anal. of* A. 20.
21. Son's Son's Wife.		21. Son's Daughter's Husband.	
22. Daughter's Son's Wife.		22. Daughter's Daughter's Husband.	
23. Wife's Son's Daughter.	*Lev.* xviii. 17.	23. Husband's Son's Son.	*Anal. of* A. 23.
24. Wife's Daughter's Daughter.	*Lev.* xviii. 17.	24. Husband's Daughter's Son.	*Anal. of* A. 24.
25. Brother's Daughter.	*Anal. of* B. 25.	25. Brother's Son.	*Conv. of* A. 4.
26. Sister's Daughter.	*Anal. of* B. 26.	26. Sister's Son.	*Conv. of* A. 5.
27. Brother's Son's Wife.		27. Brother's Daughter's Husband.	
28. Sister's Son's Wife.		28. Sister's Daughter's Husband.	
29. Wife's Brother's Daughter.	*Anal. of* B. 29.	29. Husband's Brother's Son.	*Conv. of* A. 6.
30. Wife's Sister's Daughter.	*Anal. of* B. 30.	30. Husband's Sister's Son.	*Conv. of* A. 7.

5

What we have been saying will be perhaps best illustrated by considering the Table as a whole. As set forth originally by Archbishop Parker in 1563, the Latin was given as well as the English. This we have omitted as not necessary, nor the division into first and second degrees in ascending or descending order, nor the column showing which are related by affinity and which by consanguinity. But instead we have supplied a column giving the reference to the Scriptures where the relationship is in so many words forbidden, or else the reason why it is forbidden; some relationships being so merely from their being the *converse* of what is elsewhere forbidden—or are so by direct *analogy*. As the relationships are all numbered (and this is so in all ancient copies in the churches which we have ever seen, as well as those which appear in the old Prayer-Books), the references will be found very easy.

What is meant by *converse* and by *analogy* may perhaps have been sufficiently explained above; but still, in order to make the matter clear, it may be said that *converse* means the same relationship differently expressed. A good instance of this will be found in the fact that a woman is forbidden to marry [13] her son, because it is the *converse* of the son being forbidden to marry [10] his mother. Direct *analogy* means that the relationship is exactly similar, though not the same ; for instance, because a son is directly forbidden to marry [10] his mother, and because a mother is consequently forbidden to marry her son, we infer by *analogy* (and by this only) that the daughter is forbidden to marry [10] her father, and the father to marry [13] his daughter. A man is forbidden to marry [4] his father's sister or [5] his mother's sister. It follows by *analogy* (though not stated) that a woman is forbidden to marry [4] her father's brother or [5] her mother's brother. The Table thus represents a kind of net-work, from which it is impossible to cut one mesh without making a very large rent indeed.

It will be seen, however, that some relationships are left blank on either side in the Table. These we have left so because the analogy is rather indirect than direct, inasmuch as they represent the *same kind* of degrees as are forbidden, rather than *the same* degrees. They are as follows :—

A. *A man may not marry his*	B. *A woman may not marry with her*
3. Wife's grandmother.	3. Husband's grandfather.
8, 9. Wife's aunt.	8, 9 Husband's uncle.
21, 22. Grandson's wife.	21, 22. Granddaughter's husband.
27, 28. Nephew's wife.	27, 28. Niece's husband.

A few moments' consideration will, however, show that such marriages cannot, under a reasonable and honest interpretation of the principles to be deduced from what is directly forbidden, be lawful. It will be first seen that Nos. 21, 22 on the man's side are simply a *converse* of No. 3 on the woman's side; and of course equally Nos. 21, 22 on the woman's side are simply the *converse* of No. 3 on the man's side. For if a man cannot marry his grandson's wife, neither can a woman marry her husband's grandfather, and *vice versâ*. Also, that Nos. 27, 28 on the man's side are simply the *converse* of Nos. 8, 9 on the woman's side; and equally Nos. 8, 9 on the woman's side simply the *converse* of Nos. 8, 9 on the man's side. For if a man cannot marry his nephew's wife, neither can a woman marry her husband's uncle, and *vice versâ*. Further, it will be observed that each number on one side is a direct *analogy* of the same number on the other, *i.e.* A. 3 of B. 3; and A. 21, 22 of B. 21, 22. Also A. 8, 9 of B. 8, 9; and A. 27, 28 of B. 27, 28.

Thus there is, so to speak, an interlacing; each set must all fall together, or they must all hang together. You cannot say one of them is lawful without admitting that all of that set are lawful. You cannot say that one is forbidden without admitting that all are forbidden.

Now, while we admit there is no direct analogy between any of the links in these two chains and those relationships which are definitely forbidden in the Book of Leviticus, still we contend there are such strong indirect analogies that the framer or framers were fully justified in including the above-named relationships amongst those forbidden in Scripture.

A man is definitely forbidden to marry [23, 24] his wife's granddaughter. Is it at all reasonable to suppose he may marry [3] his wife's grandmother?

Again, a man is definitely forbidden to marry [6, 7] his uncle's wife. Is it at all reasonable to suppose he may marry [27, 28] his nephew's wife?

But, as we have already shown, Nos. 21, 22 and Nos. 8, 9 are on the woman's side the converses respectively of Nos. 3 and 27, 28 on the man's side; and each converse carrying with it each analogy, the whole are linked thus together.

The marriage, however, with the [deceased] wife's sister, it will be seen, rests upon the principle of direct analogy, *i.e.* the *same degree*, and not only the same kind of degree; and we have in the foregoing remarks taken some pains to make that analogy clear, because many thoughtless people are found who say that marriage with the [deceased] wife's sister is not forbidden in Scripture. We do not accuse all those who say this of willingly perverting the meaning of God's Word, or resorting to what in ordinary language is called 'a quibble;' they do not in speaking thus make a mental reservation of 'that is, it is not forbidden directly in so many words,' but they speak hastily: the partial statement serves the purpose of an argument, and, in such cases, it would appear that it is the argument which they want to find to support their own will, and not the truth which they are seeking.

The most direct answer to such is that relying on a partial statement of that kind admits at once a principle which opens up a very long series of marriages : for out of the 60 only 17 are forbidden. It is all very well for the promoters to say—'We only just want this because some few have broken the law in this respect;' but if you once open the flood-gate you cannot say—'Thus far shall the water come and no further.'

This and Tract VII., entitled ' What does the Table of Kindred and Affinity say when compared with the Law of the Church ?' are reprinted, with some slight variation, from articles which appeared in the ' Penny Post' for 1882, with the full concurrence of the writer, Mr. JAMES PARKER.

To be had also of E. W. ALLEN, 4 *Ave Maria Lane,* E.C.
Price One Halfpenny.

Spottiswoode & Co., Printers, New-street Square, London.

Marriage Law Defence Union Tracts.
No. VII.

OFFICE: 1 KING STREET, WESTMINSTER, S.W.

What does the Table of Kindred and Affinity say

WHEN COMPARED WITH THE LAW OF THE CHURCH?

IF any one asks what was the law of our Church before this Table of Affinity was issued (for this did not take place until the middle of the sixteenth century), the answer is, that so far as the forbidding all the marriages named in it, the law was practically the same, though in no authoritative statement were the relationships exactly expressed.

The earliest instance in connection with this country of an authoritative expression of doctrine upon the subject is to be found in the Letter of Pope Gregory. It will be known perhaps to most of the readers of this that St. Augustine, when he came as a missionary to these shores in A.D. 596, wrote letters to Pope Gregory, asking for advice upon different matters, in which he could not trust his own judgment. Amongst them were two questions relating to degrees of relationship within which marriage was lawful. St. Augustine asks,

'Whether two own brothers may marry severally two own sisters who are of a family far removed from themselves?' That is, if a man has married a woman of a sufficiently distant relationship, may his brother marry that woman's sister? At first sight it may appear a trivial question to ask. But on consideration St. Augustine may well have argued that as the brother's wife came within the definite relationship forbidden, so her sister might also. Pope Gregory, however, sets the matter at rest, and is clear and definite in his reply to the question. He says, ' This is lawful beyond all doubt; *for there is nothing found in Holy Scripture which seems to contradict it.*' Thus in his reply he lays down distinctly the rule for guidance.

But St. Augustine asks a further question, which could not be answered in such few words, namely, ' To what degree may the faithful marry with their kindred, and whether it is lawful for men to marry their stepmothers and their cousins ?'

Gregory the Great does not proceed to compile a ' Table of Affinity,' but gives certain examples, and lays down certain principles. He refers to the Roman civil law, which allows brothers' or sisters' children [*i.e.* cousins] to marry; but he condemns it, not severely, nor on the grounds that it is distinctly forbidden in Scripture, but because such marriages are not in his experience blessed. He argues from Leviticus xviii. 6, 7, that the distance of three or four degrees is necessary to make a marriage lawful amongst Christians. But marriage with a mother-in-law he condemns as a horrible crime, referring especially to the text, ' they two shall be one flesh.' ' It is also forbidden,' he goes on to say, ' to marry a brother's wife, because by her former marriage she was made one flesh with thy brother.' And he gives an example : ' John the Baptist was beheaded and crowned with martyrdom because he said to the king that it was unlawful for him to take his brother's wife.'

It must be remembered that this Letter was written in A.D. 601 ; and though Pope Gregory gives no details, we see that precisely the same principles and rules are laid

3

down for guidance as those which the compilers of this 'Table of Affinity' follow.

And Gregory's words seem to have been accepted for some centuries as the basis of the law of our Church. For instance, the excerptions of Ecgbert, Archbishop of York, issued in A.D. 740, and which prescribed the law for the Northern province, quote the very words of Gregory's Letter. In a body of Canons promulgated in A.D. 950, and known as the 'Laws of the Northumbrian Priests,' the passage relating to marriage begins, 'And we forbid, as is forbidden by the Divine prohibition, that a man may have more wives than one; and let her be rightly wedded and given by her parents : and that no man take a wife that is related to him within the fourth degree.'

It will be observed that this varies slightly from St. Gregory's words of 'three or four degrees,' and fits in with the reckoning of St. Ambrose, which he adduced from the Book of Leviticus. At the same time the mode of reckoning degrees is, as a rule, obscure, and the question of 'blood' and affinity comes in, which complicates the matter.

Passing on later we find in the Canons put forth at Enham in A.D. 1009 (known as the Ordinances of the 'Witan') the following : 'And never let it be that a Christian marry within the fourth degree of relations among his own kindred, nor to the widow of one that is so near akin, *nor one nearly related to the wife whom he formerly had.*' Here we see a distinct allusion to the 'Wife's Sister.'

The laws ecclesiastical in the time of King Cnut are similar, but it would appear, if we may trust the MSS., that so early as this the prohibition is already extended to the sixth degree; and the Canons issued by Archbishop Lanfranc in A.D. 1075, though professedly following the rule laid down by Gregory the Great in his famous Letter, have the seventh degree named; and the same passage is repeated in successive series of Canons promulgated afterwards, *e.g.*, in those of Archbishop Anselm, A.D. 1102, and in those of Archbishop Corbeuil, A.D. 1126.

Consequent upon, or at least concurrent with, this exaggeration, grew up a system of 'dispensations,' the source of great abuses. For from relief accorded with respect to obedience to the Church's laws the step to relief from obedience to God's laws was easy; and we are much afraid, amidst the many black spots in the history of the mediæval Church in this country, those connected with disregard to God's laws on marriage were amongst the blackest. But this disregard on the part of the powers who were responsible for it brought with it, it may be said, its own reward. The dispensation given to Henry VIII. to marry his deceased brother's wife led to his demanding dispensation for a divorce when he had set his eyes on another and fairer woman. And when the Pope seemed to be exhibiting a readiness to be guided by policy, instead of by God's Word, the king's anger was aroused; and this country being on other accounts ripe for the overthrow of the sway of the Papal Court, this question of the marriage became the turning point with the king, and in God's providence the abuse of His laws in this direction brought in the end its true punishment, in the total downfall of the Papal sway over this kingdom.

But besides the fact of the Pope's sanction of the king's marriage with his deceased brother's wife leading to such a result, it is interesting to note that incidentally it led to an exposition of the law on the matter; and we find this in a place where we should hardly have expected to find it, namely, in an Act of Parliament, where the laws of God are very clearly explained on this point, more clearly, it may even be said, than in the several Canons to which we have referred.

In one of the Acts passed in the twenty-fifth year of Henry the Eighth's reign (1533, cap. 22) the Parliament pray that it

5

may be enacted that the marriage of the king with the lady Katherine be definitely, clearly, and absolutely declared to be against the laws of Almighty God, and they go on to say :

'III. And furthermore, since many inconveniences have fallen, as well within this realm as in others, by reason of marrying within the degrees of marriage prohibited by God's laws, that is to say, the son to marry the mother or the step-mother, the brother the sister, the father his son's daughter or his daughter's daughter, or the son to marry the daughter of his father procreate and born by his stepmother, or the son to marry his aunt, being his father's or mother's sister, or to marry his uncle's wife, or the father to marry his son's wife, or the brother to marry his brother's wife, or any man to marry his wife's daughter, or his wife's son's daughter, or his wife's daughter's daughter *or his wife's sister* ; which marriages, albeit *they be plainly prohibited and det sted by the laws of God*, yet nevertheless, at some times they have proceeded under colours of dispensations by man's power, which is but usurped, and of right ought not to be granted, admitted, nor allowed ; for no man, of what estate, degree, or condition soever he be, hath power to dispense with God's laws, as all the clergy of this realm in the said convocations, and the most part of all the famous universities of Christendom, and we also, do affirm and think.'

It will be observed that the table here given is not by any means so complete as was afterwards drawn up ; but many of the principles on which we have insisted so fully in a previous tract (No. VI.) of this series, are shewn in it. And the [deceased] wife's sister, it will be seen, is included naturally amongst the others.

We do not wish to dwell upon this system of 'dispensations,' which was one of the abuses which had sprung up in the Church ; but it must be observed that the letter which we now for other reasons quote, was in consequence of an

6

application to Archbishop Cranmer to grant, as was usual, such a dispensation. He very properly refused, although at the risk of offending no less a person than the great Lord Cromwell, who was then in very high favour with the king. The letter runs :

'TO THE LORD CROMWELL.

'. . . Whereas your lordship writeth to me in the favour of this bearer, Massey, an old servant to the king's highness, that, being contracted to his "sister's daughter of his late wife deceased [*i.e.* wife's sister's daughter],* he might enjoy the benefit of a dispensation in that behalf; specially, considering it is none of the cases of prohibition contained *in the statute*; surely, my lord, I would gladly accomplish your request herein, *if the word of God would permit the same.*

'And where you require me, that if I think this licence may not be granted by the law of God, then I should write unto you the reasons and authorities that move me so to think ; that upon the declaration unto the king's highness, you may confer thereupon with some other learned men, and so advertise me of the king's farther resolution in the same accordingly ; for shortness of time, I shall show you one reason, which is this : by the law of God many persons be prohibited, which be not expressed but be understood by like prohibitions in equal degree. As St. Ambrose saith, " that the niece is forbid by the law of God, although it be not expressed in Leviticus that the uncle shall not marry his niece. But where the nephew is forbid there, that he shall not marry his aunt, by the same is understood that the niece shall not be married unto her uncle.† Likewise, as the daughter is not there plainly expressed, yet where the son is forbid to marry his mother, it is understood that the daughter may not be married to her father, by cause they be of like degree." ‡ Even so it is in this case and many

---

* See the Table in Tract No. VI., where this is forbidden. Column A, No. 30.

† Ibid., where A 25 is marked as the Analogue of B 25, which is the converse of A 4.

‡ Ibid., where A 13 is marked as the Analogue of B 13, which is the converse of B 10.

7

others ; for where it is there expressed that the nephew shall not marry his uncle's wife, it must needs be understood that the niece shall not be married unto the aunt's husband, by cause that all is one equality of degree * . . .

‘And as touching the act of parliament concerning the degrees prohibited by God's law, they be not so plainly set forth as I would they were. Wherein I somewhat spake my mind at the making of the said [Law] but it was not then accepted. I required then, that there might be expressed mother, and mother-in-law, daughter, and daughter-in-law ; and so in further degrees directly upward and downward, *in linea recta;* also sister and sister-in-law, aunt and aunt-in-law, niece and niece-in-law. And this limitation, in my judgment, should have contained all the degrees prohibited by God's law, expressed and not expressed : and should have satisfied this man, and such other, which would marry their nieces-in-law. . . . Thus, my lord, right heartily fare you well. At Ford, the viith day of September.

‘Your lordship's own,
‘ T[HOMAS] CANTUARIEN[SIS].’

The year when this was written was A.D. 1536, *i.e.* three years after the passing of the Act to which we have already referred ; and the original letter is still preserved amongst the MSS. in the Cottonian Collection in the British Museum.

As we have already said, we do not wish here to dwell upon the scandal of these dispensations. The acts were either against the direct law of God, or they were not. If they were not, there was no need of dispensation ; if they were, the dispensation to disobey directly a law of God is unwarrantable. But what we are concerned with is, first of all, Cranmer's *reasons* for laying down that such marriages are against the Word of God, namely, that what is implied

---

* See the Table in Tract No. VI., where A 6 and 7 carry the analogies of B 6 and 7.

by the Scriptures is just as much the law as what is stated. It will be observed how the Archbishop rests his argument wholly upon the 'Word of God,' and how he fortifies his interpretation by an appeal to one of the Fathers, namely, St. Ambrose.*

Further, it will also be noticed that he thought it very advisable that a 'Table' should be set forth explaining more fully the relations which, with a due attention to the principles of the Law as laid down in the Book of Leviticus, appear to be forbidden by such Law. This letter was not written, as we have said, till 1536, and there does not seem to have ar s n any opportunity for issuing such Table at the time. Afterwards the death of King Henry, and the succession of a young king who was much at the mercy of the political parties in the State, rendered many of the reforms in ecclesiastical laws, which had been debated by Convocation in Henry's reign, impracticable ; and finally the return of the Papal power once again under Queen Mary threw everything into confusion.

We would not be supposed to attempt to give all the documentary evidence which exists illustrating the steps which led to the Table being made in its present shape ; but we must not leave Henry's reign without adverting to a book which was printed in that reign, entitled, 'The Institutions of a Christian Man.' It is remarkable, from the fact that a copy exists corrected by King Henry the Eighth himself, with Archbishop Cranmer's annotations. The paragraph relating to marriage begins :

* Cranmer, no doubt, refers to the letter of St. Ambrose written on the subject to Paternus, A.D. 393. St. Ambrose seems to consider that cousins were forbidden to marry not only by the laws of the Emperor Theodosius, but by the Bible; probably on the ground that they came within the fourth degree. On the question of the marriage with deceased wife's sister, Cranmer might have referred to St. Basil's direct statement in his letter to Diodorus (Ep. 160). St. Basil was Bishop of Cæsarea, A.D. 371–380.

'God prohibited that any matrimony should be made between the father and the daughter, the mother and the son, the brother and the sister, and between divers other persons being in certain degrees of consanguinity and affinity.'

On this paragraph the king has noted—

'The rest of the degrees prohibited are necessarily to be expressed here also.'

And to this again Cranmer has subjoined—

'All the degrees prohibited in my judgment may be best expressed in these general words : that no man may marry his mother nor mother-in-law, and so upward, *in linea recta* [*i.e.* in a straight line] ; daughter, nor daughter-in-law, and so downward, *in linea recta* ; sister, *nor sister-in-law* ; aunt, nor aunt-in-law ; niece, nor niece-in-law.'

When, after the death of Queen Mary, Matthew Parker had been elected Archbishop of Canterbury, A.D. 1559, he had the task before him of obtaining something like order amidst those who, on the one side, still clung to the state of things which had just passed away, and the lawless Puritan party on the other. Soon after his appointment he set to work, seemingly as if to fulfil Cranmer's intention, to draw up the Table which we now possess. It was formally issued and printed perhaps as early as 1560 or 1561.* It was entitled, 'An Admonition to all such as shall intend hereafter to enter the state of Matrimony, godly and agreeable to laws.' And the first clause runs, 'First, that they contract not with such persons as be hereafter expressed, nor with any of the like degree against the law of God and the laws of the realm.'

There were controversies at that time on this subject just

---

* The earliest copy is, perhaps, that which the Archbishop filed amongst his papers. But so far as we remember there was no printed date, or any MS. note giving the exact date of issue.

as there are now. Those who had made up their mind
to break God's law were ingenious in finding means of
escaping the plain and obvious meaning. The same arguments then used have been furbished up afresh now, and
one of them was, that there was a verse of the Bible which
forbade the taking of a wife's sister during the wife's lifetime,
and hence it was argued, that when the wife was dead the
prohibition ceased, and *therefore* the marriage was permissible. Then, as now, the fallacy had to be exposed;
then, as now, those who advanced it pretended that this one
verse was *all* the law on the subject. Amongst the Archbishop's papers there is found a letter from Bishop Jewel,
then lately made Bishop of Salisbury, and it is dated
'Sarum, November, 1561.' It was probably occasioned by
questions being asked, after the issue of Archbishop Parker's
Table of prohibited degrees, but to whom the letter was
addressed does not appear. Bishop Jewel, after stating the
case (somewhat lengthily), says, 'And therefore thus you
ground your Reason : A man may not marry his Wife's
sister, while she is alive; *Ergo* he may marry her after she
[*i.e.* the wife] is dead. This reason, a *negativi*, is very weak
and makes no more proof in logic than this does.' [He
then gives examples, *e.g.* ' the raven returned not to the ark
till the waters were dried up : *Ergo* it returned again after
the waters were dried up,' &c.] He then goes on to state
the next proposition :—

' There are no express words in the Levitical law, by
which I am forbidden to marry my wife's sister. *Ergo* by
the Levitical law such marriage is to be accounted lawful.
For notwithstanding the Statute in this case refers to the
18th chapter of Leviticus as unto a place where the degrees
of Consanguinity and Affinity are counted most at large,
yet you must remember that certain degrees are there left
out untouched, within which, nevertheless, it was never

thought lawful for men to marry. For example, there is nothing provided there by express words, but that a man may marry his own grandmother, or his grandfather's second wife, or the wife of his uncle by his mother's side. No, nor is there any express prohibition in all this chapter, but that a man may marry his own daughter. Yet will no man say, that any of these degrees may join together in lawful marriage.

'Wherefore we must needs think, that God in that chapter hath especially and namely forbidden certain degrees, not as leaving all marriage lawful which he had not there expressly forbidden, but that thereby, as by infallible precedents, we might be able to rule the rest. As when God saith, no man shall marry his mother, we understand that under the name of *mother* is contained both the grandmother and the grandfather's wife, and that such marriage is forbidden. And when God commands that no man shall marry the wife of his uncle by his father's side, we doubt not but in the same is included the wife of the uncle by the mother's side. Thus you see God Himself would have us to expound one degree by another.

'So likewise in this case, albeit I be not forbidden by plain words *to marry my wife's sister*, yet am I forbidden so to do by other words, which by exposition are plain enough. For when God commands me I shall not marry my brother's wife, it follows directly by the same, that He forbids me to marry my wife's sister. For between one man and two sisters, and one woman and two brothers, is like *analogy* or proportion, which is my judgment in this case.'

Bishop Jewel concludes his letter by referring to the Bishop of Rome, 'who will take upon him to rule God's commands *at his* pleasure, and by dispensation to make that lawful in one man for the time, which God has plainly forbidden in all men *for ever.*'

These are striking words of Bishop Jewel's, on the subject which was before him, and which is now before us in the same way, after a lapse of more than three hundred years. But the ways of the present generation are different; no longer those who would disobey God's law appeal to the Pope, but they appeal to Parliament for dispensation; and there may be some who are weak enough to think that Parliament can give that dispensation.

There are many, however, who believe with Bishop Jewel, that God's Word stands for ever; and when they see their representatives in Parliament tampering with God's laws, and in the name of the nation defying God's Word, will ask themselves whether they have directly or indirectly had a share in the unholy work.

But there are still many more who perhaps never think or care about the matter, or, if they do think at all, come to the conclusion that it is no business of theirs. They are wrong, for they are amongst the people of the nation, and the nation's crimes are in a manner their crimes.

Lastly, there are those who say they cannot understand the matter, as it is too hard for them. To these we answer, the Scriptures read in the light of an honest desire to understand them are not hard, nor are they doubtful on the point in question; and more than that, for the assistance of all such who cannot discover for themselves the meaning of the Scriptures, pious and learned men, in the name of the Church, have provided for them a 'Table of Affinity' such as a child can understand, and which yet will bear the investigation of the wisest, and will be found a true and faithful exponent of the written Word of God.

This, and Tract VI. entitled 'What does the Table of Kindred and Affinity say when compared with Leviticus?' are reprinted, with some slight variation, from articles which appeared in the 'Penny Post' for 1882, with the full concurrence of the writer, Mr. JAMES PARKER.

To be had also of E. W. ALLEN, 4 *Ave Maria Lane, E.C.*
Price One Halfpenny.

Spottiswoode & Co., Printers, New-street Square, London.

Marriage Law Defence Union Tracts
No. VIII

What the Presbyterians say

Of the Relationships which Bar Marriage Scripturally and Socially

LONDON
MARRIAGE LAW DEFENCE UNION
1 KING STREET, WESTMINSTER, S.W.
E. W. ALLEN, 4 AVE MARIA LANE, E.C.
1883

Price One Penny

THE following Address was sent in 1871 to the Ministers of the Nonconformist Churches of England, with the signatures of the most eminent theological and leading Ministers of the Church of Scotland, the Free Church of Scotland, the United Presbyterian Church, the Reformed Presbyterian Church, and the original Secession Church. It is now reissued with the additional concurrence of Ministers and Professors of the Presbyterian Churches in Ireland as well as Scotland.

G. J. MURRAY, Sec.

OFFICE OF THE MARRIAGE LAW DEFENCE UNION,
1 KING STREET, WESTMINSTER, S.W.
January, 1883.

What the Presbyterians say

Of the Relationships which Bar Marriage Scripturally and Socially.

To the MINISTERS OF THE NONCONFORMIST CHURCHES OF ENGLAND, the respectful ADDRESS of the undersigned MINISTERS OF THE PRESBYTERIAN CHURCHES OF SCOTLAND, on the proposed change of law as to the RELATIONSHIPS WHICH BAR MARRIAGE.

REVEREND AND DEAR SIRS,

It is necessary that we explain in an opening sentence the somewhat unusual step we take in thus writing to you. Although we have not learned to place very great reliance on statements of fact put forth by those parties in the country who have long agitated for a change in its marriage laws, we have been unable to avoid feelings of anxiety and deep regret on finding them boast of a widespread sympathy with their views among the Nonconformist Ministry of England. And well knowing the power of such a sympathy, if it really exists—the important influence it cannot fail to exert both on the public mind and on the action of the Legislature, we are thus moved to address you, and respectfully submit for your consideration some thoughts and views on the whole subject.

4

I. We will reserve for a later part of this paper the question of expediency—the more immediately practical and social bearings of the proposed change of law. As ministers of the Word, writing to brethren in the same ministry, it is fitting that we begin with Scripture, stating, as plainly as we can, what the grounds in God's Word are on which we hold the opinion expressed in the following words of the Westminster Confession of Faith (Chap. xxiv. Sec. 4), of course attaching no weight whatever to them save as resting on Scripture authority : ' Marriage ought not to be within the degrees of consanguinity or affinity forbidden in the Word. . . . The man may not marry any of his wife's kindred nearer in blood than he may of his own, nor the woman of her husband's kindred nearer in blood than of her own.' Suffer us here earnestly to invite your attention to four general positions.

1. *It were a strange thing, to say the least, if Scripture should be found to utter no authoritative voice, binding Christian countries and churches and individuals, as to the relationships which bar marriage.* For the whole subject of marriage lies within the sphere of religion and religious law. It is certain that our blessed Lord, while keeping jealously aloof from matters purely political, saying, ' Man, who made me a judge or a divider over you ?' legislated for His Church, and the whole world eventually, on marriage. And it is very noticeable how, in doing so, He fell back on that older Divine law, ' For this cause shall a man leave his father and mother, and cleave to his wife ; and they twain shall be one flesh '— authoritatively adding there (after the Septuagint) the word ' twain,' so as to bring out the force and import of the primeval law in bolder relief ; further, drawing the inference from it of the unlawfulness of divorce on any such minor grounds as the law of Moses had for a time suffered ; and still further, by implication drawing the inference of the

unlawfulness of polygamy, which thenceforth was to be disallowed among His disciples (Mark x. 2–12). Thus our opening position seems abundantly evident, that it were a strange thing, to say the least, if Scripture should be found to utter no authoritative voice, binding Christian countries and churches and individuals, as to the relationships which bar marriage—entering, as these do, into the very heart's core of moral and religious life.

2. *It is certain that, whether there be now a written and definite law of Scripture on this subject or no, there* WAS *one, at least, from and after the time of Moses.* It is chiefly found in the eighteenth and twentieth chapters of Leviticus, and thus opens (xviii. 6): ' None of you shall approach to any that is near of kin to him, to uncover their nakedness : I am the Lord.' Then follow a variety of examples of the ' nearness of kin ' which is referred to. And three things seem to us clear on the face of the whole statute. More generally, *first*, i. is clear that, as in the general prohibition just cited, so in the various particular ones which follow, the legislation is not about fornication, or adultery, but about forbidden sexual connection, under any circumstances whatever, between persons standing in the relations specified, since there could have been no necessity for specifying relationships at all, if the sins of fornication and adultery had been all that was intended. Or, in other words, the statute is one of *incest*, and so of the relationships which bar marriage. *Second*, and more specifically, it is clear on the face of the statute, that its prohibitions belong *equally to consanguinity and affinity*—to relationships by blood, and relationships by marriage. In both chapters, indeed, the larger number of the prohibitions belong to affinity ; nor are they set down in distinct classes, as if resting on grounds anywise different, but are intermingled, as if the more plainly to intimate that, in the whole matter of prohibited degrees,

consanguinity and affinity were to stand on the same footing—that 'the man might not marry any of his wife's kindred
nearer in blood than of his own, nor the woman of her
husband's kindred nearer in blood than of her own.' It
is impossible to make sense of the statute on any other
understanding of it. *Thirdly*, it is clear that the statute is
not constructed on the principle of a full and exhaustive
enumeration of forbidden connections or degrees, but on
that of a sufficiently large number of regulative specimens,
from which the whole may easily be determined. Thus, the
prohibition of a son's marriage with his mother carries with
it the analogous case, though not specified, of a father's
marriage with his daughter. The prohibition of a nephew's
marriage with his aunt carries with it the analogous case,
though not specified, of an uncle's marriage with his niece—
and so on.*

But it is questioned whether the Levitical law of incest be
any longer binding—whether it was ever intended for other
nations than the Jews—intended to be a law of universal
and enduring obligation. Our third and fourth positions
belong to this vital question.

3. *The law of incest in Leviticus was unquestionably moral*

---

* It may be well to give here a summary of the forbidden connections specified in Leviticus xviii. and xx. They are as follows :
A man with his mother, xviii. 7.
   ,,   his father's wife (or his step-mother), xviii. 8 ; xx. 11.
   ,,   his sister, full or half, xviii. 9, 11 ; xx. 17.
   ,,   his granddaughter, by son or daughter, xviii. 10.
   ,,   his aunt, by father or mother, xviii. 12, 13 ; xx. 19.
   ,,   his uncle's wife (or his aunt-in-law), xviii. 14 ; xx. 20.
   ,,   his son's wife (or his daughter-in-law), xviii. 15 ; xx. 12.
   ,,   his brother's wife (or his sister-in-law), xviii. 16 ; xx. 21.
   ,,   his wife's mother (or his mother-in-law), xviii. 17 ; xx. 14.
   ,,   his wife's daughter (or his step-daughter), xviii. 17 ; xx. 12.
   ,,   his wife's granddaughter (or his step-granddaughter),
         xviii. 17.

in its nature, nowise belonging to those ceremonies of the ancient dispensation which were to be done away in Christ. This seems to us too clear to require proof. The whole subject of marriage, and emphatically the relationships which ought morally to bar it, must needs belong to moral law. We will only here invite attention to the remarkable fact, that when Paul is marking out, in Gal. iii. and Rom. x., the distinctive character of '*the law*,' as such—'the law' in contrast with 'the promise'—'the law,' as from the beginning it had a promise of life in it to perfect obedience, he takes his proof, in both epistles, from that word of the Pentateuch, 'The man that doeth those things shall live by them.' It so happens, however, that this great word (belonging surely to 'the law' in its most essential and unalterable character) is found nowhere in the Pentateuch save in the introduction to this very statute of incest—thus (Lev. xviii. 5, 6): 'Ye shall therefore keep My statutes and My judgments ; *which if a man do, he shall live in them* : I am the Lord. None of you shall approach to any that is near of kin to him,' &c.

4. *The divine law of incest in Leviticus is of universal and enduring obligation.* Does not this follow unavoidably, from the *moral* character of it—unless, at least, an express statute of repeal can be produced? But where is any such repeal to be found? On the contrary, we crave attention to the following considerations.

First.—A definite law of incest is at least as much required in our time, and in these Western countries, as it was in the East, and in the days of Moses. So far is the state of society in our day, and in Western countries, from requiring less stringent rules of marriage than were necessary in the East, and in older times, the necessity lies all the other way, from the freer and more familiar intercourse of the sexes which prevails among us. Nor can it be doubted that it was partly in the view of that elevation of woman, and more free intercourse in society between the sexes, which were to result from His blessed Gospel, that our Lord, so very far from relaxing the previous laws of marriage, made them, in several important respects, more stringent than before.

Secondly.—The law of incest in Leviticus could not have been designed for the Jews only, since it is declared expressly to have been binding on other nations, and binding before the Jews as a nation existed. The statute of the eighteenth chapter thus opens: 'After the doings of the land of Egypt, wherein ye dwelt, shall ye not do : and after the doings of the land of Canaan, whither I bring you, shall ye not do : neither shall ye walk in their ordinances.' And these solemn words close it : 'Defile not ye yourselves in any of these things : for in all these the nations are defiled which I cast out before you : and the land is defiled : therefore I do visit the iniquity thereof upon it, and the land itself vomiteth out her inhabitants. Ye shall therefore keep My statutes and My judgments . . . that the land spue not you out also, when ye defile it, as it spued out the nations that were before you.' But 'where no law is, there is no transgression.' Whence it follows that the Levitical law of incest must, in the matter of it, have bound the Canaanites as part of the law of nature, which of course is of universal and enduring obligation.

Thirdly.—The apostle Paul thus writes (1 Cor. v. 1, 2) : 'It is reported commonly that there is fornication among you, and such fornication as is not so much as named among the Gentiles, that one should have his father's wife. And ye are puffed up, and have not rather mourned, that he that hath done this deed might be taken away from among you.' The bearing of this passage, not only on the matter now in hand, but on the whole subject of the present address, seems

9

to us very vital.   The case was one of simple affinity—that of a step-mother.   If it should be said, as it has been, that the father might possibly have been alive, we reckon this incredible, unless it can be also believed that the Corinthian Church had sunk so low as to have retained in its communion, without compunction, a man guilty of the double crime of adultery and incest.   But supposing it were granted, though we deem it incredible, that the father might have been alive, yet the apostle places the sin distinctively on the footing of the relationship of the parties, ' that one should have his father's wife '—even as John the Baptist said to Herod, ' It is not lawful for thee to have thy brother's wife,' although we *do* know from Josephus that in this case the former husband was alive.   The Baptist's charge of guilt, however, had distinctive reference to the sin of incest—to the violation of that Levitical law (which admitted of but a single exception, and that of the most express character), ' If a man shall take his brother's wife, it is an unclean thing : he hath uncovered his brother's nakedness ; they shall be childless.'   And so it happens, accordingly, that we know further from Josephus that the case of Herodias lay outside the shelter of the single exception ; for he tells us that there was a child of the previous marriage, ' after whose birth,' he says, ' having made up her mind to violate the *laws of her country*' (but *adultery* was, of course, a violation of the laws of all countries), ' she was married to Herod, brother, by the same father, of her husband, whom, though still in life, she forsook.'   Returning, however, to the apostle's words, and as more expressly bearing on the matter presently in hand, it is to be observed that Paul assumes manifestly the existence of a law, well known in the Christian Church, and binding all its members, prohibiting connection with a step-mother.   What could that law have been but the Levitical, which, more than once, solemnly denounces such a connection as incestuous and vile ?   Even should it be thought, indeed, that he may refer only to the law of nature, this reference would but strengthen our argument in some respects the more.   The contrast, however, which he marks to the Gentiles, who had the law of nature only, seems to us to forbid the idea of his having intended nothing more than that the Corinthian Church were under that law, as to relationships barring marriage, and to shut us up to the conclusion that he refers to the Levitical law of incest, as of unchanged, well known, and universal obligation.

Fourthly—and finally as to the permanency of the law of incest in Leviticus—it is to be borne in mind that so far has the Gospel been from relaxing previously existing restrictions on marriage, that whatever changes it has brought with it have been all in the opposite direction—the Lord Jesus having both made an end of the previous toleration of polygamy, and confined the lawfulness of divorce within limits unknown under the former dispensation.   Whence it would appear to us that, even supposing doubts to remain in any mind as to the permanently binding character of the Levitical statute, more strictly and technically considered, the whole *principles* of it, at least, with its prohibitions— belonging, as they undoubtedly do, to things moral and universal in their nature—must be held both to bind the Christian conscience to the full, and to form the regulative principles according to which the marriage laws of Christian countries ought to be framed.

But now it is alleged that, admitting the law of incest in Leviticus to be of permanent and universal obligation, an *exception is made in the body of that law itself in the case of marriage with a deceased wife's sister*.   The exception is said to be found in the eighteenth verse of chapter eighteen, as follows : ' Neither shalt thou take a wife to her sister, to vex her, to uncover her nakedness, beside the other in her lifetime. We are persuaded that the allegation is thoroughly and demonstrably groundless ; and we will look at it with some care.

Let the eighteenth verse, then, be first for a moment supposed absent from the statute. In this case it is certain that marriage with the sister of a deceased wife is prohibited by it in more ways than one. Generally, it is forbidden by the great principle which we have already seen to pervade the statute throughout, and apart from which it is altogether unintelligible, that consanguinity and affinity stand, in the matter of forbidden degrees, on the same footing—so that a man no more may marry his wife's sister than he may marry his own. And, more specifically, it is prohibited in the law of the sixteenth verse against marriage with a brother's wife, the degree of propinquity being in both these cases the same —brother's wife, wife's sister—and the whole structure of the law demanding that the one prohibition be held to carry the other along with it, even as, for instance, when a son is forbidden to marry his mother, we have seen that this carries unavoidably with it the prohibition, though not ex- pressed, of a father's marriage with his daughter—which last were otherwise not forbidden in the statute at all. Or, to put the argument otherwise : the prohibitions in Leviticus xviii. and xx. are all masculine in their form—all after the manner of the Old Testament, addressed to the man. But just as when, in the tenth commandment of the Decalogue, the man is forbidden to covet his neighbour's wife, the woman is thereby no less forbidden to covet her neighbour's husband, so anyone who will glance at the summary given in our foot-note on page 4 of the forbidden connections specified in Leviticus xviii. and xx., will at once perceive that, although they take the form of the *man's* duty only, they necessarily and throughout imply a correlative and corresponding duty on the part of the woman—that, for example, when a man is forbidden to marry his step-mother, the woman is thereby forbidden to marry her step-father ; and, in like manner, when the man is forbidden to marry his brother's wife, the woman is thereby no less forbidden to marry her sister's husband. It is certain, in short, that supposing the eighteenth verse absent from the statute, marriage with a deceased wife's sister is prohibited by it as incestuous, more ways than one.

But then the eighteenth verse is in the statute, and we are certainly not entitled, disregarding the allegation which is made respecting it, to assume that God could not possibly have made an exception in His law in favour of the marriage in question. But we *are* entitled to affirm this, that the probabilities and presumptions are all against the allegation, and that the alleged exceptional permission, as running counter to the entire principles and tenor of the statute otherwise, behoved at least to be given *in a manner clear and unmistakable.* Thus, to take the Levirate law for an illustration. It did seem meet to the supreme Lawgiver that there should be a single exception to the prohibition of marriage with a deceased brother's wife. But then the exception became the subject of a clear and express law (Deut. **xxv.** 5) : ' If brethren dwell together, and one of them die, and have no child, the wife of the dead shall not marry without unto a stranger ; her husband's brother shall,' &c. But how stands the case, on the other hand, as to the exceptional permission alleged to be given in favour of marriage— not in a single defined case, but under any and all circumstances—with a deceased wife's sister? Is it given in a manner clear and unmistakable? Is it really given at all? The following considerations will, we think, make it apparent that both questions must be answered unhesitatingly in the negative.

(1) *First.*—The exceptional permission is not alleged to

13

be given in express terms, but by implication only, or inference, thus : ' Neither shalt thou take a wife to her sister, to vex her, to uncover her nakedness, beside the other in her life-time.' Surely it is a thing very unlikely, that a permission running in the face of the whole principles and tenor of a statute should be given in the form of. a mere inference from one of its prohibitions.

(2) *Secondly.*—The exceptional permission, if given at all, is given in a verse confessedly of very peculiar language and disputed interpretation. We do not require to remind the brethren we address that there is a marginal rendering of it, adopted by distinguished men, which makes it a simple prohibition of polygamy, without reference to the subject of a wife's sister at all.*

(3) But, *thirdly.*—Let it be assumed that the textual rendering is the correct one, ' Neither .shalt thou take a wife to her sister, to vex her, to uncover her nakedness, beside the other in her life-time.' The argument for the alleged exceptional permission lies in the closing words, ' in her life-time.' But it is well known to the student of Scripture that when a thing is stated with reference to a particular time, it does not by any means follow, as a matter of course, that the reverse holds good *after that time.* Everything as to this depends on the particular circumstances. And thus the inference drawn from the words ' in her life-time,' in proof of the lawfulness of marriage with a wife's sister after her death, is wholly precarious—wholly insufficient to establish a permission running in the face of the entire principles and tenor of the statute otherwise.

(4) *Fourthly.*—Since, according to the hypothesis, this verse is a restriction placed on polygamy—tolerated at that

---

* The marginal rendering is ' one wife to another' ; or, yet more literally, ' one woman to another.'

time among the Jews 'for the hardness of their hearts'—the closing words 'in her life-time' cannot be shown to be anything more than a fuller and more express intimation that it *is* a case of polygamy which is the subject of legislation in the verse—as if it had been simply said, 'If thou mayest take two wives, yet on no account shalt thou take two sisters at the same time.' No doubt, the obvious objection presents itself—If, as you maintain, marriage with a wife's sister, under all circumstances, has already been prohibited by the statute, to what purpose the superfluous and confusing repetition in verse 18th? A comparison of verse 11th with verse 9th furnishes at once an analogous case and a solution of the difficulty. In legislating for the Israelites on the relationships which bar marriage, two cases might very naturally receive peculiar prominence, and be guarded with special care. The revered fathers of the nation, Abraham and Jacob, had married, the one his sister by the father's side, and the other, two sisters. In verse 9th the prohibition is full and express against marriage with a sister, whether daughter of father or mother, lawfully or unlawfully begotten. Nevertheless, lest an Israelite might plead the example of Abraham and Sarah (Gen. xx. 12) as an excuse for transgressing the statute, their special case is singled out in verse 11th, and again marriage with a half-sister is prohibited, in order to leave no room for dubiety or evasion. In like manner, marriage with a wife's sister had by clear implication been prohibited, both by the general principle pervading the statute, and specifically by verse 16th. Lest, however, Jacob's having married Rachel and Leah might tempt the Jews to follow his example, the simultaneous marriage of sisters is expressly prohibited in verse 18th, special mention also being made of the evils, very apparent in Jacob's family, of every case of polygamy, which, though still tolerated among the Israelites, is here tacitly discouraged, when they are reminded of the mutual jealousy and vexation to which it had given rise even under the most favourable circumstances. Altogether, the words 'in her life-time' (on which, in the face of the entire statute otherwise, rests the whole argument for the lawfulness of marriage with a deceased wife's sister) cannot be proved to import necessarily anything more than that the connection which is referred to and forbidden in the verse is with *two sisters taken together*, while the prohibition of marriage with sisters under *other* circumstances had already been enacted in a manner much too clear to admit of any words in this verse being stretched beyond that case of polygamous connection which is the express subject of it.

(5) *Fifthly.*—Before the inference drawn from the closing words of the eighteenth verse, in the face of the entire statute otherwise, can be made good, it requires to be proved that the verse will not admit of *any other fair construction*—any construction save that of an implied permission to marry a wife's sister after her death. But, apart altogether from the marginal translation, and still assuming the textual rendering to be the correct one, there are other views of the meaning of the verse which may be, and have been, taken. We, who stand on the clearly expressed and quite unambiguous general law, are not obliged to make an absolute choice among these. It is enough, for the setting aside of the anomalous alleged permission, if the verse admits of being interpreted, *in any way*, in harmony with the general law. As, for example, the prohibition may be viewed as having reference simply to *an additional aggravation* of the violation of the general law, by reason of the peculiar vexation and sorrow that might arise from such incest to a living sister—as if it had been said, Thou shalt not uncover the nakedness of thy wife's sister, it is the nakedness (by the law of affinity) of thy sister. But, *least of all*—in imitation

of the evil practice of the heathen, a practice into which even a patriarch was tempted to fall—shalt thou take her, to uncover her nakedness, in thy wife's life-time; since such an alliance, besides involving the incestuous violation of the law of affinity, in general, would additionally entail on her a life of aggravated vexation and misery. We repeat that we are not required to make a choice among different methods of explaining a difficult verse in harmony with the statute generally—of which other examples might have been given. But one and all of them must be proved inadmissible, else the verse can avail nothing as a sanction for the marriages in question.

(6) *Sixthly.*—It is impossible to hold that this verse gives an exceptional permission to marry a deceased wife's sister, without rendering the whole statute self-contradictory and unintelligible, and, more specifically, without placing the seventeenth verse, running, though it does, without a break into the eighteenth, in irreconcilable contrariety to it. The seventeenth verse is in these words : ' Thou shalt not uncover the nakedness of a woman and her daughter, neither shalt thou take her son's daughter, or her daughter's daughter, to uncover her nakedness ; for they are her near kinswomen : it is wickedness.' Then, 'Neither shalt thou take' (literally, 'and thou shalt not take') 'a wife to her sister, to vex her, to uncover her nakedness, beside the other in her life-time.' In the one verse, that is to say, it is forbidden to a man, in the most solemn manner, to have connection with his step-daughter, or his step-grand-daughter, and on the express ground that, although there is no blood relationship between him and them, they are the near kinswomen of his wife, and so his near kindred by affinity, and it were 'wickedness.' And yet it is affirmed that in the very next verse—quite incidentally—as in part of the same sentence, and as if there were no anomaly at all

in it, permission is given to a man to marry his wife's sister, though quite as nearly re'ated to him as his step-grand-daughter, whom it were *wickedness* for him to take ! Is this credible ? No doubt the words 'in her life-time' occur in the eighteenth verse, and it is said that the decease of the first wife makes now all the difference. But it palpably can make no difference at all *between the cases in the seventeenth and eighteenth verses respectively.* If the 'wickedness' of marriage with a wife's sister ceases with and by the death of the wife, necessarily by the same death must cease also the 'wickedness' of marriage with his step-daughter or step-granddaughter. And it must be in fact held that the Lawgiver intended in the seventeenth verse, though he does not say so in as many words, to permit marriage with a step-daughter also, after the death of her mother. But what in this case comes of the alleged *exceptional* permission in favour of marriage with a wife's sister ? Assuredly the words ' in her life-time' cannot avail to prove this marriage lawful, without proving a very great deal more—even that the 'wickedness' of marriage with a step-mother, or a mother-in-law, or a daughter-in-law, or a step-daughter, ceases with the death of the woman by whom the affinity came. It is impossible to escape this conclusion if the eighteenth verse permits marriage with a deceased wife's sister. This permission cannot possibly be held as *exceptional*, without setting the seventeenth verse, notwithstanding its intimate connection with the eighteenth, in flat contra-riety to it. The lawfulness of marriage with a wife's sister can be maintained only on the much more sweeping, and alto-gether untenable, ground, that the death of either spouse in a marriage *makes an end of the whole affinity which came by it with the kindred of the other.* We are persuaded, accordingly, that this last is the ground, however extreme, which is held at bottom by the friends of the proposed change of law. No doubt they find that the eighteenth verse respecting the wife's sister affords, in its closing words, a plausible pretext for the marriages they desire to have legalised, and so they usually prefer taking the ground of an exceptional permission given in that verse in favour of marriage with a wife's sister. But their reasonings run up unavoidably into the far broader ground, that the death of either party abolishes the whole relationship together with the kindred of the other. Unfortunately they do not often venture to avow this ground frankly and openly. If they did, the country would at once take alarm, discovering that the lawfulness of marriage with a wife's sister was pleaded for, and could only be pleaded for, in conjunction with that of marriage with a mother-in-law, a step-mother, a daughter-in-law, a step-daughter. And as for the voice of God's Word about the abolition, by the death of either spouse, of the whole relationship to the kindred of the other, it would easily be seen that Scripture and natural feeling were as to this thoroughly at one. It would be seen that the whole Book of Ruth, for example, proceeds on the assumption, and again and again expressly declares, that the death of Elimelech left altogether untouched the relationship, with its whole claims and duties, between his blood relative Boaz, on the one hand, and Naomi his widow, and her daughter-in-law Ruth the Moabitess, on the other. And as regards the Levitical statute, it would be seen that its prohibition—for example (xx. 21) : 'If a man shall take his brother's wife, it is an unclean thing; he hath uncovered his brother's nakedness ; they shall be childless'—necessarily assumes the relationship with the wife to remain untouched by the brother's death ; since, otherwise, and if it be affirmed that the prohibition is merely directed against marriage with the wife of a brother *still alive*, the wild conclusion must follow that, although the enactment is now no more than a law against adultery, the punishment of child-lessness, in place of death, is attached to an adultery peculiarly aggravated, while the entire prohibition of adultery *with a brother's wife* is something at least very like a licence to commit that crime with any other woman. Beyond question it is a marriage with a *deceased* brother's wife which is prohibited, and prohibited on the ground that his decease leaves the whole relationship which came by the marriage untouched.

Before passing from our reference to the seventeenth verse, and its prohibition of marriage with a step-daughter or step-granddaughter, we cannot help noticing how it disposes at once of an assertion often and confidently made, that there might be *physiological* reasons for the prohibition of marriage with a brother's wife while marriage with a wife's sister is not forbidden. In different ways the assertion might be refuted; and no one, we think, can calmly read the statute without perceiving that its grounds and reasons are throughout moral, not physical. Suffice it, however, to say that, physiologically, there can be no difference between marriage with a wife's sister, and a wife's daughter, or grand-daughter; and yet the seventeenth verse is in these decisive words : ' Thou shalt not uncover the nakedness of a woman and her daughter, neither shalt thou take her son's daughter, or her daughter's daughter, to uncover her nakedness; for they are her near kinswomen : it is wickedness.'

(7) *Finally.*—The words in the eighteenth verse, ' to uncover her nakedness,' are viewed by the advocates of the proposed change of law (and their cause requires that they view them) as simply equivalent to the consummating of marriage. And so, considering them of no importance in the verse, they are accustomed to quote it thus : ' Neither shalt thou take a wife to her sister, to vex her, beside the other in her life-time.' We are persuaded, however, that

this peculiar expression is not a mere synonym for the consummating of marriage—is not a superfluous redundancy in the verse, but belongs to its very soul, being expressive of an *intrinsic vileness* in the marriage of sisters, which must render it unlawful under any circumstances. On an examination of all the places where the phrase 'uncovering nakedness' occurs, it will nowhere be found descriptive of simple marriage, but found everywhere to relate to something intrinsically odious and vile. It is the proper and constant phrase for an incestuous connection—occasionally, indeed, used otherwise, but never apart from what is in its own nature loathsome. So that the true and full ground of the prohibition in this verse is, Neither shalt thou take a wife to her sister, *to vex her by uncovering her nakedness*—to vex her, that is to say, *by the shame and grievance of an incestuous husband.* And thus does it come out at last, that so very far is this verse from giving permission to marry a wife's sister, that it actually by implication forbids it—although, certainly, such a prohibition was not necessary, the statute having before forbidden it in different ways ; and although it is but a gross misrepresentation, or entire misapprehension, of the grounds on which the present marriage law is vindicated, to affirm, as has often been done, that the defence of it rests mainly on this eighteenth verse. The fact is far otherwise indeed. But the *adversaries* of the existing law have absolutely and confessedly nothing save this verse in all the Scriptures on which to rest their cause. That it is but a foundation of sand, has, we trust, been made evident. A single verse, of difficult interpretation, is taken forth, and, in place of being explained in harmony with the rest, is so interpreted as to stand in flat contradiction to the rest, stultifying the principles and legislation of the chapter. And, indeed, so certain is it that marriage with the sister of a deceased wife is forbidden by the Levitical statute, that, fain as its advocates are to plead this eighteenth verse, as seeming, on a first view of it, to favour their opinions, their only real ground is the alleged temporary and obsolete character of the entire statute. They are very willing, in other words, to avail themselves of the eighteenth verse, and, in using it, to seem as if they acknowledged the authority of the whole. But they are just as ready, when it seems to them more expedient, to exchange this ground for the assertion, that the authority of the entire statute has long since passed away. But this ground also has, we trust, been proved wholly untenable. And thus, bringing our argument from God's Word to a close, we humbly think it has been demonstrated that the words of the Westminster Confession rest on irrefragable grounds of Scripture—both Old Testament and New—'THE MAN MAY NOT MARRY ANY OF HIS WIFE'S KINDRED NEARER IN BLOOD THAN HE MAY OF HIS OWN, NOR THE WOMAN OF HER HUSBAND'S KINDRED NEARER IN BLOOD THAN OF HER OWN.'

II. And now a much briefer space will be sufficient, as we hope, to make it manifest that the proposed change of law would be as *destructive socially* as we hold it to be demonstrably opposed to the authority of God in His Word. We touch, in the second place, on the question of expediency—the more immediately practical and social bearings of the legalising of marriage with a deceased wife's sister.

1. And first, let us assume for a moment, what the advocates of this change would fain persuade us of, that it need not carry any farther changes along with it—that marriage with a deceased wife's sister might be legalised without the risk of otherwise unsettling and altering our marriage laws. But this one alteration would involve a revolution in the whole domestic life of the country. It were the abolishing in effect, as has been often said, of the entire relation of

brothers and sisters-in-law. A woman who may eventually become a man's wife, never can be his sister. The familiar attentions of a brother he may not show to her, nor may she accept them at his hand. In the same hour in which marriage becomes possible with her sister's husband, she must for ever pass out of the shelter and the sacredness of sisterhood, and, at the best, be in his house simply as any other friend, or more distant relative, would be. At present she may, without embarrassment or suspicion, be constantly under his roof, showing his children, as their aunt, all fond attentions, and, as his sister-in-law, receiving from him expressions of familiar brotherly endearment. But once let it be made possible for the sister-in-law to become the wife, and the aunt the step-mother, and all is immediately changed—and not changed, be it borne in mind, for those households only where these marriages are not disapproved of, but, out of regard to their interests, changed for the whole families and households of the country. They tell us it is a hard thing that, because *we* reckon marriage with a wife's sister contrary to God's will, they, who entertain a different opinion, and have contracted such marriages, shall be held as living in concubinage. But where does the *real* hardship lie? Is it theirs, or is it ours? They were under no pressure *of conscience* to contract these marriages. They entered into them because they would—believing them, we are quite ready to suppose, not forbidden by Scripture, but assuredly not believing them *enjoined* by it, and well knowing that they were forbidden at least by the laws of the country, which no man is entitled to break unless they forbid his doing a thing which God requires, or require him to do what God forbids. And now, for their relief from the effects of a wilful violation of their country's law, they claim to have a change made in it which cannot affect their condition only, but must tell vitally on ours also—forcing an entirely new state of family life on all the households of the country. Even while our wives are in good health, our beloved sisters-in-law must cease to be in our homes what they once were. So soon, however, as the health of a wife gives way, and she becomes unequal to the charge of her family, the new and strange question is invited within the household, whether the attentions of sister-in-law and aunt shall not be exchanged for those of wife and step-mother. The less can the question fail to arise, since the very ground on which the change is advocated is the special suitableness of the sister-in-law to occupy the place of the deceased wife. And thus does it come to pass, strange to say, that the very attentions which it *is* so natural and desirable for the sister-in-law to pay during the sickness of the wife, become impossible to be shown during that period without the most painful misunderstandings. And when at length the wife dies, how can there now any longer be a medium course between the widower's at once proposing marriage to the sister, and her retiring out of that very position of usefulness for the sake of which these marriages are pleaded for? An extraordinary method truly this, of relieving from their self-imposed hardship the comparatively few persons who have contracted these marriages, to make a change in the law which shall not only abolish, for the country at large, the whole relation of sisters and brothers-in-law, but deprive the overwhelming majority of its households of that very care of the sister-in-law and aunt, for whose sake it is affirmed that the change ought to be made! All this on the supposition that, by a change of law, the relation of sisters and brothers-in-law can be so thoroughly dissolved as to place the parties affected in the same condition with utter strangers. But is this possible? Take the case of the female. She is no longer a sister-in-law—no longer a sister so far that to tamper with her purity, or dream of sexual connection with her, would involve all the horror of incest, but she continues to move in the same family circle, after this shield of chastity is withdrawn. She may be in constant and familiar intercourse with those whom the present law constitutes her brothers. She may live under the same roof. Temptation would come with opportunity, and we can only hint at the widespread demoralisation of society which might thus ensue—not to speak of sad results, which, under the circumstances supposed, actually have ensued.

2. Thus far we have reasoned on the assumption that marriage with a wife's sister might be legalised without necessitating any further changes on the marriage law of the country. The fact, however, we believe to be far otherwise indeed. Those who are acquainted with the history of this agitation (extending now over a period of more than thirty years) are well aware that other changes have been again and again proposed in the Legislature, and withdrawn only to give this one, with its semblance of support in a single clause of the Levitical statute, better hopes of success. But as the real ground of the agitation has had little indeed to do with that statute from the beginning—as, on the contrary, its manifest drift has been all along, if possible, to get rid of its whole obligation, and to have our marriage laws henceforth weighed and dealt with independently of it, so it is certain that the legalising of marriage with a wife's sister would immediately be found a change much too arbitrary, and destitute of any solid foundation of principle to be permitted to remain alone. As it would be tantamount to the practical abandonment of the Levitical statute—which is the basis of our present marriage laws—marriage with a brother's wife, and with a wife's niece, would become the next subjects of agitation. And should other marriages still more obnoxious, but which in Continental countries that

have admitted this one, have followed in its wake, be clamoured for, at least they could no longer be resisted on any definite ground of principle.

3. It is of the last importance that the law as to forbidden degrees in marriage *should proceed on some thoroughly simple and intelligible principle.* Apart from such a principle, legislation could not possibly be wise or self-consistent; nor could the country be reasonably expected to yield a hearty and unhesitating compliance with the law. Failing to commend itself to the understanding and conscience of the community, the law, instead of continuing settled from age to age, behoved to be liable to ceaseless change—to be open to endless and not unreasonable questions, as to why such a marriage was permitted, and such another forbidden; and thus the conscience of the nation, in a matter of singular delicacy, should become gradually debauched, and its domestic peace and purity be by degrees undermined and destroyed. Well; here is a principle thoroughly simple, self-consistent, intelligible—'The man may not marry any of his wife's kindred nearer in blood than he may of his own.' This is the principle which, from time immemorial, and taken from the Levitical law of incest, has actually ruled the marriage laws of Britain. But this whole principle must be abandoned if marriage with the sister of a deceased wife is to be permitted. Thenceforth forbidden degrees might remain, but none of them on the ground of *this principle.* And the advocates of the proposed change have never even attempted to indicate another which shall take its place. Of course there are numberless matters of civil legislation which may proceed with sufficient safety on calculations of simple expediency. But if there be any one matter as to which, more than another, the guidance of some fixed and definite principle is required, surely it is that of the relationships in which marriage shall be allowed or

forbidden by law. To legalise marriage, in short, with a deceased wife's sister, were unavoidably to unsettle the whole marriage laws of Britain, and throw them loose from all fixed and intelligible principle together. In 1849, Mr. Gladstone, dwelling on the danger of breaking down the existing law of prohibited degrees, which he described as 'a law perfectly definite,' emphatically asked, 'Where is this legislation to stop?' The present Lord Chancellor, in a very able pamphlet published by him (Sir Wm. Page Wood) some years ago, thus writes :—'I have taken mere heathen ground in this letter.* But by all the joys of that tie of real brotherhood which binds us to the sister of our wife, by all the aspirations of a high and holy morality, be the man's religious faith what it may ; by all the horrors of an ever-deepening, hopeless sinking into the abyss of cold, cynical indifference as to the purity of our national life, I implore all men to aid us in resisting the proposed change of the home life of England. A friend smiled when I said, "I would rather hear of the landing of 300,000 French at Dover than of the passing of this Bill." It was no exaggeration of my feelings. We can, and should, repel an external foe ; but inward decay and rottenness will destroy us, sap our morals, and our only life worth having is at an end. Rome was burnt by the Gauls, but the Roman senate was unappalled. Hannibal caused her power to shrink to the dimensions of her walls, but a Roman nobly bought at full price the ground on which he had encamped. In the reign of Claudius, on the contrary, she seemed to command the known world, but that decree by which he was permitted to impugn her moral code, showed that she was tottering to her fall. And most firmly do I believe, that the first breach in the social laws of England that govern marriage will be a clear indication of a moral failure, and a

* The first of two.

fall graver than any that ancient or modern history has recorded.'

And now, suffer us to bring this Address to a close with a sentence or two of respectful and affectionate appeal. If your views on this great question agree with ours in the main, then would we, with the utmost earnestness, entreat you to bring your influence to bear, by petitions to the Legislature and otherwise, against the threatened change of law. If, on the other hand, we have failed to carry conviction fully to your minds, yet we take leave to submit a view of the course of duty which seems to us worthy of very serious consideration. Scripture assuredly does not *require* any man to marry the sister of his deceased wife, even assuming that it does not forbid him. Thus the existing law brings no pressure to bear on *conscience*, but, at the worst, only places an unnecessary restraint on freedom. Conscience is then touched for the first time, when human law either commands what God forbids, or prohibits what God has commanded. It is further certain that no state of the marriage law could exactly meet the views of all. For example, if marriage with a deceased wife's sister were legalised to-morrow, there would remain many persons who believe that marriage with a deceased brother's wife, or with a wife's niece, involves no impropriety. If there be real hardship from the present law in the one case, there could not fail to remain, until it should be further altered, a hardship precisely similar in the others. *Some* fixed law of forbidden degrees there must be. No single change made on the present one would please all ; and no injury is done to anyone's *conscience* by the law as it stands. Thus it seems to us to follow unavoidably, that if the present marriage law be, as a whole, scriptural, and socially expedient—if it be not radically and vitally unsound (as no one we know of has ever affirmed it to be), then it were most unwise—even apart from the far higher ground we have taken in this address—to tamper with it, for the sake of a small number of persons who deem their freedom to be needlessly restrained by it in some one particular, and have possibly, without any pressure on their *consciences*, married in deliberate defiance of it. But how, on the other hand, does the case stand as to *us*, assuredly representing in this matter multitudes over the country, who believe these marriages to be *forbidden by God in His Word?* It is with us no mere matter of ' Church Law,' but an article of our faith. *As* an article of faith, however, it has of course become, over and above, the law of our Churches, which we have no choice but to administer, in the way of shutting out from the table of the Lord Jesus those who have entered into these alliances—just as we should still be compelled to shut them out were the civil law changed, and the alliances rendered valid as to civil effects. Moreover, as to the hardship to us, and to the multitudes who think with us, it were no consolation to be told (as at present we are so often told in public prints) that no one seeks to compel *us* to contract these marriages. No doubt. But, unfortunately, the simple legalising of them would at once revolutionise the state of all our households together ! We know how much you revere the memory of your forefathers' struggles in the cause of liberty of conscience. May we not, on that sacred ground, make our closing appeal to you, since *conscience* is not aggrieved by the law as it stands, while the proposed legislation must force a change we recoil from the thought of on the condition of all our households and families, and compel our Churches, so far as we know their mind, to enter into a painful and enduring conflict with the law of the State—unless, indeed, we should be tempted to avoid the conflict by suffering a civil law, anti-scriptural, in our judgment, and religiously

void, to become the rule of our spiritual discipline? May
we venture, with the utmost respect, to submit this question
for your consideration, whether anything short of a clear
and full conviction that the present law is both without
ground in Scripture and socially inexpedient, can warrant
the lending of any countenance to the agitation for its
change?

With great regard, we are, Reverend and Dear Sirs,
yours in the bonds of the Gospel,

> CHAS. J. BROWN, D.D.,
>> Minister of Free New North Church, Edinburgh.
>
> JAMES BEGG, D.D.,
>> Minister of Newington Free Church, Edinburgh.
>
> WILLIAM BINNIE, D.D.,
>> Professor of Theology in the Reformed Presbyterian
>> Church.
>
> DAVID BROWN, D.D.,
>> Professor of Theology, Free Church, Aberdeen.
>
> ROB. BUCHANAN, D.D.,
>> Minister of the Free College Church, Glasgow.
>
> JOHN CAIRNS, D.D.,
>> Professor of Theology in the United Presbyterian
>> Church.
>
> ROBERT S. CANDLISH, D.D.,
>> Principal of the New College, and Minister of Free
>> St. George's, Edinburgh.
>
> THOMAS J. CRAWFORD, D.D.,
>> Professor of Divinity in the University of Edinburgh.
>
> GEO. C. M. DOUGLAS,
>> Professor of Hebrew, Free Church College, Glasgow.
>
> ALEXANDER DUFF, D.D., LL.D.,
>> Professor of Evangelistic Theology, New College,
>> Edinburgh.
>
> PATRICK FAIRBAIRN, D.D.,
>> Principal and Professor in the Free Church College,
>> Glasgow.

30

JAMES GIBSON, M.A., D.D.,
Professor of Systematic Theology, and of Church
History, Free Church College, Glasgow.

WILLIAM H. GOOLD, D.D.,
Professor of Biblical Literature in the Reformed
Presbyterian Church, Edinburgh.

THOMAS GUTHRIE, D.D.,
Minister of Free St. John's Church, Edinburgh.

N. M'MICHAEL, D.D.,
Professor of the History of Doctrine, United Presbyterian Church.

ALEXANDER McEWAN, D.D.,
Claremont United Presbyterian Church, Glasgow.

J. MACRAE, D.D.,
Minister of Hawick.

WILLIAM MARSHALL, D.D.,
United Presbyterian Church, Coupar-Angus.

ALEX. F. MITCHELL, D.D.,
Professor of Ecclesiastical History in the University
of St. Andrews.

MATTHEW MURRAY, D.D.,
Professor of Divinity of the Original Secession
Church, Glasgow.

ROBERT NISBET, D.D.,
Minister of West St. Giles's Parish, Edinburgh.

ANDREW SOMERVILLE, D.D.,
Ex-Foreign Mission Secretary of the United Presby-
terian Church, and Lecturer on Missions and
Evangelism.

WM. STEVENSON, D.D.,
Professor of Divinity and Church History in the
University of Edinburgh.

ANDREW THOMSON, D.D., F.R.S.E.,
Minister of United Presbyterian Church, Broughton
Place, Edinburgh.

EDINBURGH, *October* 1871.

31

We, the undersigned, also concur generally in the foregoing statement.

JAS. S. CANDLISH, D.D.,
>Professor of Theology, Free Church College, Glasgow.

JOHN CHRISTIE,
>Professor of Divinity and Church History, Aberdeen.

WILLIAM LEE, D.D.,
>Professor of Church History, University of Glasgow.

WILLIAM MILLIGAN, D.D.,
>Professor of Divinity and Biblical Criticism, Aberdeen.

K. M. PHIN, D.D.,
>Formerly Minister of Galashiels, now of the Church of Scotland Offices, Edinburgh.

ROBERT RAINY, D.D.,
>Principal and Professor, New College, Edinburgh.

THOMAS CROSKERY,
>Professor of Systematic Theology, Magee College, Derry.

JOHN JAMES GIVEN, Ph.D.,
>Professor of Hebrew and Hermeneutics, Magee College, Londonderry.

JAMES GLASGOW, D.D.,
>Professor of Oriental Languages in the General Assembly College, Belfast, and Magee College, Londonderry.

W. D. KILLEN, D.D.,
>Principal of the Presbyterian Theological Faculty, Ireland.

JAMES G. MURPHY, D.D.,
Professor of Hebrew, Belfast.

HENRY WALLACE,
Professor of Christian Ethics, Presbyterian College, Belfast.

ROBERT WATTS, D.D.,
Professor of Systematic Theology in the Assembly's College, Belfast.

THOMAS WITHEROW,
Professor of Church History, Magee College, Londonderry.

Spottiswoode & Co. Printers, New-street Square, London.

Marriage Law Defence Union Tracts.
No. IX.
OFFICE: 1 KING STREET, WESTMINSTER, S.W.

What the Bishops of the English Church say.

THE ARCHBISHOP OF CANTERBURY wrote:

The alteration of the marriage laws as to the sisters of wives would, in my opinion, be disastrous to morals and peace.
Truro, *January 31st*, 1883.   EDW. CANTUAR, *Elect.*

THE LATE ARCHBISHOP OF CANTERBURY, Dr. LONGLEY (then of York), in a Charge delivered in 1861, said:

It is argued that Lev. xviii. 18 sanctions a man's marriage with the sister of his deceased wife. To this objection various answers may be given. In the first place, this verse is, on all hands, acknowledged to be obscure in its meaning, and to admit of a great variety of explanations. Now, according to the rule of construction that is generally applied to human laws, a leading principle of an enactment can never be set aside by reason of some doubtful passage in a later portion of it, which may according to one out of many interpretations, seem to militate against that principle ; especially when we find that, what is relied upon as reversing the positive enactment appears in a negative form forbidding something else, and admitting the exception to the great principle of the law in question solely by inference and implication. I conclude, therefore, that whatever be the meaning of the eighteenth verse, whether it be a law against polygamy, or whether it bear some other of the various senses that have been attributed to it, it can in nowise have the power to abrogate the general law laid down in the sixteenth verse. To my mind, then, the question is concluded on Divine authority. I believe ' it is written ' that a man shall not approach those who are near of kin to him, and that the sister of his wife is included among those who are nearly allied to him, not merely by the argument from analogy, but also because God has declared that man and wife are one flesh, thus establishing the relationship of consanguinity in addition to that of affinity. And, if I am asked what is my view of it as a social question, I reply that my repugnance and aversion to such a relaxation of the existing law is of the strongest and the most insuperable kind. Who so fit, say some, to take charge of the children of the deceased mother as the aunt? This may well be granted, since the argument seems to tell with overwhelming force against the change; for, while in one or two instances the object might be furthered by the marriage of the aunt to the husband of the deceased sister, in the vast majority of cases it would be entirely frustrated by the necessary withdrawal of the sister from the family in which she might, by the alteration of the law, exchange the relation of aunt for that of mother-in-law.

THE LATE BISHOP GRAY, Metropolitan of Capetown, wrote :

Our Canon declares such marriages to be incestuous. The whole Church in every country and in every age, up to the Council of Trent, believed them to be so, and forbidden by God's Word. [Note that : 'forbidden by God's Word,' and *cf.* 'forbidden in Scripture' (and our laws) in the Table of Affinity in our Prayer-book.]

Again : The Canons say they have committed incest ; the early Church excommunicated them and made them separate. I believe God has forbidden these marriages. The Church of England has always believed the same.— Pp. 373, 374 of Bishop Gray's Life.

THE BISHOP OF FREDERICTON, Metropolitan of Canada, in a Charge delivered in 1880, said :

Everyone must see the necessity of some restraint on human passion in regard to marriage, for where no law existed in old times, mankind invariably ran into the most revolting excesses. 'They took them wives,' we read in the Scriptures, 'of all which they chose,' not only as many as they chose, but without any restraint in respect of affinity

3

or consanguinity. These vile practices were continued after the flood, among the Canaanites, and formed one of the chief reasons for their disinheritance by the hand of God. To counteract this detestable profligacy among the Jews, and to give a Divine sanction to a purer code of morals in respect to marriage, Moses was commissioned in the name of God, and as His mouthpiece, to make a table of degrees for restraint of marriage within certain limits founded on this general principle, announced in the beginning of the table—'None of you shall approach—viz., by marriage—to any that is near of kin to him—I am the Lord.' The table then gives instances of such affinity or consanguinity, for no difference is made between them, and the prohibitions are given exclusively to men, though women are equally concerned. It is not an exhaustive table of marriage, for marriage with a man's own daughter or his grandmother are not forbidden ; but it is evidently governed by the principle which the Lord lays down as the true foundation of the marriage relation. that man and wife become 'one flesh,' and consequently all the blood relationships which would be forbidden are equally unlawful after marriage to relations by affinity. This simple and Divinely authorised rule, in contradiction to the loose practices of the heathen, and even of some of the patriarchs, is the rule of Christian morals given to us by our Lord. Those who argue that all Jewish laws are obsolete, need to be reminded that the law of the Ten Commandments is read in the churches every Sunday, and that the Gospel spirit not only binds us to receive them in substance, but to carry them out on a higher, purer, and more exacting principle than a servile adhesion to the letter would indicate. Polygamy, for instance, and an easy system of divorce were tolerated among the Jews, because of the 'hardness of men's hearts ' ; but the Christian system supposes a higher power of self-restraint, and, therefore, demands a higher, not a lower, code of morals.

Besides, where are we going to stop in this downward course of licence? Already our legislators propose to go beyond the demands of agitators of the question in England. One law is to sanction the marriage of a woman to a deceased husband's brother. 'Why, then,' as Lord Hatherley says, 'should not a man's own brother desire his daughter in marriage, or look even to the reversion of his wife?' We may be sure that ingenious arguments would be found even for this revolting connection; but some are prepared to go even beyond this, and even bid us be of good courage and dare to do what Paul tells us 'is not so much as named among the heathen,' to take in marriage our father's wife. This language has, I understand, been supposed to be said in a joke, as if no man would desire it. In most instances it would, no doubt, be improbable, but it is far from being impossible. A man, we will suppose, marries early in life and his wife bears him sons, who are grown up when his wife dies. He then selects a wife very many years younger than himself. Meanwhile one of his sons marries early, and his wife dies leaving children. Finally the father dies. Why, then, if man's appetite is to be his sole guide, may not the son select his father's wife, no older than himself, to be the guardian of his children; and pretend that no one can possibly feel so much affection for them as his step-mother, and be so suited to be their guide? Then if she bears children, it is to one who ought to consider himself her son, and her children would be brothers and sisters to his children. This may be considered an exaggerated case, but is perfectly possible, and if we are to follow advice given either in seriousness or in sport, all the hideous consequences would follow. When we try principles we have a right to consider extreme and possible cases. The fact is, that the transgression of a Divine law always proceeds in a downward course and never ascends to the source of all purity, to Him who says, 'Be ye holy for I am holy.'

The BISHOP of LONDON, in the HOUSE OF LORDS, May, 1879:

This measure proposes to alter a law which is undoubtedly the law of the Christian Church—a law which is closely connected with the happiness, the peace, and the purity of family life; and if Bishops of the Church of England are not to be allowed to stand forward and express their opinion

5

on such a proposal, I hardly know of any question on which they can claim to exercise that right. The Bill has been advocated on the ground of its popularity, but the petitions presented in favour of the change have emanated from men. I believe that the immense majority of the women of England are against the measure. The measure has never passed a second reading in your lordships' House, and I sincerely trust it may never do so.

It is true that there is no direct prohibition of these marriages in Scripture, but it must not be assumed that therefore it is intended to approve of them. Scripture does not prohibit a man from marrying his own daughter, although a son is prohibited from marrying his mother; but it would be absurd to contend that that authorises marriages between fathers and daughters. The inference that the Church has from the earliest times drawn from the Scriptures is that these marriages are unlawful.

Under the existing law the relationship of a husband with that of his wife's sister is that of almost brother and sister, and it leads to much comfort and happiness in households. This is not a state of things that should be touched without very great consideration. The position of the wife's sister in a household must become much changed if she may become the wife of her sister's husband, and although there may of course be well-balanced minds upon whom the change in the law will produce but little effect, nevertheless there are numbers of persons of a jealous disposition who will find that such a change tends to disunite their households. If it be true that the happiness of married life and the peace and purity of the family are maintained by the restriction which at present exists, as I hold they are, your lordships would not be justified in taking away that prohibition. It is said that the sister of a deceased wife is the true guardian of her dead sister, and on that ground I trust your lordships will not deprive children so placed of that protection. For my part I believe from my experience of a large population, and such also is the experience of other clergymen with large parishes, that the proportion of widowers who desire to marry their deceased wife's sister is very small. This is

6

not a time to interfere with the sanctity of domestic life. Very recently the painful case has been brought under my notice of a man who has married his deceased son's widow, and who defends the act on the ground that he is the natural guardian of his son's children. An advertisement recently appeared in a newspaper calling upon those who desire to marry their nieces to support Sir Thomas Chambers's Bill, as a Bill to legalise such marriages would be sure to be introduced and carried soon after the present Bill became law. I regret that the Bill has been brought in, and I hope that your lordships will not only reject it, but do so by such a majority as may settle the question for the present generation. It will show that your lordships refuse to alter a law which has some claim to be a law of God, and is undoubtedly a law of the Church. It will show, too, that your lordships are not disposed to legislate for the few to the detriment of the many, or to disturb the peace and happiness of families, and possibly the purity of the community.

THE BISHOP OF WINCHESTER (then of ELY), in the HOUSE OF LORDS, May 19, 1870 :

With regard to the famous 18th chapter of Leviticus, its principle was to forbid certain marriages which were common among the Canaanites, and which are condemned as defiling the land. The interpretation of that chapter must, in some cases, inevitably be inferential, as all the degrees of consanguinity and affinity, within which it is unlawful to marry, are not enumerated ; but interpreters have uniformly agreed that parity of reasoning must govern our understanding of it. For instance, there is no prohibition of marriage between a father and daughter, nor between an uncle and niece ; but, as there is prohibition of the marriage of a son with his mother and of a nephew with his aunt, it is inferred, as a matter of course, that the parallel cases of father and daughter, uncle and niece, are by parity of reasoning included in the prohibition. The same is the case with regard to a wife's sister. The pro hibition is inferential, not direct. In verse 16 it is forbidden to marry a brother's widow, and in verse 14 it is forbidden

7

to marry an uncle's widow, because 'she is thine aunt.'
It is therefore incontrovertibly concluded that a wife's
sister, being the same relation as a brother's wife, and a
still nearer relation than an uncle's wife, is comprehended
in the prohibitions of verses 14 and 16. It equally follows
that, if thine uncle's wife 'is thine aunt,' thy wife's sister
must be thy sister. The re-affirmation of this general
principle in the New Testament is familiar to everyone
in the words of John the Baptist to Herod : 'It is not
lawful for thee to have thy brother's wife.' These, then,
are the general principles of the Mosaic law, and on these,
not on one or two disputed passages, the Christian Church
in all ages has founded its table of prohibited degrees.
Now the objections which are thought fatal to this principle
by the advocates of the Bill are really founded on two
passages, which are doubtful at the best, but which, rightly
interpreted, have nothing to do with the question. The
one is the passage in Deuteronomy xxv. 5, which is commonly known as the *lex leviratus*, the law of brothers-in-law,
and is supposed by some to be a formal repeal, as regards
at least the particular case, of the law in Leviticus xviii. 16.
It is said that ' if brethren dwell together and one of them
die and have no child, the wife of the dead shall not marry
a stranger, but her husband's brother shall take her to wife.'
Now the word ' brother ' in Hebrew is of very wide
meaning, and the translators of the Bible have put as the
marginal rendering 'next kinsman.' ' Brother ' in Hebrew
is continually used for kinsman, and ' sister ' for kinswoman.
The words, ' If brethren dwell together,' would, indeed,
more naturally be understood of a family of kinsmen as distinguished from the ' strangers ' with whom it was forbidden
to the Israelites to intermarry. In a very able pamphlet on
the Marriage of Brother and Sister-in-Law, by Mr. Galloway,[*]
it is shown that the ancient Jews did not consider this *lex
leviratus* as over-riding the prohibitions of Leviticus xviii.,
and that, in fact, the next of kin to whom the widow was
given was not the brother, but some relation not so near to
the deceased husband. This, then, is one of the disputed
texts. Rightly understood, it makes nothing for the advocates of the Bill. The other disputed text by which our

---

[*] Published by Rivingtons in 1870.

opponents strive to shake the testimony of Leviticus against marriage with a wife's sister is the famous 18th verse of the 18th chapter, the words of which in the common translation are, 'Thou shalt not take a wife to her sister to vex her, besides the other, in her life-time.' From this it has been inferred that after her life-time a man might take his wife's sister to wife. Besides other objections to this interpretation, it may be observed that the words rendered 'wife to her sister,' or more correctly 'woman to her sister,' occur over and over again in the Old Testament, as does the parallel case, 'man to his brother,' according as the antecedent is masculine or feminine, and that wherever else they occur they are and must be rendered simply 'one to another.' Thus, in Exodus xxvi. 3, it is said five curtains 'shall be coupled one to another,' literally, 'woman to her sister.' In Ezekiel i. 9, iii. 13, the wings of the living creatures are joined one to another, literally 'woman to her sister.' In Exodus xxv. 20, the faces of the cherubim were one towards another, literally ('face' being masculine) 'man to his brother.' So in Genesis xiii. 11, where human beings are spoken of, they are said to separate one from another, literally 'man from his brother.' This was, then, an idiomatic expression of constant occurrence ; and our translators, who were ripe scholars, and who often put their most important renderings in the margin, have placed in the margin here, 'one wife to another,' and have referred, in vindication of this translation, to Exodus xxvi. 3, where the same words must be rendered 'one to another.' The passage, therefore, is either prohibitory of polygamy, or else is to be joined to the verse immediately before it in explanation and amplification of that.

The BISHOP of OXFORD, in the HOUSE of LORDS, March 13, 1873 :

It has been claimed by those who have supported this Bill that England stands alone among the nations of Europe in their opposition to it, but I am not aware that there is a single European nation in which the law is as this Bill would make it. The state of law which would result

9

from passing such a Bill as this would be one of entire confusion and of intolerable wrong. Those (noble lords) who support the Bill seem to think that the existing restrictions consist of a series of haphazard prohibitions strung together anyhow; but the fact is that the table of prohibited degrees proceeds upon a very precise and intelligible principle. No man is allowed to marry a woman descended from his own parents, and no woman may marry a man descended from her parents; and, in addition to that, the blood relations of the wife are considered as the blood relations of the husband. These are the principles upon which the table of prohibited degrees is based. If this Bill should pass, one of these principles, that which makes the blood relation of the wife the blood relation of the husband, will be lost. If a man were to be allowed to marry his deceased wife's sister, it would be very unjust to interpose any bar between the marriage of a woman with her deceased husband's brother, or between the marriage of a man with his deceased wife's niece; yet the passing of this Bill would legalise marriage with a deceased wife's sister, and leave the other marriages incestuous, and the children resulting from them bastards. Now I do not insist on noble lords paying respect to logic or reason; but whereas, when my opinion is now asked on any such unions, I could say that they are forbidden on an intelligible principle, which has been for 300 years the law of England, what, if this Bill passes, can I say to a woman marrying her husband's brother? I should be obliged to say that a precisely analogous union has been legalised, but that as persons have not subscribed, agitated, and petitioned, and have not tickled Nonconformist antipathies, that particular union remains an incestuous one. As for the Act of 1835, what it did was to recognise the existing illegality alike of all marriages within the prohibited degrees, but to draw a retrospective distinction between consanguinity and affinity. Unions between a wife and her deceased husband's brother, and between a man and his wife's niece, were logically involved in this Bill, and could not be excluded, on the principle of it, without intolerable injustice and wrong to persons who had contracted them. As to the alleged absence of a desire for these other unions, I repeatedly meet with or hear of cases in which persons have contracted, or wish to contract them, especially the marriage of a man with his brother's widow. The canon law has nothing to do with the question, and though Scripture has much to do with it, I have not urged that view of the matter. I can make every allowance for the feelings which lead the real promoters of the Bill to put it forward year after year, every allowance for the tender affection and strong passion which actuate persons perhaps engaged to one another for years, even when such feelings provoke them to irrelevant abuse of this House, especially of the Episcopal bench ; but I have to consider, not individual affections and passions, but a consistent and tenable marriage law. I entreat your lordships not to pass a measure which will inflict intolerable wrong on those the prohibition of whose marriages is not repealed, and which, proceeding upon no sound principle, will be an outrage on morality and reason which Parliament has no right to permit.

THE BISHOP OF PETERBOROUGH in the HOUSE OF LORDS, June 12, 1882 :

It has been the fashion of the supporters of the Bill to say that the opposition of the Bishops to the Bill is a bigoted and narrow opposition, and that we who live in palaces know nothing of the wants and needs of the poor man ; that in disregard to those wants we cling to an obsolete Table of Affinity in our Prayer-books. But my opposition to the Bill would have been equally strong if the whole Table of Affinity were struck out. I oppose it because I claim to know as much as any of your lordships of the wants and sorrows of the poor man. The Bill is supposed to give to the poor man who has lost his wife the advantage of having someone come into his house to take care of his children upon whom he can rely to treat them with kindness. But the fact is that the Bill immediately deprives such a man of that advantage, and I wonder that it has not occurred to the supporters of the Bill that common decency and regard to the proprieties of life would always prevent a widower bringing a new wife into his house within a year, at least, of his former wife's death. Thus a man would be for one year, at least, prevented from bringing into his house a woman whom the law had declared to be no nearer to him than any other woman. A poor man has delicate feelings as well as a rich man, and could hardly be expected to ask his wife's sister to remain in the house for at least twelve months after his wife's death ; and thus for a year the children, whose case is so strongly advocated, would be left deprived of the most natural and effectual guardianship. As things are, during the presence of the sister-in-law, the widower would be able to find a suitable wife to take care of the children. Except, therefore, in the case of a guilty and criminal attachment during the lifetime of the wife, there is not the inducement which it was supposed there was even for the poor man to marry his sister-in-law. Then it is said that the sister-in-law would naturally prove the most affectionate guardian of her nephews and nieces. I doubt that proposition extremely. It may be the case so long as the sister-in-law, when married to the widower, remains childless, but when once there is raised in the breast of the woman the deepest passion of human nature, as well as the holiest—the love of her own children—there will arise all those formidable possibilities of jealousy of the children of her predecessor— her deceased sister. The feelings of the *injusta noverca* arise in great measure from the love of a mother as well as from baser motives, and are not to be overcome by the mere fact that the step-children are the children of the step-mother's own sister. On the contrary, it would often make the misery of a sister the more bitter. The whole of the step-mother's argument, therefore, falls to the ground in the presence of the broad facts of nature.

But I plead not only for the poor man, but for the rich man also. I plead, likewise, most earnestly for a class which especially needs protection—I plead for sisters-in-law as they are. The relation of sister-in-law and brother-in-law is one of the most beautiful and endearing of all family relationships. There is a sweet tenderness and a depth of affection in it which can only be found elsewhere in the nearest ties of blood relationship. There are hundreds of brothers-in-law and sisters-in-law who have no thought of marriage with each other, and it is these whom the Bill would necessarily sever, as it will be no longer possible for the sister-in-law to remain in her brother-in-law's house when her sister is dead. Social disturbance of a most painful kind will arise. I am not speaking of the disturbance which might arise before the second marriage. I am not speaking of the bitterness and jealousy which may be brought about, by the attractions of the younger sister, in the heart of the wife whom that younger sister might succeed. I am only speaking of the unfortunate sister-in-law who might for years have lived happily with her sister and nephews and nieces, but who, by this Bill, will be driven from her home. And that effect is to be brought about for the sake of an experiment, and to gratify the passions of rich men, who cannot control themselves, and these experimentalising philosophers who find nothing so safe as to experiment upon a matter of this kind, without a particle of principle to guide them. I protest against the Bill because it contains no shred of principle, because it would do harm to a number of most deserving persons, and because it picks out of a number of prohibited degrees one, and one only, while it does not introduce any fixed principle of legislation with regard to the marriage law. In the country districts, other Bishops and myself know that not only marriages of too near affinity, but marriages of too near consanguinity, are of sadly frequent occurrence in the homes of the poor ; and I dread the effect upon the home of the poor man when he is told that the highest legislative assembly in the whole realm has, without any fixed principle, and without any reason alleged for it, save this, that a great many desired it, introduced a perilous relaxation of the law of marriage, as to which not only he, the poor man, with his dull and uneducated mind, but the most accomplished and eloquent supporters of the Bill, cannot find any logical principle that would prevent their going on to other degrees, and to others and others again.

Spottiswoode & Co., Printers, New-street Square, London.

Marriage Law Defence Union Tracts.
No. X.
OFFICE : 1 KING STREET, WESTMINSTER, S.W.

What the Roman Catholic Church says on the Law of Marriage.

WHEN it is remembered that the Church in communion with Rome inherits the traditions of the early ages of an undivided Christendom, that it embraced for many centuries all the Christian nations of the West, including our own, and that it still comprises a considerable majority of professing Christians, its judgment on a grave question of religious and social morality must be allowed to have some weight, even with those beyond its own pale. It has, moreover, been frequently and most erroneously asserted or implied of late years by advocates of the proposed innovation on what has been from the first a fundamental principle of the English marriage law—which, to cite the high authority of Cardinal Manning, 'on this point is, to this moment, Catholic, and supports the discipline of the Church'—that Roman Catholics generally are in favour of legalising marriage with a deceased wife's sister, and, in taking this line, are only carrying out the professed principles of their Church. Both statements, the second especially, are in the teeth of facts. No apology, then, is needed for a brief statement—and it shall be made as brief as is consistent with a due regard to the historical evidence—of the real authoritative teaching of the Roman Catholic Church on the subject from the beginning.

In the early ages Christendom had a common centre and a common faith, and the teaching of Rome was therefore identical with the Christian tradition generally. What that tradition was in reference to marriage within the prohibited Levitical degrees, including the wife's sister, there cannot be a shadow of doubt. It is true that during the first three centuries—putting aside the so-called Apostolic Canons, the precise date of which is uncertain—no conciliar enactments on the subject exist, for much the same reason that Solon made no law against parricide. But it has further to be borne in mind that, for obvious reasons, comparatively few Councils were held during the ages of persecution; while, on the other hand, there was less need of corrective legislation as long as the standard of Christian purity was sustained by the rougher discipline of martyrdom. Moreover, in most particulars—the exceptions will be noted presently—the marriage law of the Roman Empire conformed to the rule of Leviticus and of the Church. In the first century there is no record of any Synod except that mentioned in the Acts of the Apostles; the few held in the second century were concerned exclusively with the Montanist heresy and the controversy about the time for the observance of Easter; the Synods of the third century, which were not summoned to examine charges against particular individuals, such as Origen and Paul of Samosata, were occupied with Novatianism or with the question of heretical baptism. But at the beginning of the fourth century, according to Hefele in 305 or 306, we find the Council of Elvira (or Illiberis), in its 61st canon, forbidding marriage with a wife's sister, under the penalty of five years' exclusion from communion; while, a few years later, the second canon of the Synod of Neocæsarea excommunicates a woman, who has married her husband's brother, until death, when she may, on condition of breaking off her illegitimate union, be absolved. Hefele here observes : ' This is a question of marriage in the first degree of affinity, *which is*

3

still forbidden by the present law,' i.e., by the decrees of the Council of Trent, to which we shall have occasion to advert later on.* These prohibitions of marriages of affinity were repeated by several later Councils in different parts of the Church, but not so frequently as to give any support to the paradoxical inference, which has sometimes been drawn, that there was a general tendency to break the law, still less to suggest the wilder paradox, for which there is not a shred of evidence, that there was a practice at the time of granting dispensations for them.

It has been already observed that the marriage law of Pagan Rome was, in most respects, accordant with that of Scripture and of the Church, and it is specially noteworthy that the two are agreed on the fundamental principle of drawing no distinction between prohibited degrees of consanguinity and affinity. The Roman law was based, like our own, to use Dean Milman's words, on the principle that 'connections formed by marriage were as sacred as those of natural kindred';† and hence marriage with a son's wife or wife's daughter was forbidden on the express ground that ' both are daughters,' and marriage with a step-mother or mother-in-law on the ground that ' they are in the place of a mother.' It was no negation of this principle that, in applying it, the Roman law fell short of the strictness of the Christian by allowing a man to marry his wife's sister, and also—like almost every modern code which permits the former—to marry his own niece. But as soon as the Empire became Christian these incestuous unions were forbidden by a succession of imperial laws, which would alone

---

* *See* Hefele's *Councils of the Church* (Eng. Trans.), Vol. I., pp. 164, 224. The date commonly given for the Synod of Neocæsarea is 314 ; Hefele thinks 324 more probably the correct one, but in any case it was anterior to the Council of Nice.

† *Latin Christianity*, Vol. II., p. 19.

suffice to prove the existing rule and tradition of the Church. We have, moreover, the direct and very emphatic testimony of St. Basil, about the middle of the fourth century, in a letter to Diodorus, where, after first saying that he 'shudders' at the notion of anyone supposing marriage with a wife's sister to be lawful, he proceeds to allege 'that which is of the greatest weight in such matters, *the custom established among us* (Christians) that if anyone, *mastered by an impure passion*, shall have fallen into a lawless union with two sisters, neither is this to be accounted a marriage, nor are such persons to be received into the communion of the Church till they are separated from one another.' And he goes on to show that, by the law of the Church, such unions have always been treated as incestuous and invalid, and then to insist at length on the argument from Leviticus; and a penance of seven years' excommunication after the separation of the parties is prescribed for those who have formed such unions.* And the rule here laid down by St. Basil is re-enacted in the second, and again more explicitly in the fifty-fourth canon of the Quinisextan or Trullan Council (692), regarded by the Greeks as a continuation of the sixth Ecumenical Council, and is therefore held binding in the Eastern Church to this day.† It is more directly to our present purpose to observe that it is also incorporated in the Latin Canon Law, of which it became part and parcel, and in the constant teaching of Schoolmen, Canonists, and Popes, as well as—we may add—in the Canon law of our own country from Saxon times downwards.

For the first five centuries those marriages only held to be forbidden by the Divine law, including of course mar-

---

* S. Basil *Epist.* 160, *Opp.* III., 249, Ed. Bened.
† *See* Labbé, *Concilia*, Tom. vi., p. 1168 ; Hefele, *Conciliengesch.* Vol. III., p. 337.

5

riage with a wife's sister, were forbidden by the Church, but after that period further restrictions began to be introduced into the canon law, and from these impediments of her own making the Church very naturally claimed the right of dispensing for sufficient cause in particular cases, though no dispensations appear to have been issued earlier than the end of the eleventh century, and even then only to crowned heads, and on grounds of public interest. Meanwhile a marked distinction was always drawn by canonists and theologians between impediments of the Divine law and the ecclesiastical. Thus St. Thomas Aquinas, who may be taken as a typical authority, distinguishes between impediments resting on the law of nature, the Divine law, ' quod in veteri Lege continetur' (*i.e.*, the Levitical code), and human or ecclesiastical law, and holds that the Pope has the right of dispensing from the last only, and in this distinction the Schoolmen generally follow him. He maintains accordingly that converts from heathenism, who have married within the degrees prohibited by canon law, may be permitted to live together, but that if they have married within the Levitical degrees they must be separated.* A similar judgment is expressed by Gregory the Great, in reply to St. Augustine, † who quotes Levit. xviii. ; by Pope Zachary (741–752); and by Innocent III. (1198–1216), in three epistles which are cited in the Decretals, where it is assumed that within the Levitical degrees there is no power to dispense. In 1333, John XXII. decided in the same sense, ' juxta constitutionem felicis recordationis Innocentii Papæ III. prædecessoris nostri super hoc editam, quæ incipit *Gaudeamus*.' And Alexander of Hales, to add the name of one of the most eminent of the Schoolmen among our own

* *Summa*, Suppl. Pars. iii. Q. 54, Art. 3 ; Q. 59, Art. 3.
† *See* Bede, *Hist. Eccles.* i. 27.

countrymen, distinguishes the Levitical prohibitions as binding universally from those imposed by ecclesiastical authority only, saying of the former, ' quod incestus, in quantum hujusmodi *malum est secundum se*, quia transgreditur limites *ratione vel Lege Dei* sine Ecclesiæ auctoritate determinatos.'

The first case alleged of a dispensation within the Levitical degrees is of one granted by Pope Martin V. in 1427 to the Count of Foix, as to the details of which there is a conflict of evidence, some writers describing it as a permission to marry his wife's sister, others as the rehabilitation of a marriage previously contracted with the sister of a woman he had seduced. Into that discussion we need not enter here. What is more important to observe is that the act of Martin V., whatever its precise scope, was unquestionably the earliest example of any innovation on the uniform custom and tradition of fourteen centuries, and that we have the highest authority for insisting that it cannot be drawn into a precedent. Application was made to Martin's immediate successor, Pope Eugenius IV., to sanction the marriage of the Dauphin (afterwards Louis XI. of France) with his wife's sister, and was refused, as being *ultra vires*. We learn from his trusted adviser, the famous theologian and canonist, Cardinal Torquemada (who must not, of course, be confounded with the Inquisitor of that name a century later), that he was himself commissioned by the Pope to examine the question, and reported that dispensations could not be granted for degrees prohibited by the Divine law, and therefore in the case submitted to him ' non poterat Papa dispensare.'* Torquemada adds, probably with re-

* 'De eo quod dicitur quod aliquando fuit dispensatum, non vidimus hoc, imò rege Franciæ nunc regnante, cum esset Delphinus, et peteret ut mortuâ uxore suâ, posset cum sorore illius contrahere, materia ista fuit ventilata, ex mandato Domini Eugenii, coram nobis, cui commissa fuit causa, et judicatum est quod non poterat Papa dispensare.'—

7

ference to the alleged action of Martin V., that 'supposing this had ever been done, or should be done, by any Pope ignorant of the Divine Law, or blinded by avarice, or in order to please men, it does not follow that he could do it rightly, for the Church is ruled by laws and rights, and not by such precedents.'

The first authentic example of a dispensation to marry a wife's sister, setting aside the doubtful case of Martin V., is that granted in 1500 to Emmanuel, King of Portugal, by Alexander VI., who also dispensed Ferdinand, King of Sicily, to marry his own aunt. The second instance of the kind on record is the dispensation granted by Pope Julius II. in 1503 to Henry VIII., then Prince of Wales, to marry Catherine of Aragon, his brother's wife, where, however, it is important to bear in mind the great stress laid by all concerned on the fact, to which Catherine herself deposed on oath, and which Henry never ventured to dispute, that the previous marriage with Prince Arthur had not been consummated, and there was therefore no real affinity, though it is true that the Bull was so drawn as to cover either contingency.† Within less than half a century from that occurrence, and while the European controversy provoked by it was still fresh in men's minds, the Council of Trent assembled, and in due course the Sacrament of Matrimony, involving the whole question of matrimonial impediments and dispensations, came under its notice. It was no doubt partly from

Johannes de Turrecremata, *Commentaria super Decret. Gratian.* Secunda Pars, Causa xxxv., Quæst. ii., vol. iii. p. 465 (b). Venise, 1578. Cf. Legeay's *Hist. de Louis XI.*, vol. i. p. 128, where we read that after the death of his first wife, Margaret of Scotland, in August, 1445, 'Louis voulut épouser en secondes noces la sœur de Marguerite, mais le Saint-Père ne lui en accorda pas la dispense.'

† The real objection on grounds of affinity, as Cardinal Pole reminded him, was to Henry's incestuous no less than adulterous union with Anne Boleyn, whose elder sister, Mary, if not her mother also, had previously been his mistress.

a natural reluctance to cast a slur on the memory of two recent Popes, that, for the first time in Church history, the Council gave a kind of canonical sanction, but—as will presently appear—a studiously guarded and limited sanction, to dispensations within the Levitical degrees. The Tridentine canon on the subject runs as follows :

Si quis dixerit, eos tantum *consanguinitatis et affinitatis gradus* qui Levitico exprimuntur posse impedire matrimonium contrahendum et dirimere contractum, nec posse Ecclesiam *in nonnullis illorum* dispensare, aut constituere ut plures impediant aut dirimant, anathema sit.[*]

On this canon it is obvious to observe, first, that, in accordance with the uniform tradition of theology and canon law from the beginning, it draws no distinction between prohibited degrees of consanguinity and affinity, either as to their obligation or the right of dispensation ; secondly, that it only recognises in the abstract a right of dispensation 'in some of them,' without specifying which ; and, thirdly, that by the fifth chapter of the ' Decree on Reformation of Marriage,' passed in the same Session of the Council, the exercise of this right—whatever its extent —is very strictly limited.

It may further be worth noting that the form in which the canon was originally proposed was somewhat different, as we learn from Massarelli's *Acta*, edited by the late Father Theiner. The earliest draft, as introduced, July 20, 1563, omits the second clause about dispensations altogether, thus simply asserting the right of the Church—which had been exercised for the last thousand years—to constitute 'diriment' impediments over and above those prescribed in Leviticus.[†] But in the discussion that followed, about thirty bishops, as we learn from the same source, desired that a right of permitting marriage within these limits should also be asserted. In the second draft, therefore, introduced

* *Canones et Decreta Conc. Trid. Sess.* xxiv. can. 3.
† *Acta Genuina SS. Œcum. Conc. Trid.* Tom. ii. p. 313, ed. Theiner.

on August 7, the words 'nec posse Ecclesiam constituere ut plures *aut pauciores* impediant et dirimant' were added,* but no less than 93 fathers voted for excluding the critical word 'pauciores,'† many of whom expressly disputed or denied the right of dispensation within the Levitical degrees. The same draft canon was brought forward again on September 5, when several of the bishops again repeated their objections. On October 13 it was introduced for the fourth time, with an alternative final clause, corresponding to that in the existing canon, and in this form it was eventually passed.

But in the same Session of the Council was passed also the *Decretum de Reformatione Matrimonii*, the fifth chapter of which concludes with these words : 'In contrahendis matrimoniis vel nulla omnino detur dispensatio, *vel raro*, idque ex causa et gratis concedatur. *In secundo gradu nunquam dispensetur* nisi inter magnos principes, et ob publicam causam.'‡ By thus enjoining that dispensations of any kind, even for ecclesiastical impediments only, were to be restricted to rare and exceptional cases, and that 'in the second degree' they were only to be granted to 'great princes,' and on grounds of public interest, the Council plainly implied that in the first degree—which includes the case of sisters and sisters-in-law—they were never under any circumstance to be allowed, and must be understood, from its assuming this as too self-evident to require explicit statement, to imply that they *could* not be given.§ It has accordingly

* *Acta Genuina SS. Œcum. Conc. Trid.* Tom. ii. p. 335, ed. Theiner.
† Ib. p. 368.
‡ *Conc. Trid.* Sess. xxiv., Decr. De Ref. Mat. cap. 5.
§ We have already seen that a dispensation within the first degree was refused, after full deliberation, and as wholly inadmissible, to the son of the 'Most Christian King,' and heir to the sovereignty of the nation styled 'the eldest daughter of the Church.' A more crucial example of a rule held to admit of no exception could hardly be imagined.

been maintained by distinguished canonists, like Fagnan, that the Council forbade such dispensations altogether, and Hefele, as we have already seen, declares that 'marriage in the first degree of affinity *is still forbidden* by the present law.' Estius, who died in 1613, said he had only heard of one example of such a dispensation since the Council of Trent; later in the same century, Innocent XI. (1676–1689), one of the wisest and holiest of modern Popes, made it a principle always to refuse them ; and in our own day Cardinal Wiseman, when interrogated before the Royal Commission of 1848, said that 'in Catholic countries you very seldom find marriages within [any of] the prohibited degrees,' and that he himself could 'hardly recollect such a thing in Italy.' On the other hand, those post-Tridentine divines, like Estius and Soto, who most strongly insist on the abstract right of papal dispensation within the Levitical degrees, are unanimous in declaring that there is 'a certain natural turpitude' in such unions. Sanchez cites a considerable number of theologians, though he does not himself agree with them, who maintain that, as by the law of nature the marriage of brother and sister is not absolutely excluded—for it was, of course, necessary in the first generation of mankind—the Church has the abstract right of dispensing such marriages, though it is never exercised. Certainly, whatever may be said of the law of nature, no distinction is drawn either in Scripture or canon law between the corresponding degrees of consanguinity and affinity, on the principle laid down by our Lord Himself that man and wife are 'one flesh.' * If, therefore, the letter of

* How little the law of nature can be relied upon as a practical guarantee may be inferred from the fact, mentioned in Geikie's *Hours with the Bible* (II. 94), that 'a marriage of brother and sister was thought in Egypt, as in ancient Persia, the best possible for a prince,' and continued in use there down to the time of the Ptolemies. He adds that, in spite of the Levitical prohibition, marriages of brothers and sisters were not unknown in Israel, as is seen from 2 Sam. xiii. 13.

the Tridentine decree may be strained to include permission for marriage with a sister-in-law, it may equally be strained to include permission for marriage with a sister. The reasonable and natural construction, as has been already pointed out, is that it is designed equally and absolutely to exclude both.

That the mind and discipline of the Church is wholly opposed to such unions is, at all events, no mere individual inference, however unimpeachable, from the overwhelming weight of historical and documentary evidence which has been adduced. It is confirmed by the formal and official statement of the highest Roman Catholic authority in this country. The following weighty words occur in a letter addressed last year to his Vicar-General by the Cardinal Archbishop of Westminster, and published at the time in the newspapers :

' I. The law of the Catholic Church forbids and annuls the marriage with a deceased wife's sister.

' 2. The law of England on this point is, to this moment, Catholic, and supports the discipline of the Church.

' 3. The Holy See can alone dispense in such cases ; and it never dispenses except, 1, rarely ; 2, with reluctance ; and 3, for grave reasons and to avoid greater evils.

' 4. To abolish the law which prohibits such marriages would have the effect of throwing open as lawful to everybody that which in a few, rare, and exceptional cases is reluctantly given to avoid greater evils.

' 5. And this throwing open of the civil law would encourage and multiply such marriages, in direct opposition to the discipline of the Catholic Church, and to the grave and dangerous disturbance of domestic life.

' Better far is it that a few cases should still suffer a legal hardship than that the home life of our whole commonwealth should be seriously endangered.

' I trust that all Catholics in either House of Parliament will vote firmly and always against such a change in the statute law.'

In the peroration of a remarkable speech delivered thirty-six years ago before the Court of Queen's Bench, in the case of 'the Queen *versus* St. Giles's-in-the-Fields,' the late Mr. Badeley—himself no mean authority on such a matter

12

—thus summed up a portion of his argument : 'I have shown, my Lords, that the ecclesiastical law of this country, from the earliest period to the present, has gone on one uniform course ; and that whether before the Reformation, at the time of the Reformation, or since, the decisions have been uniform regarding marriage with a wife's sister as incestuous.' And therefore, to repeat once more the emphatic declaration of Cardinal Manning, 'the law of England on this point is, to this moment, Catholic, and supports the discipline of the Church.' It follows that the repeal of this immemorial law of England and of the Christian Church, now so persistently demanded for the selfish satisfaction of a wealthy clique, who desire to throw a decent disguise over their own deliberate violation of it, is as little in accordance with Catholic principles as with the highest interests of national morality and of domestic purity and peace.

Spottiswoode & Co., Printers, New-street Square, London.

Marriage Law Defence Union Tracts.

No. XI.

OFFICE : 1 KING STREET, WESTMINSTER, S.W.

What the Eastern Church says.

IT is well known that the Eastern Church, which allows of no changes, and permits no dispensations, has from the beginning strictly forbidden the marriage of a man with the sister of his deceased wife. The question has been put, on the part of the Executive Committee of the Marriage Law Defence Union, to the clergy of the Greek Church of S. Sophia, Bayswater, and of the Russian Church in Welbeck Street, whether such a marriage would be possible now in either of the great branches of the Eastern Church represented by them. The Reverend Archimandrite, Dr. Hieronymus Myriantheus, of the former, and the Reverend Eugene Smirnoff, of the latter, have kindly replied, that such marriages are most strictly prohibited. The following Canons are considered as still binding the consciences of all Greek Christians, and form the present law of the Eastern Church with respect to these marriages.

1. The 19th of the (so-called) Apostolical Canons :

' One who marries two sisters or his niece cannot become a cleric.'

Translated in Bishop Hefele's ' History of Christian Councils ' (Edinburgh, T. & T. Clark), Vol. i., p. 465. This Canon will be found in Bishop Beveridge's ' Pandectæ Canonum,' Vol. i., p. 13. Dr. von Drey (*see* Hefele) considers this Canon to be an imitation of the Second Canon of Neo-Cæsarea.

2. The 2nd Canon of Neo-Cæsarea (A.D. 314–325).

'If a woman has married two brothers, she shall be excommunicated till her death ; if she is in danger of death, and promises in case of recovery to break off this illegitimate union, she may, as an act of mercy, be admitted to penance. If the woman or husband die in this union, the penance for the survivor will be very strict.'

Translated in Hefele's ' History of the Christian Councils,' Vol. i., p. 224. Beveridge's ' Pandectæ Canonum,' Vol. i., p. 402. This Canon, by the law of analogy, forbids a man to marry two sisters. The Council of Neo-Cæsarea, in Cappadocia, was held a little later than that of Ancyra, but before that of Nicæa.

3. The 87th Canon of S. Basil the Great (*see* p. 4).

It will be seen from these Canons that the Greek Church condemns, as it has always condemned, the marriage of a man with his deceased wife's sister, which it is now proposed to legalise in England.

In his evidence before the Royal Commission, on Nov. 26, 1847 (p. 41), Dr. Pusey says : ' In the Eastern Church, the Council of Trullo, acknowledged throughout (A.D. 694, can. 54), enlarges the Canons of S. Basil, founding them upon Holy Scripture, *i.e.* Lev. xviii. 6. A little earlier, the famous Theodore, a learned Greek, a native of Tarsus, resident for some time at Rome, and afterwards Archbishop of Canterbury, A.D. 668, gives an account of the then rule of both Eastern and Western Churches, with both of which he was familiar. Bede mentions his "secular and Divine learning" (iv. 1.). While, as it is well known, in his Pœnitentiale (c. 11, p. 12, ed. Pet.) he says, "According to the Greeks, marriage may take place in the third degree (second cousins), as it is written in the law ; in the fifth,

3

according to the Romans; yet they do not dissolve marriage in the third. But the wife of one in the third degree may not be taken after his death. A man is, in· marriage, equally united with those of his own blood, and those of the blood of his wife after her death" (*i.e.* equally prohibited from marrying either). It appears from this, that although the degrees prohibited in the Western Church were still being gradually extended, the distinction was preserved between degrees prohibited, or thought to be prohibited, by the Divine Law, and those of the Church, in that marriage within the former was dissolved, not within the latter.'

LETTER OF S. BASIL THE GREAT TO DIODORUS OF TARSUS (4TH CENTURY).

There was brought to us recently a brief or epistle, bearing the signature of Diodorus, but in all other respects fit to be ascribed to anyone rather than to Diodorus, for it seems to me that it must have been some ignorant fellow, who, by personating thee, hoped to impose upon others with a show of authority. Whoever it was, having been consulted, as he represented, by some man, whether he might lawfully marry his deceased wife's sister, he not only showed no horror at the question, but coolly entertained it, and even countenanced the man, and defended zealously enough and argumentatively that his licentious idea. If it had been still in my possession, I would have sent thee the writing itself, and so thou wouldst have been able to defend thyself and the truth. But since he who showed it me, took it away again and carried it about as a sort of trophy against us, who have all along forbidden any such thing to be done, saying that he had authority in writing to do it, I have now sent [the accompanying Constitution] to thee, that we may join our forces against that

4

spurious document, and leave it no force to deceive, as it otherwise might, perchance, any incautious persons to whom it may come.

[*Canon* lxxxvii.] The first argument (and it is the strongest of all in such questions) which we have to put forward in this matter, is that of *our custom*; a custom which has the force of a law, inasmuch as our rules have been transmitted down to us by holy men. And our *custom* is this, ' that if any man being overcome by filthy passion fall into an unlawful union with two sisters, neither is such union to be accounted marriage, nor are either of the parties ever to be reconciled to the unity of the Church, unless they have first parted the one from the other.' So that even though we had no other argument to bring, our *custom* of itself would suffice as a defence against any such mischief.

But since the writer of that epistle has sought by his fraudulent composition to bring into our social life so great an evil, it is needful that neither should we on our side be slack to oppose a defence of sound words; although, in things that are so very clear, that prejudgment, which every one of us must feel, is far stronger than any argument.

' It is written,' he says, ' in Leviticus, Thou shalt not take a wife to her sister to vex her [ἀντίζηλον], to uncover her nakedness, beside her [ἐπ' αὐτῇ, ἔτι ζώσης αὐτῆς] in her lifetime. (Lev. xviii. ver. 18.) It is manifest then (thus he reasons), from this text, that it *is* permitted to take her after the first sister is dead.' In answer to this I will say, first, that—

[I.] Whatsoever the law saith, it saith to them that are under the law, else, by parity of reasoning, circumcision too, and the Sabbath, and abstinence from meats, might be urged upon us; for it will hardly be pretended, I suppose, that if we find anything in the law favourable to our own pleasures, we are in this to put ourselves under the yoke of the bondage of the law, but if any of the things enacted by the law

5

seem to be grievous, we are then to run off to the liberty
which is in Christ.

[II.] I was asked, '*Is* it written [or is it *not* in the
Scripture] that a man may take a woman to [or after] her
sister?' I replied (and this is both a true and a safe
answer), that it is *not* so written. And to infer and conclude
from the clause added after [the prohibition] something else,
about which nothing is actually said, is to legislate, not to
take the law as it stands ; for—

[III.] If such a principle of interpretation be admitted,
he who wills may lawfully venture, even while the first sister
lives, to take the other. The same sophism will serve equally
for that. It is written, he will say, 'Thou shalt not take
. . . . *to vex her'* [ἀντίζηλον], so then if there be no danger
of her vexing her, there is no prohibition [ὡς τήνγε ἔξω τοῦ
ζήλου λαβεῖν ὀυκ ἐκώλυσεν]. Whereupon, he who is plead-
ing in favour of his own passion will settle it that the two
sisters are so disposed as to be in no danger of vexing or
being vexed; and so the reason given for the prohibition not
existing, what (he will ask) is there to prevent his taking and
having the two sisters together? But this is not written, we
shall answer—neither in the other case is the allowance that
is contended for expressed. But the sense of the clause
added [after the words of prohibition] opens the door
equally to both. However—

[IV.] If we had first gone back a little to some words of
the previous legislation [at the beginning of the same chapter
of Leviticus, xviii. v. 3] we might have got rid of our difficulty. For the lawgiver in this place seems not to be enu-
merating every form of sin, but specially forbidding the sins
of the Egyptians from whom Israel had come forth, and of
the Canaanites to whom Israel was being removed. For it
is thus written : 'After the customs of the land of Egypt
wherein ye sojourned shall ye not do ; and after the customs
of the land of Canaan into which I will bring you

6

shall ye not do : neither in their ordinances [νομίμοις, ways, maxims] shall ye walk.' So then probably this particular form of sin may not have been common then among the Gentiles ; and on this account the lawgiver may not have needed to make any additional provision against it, but may have contented himself with the existing and untaught custom to condemn the abomination. But how then was it (it will be asked) that when he *had* forbidden the greater [offence against such existing and untaught custom or feeling] he said nothing about the less [which might seem to need it more]? Because (we answer) there was something likely to be hurtful to many of the more carnal sort, and to give occasion to their taking to wife one sister after another while both were living, in the example of the Patriarch [Jacob]. But as for us, which is rather our duty, to speak that which is written, or to be curious about that which is not written?

[V.] Take another case : That it is not right for a father and his son to come near to the same woman ; neither shall we find that written here in these laws ; and yet the Prophet treats it as a sin of the very deepest dye. For 'a son (he says) and his father will go in unto the same maid' [Amos ii. 7]. And how many other forms are there not of unclean lusts, devised by the school of devils, which the Divine Scripture has passed over in silence as being unwilling to pollute its own sanctity by the names of things shameful ; distinguishing uncleannesses only under general heads? As the Apostle Paul says, 'But fornication and all uncleanness, let it not be so much as named among you, as becometh saints'; comprehending, under the one general name of 'uncleanness,' all the unmentionable sins both of ma'es and of females ; so that it is not true at all that the silence of Scripture carries with it a licence for the lovers of pleasure.

[VI.] Not that, as regards our present question, I can

7

ever allow that such sins have, in point of fact, been passed over in silence ; far from it ! I assert that the lawgiver has forbidden them very expressly. For this text, 'None of you shall approach to any that is near of kin to him, to uncover their nakedness' [Levit. xviii. 6], takes in this kind of 'nearness' also. For what can there be 'nearer' to a man than his own wife ; or rather, than his own flesh? For 'they are no longer two but one flesh.' So then, through the wife, her sister necessarily comes to be 'near to the husband.' For as he is not to take the mother of his wife [Levit. xviii. 17], nor his wife's daughter [*ibid.*], because neither can he take his own mother or his own daughter, so [by parity of reasoning] neither is he to take the sister of his wife any more than his own sister, and *vice versâ* ; neither will it be lawful for a woman to be married to any that are 'near of kin' to her husband. For the rights of kindred are common on both sides.

[VII.] But, for me, as regards marriage, if there be anyone who is willing [to listen to me], I testify 'that the fashion of this world passeth away, and that the time is short, and that they who have wives be as though they had them not.' But if anyone object to me the text 'increase and multiply,' I smile at his ignorance in not distinguishing between the times of the [different] legislations. A second marriage is [allowed] as a remedy against fornication, not as a passage to licentiousness. If they cannot contain 'let them marry,' he says, but not so as in marrying also to transgress.

[VIII.] But neither do such, while they foul their souls by dishonest passion, respect even Nature herself, which has fixed from of old distinctive appellations of kindred ; nor do they consider by what names they shall call the double issue of such double marriages ; of brothers and sisters to one another, or of cousins ; for both names will suit them equally on account of the confusion. Make not, O man,

8

thy young children's aunt into their stepmother ; nor arm against them her who ought to stand to them in affection, instead of their mother, with those implacable jealousies. For it is the stepmother's hatred only which carries its enmity beyond the grave. Other kinds of enemies are all willing to make peace with the dead, but the stepmother begins her hatred after death.

To conclude what has been said : If any man contemplates marriage according to law, the whole world is open to him ; but if his desire be of lust, that is just the reason that he is to be all the more forbidden ; that he 'may learn to possess his vessel in sanctification, and not in the lust of concupiscence.' I would fain say more ; but am withheld by the limits of this letter. I heartily pray that either my admonitions may have more force than such lust, or, at any rate, that so abominable a pollution come not into my province, but keep itself in those parts where the sin was perpetrated.

As regards the penance for such marriages, Canon lxviii. appoints for marrying two sisters successively the same penance as by the preceding Canon lxvii., had been appointed for bigamists ; that is, a penance of *seven years'* excommunication after the separation of the parties.

The discipline of the Nestorians, who have been separated from both Greeks and Latins since A.D. 431, and also of the Abyssinians, Copts, Syrians, and Armenians, who separated from the three first-named A.D. 451, is stated to be identical in this matter with that of the Greek Church.

Price One Halfpenny.

To be had of E. W. ALLEN, 4 *Ave Maria Lane, E.C., as well as at the Office of the Union.*

Spottiswoode & Co., Printers, New-street Square, London.

Marriage Law Defence Union Tracts

No. XVI

Deceased Wife's Sister Bill

A VILLAGE TALK

BY

THOMAS VINCENT, M.A.

RECTOR OF PUSEY

LONDON

MARRIAGE LAW DEFENCE UNION

1 KING STREET, WESTMINSTER, S W.

1884

Price One Penny.

Deceased Wife's Sister Bill.

𝔄 𝔙illage 𝔗alk.

BY

THOMAS VINCENT, M.A.,

RECTOR OF PUSEY.

GEORGE (looking at a newspaper in the Village Reading Room at ———).—So I see they are going to bring on that 'Deceased Wife's Sister's Bill' again. I can't think what people can want with altering our marriage laws, which have been our marriage laws ever since the reformation of the Church of old England : yes, and as I've heard the Parson tell us, the marriage laws of the Church from the beginning. Why what's been believed *wrong*, and counted against God's law, from the Apostles' day till this, can't be made *right* now by an Act of Parliament.

James.—There's something in what you say, George, but I don't look at it just as you do. It's very true our Church of England has always said it is wrong for a man, if his wife dies, to marry his wife's sister. But it isn't so said by some other Protestant countries abroad as I've heard say : and some of our colonies too, they say, have made it lawful now.

3

And it seems wrong to have different laws in our colonies from what we have here. That a man may marry his wife's sister out in Australy, but mustn't do it here!

George.—Well, James, in a matter of right or wrong, I suppose you'll allow,—if a thing is wrong, we mustn't do it, no matter how many countries or people there may be who do?

James.—No, we mustn't. But I don't see why *they* should be wrong, and *we* right.

George.—Of course, they're not bound to be wrong, nor we to be right; but I think I can show that we are right here anyway, and they wrong. And, first of all, those Protestant countries abroad have done some odd things, as I think, besides this. And on this matter of marriage their great leader—and he was a great man many ways—their great leader, Luther, seems to have been more worldly wise than true to God in this matter of marriage. Why, he let a man, who was a prince, have more than one wife at a time! Now I think that you don't want to defend him in that.

James.—No. I have heard of that before, and I never could think how he could have done so.

George.—No, nor I neither—nevertheless he did; so we'd best not be troubling ourselves with what others are doing, but just consider what is right or wrong in the matter.

James.—Well, but I don't see that there is anything wrong in the matter. I've looked at the Bible where it says what relations we are not to marry, and I can't see that it says we are not to marry a wife's sister, if our wife dies, and she has a sister. It seems to me a most natural thing, and I can't see that it's forbidden ; and, as I've often heard say, 'there's no *blood* between them.'

George.—It seems to me that there's a good many more

points than one to be considered in what you've just said, James. And, first of all—suppose you and I differ in what we understand God's Word to mean—who's to say which of us is right?

James.—Well, but I only want to go by what the Bible says.

George.—And so do I. But sometimes people understand it differently—as you and I on this very matter. Who's to decide then?

James.—Well, I don't quite see.

George.—I think I do. Do you recollect what St. Paul said of the Church when he wrote to Timothy the first time (1 Tim. iii. 15)? He called the Church 'the Pillar and Ground of the Truth.' Anywise he meant *something* when he said that. And I don't see what he could mean, unless he meant that the Church was, as it were, the *stay* and prop of the truth : and that when we differed as to what God's Word meant, we were to look to the Church, to see how she took it. Howsoever, let that be just now. I believe that a great deal more may be proved out of God's Word direct than some people think, and more a good deal than many people like, if we only look carefully into it, and try to see what it means, and not only what we wish it to mean. And now suppose you and I try to do this, and leave what you say about the wife's sister being likely to care most for her sister's children, and its being 'natural,' and all that, till afterwards.

James.—Very well, George; but I've looked over those chapters a score of times, and I don't see how you can make out that it's wrong, by what you'll find in them.

George.—Well, let's set to work; and first of all, as it's very puzzling to be looking backwards and forwards, first at the Bible, and then at the Church 'Table of Kindred and

5

Affinity,' as they call it, let's begin by taking those tables and marking down on a piece of paper, in three separate rows : First, a man's own relations by 'blood,' as his mother or sister ; then, secondly, his *own* relations by 'affinity,' as his father's wife, his son's wife, &c. ; then, thirdly, his relations by 'affinity,' through *his wife*, as his wife's mother, his wife's daughter, &c. And the woman's relations in three more columns.*

Then we will take the 18th and 20th chapters of Leviticus, and, as we read down each relation forbidden, we'll draw a line under it where it stands in the columns ; and when we find it named a second time, as many are, we'll draw a second line ; and if it is mentioned a third time, as you'll find one to be, we'll draw a third line ; and then we'll put figures under these lines, to show what chapter and verse forbids marriage with such or such a relation.

[George and James do this very carefully, and look it over more than once to see that every degree is put down which is noted either in the Bible or the Prayer-book ; and they find all correct. But they notice that they have a few more degrees marked than they find in the Prayer-book ; they soon, however, see that this is only because the Bible speaks of some cases under two or three separate forms, while the Prayer-book includes them in one. For instance 'sister,' where the Bible has 'father's daughter,' and 'mother's daughter.']

* It has often been asserted lately that Christians are not under the 'Law of Moses,' and therefore are not bound by the Marriage Law of Leviticus. This idea must be wrong, because (1) Jesus enforces the moral precepts of Moses' Law on all who would 'inherit eternal life,' St. Matt. xix. 16; St. Mark x. 17; St. Luke x. 25, xviii. 18, and elsewhere. (2) The Apostles carry on this teaching, Ephes. vi. 2; 2 Tim. iii. 16, and elsewhere. (3) The Church has continued it, holding that we are bound by the moral precepts, while freed from the ceremonial rites.

6

A MAN MAY NOT MARRY HIS

Blood		Affinity	
Own Relations		*Own Relations*	*Wife's Relations*
Grandmother		Grandfather's Wife ..	Wife's Grandmother
Aunt ..	Father's Sister .. (xviii. 12 ; xx. 19)	Father's Brother's Wife (xviii. 14 ; xx. 20)	Wife's Father's Sister
	Mother's Sister .. (xviii. 13 ; xx. 19)	Mother's Brother's Wife (xx. 20)	Wife's Mother's Sister
Mother .. .. (xviii. 7)		Father's Wife .. .. (xviii. 8 ; xx. 11)	Wife's Mother (xviii. 17 ; xx. 14)
Daughter		Son's Wife .. .. (xvii. 15 ; xx. 12)	Wife's Daughter (xviii. 17 ; xx. 14)
Sister .. (xviii. 9)	Father's Daughter .. (xviii. 9, 11 ; xx. 17)	Brother's Wife... .. (xviii. 16 ; xx. 21)	Wife's Sister
	Mother's Daughter.. (xviii. 9 ; xx. 17)		
Granddaughter	Son's Daughter .. (xviii. 10)	Son's Son's Wife ..	Wife's Son's Daughter (xviii. 17)
	Daughter's Daughter (xviii. 10)	Daughter's Son's Wife..	Wife's Daughter's Daughter (xviii. 17)
Niece ..	Brother's Daughter..	Brother's Son's Wife ..	Wife's Brother's Daughter
	Sister's Daughter ..	Sister's Son's Wife ..	Wife's Sister's Daughter

A single line ————— under a degree of relationship signifies that it is mentioned but once.   A double line ═══════ that it is mentioned twice.   Three lines ═══════ that it is mentioned three times.   No underlining or reference means that it is not mentioned at all, but more or less directly implied by the analogy with relationships which are prohibited by name.

The figures refer to the 18th and 20th chapters of Leviticus.

7

A WOMAN MAY NOT MARRY HER

Blood	Affinity	
Own Relations	*Own Relations*	*Husband's Relations*
Grandfather	Grandmother's Husband ..	Husband's Grandfather
Uncle { Father's Brother	Father's Sister's Husband ..	Husband's Father's Brother
Uncle { Mother's Brother	Mother's Sister's Husband ..	Husband's Mother's Brother
Father	Mother's Husband	Husband's Father
Son	Daughter's Husband	Husband's Son
Brother	Sister's Husband..	Husband's Brother
Grandson { Son's Son ..	Son's Daughter's Husband ..	Husband's Son's Son
Grandson { Daughter's Son	Daughter's Daughter's Husband	Husband's Daughter's Son
Nephew { Brother's Son	Brother's Daughter's Husband	Husband's Brother's Son
Nephew { Sister's Son ..	Sister's Daughter's Husband ..	Husband's Sister's Son

In former editions ' Father's Brother' and ' Father' were marked in the first column on this side as being directly forbidden to the woman by vv. 14 and 17. This they appear to be, at first sight, in our English translation ; but in reality they are not so, as is shown in the Hebrew, where the pronoun 'thou' is masculine throughout. The irreverence mentioned is effected by taking their wives.

George.—There, now it's done, and we can see at one look what is forbidden by the words of the Bible, and what is not.

James.—Yes, I never thought of putting it all out in this way before. It does make it clear, that it does! But (after a steady look) what a many more relations are put down in the Prayer-book than are put down in the Bible! Well, I shouldn't have thought to find it so.

George.—Well, I hope to show you a little more than that presently. But first let me ask you—Which way are we to understand what *is* noted from those two chapters of Leviticus? Are we to understand that what is forbidden in the very letter, *that is forbidden,* and *that only* : and everything else allowed? Or, are we to take what is forbidden, and say, 'This is not lawful, *nor any relationship of the same nearness?*' And 'When one is forbidden to the man, *the same in degree is forbidden to the woman?*' This is called taking it in the *spirit.* The first way is called taking it in the *letter.*

[James is a little puzzled ; he sees at once that there are many underlinings on the man's side and none on the woman's. While he hesitates, George breaks the silence, and says]—Well, James, I think you look a bit puzzled ; but let me remind you, you can't have it *both ways.* I mind an old saying, 'You can't eat your pudding, and have your pudding' : you can't tie me down to the *letter* when it seems reasonable to you, and borrow a bit of the *spirit* from me when the letter alone would seem unreasonable. Which way will you take the chapters, by the *letter* or by the *spirit?*

[James is still silent, for now he sees a few more difficulties.]

George.—Suppose I take it each way for you; and, first, as I am speaking, let us take it my way of looking at it—by the *spirit.* Now, first, it seems to me, *we* are *bound* to take these chapters by their *spirit* ; because, as members of the

9

Church, haven't we promised 'to keep God's holy *will*,' as well as His Commandments?   And how are we to gather what is *His will*, when it is not expressed in command, unless we gather it from the spirit of what is commanded?   If we do this, then it follows that we are bound to keep away from, not only all unions which are forbidden by name, but from those also which are of the same kind of nearness, either in 'blood' or 'affinity,' even although they are not mentioned. Moreover, we must allow that when a relationship forbids a man to marry a woman, the *same degree* of relationship, though it is not named, forbids a woman to marry a man.

James.—Well, I own I don't see how a man is to get out of that—that is, if we are to go by what you call the *spirit* of these chapters ; but mind you I don't grant that we are.

George.—Very well, let that bide at present.   I don't want to shirk it, mind ye, but I think we shall come better to that point presently ; let us go on as I was going.   Let's see what these chapters mean if we take them my way—in the spirit.   You will own then, I suppose, for argument's sake, that, if they are to be understood in the *spirit*, we are bound not only to keep off from those relations which are forbidden (whether of blood or affinity), but also from all relations of the same degree of nearness ; and also that whatever degree is forbidden to a man, the same is forbidden to a woman.   You will allow that ?

James.—Yes.   I don't see how a man is to get off owning that, *i.e. if we go by the spirit.*

George.—Well, then, in that case, the thing seems to me to be settled at once.

James.—How?

George.—I'll tell ye.   Look here, in Lev. xviii. 16, and xx. 21, a man is told flat he must not marry his 'brother's wife.' Now—Ain't a sister's husband the same relation to her?

James.—There is no denying that.

George.—Well, then, you own that, as I take it, a woman mustn't marry her ' sister's husband,' and that is the same as saying a man mustn't marry his ' wife's sister.'

James.—I see that, taking it your way ; but then it seems to me there isn't any *blood* between them.

George.—No ; neither is there any *blood* between a man and his brother's wife ; but that's not the point. The point is, the Bible says a man is not to marry his ' brother's wife.' And so I hold it means a woman is not to marry her ' sister's husband.'

James.—Well, in your way of taking it, I own that seems right enough. But how do you get out of this : the Bible does say *here* that a man is not to marry his ' brother's wife,' and yet it says in Deut. xxv. 5, that if a man dies and leaves no child, then his brother *shall* take the dead brother's wife ?

George.—Yes, we all know that ; that was for one great reason, and for that *one* only : that before the Saviour came no family might seem cut off beforehand from the blessing of having that Saviour born in his family. But this *one*, and mind ye, *only one* exception, makes the rule, to my mind, all the tighter in every other case.*

James.—Well, there you seem right again, on your own grounds. But how will it be if you go upon mine, and say nothing is wrong but what is forbidden in actual words?

George.—Well, if you keep to that, I think you'll find yourself in no end of difficulties. So let's begin. First of all, when you look at all those degrees which the Church forbids, marked underneath where the Bible forbids, you'll

---

* It may be said that this object of Deut. xxv. 5, is nowhere declared in the Bible. True, it is not, but it is the commonly received idea. and, at least, this Law was given for the declared object that ' his ' (any man's) ' name be not put out of Israel ' (v. 6) ; or, in other words, that , all *birthright* blessings might be retained to each man's name.' Why were *birthright* blessings of so 'much consequence in Israel ? There can be but one answer to this question, viz. : ' Because of the " Seed-promised " to their common father, Abraham.'

see at once that while a great many are forbidden to the man, there are none forbidden to the woman. So that if you go by the *strict letter* only, you get into this difficulty at once, viz., that a woman may marry many men who may not marry her! How do you get over that?

James.—No, no, that's quite *folly;* the Bible never could mean that. If a man is forbidden to marry any woman, that woman must be forbidden to marry him.

George.—And so say I. But you must mark that's taking it my way, by the *spirit* of it—not by the *letter*; and mind ye what I said a time back: you can't have it *both* ways; yours when the letter suits you, and mine when it doesn't. And it seems to me that God, by not forbidding anything directly to the woman, obliges us to say that what is forbidden to the man is forbidden to the woman; and therefore that we *are* to take His law by what we call the *spirit*, and not by the *letter* only. Howsoever, I won't be that hard upon you, as to tie you down so close as this. I have plenty more difficulties for you yet. I'll take now only what is said about the man. Look again, you'll see a man is not forbidden to marry his grandmother, though he is forbidden to marry his granddaughter.

James.—Well, but he is, as you say, forbidden to marry his granddaughter, and she is the same relation to *him* as *he* is to his grandmother; and he is forbidden to marry his mother; so much more I should think his grandmother.

George.—Easy, James, easy! That's all very well for me to say, taking it my way; but it won't do for you to say, taking it by the *letter*; you can't, as I said, 'eat your pudding, and have your pudding.' If you *hold* to the *letter*, you must *keep* to the letter, and you must let a man marry his grandmother—if he and she be willing—yea, and his grandfather's wife, his wife's grandmother too!!

James.—Oh, that's nonsense!

George.—And so say I ; and a great deal worse than nonsense too; but it's what you must come to if you go by the letter, and the letter only. But I have something more for you : a man is not forbidden in words to marry his own daughter, though he is forbidden to marry his daughter-in-law, or even his step-daughter : and again, he is not forbidden to marry his own niece, though he is forbidden to marry his aunt by marriage, who might easily be as young, or younger than himself ; now his own niece is his blood-relation three degrees off, but this aunt, while also three degrees off, is only his relation by marriage or affinity. The Bible could never mean that man might marry relations by *blood* while he might not marry relations by marriage, or *affinity*, of the same nearness : that would not be sense.

James.—Well, I must own I never thought all this out before, and I own I do seem beat; I only thought of that one case which has been so often brought before us, the ' wife's sister,' and I never thought of all that followed with it. But you, George, was always given to musing. I see now, clear enough, when you come to take these chapters by the *letter* only, you do seem to get into difficulties which you can't clear away, and I see there are more still than you have named. But when you take them as you do, and as the Church of England takes them, then it all does seem reasonable enough. The daughter is prohibited, because the mother is forbidden ; the niece is prohibited, because the aunt is forbidden, and so on ; and therefore the wife's sister is prohibited, because the brother's wife is forbidden.

George.—I think so too, and now with regard to relations by ' blood,' and ' affinity.' Some of our great Parliament leaders have told us that relations by ' affinity ' are no real relations. One of them, a great Minister of State, has said openly, ' my wife's relations are not my relations.' Now, I hold that saying to be a *great untruth* covered with a

13

painting of truth. His wife's relations are not his *blood* relations, here is the painting of truth ; but they are his *relations* in the sight of God, as relations by affinity ; and for the purposes of marriage restraints, as God's Word shows over and over again ; and therefore to say they are *not his relations* is a great *untruth.*

Look, again, at those tables (on pages 6, 7), you will see that while God has expressly forbidden marriage between *seven* cases of blood-relations, He has forbidden *nine* cases of affinity. And if you count the number of lines you will find that the cases of blood-relations are forbidden in *twelve* places, while the cases of affinity are forbidden in *fifteen.*

James.—Ay, it is so ; and I can't get out of that. And, to be honest, I must own that it seems not only as if God counted relations by affinity the same as relations by blood, but that He seems to have foreseen how men would try to make out as though they were not, and so He was all the more strict in naming them ; naming the larger number, even two-thirds of them, twice over.

George.—Yes, I quite think with you there; and, if you look in Lev. xviii. 14, you will find an uncle's wife, a relation only by affinity, forbidden because 'she is thine aunt,' so counted by God as near as if by blood. And, more than this, you mind it was said in Genesis of the man and his wife, 'and they shall be *one flesh*' (Gen. ii. 24) ; and how our Lord in the Gospels makes that 'and they *twain* shall be *one* flesh,' and strengthens this by adding, 'Wherefore, they are no more *twain* but *one* flesh,' *i.e.* in the sight of God. Whosoever then are *flesh* relations to the wife, are now, in God's sight, *flesh* or blood relations to the husband ; and those of the husband to the wife, and so we can't wonder that God's law forbids in the *letter* even more relations by affinity than by blood, and in the *spirit* forbids each alike.

But I mind you said it was so 'natural' to think a wife's sister would make the best mother to her sister's children, and I said I would come to that in time. Well, now I ask, how is she likely to be a better mother to them if she marries their father, than if she remains his sister? Suppose she marries—what more likely than that she soon has children of her own? Is she likely to be a better mother to her sister's children *then* than she would be if she had none of her own? 'Human nature is human nature,' and weak enough at best! Very like, I think, she'd love her own better than her sister's. Leastwise she couldn't do so much for her sister's as before.

James (musingly).—May-be it would be so.

George.—And then as to 'natural,' take another case. Sometimes two brothers marry two sisters; that's not uncommon. I've known such cases more than once, and I daresay you too. Well, now, suppose one brother dies, and one sister, each leaving children: according to that 'natural' way of argument—who could better father and mother the two families at once than the remaining brother and sister? Why should they not marry? That's a stronger case by the 'natural' way of argument, James, than the other, isn't it?

James.—Yes, certainly it would be.

George.—But what do we come to then? Why we come dead up against the very *letter* of God's Word, that says, as you recollect, twice over, 'a man shall not marry his brother's wife.' We've seen already that the 'natural' argument won't hold in sense; and now we see, that if we go along with it, it would bring us dead up against God's *Own* Word. And no wonder: God's Word was written, among other reasons, to restrain the *natural man* from going contrary to His will, and to instruct him how to become a 'new man.' a spiritual man. what, in short, a child of God, and now a 'member of Christ,' ought to be.

James.—But there's one thing which puzzles me yet, and that is this 18th verse of Lev. xviii., where a man is told not to take a 'wife to her sister, to vex her, to marry her besides the other in her lifetime.' That seems as if to say he may take her when the first is dead.

George.—Look again, James ; what do you find said in the margin ?

James.—Why the margin says it may be rendered, 'one wife to another.'

George.—Just so ; it's one of those passages about which our translators couldn't feel sure which was the truest way of rendering the old Hebrew into English ; specially because the words 'brother' and 'sister' were used so very widely by the Jews. But I've heard say that the men who know Hebrew best take it as it is in the margin, and count it as a law against having more wives than one at a time. But then you'd say that many of the great men among the Jews, as David and others, did have more wives than one: they did, but it was not agreeable to God's will, and seemed only allowed, like their *divorces*, as our Lord Himself tells us these were, 'for the hardness of their hearts.'

Moreover, that verse may likely enough mean that if a man (when more wives than one were in a way permitted) did take a second or more, he was not to do so to 'vex' the first, *i.e.* I suppose, against her will.* You recollect when Abraham took Hagar it was not against the will of Sarah, but at her desire. So, again, when Jacob had two wives, it was not because he wished it, but because he was cheated into it, and when he took two more it was each time at the request of one of the two first.

* There is strong reason for believing that this is not only a *possible*, but that it is the *real*, intent of the passage.

And, moreover, if a man is told not to do a thing at one time, he is not, as a matter of course, allowed to do it at another : unless it is distinctly so stated; which is not the case here.

There is a point yet about which, I think, we shall do well to trouble ourselves a little more, and that is the *cruel wrong* it would do to thousands and thousands of families, and to tens of thousands of pure-hearted women throughout the whole country, if this Bill was to pass. Now only think—just because a few rich people want to marry their 'wives' sisters' against what our Church has always held to be the *will of God*—and, as we have seen, truly so held— if this Bill was to pass, at one sad blow 'sisters-in-law' would to all intents and purposes be *abolished*; no man in the land could any longer have a *real sister-in-law.* No wife could enjoy the comfort of a sister's presence in her home, and see her husband show her a brother's love, without the possibility of feeling that the sister might be stealing away her husband's affections from her. No widowed husband could venture to accept, what often now is so great a blessing, the watchful care of a sister-in-law over his motherless children ; because intimacy, with the power of marriage, would tempt to marriage against his conscience, or lay him open to suspicion. And poor, simple-minded, unlearned people would be led into sin without seeing their danger, because it would be covered over by an Act of Parliament. A cruel wrong would be done to the many by yielding to the unsanctioned desires of a few.

A multitude more wrongs, and much more harm would come of passing such an 'Act.' But our talk has been already long, so at least for the present we will say 'Good-bye!' and pray that our country may never so sin against God as to pass this Bill.

Spottiswoode & Co., Printers, New-street Square, London

𝕸arriage 𝕷aw 𝕯efence 𝖀nion 𝕿racts.

No. XVII.

OFFICE : 1 KING STREET, WESTMINSTER, S.W.

Some Reasons against Marriage with a Deceased Wife's Sister.

OUR present Table of prohibited degrees of marriage is based on an intelligible and consistent principle, stated in terms at the original institution of marriage, embodied in God's law, and sanctioned by our Lord Himself when He affirmed that in marriage 'they twain shall become one flesh.' These words cannot mean less than that in God's sight relationship by marriage is as close as relationship by blood. The 18th chapter of Leviticus, which assigns the limits within which relationship either by affinity or blood is a bar to marriage is throughout based on this principle, forbidding nine cases of affinity against seven of blood relationship. It is put forth as God's law of purity in marriage, and as the heathen Canaanites are at the same time, both at the beginning and end of the same chapter, sternly denounced for violating its precepts, it must be taken, not as a mere Jewish ceremonial ordinance, but as an universal law binding on the whole race of mankind. Every prohibition in our Table can be shown to be contained in that chapter, either in express words or by analogy. It follows then that to allow marriage with a deceased wife's sister would not only be a breach of a single rule, but would involve the overthrow of the *divinely sanctioned principle* on which the law of purity in marriage is based. If such an infraction were admitted it would be impossible with any show of consistency to maintain other remaining prohibitions, as *e.g.*, that a man may not marry his wife's niece, or his step-daughter, or his step-mother, though this last is denounced by St. Paul, 1 Cor. v. 1., as 'such fornication as is not so much as named among the Gentiles.' The experience of other countries has shown that such unhallowed connections are the inevitable result of relaxing the law with respect to a deceased wife's sister.

The alteration of the law, therefore, should be strenuously resisted.

1. Because it is opposed to the revealed will of God.

2. Because by leading, as it has a sure tendency to do, to other unhallowed connections it would greatly lower the sanctity of the marriage tie.

3. Because it would remove the shield which the impossibility of marriage within the degrees of affinity now throws over the purity of intimacy in the domestic circle, and cause many social difficulties, confusions, and temptations.

Price Twopence per dozen.

Spottiswoode & Co., Printers, New-street Square, London.

Marriage Law Defence Union Tracts.
No. XX.

OFFICE: 1 KING STREET, WESTMINSTER, S.W.

THE CHRISTIAN LAW OF MARRIAGE.

What does our LORD say on the subject?

MANY people think, or take it for granted, that the Old Testament Scriptures alone bear upon the above question, and that our LORD'S words and the New Testament say nothing about it.

I think this impression wrong, and that there *is* a word of our Lord bearing decidedly, and not remotely, upon the subject ; and I believe there are very many Christian people who, as soon as they see the true relation and force of our Lord's words, will at once confess that *the Divine Law* is essentially *against marrying two sisters.* The Word is :

'WHEREFORE THEY ARE NO MORE TWAIN, BUT ONE FLESH,'
S. MATT. xix. 5, 6.

If this text even stood alone it would be weighty and decisive as to all marriages, but its force and application are signally increased by the connection in which it was spoken.

Yes ! our Lord's word is here emphatic and confirmatory upon a Divine Word from the Beginning—'and they twain shall be one flesh.' He always 'spake as one having authority,' but when He interprets, emphasises, or adds to the Old Testament Scriptures, then His words are specially awful to the conscience. Such power and weight are in the words, 'Ye have heard . . . of old . . . but *I* say unto you,' &c. ; and so as to a word of His own, in His reply to Nicodemus—without explaining the point of the inquirer's doubt—'Verily, verily, *I* say unto thee, except a man be born of water and of the Spirit he cannot enter into the Kingdom of God';—and in other words.

Look, now, at the word as it stands—'*Wherefore* they are no more twain, but one flesh.' It is emphatic and confirmatory ; it is also authoritative—our Lord's own added sanction and seal. It is the word of the Son adopting and giving new life to the word of the Father, which had then been made practically a dead letter. Moreover, our Lord Himself connects the two, and sets forth His own word as a direct *consequence* of the Father's decree.

Why did our Lord add His own word? It enforces no further meaning than the old word conveyed. No ! but He, as ever, watchful for good, seized the opportunity to enforce marriage, against man's abuse, as a *divine institution*, unalterable, not to be relaxed by human licence ; and to decide that the rule and law of marriage and divorce are *the written Word* ; and to make that word conclusive, as if He had said in His well-known phrase, 'It is written,' and had then

3

applied the supreme command, as being also His own, in absolute and direct consequence, ' Wherefore '—because it is written—' they are no more twain, but one flesh '; and assuredly this is very striking !

Look next at the *occasion* of this word of the Lord. He was questioned as to man's power to unloose his marriage bond. He replies virtually, and direct to the conscience, ' Marriage is the divine ordinance, not a mere human tie; man and his wife are divinely made "*one* flesh."' Then, when further urged, He affirms the Divine Law to be 'from the beginning,' before Moses' law, and pronounces His own awful fiat, 'And *I* say unto you,' &c.—in restoration of the original Divine Law (v. 9).

And observe specially here that our Lord allows only one act of a woman—adultery, *whose punishment was death*—as able to break the marriage bond ; and also observe intently that this one act is criminal, and so heinous as to incur death, just because it is done *in the very flesh* which has, by marriage, out of two persons been made an awful ONE—' one flesh ' in the sight of GOD!

Observe, again, that our Lord's words are imperatively against *any* relaxation of the marriage law ; just as, in another case, He makes its power more wide and strict, by His decree that a lustful look is a breach of the commandment, and affirms more than once (S. Matt. v. 28, 32 ; xix. 9), that marriage with any divorced woman is adultery : so does He restore and re-assert the original and highest view *of the essential nature of marriage.* It is, He says virtually, a uniting of two bloods, so that, by the Divine Word and power, two are made 'one flesh,' and their previously separated being is virtually ended, and lost in their new existence as the perfect creature of God.

Now consider that upon this truth—the original view of marriage—the law given by Moses was based, and that upon it the restrictive 'Tables of Affinity' in the Book of Leviticus were almost certainly wrought out, and then, without misgiving, you may pass from our Lord's words straight to the Levitical ordinances, and be sure that He *does* say something on the question of marrying two sisters. Yea ! He says—and that while speaking emphatically and with His own divine authority—that *the wife's sister is a man's own sister*, and that *because* he has become ' one flesh ' with the two sisters.

As this is the very central point of the subject, let it be stated, with rigid distinctness, that *nature* and *marriage* have the same rule in the Scriptures and with our Lord ; that—

Blood relationship bars marriage ;
and that—

Through marriage, relationship is counted as of blood ; thus—

(1) Mother, sister, half-sister, son's daughter, are forbidden by *blood*.

(2) Daughter-in-law, aunt by marriage, brother's wife, are forbidden by *marriage*.

5

Nature is against the one class ; God forbids the latter, where yet, with each man and woman named, there is no kinship, save through marriage.

It will, if possible, add simplicity and clearness to the rules or 'tables,' if it be kept in view that NO TWO OF THE SAME BLOOD are to have *one* woman; and that the law is THE SAME FOR WOMAN AND FOR MAN ; and finally, that it is strictly *every* same degree or nearness of relationship that is barred ; thus—

To *man*, his daughter-in-law, aunt, brother's wife.

To *woman*, her son-in-law, uncle, sister's husband.

Then, how singularly impressive it is, as before noted, that our Lord's word of confirmation, ' Wherefore they are no more twain but one flesh,' does, in fact, assert the latent principle upon which, as to the second class of marriages, the Levitical 'tables ' were made to turn, and gives the true key that makes their spirit plain—they are fashioned to turn upon the two *centres* of *nature* and *marriage* as God ordained it !

Also, out of this principle it arises that the 'tables' speak only of the *man* and his relations, because man and wife being one flesh the relationships are common, and the forbidding law is common. Hence the law against a man having his brother's wife is also the law against a woman having her sister's husband, and the law against a man marrying his father's brother's wife (aunt by marriage) is the law against the aunt marrying her nephew and the uncle marrying his niece. In fact, each law throughout the chapter is mutual and reciprocal—for the woman as for the man—and nearness to the *centre* of marriage determines a prohibition, just as if it were nearness of natural blood connection, so that, as a *father's* sister—a man's own blood—is forbidden, so equally is a *brother's* wife and a sister's husband.

Now a reverent study of our Lord's utterances will show that He ever expanded narrow and partial rules, and *set-by* the mere particular to confirm a universal duty ; and it is absolutely contradictory of His way, and radically inconceivable that He should have made a declaration so unequivocally *universal* as the saying, ' Wherefore they are no more twain but one flesh,' and yet leave us at liberty to apply it only to the particular question of divorce, and not also to the allied question of the universal nature of marriage. No ! the law of marriage and that of divorce hang together, barred alike by the sanctity of the divine ordinance against breach.

Let it, then, be once more repeated, that our Lord's living word, which cannot ' pass away,' *does* determine by His own authority—in sanction of the old law—that a man and his wife's sister are in the connection of ' one flesh,' and that marriage operates even as a direct blood relationship in bar of the wife's sister becoming the wife of her brother-in-law.

Now, for the sake of enforcing or disproving the conclusion here drawn, let it be supposed that the question had been put to our Lord, not on the point of divorcing a wife,

7

but of taking one in marriage ; that one had come to Him and said, ' Master, if a man's wife die and leave a sister, is it lawful for him to marry the sister ? ' Our Lord might perhaps have replied—in order to enforce the whole matter and ground of the question—' What saith the law, how readest thou ? ' and, suppose the questioner to have responded 'the law does not mention the case of two sisters, or forbid marriage to those not related by *blood*,' would not He then have taken occasion—as ever He did—to correct the misunderstanding of the law, and have said, 'Ye do err not knowing the Scriptures nor the power of God. He that made them at the first made them by marriage one flesh, and *I* say unto you that *the living sister is the husband's sister*, and that even as through *blood*.' And again He might have said—enlarging to prevent the possibility of any misunderstanding— ' The law which forbids a man from having his brother's wife also forbids a woman from having her husband's brother ; and, in forbidding two brothers from marrying *one* woman, the law equally forbids two sisters from marrying *one* man.'

Let Christian England then feel the really momentous issue of *a new law of marriage*. Whether a man shall be allowed to marry his wife's sister or no, is not simply a point of Jewish polity and social regulations ; it is not a mere change of our own immemorial legislation, which a Christian Parliament has any *right* to order. No ! it is nothing less than the granting of a greater licence where Christ our Lord afresh laid restraint. It is the enacting for Christian England, by a Parliament no longer wholly Christian, a law of the civil power *against* the law of the Church, and at the tremendous risk of deliberately and presumptuously rejecting what the Apostle calls

'The Law of Christ.'

W. F. HOBSON, M.A.

POSTSCRIPT.

Lord Bramwell has recently published an objection, that our Lord's word, ' Wherefore they are no more twain, but one flesh,' is *figurative.* This may be an honest objection, but it is a poor paltering with language and thought. HE used the word *absolutely*—as *divine prohibition.* HIS *meaning* is clear as daylight, and that meaning is the law of Christian thought. The objection ignores the essential motive of figurative language, which is to *quicken and intensify* a meaning. So it was with HIS warning against the danger of riches ; the ' camel ' and the ' needle's eye,' by a figure, focussed HIS meaning ; and so with a multitude of figures, in the Old and New Testament.

But what if there be a physical fact underlying the figure ? What if, in the mystery of Nature, Our Lord's word is an experienced fact ? I had once a favourite creature whose race I wished to keep pure, and an old keeper said, ' Remember, sir, *the first father leaves his blood behind him !*' *i.e.*, the male and female become ' one flesh,' or one blood. Alas! there are those yet who ' know not the Scriptures, nor the power of GOD.'

W. F. H.

November 1886.

To be had also of E. W. ALLEN, 4 *Ave Maria Lane, E.C.*

Price One Halfpenny.

Spottiswoode & Co., Printers, New-street Square, London.

𝔐arriage 𝔏aw 𝔇efence 𝔘nion 𝔗racts.

No. XXI.

OFFICE: 1 KING STREET, WESTMINSTER, S.W.

May I Marry my Deceased Wife's Sister, or may I not?

THIS is a subject which is now being talked of far and wide, so there is no doubt that it is one on which we ought to make up our minds. Some persons see no objection to marriage with a deceased wife's sister because they say she is no *blood* relation. 'Why may not I marry her? why curtail my liberty?'

First, let me ask those who say thus, Do you believe in the Bible? Do you hold to it at all risks? Do you think that God gave His Word to be our rule of life? Has God revealed His Will to us on this subject, or has He not? Did He consider affinity, that is relationship through your husband or wife, and consanguinity, that is relationship with yourself, as equally binding ; that is, that a person connected by marriage, is regarded as one connected by blood?

Now, look at Leviticus, chapter xx. verse 22, and ask yourselves this question, Why did God threaten, that if His people committed certain sins, the land should '*spue them out*'? What were the 'manners' of the nations which God '*abhorred*'? Look to verses 20 and 21, which precede these awful words ; both the cases there mentioned are those of *affinity*. Your deceased uncle's wife is no blood relation ;

2

your brother's wife is no blood relation: yet you are for-bidden to marry them, under a curse.   Does not a deceased wife's sister come logically under the same head?   I do not see how any reasonable man can avoid the conclusion.

Besides this, it appears to me that our Lord in the New Testament has set His seal and sanction on this prohibition, in the most marked way.   In what terms does He speak of marriage?   Is it as a very close bond and tie, or not? He said of man and wife, 'they are no longer twain but ONE FLESH.'   Now the heathen world, and even the Jews them-selves, had been very lax in these matters, especially as regards divorces.   But our Lord came to enforce a higher law and purer practice.   Now I ask you to consider what are the promoters of this alteration of our marriage law aiming at?   Are they the friends of progress?   I verily believe that such an alteration would be a retrograde move-ment, a stepping down from our high position, an opening of the door to every kind of laxity and licence.   (I am certain it would punish many sisters-in-law, whom it would turn out of their brothers-in-law's houses, for the sake of the few who wish to stop on as wives.)   What do you think of an Englishman who turns Mahometan or Zulu?   Was not our Lord's object, not to debase, but to raise and elevate marriage to a higher standard ; that the world might now witness holier affections and purer lives than it had ever seen before?

I am for progress.   I believe in the Bible, and I believe that adherence to this can alone make us a great and happy nation.

AN ENGLISHMAN.

Price One Penny per dozen.

Spottiswoode & Co., Printers, New-street Square, London , E.C.

Marriage Law Defence Union Tracts.
No. XXII.

OFFICE: 1 KING STREET, WESTMINSTER, S.W.

LEV. XVIII. *v.* 18.

'*A Wife to her Sister.*'

Explained by the BISHOP OF LINCOLN.

OBSERVE the place of this verse. It stands at *the end* of the prohibitions concerning affinity, and at the head of a series of general prohibitions, which have no reference to affinity. It may, therefore, belong, and it is almost certain that it does belong, to the latter and not to the former at all. Next, examine the words of the original. The Hebrew phrase is *ishah el achothah* ; and this is rightly rendered in our margin *one wife to another* ; or *one woman to another* ; *not* one *wife* to her *sister*.

For, if you look through the books of Moses, you will find this Hebrew phrase used to describe the coupling of one thing with another. Hence Paganini (*Lex. Heb.*, p. 83) observes that it is carefully to be noted, that by a Hebrew idiom, anything is called *ish* (man) or *ishah* (woman), as the faces of the cherubim in Exod. xxv. 20, where the original literally means '*one man to his brother*' (*Cf.* Exod. xxxvii. 9). And so the curtains in Exod. xxvi. 3, are said to be coupled '*one woman to her sister*,' that is, *one* curtain *to another* (See also Gesenius, *Heb. Lex.* pp. xxvii. xxx., ed. London, 1847. *Cf.* Gen. xiii. 11 ; xxvi. 31 ; Exod. xvi. 15 ; xxxii. 27–29 ; Isa. iii. 5 ; xix. 2 ; Ezek. i. 19 ; iii. 13 ; xvi. 45, 48, 49 ; Joel ii. 8).

Thus in the twenty-sixth chapter of Exodus it occurs four times (verses 3, 5, 6, 17), and in none of these does it signify a *wife* to *her sister*, but simply a *thing* to *its fellow*. And so it is used in other places of Holy Writ. And in like manner the Hebrew phrase which signifies literally 'a man to his *brother*,' does not mean a man to his brother by *blood*, but simply, 'one man to his fellow,' or 'one man to another man'; and so it is commonly rendered in our Bibles.

The following important statement on this point is from the Rev. Charles Forster's remarks on this question (London, 1850, p. 32): 'This phrase, "a woman to her sister," together with the similar formula in the masculine, viz., "a man to his brother," occurs, with slight variations of the intervening preposition or conjunction, *two-and-forty* times in the Hebrew Bible, and *never once* does it designate the blood relationship of *two sisters* or *two brothers*, but always and invariably means (when used of persons) simply *two men together*, or *two women together*; and when used of things (for it is used of things as well as of persons) it means two masculine or feminine things of the *same kind*. And it is actually thus translated in our Bible in thirty-two out of the forty-one other places where it occurs; and in the other nine places *brother* obviously does not refer to consanguinity, but to proximity. If, therefore, this expression designates in Lev. xviii. 18 the blood relationship of two sisters, I can only say that *this is the solitary instance in the whole Bible where it has such a meaning.*'

Out of two-and-forty times, then, in which this Hebrew idiom occurs, it is agreed on all hands that in forty-one instances it has no reference to the blood relationship of two brothers or two sisters, but simply means two persons or things of the same kind. (See also the analysis of the passages in Dwight's *Hebrew Wife*, pp. 84–91.)

Spottiswoode & Co., Printers, New-street Square, London.

Marriage Law Defence Union Tracts.

No. XXIII.

OFFICE: 1 KING STREET, WESTMINSTER, S.W.

'*A FEW FACTS*' *from Early Church History,*

AS STATED BY THE MARRIAGE LAW REFORM ASSOCIATION.

A PAPER was recently issued by the Marriage Law Reform Association, under the title of 'A FEW FACTS (*sic*) in Connection with the Proposal for Legalising Marriage with a Deceased Wife's Sister.' It has often been publicly asserted, and certainly has never been disproved, that the agitation for legalising these incestuous unions was from the first a paid agitation, originating with a limited but wealthy clique, who, as Mr. Matthew Arnold somewhere expresses it, 'have an eye to their wives' sisters,' or whose friends have; and that it is mainly sustained by the same agencies which created it. Without positively asserting this to be a 'FACT'—for, unlike the compiler of the manifesto now before me, I am anxious to assert nothing which I cannot prove—I will say that there is at least much better evidence for it than for many or most of the so-called

'FACTS' with which that remarkable document bristles, 'thick as leaves in Vallombrosa,' but most of which, to put it mildly, 'require confirmation.' It is not easy, indeed, to conceive, still less to understand, how men with no private aim or interest to serve should be smitten with an abstract passion for the legal condonation of this particular variety of incest.* And it is wholly inconceivable that any one possessing even the moderate acquaintance with history claimed for Lord Macaulay's 'schoolboy' should be able, without some strong personal bias, to read into it the marvellous version of 'FACTS' here presented to the world.

It is a trite saying that 'nothing is so delusive as facts except figures;' and I sincerely trust that the figures, as well as the 'FACTS,' lumped together in this interesting document, will be submitted by competent hands to a searching critical analysis. If I am not greatly mistaken, they will come out of the crucible in a somewhat altered shape. With the figures, however, we are not concerned just now; nor do I propose to deal here with more than one particular department of alleged 'FACTS,' those concerning—to adopt the grand style of our learned compiler—the history of 'Universal Christendom.' I shall not even, as I wish to confine myself to the historical question, stay to examine the audacious paradox prefixed to this historical sketch, that 'such marriages are legal in every Christian State in the

* I am told that the advocates of these unhallowed unions complain of the term incestuous, when applied to them, as 'offensive;' and I quite believe it. To call shooting landlords, murder, is, for precisely similar reasons, 'offensive' to Nationalists and Fenians. But while in many things I disagree with Luther, I fully agree with him that it is often desirable to call a spade, a spade. And in view of the threatened legal pollution of the purity of our homes, it is impossible to insist too strongly that, just as theft is theft, and murder is murder, so too *incest is incest, and always will be*, even should the English Parliament ever unhappily consent to sanction it; just as, again, the so-called re-marriage of divorced persons, though sanctioned by the Act of 1857, has not ceased to be adultery.

3

world, except in certain parts of the British Empire.' * But
I may just point out in passing that, so far as my own
observation extends, the compiler can as little be trusted for
statements of contemporary as of historical fact, and that no
reader desirous of knowing the truth can safely take any single
assertion of his on his own *ipse dixit*. He tells us, for instance,
in one place (p. 2), that 'the whole Catholic hierarchy of
Dublin and London [meaning apparently the English and
Irish Roman Catholic bishops], almost without an exception,
appealed to Parliament, or to individual members of Parliament, to abolish the restriction on these marriages.' Of the
'hierarchy of Dublin' I cannot speak, though I more than
doubt the accuracy of his statement; but as regards the 'hierarchy of London,' it is flatly and peremptorily contradicted in
an official letter addressed in May 1882 to his Vicar-General
by Cardinal Manning, the head of that hierarchy, and published in the newspapers, and which therefore our purveyor
of 'FACTS' had no excuse for not being acquainted with.†
But this by the way.   Let us come to ' Universal Christendom.'

This summary of universal Church history for fifteen
centuries, ranging from the Apostolic age to the Reformation,
is comprised in just fifteen lines and a half, and it contains not
a single statement which is not either false, or directly sug-
gestive of falsehood.   It bristles with fallacies, but includes

---

* There is possibly an ambiguity in the use of the term ' Christian
States.' I remember once hearing a sermon in which the different
religions of the world were contrasted, Protestants only being called
Christians, and Roman Catholics classed as idolaters ; of the Eastern
Church the preacher had evidently never heard. Our compiler may
have possibly adopted some similar classification of ' Christian States.'

† After referring to this report about the views of the Roman
Catholic bishops, his Eminence observes, ' Nothing was further from
the intention of the bishops' ; and he adds that he trusts ' all Catholics
in either House of Parliament will vote firmly and always against such
a change in the statute law.'

4

not a single real 'FACT' which can in any way subserve the cause of the compiler. His ingenuity, however, is beyond all praise. To have compressed into so small a space a string of assertions, all but one or two of which are susceptible of a sense not literally false, but which conspire to present to the uninformed reader, for whose benefit it is designed, a view of the actual state of the case in every respect the exact opposite of the true one, must be allowed to be a masterpiece of misdirected skill. It is barely possible, no doubt, that the compiler may himself have been destitute of the rudimentary knowledge familiar to every tyro in ecclesiastical history ; but ignorance is no excuse. He was bound to inform himself before undertaking to instruct others. It is not the duty of everybody to study the history of ' Universal Christendom,' but it is the obvious duty of those who have not studied not to profess to teach it. I propose now to take *seriatim* the successive clauses of this historical compendium, and examine each in turn.

1. ' Until the fourth century their prohibition [*i.e.* the prohibition of marriage with a wife's sister] had never been heard of in the Christian Church.'

Neither had prohibition of marriage with a sister or a mother been 'heard of.' There were no canons on the subject. The compiler's statement is true in the same sense as it is true to say that the prohibition of parricide was 'never heard of' in the laws of Solon, and in no other. It was never heard of because 'such marriages,' which Christians of that age would not have called marriages at all, were never heard of, and therefore no prohibition was required. When our ingenious compiler has produced a single example of such a 'marriage' among Christians of the first three centuries with the express or even tacit sanction of the Church, it will be time enough to deal with his allegation. Meanwhile, we may be content to observe with the late Bishop of Lincoln, Dr. Wordsworth,

5

one of the most learned prelates and divines in the Church of England; 'Not a single testimony in favour of such marriages can be cited from any Christian writer of any note for fourteen centuries after Christ. *All Christendom abhorred them.*' It may be added, though the argument requires no such addition, that during the first three centuries, which were the ages of persecution, no General Council, and comparatively few Provincial Councils, were held. In the fourth century we have the explicit testimony of St. Basil to the universal practice and tradition of the Christian Church : ' Our custom in this matter *has the force of law*, because the statutes we observe have been handed down to us by holy men : and our judgment is this, that if a man has *fallen into the sin* of marrying two sisters, we *do not regard such a union as marriage*, nor do we receive the parties into communion with the Church until they are separated' (Ep. 160). This decision is embodied in Canon 54 of the Council *in Trullo*, which to this day fixes the rule of the Eastern Church on the subject. I will add, *ex abundanti cautelâ*, the conclusion of the learned writer on ' Prohibited Degrees' in Smith's *Dictionary of Christian Antiquities* : ' It will be seen from the above review that during the whole of the first eight centuries marriages were never allowed, either by civil or canon law, in the first degree, *whether of consanguinity or affinity*, nor, with one exception—that of cousins—in the second degree. . . . The first degree of affinity comprises the stepmother, the wife's mother, the wife's daughter, the son's wife, *the wife's sister*, the brother's wife.' The writer adds, with entire correctness, that ' the prohibitions of marriage with the stepmother, stepdaughter, mother-in-law, daughter-in-law, sister-in-law, *and wife's sister*, are as decided as those of marriage with the mother, daughter, and sister.'* In other words, no dis-

---

* Smith and Cheetham, vol. ii. pp. 1728—9.

tinction whatever is drawn in canon law—and this holds good from the first age of the Church to our own day—between the corresponding degrees of consanguinity and affinity. There is the same prohibition and the same abhorrence of marriage with a sister-in-law as with an own sister. Both alike are unequivocally condemned as incestuous. So much for 'FACT' No. 1 in the history of 'Universal Christendom.'

2. 'That prohibition [of marriage with a wife's sister] owes its origin to the doctrine, sedulously maintained in the third century, that all second marriages, of whatever kind, "exclude from any part in the kingdom of heaven." '

This is one of the statements in the series to which I referred as being not only—like all the rest—false in its necessary implication, as having any relevancy to the matter in hand, but also in every possible sense directly, flagrantly, and literally false. The prohibition of these incestuous unions does not date from the third century, but from the first, though, for reasons already intimated, no canonical enactments on this or any other prohibited degrees are found before the fourth. It could not possibly, therefore, 'owe its origin' to any opinion, right or wrong, maintained in the third century. But the compiler's wonted ingenuity has not deserted him here. He has contrived to flavour his misstatement with just that modicum of truth which makes it the more likely to mislead the unwary. It is quite true, as he states, that 'the doctrine that all second marriages, of whatever kind, exclude from the kingdom of heaven,' *was* 'sedulously maintained in the third century.' What he omits to add, but can hardly have failed to know, is that it was maintained exclusively by certain heretics and schismatics—viz., the Montanists and Novatians—who, for that as well as for other errors, were expressly condemned by the Church. There was, indeed, a feeling among Christians of the early ages against second,

7

and still more against third marriages, as being the less excellent way (and hence the second marriage of the clergy was always prohibited) ; and that feeling is shared by many Christians of our own day, as well Protestant as Roman Catholic. But so far from ever attempting to forbid these marriages, the Church sternly condemned the prohibition, and excluded from communion all who persisted in maintaining it. The eighth canon of the first Ecumenical Council, of Nice, requires of 'those who call themselves *Cathari*, if they wish to enter the Catholic and Apostolic Church, that they must, above all, promise in writing to conform to and follow the doctrines of the Catholic and Apostolic Church : that is to say, *they must communicate with those who have married a second time,*' &c. The Church, therefore, actually required of those who had maintained it, as an indispensable condition of admission to communion, a written abjuration of that very 'doctrine,' as heretical, which our veracious compiler represents as forming the basis of her own matrimonial legislation. He may just conceivably have been misinformed ; that is no concern of ours. But of his statement all that can be said is, that it is not only a lie, but 'a lie with a circumstance,' and therefore the better calculated to deceive. So much for 'FACT' No. 2.

3. 'The same Council which first prohibited marriage with the sister of a deceased wife was also the first to prohibit the marriage of the clergy.'

The adroitness of this statement, which combines a grain of irrelevant truth with a bushel of suggested and wholly gratuitous falsehood, is really admirable in its way. There is a double *suggestio falsi*, partly addressed to the general reader, partly intended for the special misinformation of Protestants. It is suggested to all alike that the prohibition of marriage with a wife's sister rests on the same authority as the rule of clerical celibacy, which is, of course, admitted even by Roman Catholics, however desirable and

8

expedient it may be deemed, to be matter of ecclesiastical, not of Divine obligation. It is further and more particularly suggested to Protestants, who think the rule of celibacy inexpedient and wrong, that the two prohibitions originated at the same time, and owed their origin to the same erroneous phase of belief, just as it was stated in 'FACT' No. 2 that the Church's prohibition of incestuous unions 'owes its origin to' a certain heretical doctrine maintained in the third century by Novatians and Montanists, which she had expressly condemned. The compiler must have been ignorant of the first rudiments of Church history if he did not know both his insinuations to be directly in the teeth of facts. Even the modicum of irrelevant truth he has got hold of he cannot state correctly. The thirty-third canon of the Synod of Elvira (A.D. 306), to which he must be presumed to refer, does not forbid the marriage of the clergy, but forbids those in sacred orders to cohabit with their wives. It was a local Spanish Synod, and so far from the rule it prescribed being of general application throughout the Church, the Ecumenical Council of Nice twenty years later expressly refused to impose it, when urged by Hosius to do so. Meanwhile the prohibition of marriage with a wife's sister, which was not held to rest on canon law, but on the law of God, was coeval with Christianity, or rather anterior to it, and had existed in the Church from the beginning. It was not till long after the Council of Nice that clerical celibacy was generally enforced throughout the West. In the Eastern Church (which our learned historiographer, as we hinted before, appears never even to have heard of) the marriage of the clergy is to this day the rule; yet, from the beginning till now, marriage with a wife's sister has been uniformly and absolutely prohibited, as being, in St. Basil's words, no marriage at all, but an act of deadly sin, which excludes those who commit it from communion till they have repented and broken off the incestuous *liaison.* We are now in a position to appreciate the connection insinuated by our compiler between the prohihition of marriage with a wife's sister and the rule of clerical celibacy. In date, in origin, in the grounds respectively alleged for them, in the authority they are held to rest upon, and the range they extend over, the two laws are not only distinct, but have absolutely nothing in common. There is no parallel, still less any connection, between them. Whether the marriage of the clergy is expedient or inexpedient is a point on which there always have been, and probably always will be, differences of opinion among Christians, but it has nothing whatever to do with the question now before us. The attempt to enlist Protestant antipathy to the existing Roman rule of celibacy against the prohibition throughout the Universal Church, from the days of the Apostles to our own, of marriage with a wife's sister, is either a fallacy or a fraud. The two things have as much connection as chalk and cheese. So much for 'FACT' No. 3.

4. 'The marriage of cousins was about the same time prohibited under pain of death by fire.'

Our learned and ingenuous historiographer waxes in boldness as he proceeds. His affirmations become at once more sweeping, more peremptory, and more vague. Do 'cousins' mean cousins generally, or only first cousins? Judging by his language, it should mean the former; to bring his statement into any even remote relation with history, it can only mean the latter. By whom, again, were these marriages forbidden under pain of death by fire? Judging from the context, he should mean by the Church; but if he does mean that, his statement is a pure invention. And there is, again, a charming vagueness in 'about the same time,' which inevitably recalls those delightful fairy tales of our childhood, which always used to begin, 'Once upon a time.' As our compiler's last reference—if he was referring to anything in particular—was to the Synod of Elvira, which was held in 306, ' about the same time' ought to mean about the beginning of the fourth century. But if he is thinking of any prohibition which exists outside his own 'internal consciousness' (evidently a capacious one), he must mean about the end of the fourth century; which is much as though an English historian, after recording the heroic exploits and death of Lord Nelson, should continue; 'About this time, in consequence of a conspiracy to blow up the metropolis, an Act of Parliament was passed to restrain the manufacture and sale of dynamite, called the Explosives Act.'

At all events, to make his statement relevant to the matter in hand, he must be taken to mean that the prohibition in question (1) was imposed by the Church;* (2) that it was understood, like the prohibition of marriage with a wife's sister, to rest on the Divine law; (3) that it remained permanently in force. Yet he must know well enough—if, indeed, he is to be credited with knowing anything at all of what he is talking about—that in all three respects the exact contrary is the case. The only law he can have in his mind is a civil enactment of the Emperor Theodosius, of 385; it remained in force in the Eastern Empire for nineteen years, in the Western probably for 144; but after the first twenty years it was importantly modified, and the penalties were relaxed.† Those contem-

---

* This is indeed distinctly implied in the very next sentence, where we are told that at the period of the Reformation ' Statute law, in the matter of marriage, was substituted for canon law *for the first time.*'

† The text of this law of Theodosius is no longer extant, but it is referred to by contemporary writers, and in the laws of his sons Honorius and Arcadius. St. Ambrose speaks of the penalty as '*severissimam,*' and Arcadius speaks of '*ignes et bonorum proscriptio,*' but there is no evidence of the punishment being ever inflicted. Arcadius repealed the law altogether for the East in 404, and in 409 an enactment of

porary writers who mention and defend the law, which is no longer extant, defend it on grounds moral and physiological, which appeared to them—and appear to many in our own day—to have great cogency, but are careful to distinguish it from the prohibitions of Scripture. Thus St. Augustine says that a very general feeling had grown up against such marriages before any law forbade them, and expresses his approval of the law ; but expressly adds that ' the Divine law did not forbid them.'* And it so happens that we have a form of dispensation used by the Gothic kings, during the period while the law of Theodosius continued in force in the West, preserved by Cassiodorus, which begins by distinguishing, in a kind of preamble, the legal prohibition of the marriage of first cousins from prohibitions resting on the Law of God. After referring to the prohibited degrees of the Mosaic Law, the formula goes on to recite that prudent men, following this precedent, have extended further the chaste observance, reserving to the prince the right of dispensing in the case of first cousins, in order that such marriages might be restricted, without being absolutely suppressed.† On the other hand, no application was allowed for civil dispensation from prohibitions, like that of marriage with a wife's sister, held to rest on the law of God. It was not till the sixth century that the canon law began to forbid the marriage of first cousins, and then it was on grounds of

Honorius either made the law, or confirmed a previous provision making it, subject to imperial dispensation. By the Codex of Justinian in 529 it was repealed for the whole empire.

* ' Expert sumus in connubiis consobrinarum etiam nostris temporibus propter gradum propinquitatis fraterno gradui proximum, quam raro per mores fiebat, quod fieri per leges licebat, quia id *nec Divina prohibuit* et nondum prohibuerat lex humana.'—*De Civ. Dei*, **xv. 16**

† Cassiod. *Variar.* Lib. vii. Form. 46.

expediency, moral and physical, not of Divine obligation ;*
and therefore the law was held to be dispensable, and was not
enforced on newly converted individuals or nations.

We find, then, that the parallel insinuated by our ingenuous compiler between prohibition of the marriage of
cousins and of marriage with a sister-in-law breaks down at
every point.   It is as utterly baseless as his historical statement is inexact.   So much for 'FACT' No. 4.

5. The fifth and final clause of this comprehensive
summary of the ecclesiastical history of fifteen centuries runs
as follows :—

'As is well known, such restrictions multiplied, with
varying severity (dispensations being always allowed), down
to the period of the Reformation, when for the first time,
Statute law, in the matter of marriage, was substituted for
Canon law.'

When a sweeping assertion is to be hazarded, for which
no proof can be offered, but which it is assumed that the
hearer will not be in a position to dispute, 'As is well known,'
or 'As everybody knows,' or, according to Lord Macaulay's
formula, 'As every schoolboy knows,' is a common and
convenient prefix.   It is one of those 'knock-me-down'
methods of argument which disarm criticism, not by refuting
the critic, but by browbeating him.   It is like the method of
interrogation said to be in use at some private schools of the
'Dotheboys Hall' type, where the hungry youth who has
despatched his first plate of mutton is courteously asked,
'You won't take any more mutton, will you?' 'the answer
No being expected,' as Arnold's Latin Exercise books tell
us, after the use of *Num.*   He would be a boy of abnormal
pluck who ventured to answer his master's polite query with

* Thus Gregory the Great, in replying to the questions of St. Augustine of Canterbury, places first among objections to the marriage of first
cousins, that 'we have learnt by experience that they are unfruitful.'
—Bede's *Hist. Eccles.*, i. 27.

'If you please, Sir.' And that reader must have the courage of his opinions who ventures to confess himself ignorant of what 'is well known' to everybody except himself. However, our confidence in the accuracy of our compendious historiographer of 'Universal Christendom' has been a little shaken already, and we cannot help being aware that two at least of the alleged facts he assures us are 'well known,' including the only one which has any bearing on his argument, are really 'well known' to be not facts, but fictions. We have seen already the absurd incorrectness of his assertion that there was no statute law about marriage before the Reformation ; it was strictly regulated by the Roman civil law, generally in accordance with the rule of the Church, both before and after the conversion of the Empire ; but let that pass. It is true that from the sixth to the eleventh century ecclesiastical restrictions on marriage were multiplied in the West, till the Lateran Council of 1215 again reduced them to the fourth degree of consanguinity or affinity ; certainly also after the eleventh century dispensations were allowed for impediments resting on ecclesiastical law only. But neither of these facts has any real bearing on the question at issue. The whole point of our compiler's argument lies in the remark, astutely inserted in a parenthesis, 'dispensations being *always* allowed.' This is to state that they were allowed in all ages, and to imply that they were allowed for all prohibited degrees, the wife's sister of course included. Both statement and implication are notoriously untrue. The true state of the case is explained in the following brief summary, taken from a learned work of the late Dr. Pusey's, which will be found to be strictly accurate. Three successive stages may be traced in Church legislation on the subject during the first fifteen centuries. 'Until the beginning of the sixth century all marriages forbidden in Holy Scripture, whether expressly or by implication, and those only, were absolutely forbidden by the Church, *and held to be incestuous.'* He had shown that this prohibition included marriage with a wife's sister. 'Until the end of the eleventh century, during which other marriages were forbidden by ecclesiastical law ; but, in case of newly converted individuals or nations, the ecclesiastical law was not enforced. Until the end of the fifteenth century, during which the Eastern Church retained its rule unchanged, in the West the degrees prohibited were limited by the Fourth Lateran Council, and individual dispensations *within the degrees strictly ecclesiastical* were allowed ; those forbidden in Holy Scripture were held to be Divine and indispensable.' The first authentic case of a dispensation to marry a wife's sister occurred in 1500, and it was granted to Emmanuel, King of Portugal, by Pope Alexander VI., who allowed another Sovereign to marry his own aunt ; half a century earlier the French Dauphin, afterwards Louis XI., had applied to Pope Eugenius IV. for such a dispensation, and it was refused, as being beyond the power of the Holy See to grant. The Council of Trent (1563), for the first time in history, asserted the power of the Church to dispense 'in *some* of the degrees named in Leviticus,' but without specifying in which. And a decree passed in the same session of the Council forbade any dispensation to be granted 'in the *second* degree,' except to crowned heads, and for some cause of grave public interest; thereby clearly implying that, in the *first* degree, they could never be allowed at all. So much for the crucial passage of our astute compiler's closing chapter on the Church history of the first fifteen centuries, 'dispensations being *always* allowed.' And so much. also, for 'FACT' No. 5, and last, in this exhaustive chronicle of the laws and customs of 'Universal Christendom.'

I have now completed the task I set myself. I have gone in order through all the five points of the historical charter of the official advocates of the Incestuous Marriages

Bill, and have shown each of them, when submitted to critical examination, to be worse than worthless. It will perhaps be objected that I have expended on some fifteen lines of this Marriage Law Reform Manifesto as many pages. True, but that was inevitable. It is a familiar truism, that a fool may ask as many questions in five minutes as a wise man can answer in a day. Not that I have the least intention of insinuating that our ingenious historiographer is a fool—far from it—though the most charitable judgment on his compendium would be to suppose him an ignoramus. But that hypothesis is hardly consistent with his skill in the manipulation of his materials. What I meant to say is this : his method is to assert without attempting to prove, and it is always easy enough to string together in a dozen lines a bundle of gratuitous assertions, each more baseless than the last, which it may take a volume to refute. That such methods of controversy are profoundly immoral goes without the saying, and they are not more immoral than ineffectual in dealing with readers who are thoughtful and well-informed. But it is often equally important, as Walpole explained when he kept a ' foolometer ' in his Cabinet, to convince the fools. And a controversialist who is unscrupulous, and is touting for votes which may be counted and need not be weighed, can generally reckon on a considerable success with the thoughtless and ill-informed. Moreover, Church history is a subject of which many educated men know little or nothing, and they may therefore be induced to swallow wholesale in good faith even so grotesque a travesty of the ' FACTS ' as is here provided for them, especially when it is presented in the grand style of sweeping affirmation, with a superadded hint that the facts alleged are already ' well known ' to every one who knows anything about the matter. Our compiler may fairly be congratulated on the neatness of his achievement, such as it is. He could hardly have achieved it more neatly, if it was to be done at all. He and those who prompted him have abundantly earned the commendation pronounced on the unjust steward in the Gospel. They have shown themselves 'wiser for their own generation than the children of light.' But if I might presume to offer then one piece of parting advice, it would perhaps be wiser still, considering what is their object, to keep clear for the future of Church history and Canon law altogether. They ought to know that such an appeal is treason to their cause.

H. N. Oxenham.

Spottiswoode & Co. Printers, New-street Square, London.

𝕸𝖆𝖗𝖗𝖎𝖆𝖌𝖊 𝕷𝖆𝖜 𝕯𝖊𝖋𝖊𝖓𝖈𝖊 𝖀𝖓𝖎𝖔𝖓 𝕿𝖗𝖆𝖈𝖙𝖘.
No. XXIV.

OFFICE: 1 KING STREET, WESTMINSTER, S.W.

Speech of the late Bishop (Thirlwall) of St. David's

In the House of Lords, April 25th, 1856.

THE Bishop of St. David's said he had reason to believe that the authority of the office he had the honour to fill had been pressed into the service of the cause supported by the noble Earl (St. Germains) much against his (the Bishop's) own intention and judgment. There was an impression that he agreed with the noble Earl upon a very essential point; but he wished to state that the extent of the agreement had been most prodigiously overrated, and he was sorry to be obliged to add that the divergency between the views of the noble Earl and his own had been very greatly increased by what had to-night fallen from the noble Earl. He had great pleasure in feeling that there was no material part of the question with respect to which he did not substantially agree with the great majority of his right reverend brethren. In one sense he was not sorry that this question had been revived, because he trusted that the rejection of the measure would be carried by so large a majority of that House as would go far to put an end to the agitation;

in another sense, however, he was sorry that the question had been revived, on account of the preparations which he knew had been made to support the Bill—preparations indicated by the petitions which had been laid upon the table ; and the agitation of such a subject could not but have a most injurious effect. The number of the signatures to those petitions bore a very small proportion to the mass of the people who were opposed to the Bill, but even if it were ten times greater, he would say that upon a question of this kind their Lordships ought not to count the numbers who had signed, but to weigh the reasons which were staled in the petitions. It was an undeniable fact that the prohibitions with regard to marriage contained in the Old Testament formed the laws of the land on that subject. Those prohibitions, until the beginning of the Christian dispensation, were the undoubted law of the Jewish people, and they were regarded with the greatest veneration by the disciples of Him who declared that He had come not to destroy the Law, but to fulfil it. It was also notorious that the tendency of the Primitive Church was not to relax, but to increase, the stringency of such prohibitions. There could be no doubt that these prohibitions formed the basis of our present social system—the only basis which could be devised by human wisdom, unless they went back to the light of nature for the regulation of all the relations concerning this subject ; and when there would be nothing to prevent men from falling into those excesses and that license into which some of the most civilised nations of the ancient world did actually fall by sanctioning all kinds of incestuous abominations. The noble Earl had no such intention ; but such was the consequence logically involved in his measure. The noble Earl proposed to touch only one restriction ; but his proposition rested upon grounds which

3

would virtually sweep away all the rest. He agreed with his right rev. brethren in thinking that the spirit and principle of the Divine Law was clearly opposed to that kind of marriage which the noble Earl proposed to sanction. The prohibitions in the 18th chapter of Leviticus were prefaced by a general statement which laid down a governing principle applicable to every case of kindred ; and in the 8th verse this principle is extended to the corresponding degree of affinity. The prohibition in the 16th verse was full and express ; and this, on rinciple, includes the case of the wife's sister; so that, if this had not been mentioned, there would have been no doubt as to the intention. But then the noble Earl maintained that this principle is counteracted by the language of the 18th verse. But the text on which the noble Earl relied was ambiguous and obscure. He said advisedly it was ambiguous, because it admitted of more than one interpretation ; and although upon the whole he preferred the text of the authorised version, still the marginal note was not undeserving of attention or destitute of some degree of probability. It might be understood in that sense as meant to qualify the general license of polygamy. The text was obscure, because it contained several words which were superfluous for the purpose that the noble Earl considered it was intended to convey, and which tended to confuse certainty as to the real meaning. For the reason assigned, ' to vex her,' did not apply to this more than to any other case of polygamy. If their lordships had now to decide what part of these prohibitions were to be incorporated into the law of the land, it would be safest to take that which was clear and indisputable—to take the spirit and principle of the whole code of prohibition, and not that which was ambiguous and obscure. A petition had been presented and circulated on the part of the Protestant Dissenters in favour of this Bill, but the ground upon which they rested their objection to the existing law was just as applicable to every other prohibition in the table as it was to that which the noble Earl had selected. He could only consider this proposal as the first step in a movement the limits of which he was utterly unable to foresee. The noble Earl disclaimed any intention to carry the alteration of the law any further, but he had not disguised from himself or from their lordships the probability, nay, he might almost say the moral certainty, that some other noble lord, bolder and more consistent, might carry out still further the principle upon which he had founded this particular measure. He could see no line of separation between the removal of this prohibition and the infringement of the remainder of the existing law. This table inclosed that which he had always been accustomed to consider holy ground. It guarded the purest affections and holiest charities of domestic life, and neither the noble Earl nor anyone else could show what portion of that ground would remain unviolated and un-polluted if that fence were once broken down. He hoped that their lordships would earn a fresh claim to the gratitude of the country by rejecting this proposition by a still greater majority than on the former occasion, as the present measure was open to greater, to more numerous, and graver objec-tions than the last. At all events, he must express his decided protest against a Bill fraught with infinite danger to the country and to society.

Price One Halfpenny.

Spottiswoode & Co., Printers, New-street Square, London.

Marriage Law Defence Union Tracts.
No. XXV.
OFFICE: 1 KING STREET, WESTMINSTER, S.W.

The Real Bearing of the Opinions of the Professors of Hebrew and Greek on the Scriptural Law of Prohibited Degrees of Marriage.

By JAMES S. CANDLISH, D.D.,

Professor of Theology, Free Church College, Glasgow.

THIS volume * contains a formidable array of authorities learned in Hebrew and Greek, and all, with two or three exceptions, seeming to agree in declaring that Scripture contains nothing to forbid marriage with a deceased wife's sister ; and it has been referred to as proving that it is only a vulgar but mistaken belief that such a marriage is prohibited in Scripture.   It contains indeed many opinions that are entitled to great weight ; and it would not be candid to deny that these give, so far as they go, a corroboration to part of the argument of those who support the Bill for legalising such marriages.   But an examination of the precise extent to which the opinions go will show that many of them are far from being decisive, and that the point on which they really give a decision entitled to respect is one that does not at all carry the desired conclusion.   It is not

* ' Opinions of the Hebrew and Greek Professors of the European Universities on the Scriptural aspect of the question regarding the legalization of Marriage with a Deceased Wife's Sister ' ; with an Appendix.   Marriage Law Reform Association, 21 Parliament Street, S.W. London : Printed by Samuel Goulburn, 1882.

proposed in this paper to discuss any questions of Hebrew or Greek scholarship dealt with in these opinions, but simply, allowing them on all such points to have the authority of experts, to examine what are the precise points on which they pronounce, and what is the relation of these to the general argument from Scripture.

The title of the volume does not correspond with its contents, but might lead the unwary to the idea that these amount to more than they really do. It is entitled, 'Opinions . . . . on the Scriptural Aspect of the Question regarding the Legalization of Marriage with a Deceased Wife's Sister'; but when we look at the letters of Lord Dalhousie—in reply to which the opinions were given—we find that he did not put his inquiries in that general form, but only asked the professors of Hebrew their opinion 'whether such marriages are or are not prohibited in the Mosaic writings'; and the professors of Greek their opinion 'whether there is anything in the original text of Eph. v. 31, from which it can be reasonably inferred that all the rela. tions of a wife become by her marriage, and so remain after her death, one flesh with the husband.' That is, the book contains the opinions of one set of learned men, as to whether such marriages are forbidden in the Pentateuch, and of another set whether one particular passage in the New Testament affords a reasonable inference against them. But they do not give a conjoint view of the teaching of Scripture as a whole, for it is quite possible to admit that such marriages are not forbidden in the Levitical law, nor in Eph. v. 31, and yet to be firmly convinced that they are opposed to the general scope and spirit of the Bible. That this is not a mere fanciful distinction may be seen by taking a parallel case. Suppose the question had been as to the lawfulness of polygamy, and had been treated in the same way. Precisely the same answers might have been given, both as to the Pentateuch, and as to any one New Testament text that might have been selected. But would any one hold a series of opinions on these points to be an adequate representation of the Scriptural aspect of the question?

Even, therefore, if we should accept the whole of the

3

opinions of the professors as perfectly decisive on the questions submitted to them, we might still hold, as we do, that the Bible, more especially the New Testament, contains principles that show such marriages to be immoral and unlawful. The professors' opinions may have advanced Lord Dalhousie and his friends some distance towards getting over the Scriptural argument against their Bill; but they certainly have not, even on the most favourable construction, enabled them to overcome it. The book contains at best only opinions on some parts of the Scriptural aspect of the question. But it is a recognised principle of modern theology, that the teaching of Scripture on any subject is to be determined, not as was too often done formerly, by a few so-called proof-texts, but by a combined view of all its parts in their historical relations.

So much appears simply from comparing the title-page of this volume with the inquiries that elicited the opinions contained in it, without looking at all at the opinions themselves. When we examine these we may see reason to think that, even to the limited extent to which they are really given, their collective weight is not so overwhelming as it appears at first sight to be. We may consider separately the opinions of the Hebrew and Greek professors respectively on the questions submitted to them.

The question on which the professors of Hebrew have given their opinions is, whether marriage with a deceased wife's sister is, or is not, prohibited in the Mosaic writings; and the passage on which the discussion turns is Lev. xviii. 6–18, which is the fullest statement on the subject in the Mosaic law, other passages merely repeating some of its enactments with various penalties, so that there need be no objection to limiting the inquiry to Lev. xviii. 6–18. Now, in these verses there are some points of linguistic and grammatical difficulty, especially in v. 18; and on these the opinion of learned Hebrew scholars is of great weight, and the concurrent judgment of the European professors of that language may be regarded as decisive. That judgment, as given here, condemns certain positions that have been maintained by some of those opposed to the proposal to legalise marriage with a deceased wife's sister. As the

4

advocates of that measure lay much stress on Lev. xviii. 18 as allowing it, some have contended that the prohibition in that verse is not limited to the lifetime of the first wife, the words 'in her lifetime' being taken to refer to the wife's sister, and to be added for the sake of emphasis, thus making the verse an express prohibition of the marriage in all cases. Others, again, have held that the verse does not refer specially to sisters, but is a prohibition of polygamy in general, adopting the rendering in the margin of the English Bible. Now, these are questions that turn on the meaning of the Hebrew words, and the rules and usages of Hebrew grammar; and in regard to them, the opinions of the professors are unanimous in rejecting both these proposed constructions of the verse. This is the subject that is dealt with in the elaborate and learned arguments with which most of the professors consulted have filled up their replies to Lord Dalhousie. But many of those who have held marriage with a deceased wife's sister to be forbidden in Leviticus, never maintained either of these opinions; and though some distinguished scholars still hold that Lev. xviii. 18 is a prohibition of polygamy, this does not form the main ground of their position, but only part of the answer they make to an argument which their opponents draw from that verse. The position maintained was, and is, that the marriage in question is forbidden by the preceding law in v. 6–17; and that the prohibition in v. 18, whatever interpretation be given to it, cannot reasonably be held, by its mere silence, to allow a marriage within the degrees of affinity already forbidden.

Now, of the forty-eight opinions in this collection, no fewer than twenty-nine take no account whatever of the verses on which the prohibition is held to be based, but are confined entirely to a discussion of the single verse, Lev. xviii. 18.* Many of them state or assume that this verse is the only one bearing on the question, or argue that the limitation of its prohibition of marriage to the lifetime of the wife proves conclusively that it must have been allowed

---

* Of the others, ten take a view of the law as a whole, and regard it as allowing the marriage in question, three take the opposite view, and six merely give a personal opinion without indicating its grounds.

5

after her death, without taking the slightest notice of the construction of the preceding precepts, on which the whole question really turns.

Their authority as Hebraists, therefore, cannot fairly be regarded as going beyond the question of the interpretation of that one verse (Lev. xviii. 18), which indeed is the only point on which Hebrew scholarship has any bearing. Their opinions really are simply, that that verse does not prohibit the marriage in question, but inferentially permits it, or that the Levitical law does not expressly prohibit it. Many of them seem to have understood this to be the meaning of Lord Dalhousie's question, and one, Professor Watkins of Durham, gives his opinion in this form : ' That the letter of the Levitical law does not forbid, but by inference permits, marriage with a deceased wife's sister' (p. 21). No doubt it may be said that many of these professors have put no such qualification in their opinions, but have declared in the most absolute terms, that in their view the Levitical law did allow the marriage. That is indeed true ; but then it must be remembered that it is a recognised and important principle in regard to the use of authorities, that no writer should be regarded as giving a decision on a question that was not really before him. This is necessary, in order to guard against the unfairness of which almost all theological parties have been guilty, in quoting the sayings of the Fathers, Reformers, or other venerated men, as pronouncing on questions that were not raised till after their day, or were not in their view. Now, all these twenty-nine professors show, in their replies to Lord Dalhousie, that they had distinctly before them the questions as to the meaning of Lev. xviii. 18, on which, as Hebraists, they might naturally think their opinion was desired ; but none of them shows that he has considered, some not even that they are aware of, the arguments from Lev. xviii. 6-17, on which those who think that the Levitical law forbids the marriage in question base their opinion. This appears from the profound silence they observe as to these arguments, while discussing, sometimes at great length, the varying interpretations of verse 18. It cannot be supposed that this silence is due to contempt, as if they thought these arguments unworthy of notice or refutation. There is no trace of such a feeling in their letters; and they have discussed, with a care and patience that are sometimes astonishing, views which are much less worthy of respect, either for their inherent probability or for the number and reputation of their supporters. The argument from the preceding law is noticed, along with the interpretation of Lev. xviii. 18, in ten other opinions, to which we shall refer further on; and there seems to be no other explanation possible of the silence of the twenty-nine we are now considering, except that the professors who gave them were not aware of the argument.

Nor is this anything wonderful, or any real discredit to those eminent men. It has frequently happened in this controversy, that men who have adopted the view that marriage with a deceased wife's sister is not forbidden by the Levitical law, have shown themselves ignorant of the grounds on which the opposite view is held; nor is that because these grounds are obscure or shadowy, but simply because they involve the question of the construction and application of the law, and not of its mere translation; and so may be overlooked by those whose business is with the grammatical exegesis. A man may be a thorough Hebrew scholar, and well acquainted with the text and interpretation of the Old Testament, and yet never have given attention to the question, What is the most reasonable interpretation of the law of marriage contained in Lev. xviii. ? On this question, the opinions of professors of theology, or ethics, or jurisprudence, would have been more valuable than of those of Hebrew; but in order to have been of real weight, they should have been given not on a mere general question put by one party, but on statements by both sides of the grounds of their opinions.

However that may be, two of the most learned and valuable of the replies to Lord Dalhousie show plainly in their authors, not merely ignorance, but entire misapprehension of the ground on which the opposition view is maintained. Professor Paul de Lagarde of Göttingen, writes :

'It is most certain that the Pentateuch does *not* prohibit

7

marriage with a deceased wife's sister. I shall direct a full proof of it to your lordship in the course of eight or ten days.'

And then in the opening of the essay, which he sends in fulfilment of this promise, he says :

'There is only one verse in the Pentateuch that has been quoted in favour of the opinion that such marriage is prohibited : Lev. xviii. 18 ' (pp. 25, 26).

So, too, Dr. Merx of Heidelberg says :

' Before entering into a detailed explanation of the passage of the Mosaic law, by which in the opinion of many persons marriage with the deceased wife's sister is forbidden, it is necessary,' &c.; and again, ' this has been the case in the passage, Lev. xviii. 18, on which the opinion is based that marriage with the deceased wife's sister is forbidden by divine law ' (pp. 38, 39).

Now, this is the very opposite of the truth. The text, Lev. xviii. 18, is that on which is based the opinion that marriage with a deceased wife's sister is permitted by the Mosaic law. Those who think otherwise, do indeed hold that it can be fairly interpreted so as not to imply that permission ; and a few of them have, as indicated above, endeavoured to construe it as a prohibition ; but none of those who hold that the Levitical law forbids such marriage make this the main, much less the only, ground of their opinion. In proof of this, it is enough to quote the following statement from the answer of the Strasburg professors to Lord Dalhousie :

' The opinion specially promoted by Calvin (Opera ed Reuss, Cunitz, Baum ; Brunsvig, xxiv. p. 664), which, as opposed to the Catholic view, gained admission into certain Protestant churches, viz., that marriage with a wife's sister was in any case forbidden is, in their contention, based, not upon the text of Lev. xviii. 18, but upon Lev. xviii. 16, from which it is sought to show, that since marriage with a brother's wife is forbidden because of the flesh relationship with the brother, it necessarily follows that marriage with a wife's sister is also inadmissible ' (p. 79).

This is not quite an adequate statement of the argument, or of the extent to which it has prevailed in the Christian Church ; but it is amply sufficient to show that judgments given on the assumption that Lev. xviii. 18 is the only passage to be considered, are really passed on a hearing of the evidence on one side of the question only, and are therefore of no value on the main question, though they have weight on the subordinate points which they discuss.

There are, however, ten opinions of Hebrew professors contained in this volume, which show that their authors have considered the Levitical law on this subject as a whole, and not merely one particular text, and indicate more or less clearly how they meet the argument of those who hold that the law as a whole forbids marriage with a deceased wife's sister. Of these, five are from Protestants, including one signed by four professors at Strasburg, and five from Roman Catholics, including one signed by three professors at Salamanca, and answering the question as. to the New Testament as well as the Old; so that we have the opinions of fifteen professors in all. Some of these indicate the ground on which they reject the inference from Lev. xviii. 6-17 against marriage with a deceased wife's sister; others do not do so, but only show that they do reject it, or that they have considered the law as a whole.

In order to estimate the weight to be attached to these opinions, it may be well to give a more distinct statement of the view taken of the Levitical law by the supporters of the present law of this country. I shall take this, not from any controversial work, but from the calm and dispassionate pages of a work on the law of the Church of England.

'By the 32 Henry VIII. ch. 38 (the portion of which relating to this subject was confirmed by 2 & 3 Edward VI., ch. 23, and after its repeal under Philip and Mary, was revived by 1 Eliz., ch. 1, § 3) all marriages are prohibited between persons not *without the Levitical degrees*. The peculiar form of this enactment is to be observed, indicating as it does the probable intention of the Legislature to give the statute a wider disabling operation than merely in restraint of marriages within the *express Levitical prohibitions*. To carry out this intention, lawyers have been guided by two rules in the interpretation of this Act. (1) The word " degrees " must not be considered as referring to steps of vertical relationship, and thus the Levitical prohibition of marriage between parent and child extends to all marriages between persons in the ascending and descending line *ad infinitum* (*e.g.* grandparent and grandchild,

9

&c.), as being persons within the same *degree.* (2) The express Levitical prohibition of marriage between persons connected by a certain degree of relationship is to be extended to all marriages which are *in paritate rationis, e.g.* marriage being expressly forbidden between a woman and her husband's brother, it is also forbidden by implication between a man and his wife's sister, as being within the same degree of relationship as a marriage between the former parties. Agreeably to this principle, a table of forbidden degrees was promulgated in 1563 by Archbishop Parker, which contained several prohibitions not expressly insisted on in Lev. xviii., but capable of being deduced from the Levitical prohibitions by the application of the above-stated rules of interpretation. This table is adopted in the 99th canon of the year 1603, which is as follows: "No person shall marry within the degrees prohibited by the laws of God, and expressed in a table set forth by authority in the year of our Lord God 1563 . . ." These prohibitions are founded upon the two principles—that (1) the relationships forbidden by God in the case of either sex are equally forbidden to the other sex; and that (2) the husband and wife being one flesh, relationships by marriage become to either of them blood relationships. The course of subsequent legal decisions has constantly affirmed these principles of interpretation, not only positively by annulling all marriages which are impliedly forbidden, *paritate rationis,* by the Levitical law, but negatively by refusing to interfere with any marriage which could not be brought within the analogy of the Levitical prohibitions.' (The 'Book of Church Law,' by the Rev. John Henry Blunt, M.A., F.S.A., revised by Walter G. F. Phillimore, D.C.L., 2nd edit., 1876, pp. 140, 142.)

The view which has thus been taken, not only by divines but by the leading statesmen, lawyers, and judges of England, and, as could easily be shown, of Scotland too, is briefly this : that Lev. xviii. 6 lays down the general principle, that marriage is not to be contracted between those who are near of kin, and that the following verses (7–17) give, not an exhaustive list of all the relations forbidden, but a number of illustrative cases, to show what is meant by near of kin in this connection.

Now, even the comparatively few opinions in this large collection, that take the slightest notice of this view, differ widely in their own view of the law. Some agree with us in regarding the specific prohibitions as not an exhaustive list, but indications of a principle ; though they draw from them a principle that allows marriage with a deceased wife's sister. Others adopt the view of the Jewish Talmudists that all marriages not expressly forbidden are allowed. Of the former, the most explicit is that of Professor Birrell of St. Andrews, who writes as follows :

' In the crucial passages, Leviticus, chaps. xviii. and xx., the principle that underlies the legislation may be said to be twofold, viz.: 1st, actual closeness of relationship nearer than cousinship ; 2nd, the having been married to anyone of which the above closeness of relationship can be averred. Coming under the second head are—marriage with an aunt-in-law, because she has been married to such a near blood relation as an uncle ; and marriage with a deceased brother's wife, for the very same reason. In the case of a deceased wife's sister the above does not apply, unless, indeed, she had been a deceased brother's wife, or the wife of any other near relation. In any other case she stands outside the prohibited circle. If a spinster, she has been married to no one, and being herself not within the prohibited degree of relationship, the marriage is quite legal under the Mosaic code. If the widow of any other than a deceased uncle or brother, or other near relative, she is also equally unobjectionable. Anyone reading over the chapters carefully, and without prejudice, must, I think, believe that the view above indicated is the only correct one.' (' Opinions,' &c., p. 74.)

This last statement is sufficiently confident, especially as the view thus pronounced to be the only correct one, is entirely opposed to those of all the Jewish and of all the Christian interpreters, much as these differ among themselves. One might even challenge Dr. Birrell to name a single author who agrees with him. What he thinks to be so evidently the underlying principle of the law is clearly inadequate to account for the prohibition in Lev. xviii. 17 of marriage with a wife's daughter or granddaughter ; for they are neither blood-relations nor persons who have been married to blood relations. Perhaps, indeed, Professor Birrell understands that verse as meaning only to forbid marriage with a woman and her daughter or granddaughter at the same time, as Professor de Jong of Utrecht says is probably the meaning ; but that is really utterly untenable, in the face of the absolute and unequivocal words in Deut. xxvii. 23, on which also, as well as on Lev. xx. 14, Professor Birrell's principle is hopelessly shattered.

The only other opinion that indicates any principle as underlying the law in Leviticus, is that of Professor Merx of Heidelberg, and the principle he finds in it is much more complex and cumbrous in statement : ' In the first place it forbids sexual intercourse with the relatives of father, mother, and other wives of the father and their descendants (Lev. xviii. 7–16). . . . . Then in the second part of this law, which refers to the relation of a man to the family of his wife (Lev. xviii. 17, 18), sexual intercourse is absolutely forbidden between a man and the direct ascendants and descendants of his wife ' (p. 40).   The principle of the first part of the law is somewhat vaguely expressed ; but the enumeration of cases shows it to be the same as that which Professor Birrell thinks sufficient to explain the whole law.   This, taken along with Professor Merx's other principle, would cover all the cases mentioned ; and it is possible that this was the principle of the law.   It is that to which we should be led if v. 18 is held to sanction marriage with a deceased wife's sister ; and that is the only thing that can be alleged in its favour, but in other respects it is very improbable.   It is a very complicated rule, making differences with no apparent reason.   It rests on a distinction that is nowhere indicated in the law, that the wife of a blood relation is to be treated differently from the blood relation of a wife ; although that again is complicated by the exception of the wife's direct ascending or descending line.   Besides, v. 17 distinctly declares that the wife's near kinswomen are not to be married ; and it is unquestionable that near kinswomen in this law include sisters.

But in holding these to be the principles of the Levitical law, Dr. Merx stands quite alone among those whose opinions are given here, and is opposed by the whole current of Christian interpreters on the one side and of Jewish interpreters on the other ; the former holding that the wife's blood relations are forbidden to the same extent as the husband's, and the latter, that only the marriages expressly mentioned are forbidden.   At least he is alone in stating it explicitly; but perhaps Professor Dillmann of Berlin, Professor Kamphausen of Bonn, and the Strasburg Professors indicate a similar view, by stating that, according to Hebrew law, a man was more nearly related ' to the house of his brother (that is, the family of his own father) than to the family of his wife's parents' (pp. 14, 16, 79). This however is not fully explained, and may not amount to Dr. Merx's principle.

The other view of the law in Lev. xviii., that of the Talmudical Jews, that it only forbids the marriages expressly mentioned as unlawful, is presumably that held by the large number of the professors who have based their opinions only on v. 18. How far this would carry us in legitimising marriages between those who are nearly related, not merely by affinity, but even by consanguinity, appears from the following words of Dr. P. de Jong, Professor at Utrecht: ' Not prohibited are marriages

> With a mother's brother's wife,
> Of an uncle with a niece,
> Of nephew and niece,[*]
> With a wife's sister after the death of the wife.'
>
> (' Opinions,' &c., p. 81.)

Even this is not perfectly consistent; for, if Dr. de Jong will not even extend the prohibition of a father's brother's wife to a mother's brother's wife, what does he make of the absence of all prohibition of marriage with a daughter, which does not occur in his list either of those prohibited or not prohibited?

The Secretary of the Marriage Law Reform Association is careful, in connection with Dr. Pusey's statement that the agitation has spread to the whole subject of affinity, to remind us in a note (p. 70) that the Association ' still confines its operations *exclusively* to the removal of restrictions on marriage with a deceased wife's sister.' He has not thought it necessary to make any reference to this in connection with Dr. de Jong's opinion, which goes far beyond the modest proposal of the Association. In what sense so limited a change can be regarded by anyone as a ' reform,' it is im-

---

[*] This seems to be a misprint, or mistranslation, but what is meant is not clear.

possible to see ; the movement must go further, else it would
be at variance with every possible construction of the
Levitical law. To do nothing more than legalise marriage
with a deceased wife's sister, would depart from the view of
the Ancient Church and of the Reformation Churches ; but it
would be equally at variance with the views of Dr. Birrell, of
Dr. Merx, and of the Jewish Rabbis, as expressed by Dr.
de Jong. The opinions of the Hebrew professors, therefore,
while they are opposed to that construction of the Levitical
statute on which the law of this country proceeds, give no
positive support whatever to the limited aim of the Marriage
Law Reform Association.

The Roman Catholic professors can accept the Jewish
interpretation of the Levitical law with less inconvenience
than Protestants, for they hold that the Church can add,
and has added, prohibitions to those contained in the
Pentateuch, so that what was allowed to Jews is not necessarily legitimate for Christians. Professor Ribero of
Granada, and the Greek Professors Pasquier of Angers, and
Garriga of Barcelona, ground the dispensing power of the
Pope for marriage with a deceased wife's sister on the
assumption that 'there is no divine precept or positive law
opposed to their union' (p. 36). But this is certainly not
the authorised doctrine of the Roman Catholic Church ;
for the Council of Trent claims for the Church the power
of dispensing, in some cases expressly forbidden in Leviticus. 'If anyone say, that only those degrees of consanguinity and affinity which are expressed in Leviticus can
impede the contraction of marriage or dissolve it when
contracted ; and that the Church cannot dispense in some
of them, or appoint that more impede and dissolve marriage,
let him be anathema.' (Conc. Trid. Sess. xxiv. Can. iii.)
The famous case that raised the question was the dispensation granted by Pope Julius II. to Henry VIII. of England
to marry his brother's widow, and that is a union expressly
forbidden in Leviticus. The ground taken by the defenders
of that act, apart from some questions of fact and technicality, was that the dispensation 'did not touch any part of
the divine or natural law.' This appears from the quotation
from Cardinal Cajetan, in Mr. Jenkins' letter to Cardinal

14

Manning in the appendix to this volume (p. 123), and the matter is put in the same way by Professor Donadin of Barcelona (p. 12). The adoption of the Jewish interpretation of the Levitical law was not indeed necessary for the Roman Catholic position ; but was a very natural thing when such a dispensing power was claimed. This dispensing power, however, was a new thing in the sixteenth century. Previously it had been only claimed and exercised in regard to those prohibitions which the Church had added to the divine law, so as to extend the bar to the fourth or seventh degree. In regard to these and similar restrictions, as the Church had imposed them, so she could grant dispensations ; but the prohibitions in Leviticus were held to be of divine authority, and to extend to the third degree, both of consanguinity and affinity. In regard to these, no dispensing power was claimed till the end of the fifteenth century, when the infamous Pope Alexander VI. (Borgia) gave the King of Portugal a dispensation to marry his deceased wife's sister.

The Reformers and the Protestant Churches simply returned to what had been the universal belief of the Church for fifteen centuries, accepting the law in Leviticus as of divine authority, rejecting all extensions of its prohibitions beyond the third degree of consanguinity and affinity, and disallowing all dispensing power in the Church. Thus, when the Strasburg professors speak of this view as especially promoted by Calvin and opposed to the Catholic view, that is only true of the Catholic view of modern times ; for Calvin's was the truly Catholic view up to a generation before his day, and was that also of the other Reformers as well. If, therefore, the concurrent opinion of nearly all the present professors of Hebrew forms a strong body of authorities in favour of the view that marriage with a deceased wife's sister is not forbidden in Leviticus, it must not be forgotten that on the other side are the Karaite Jews, the whole Christian Church, Eastern and Western, for 1,500 years, the Reformers and the Protestant Churches down to recent times, when many of them have been divided in opinion: and this mass of authorities includes many as learned Hebrew scholars and as able interpreters as any now living.

Among the opinions in this collection, this view is maintained in those of Dr. Pusey (Oxford), Professors Urriza (Madrid), and Iago (Seville), and though that is a small number of the entire collection, yet, as we have seen, the great majority have given no opinion at all on the point, and there are not more than three who explicitly agree on any other positive interpretation of the Levitical law.

What has just been said about the agreement of Christian interpreters for fifteen centuries may seem to be contradicted by a passage quoted by Professor Watkins of Durham from the 'Speaker's Commentary' on Leviticus xviii. 18, where, after a reference to authorities in favour of the translation which makes it only a prohibition of marrying a wife's sister during the life of the former, it is added: ' The interpretation appears indeed to have passed unchallenged from the third century before Christ to the middle of the sixteenth century after Christ' (p. 22). But this is said only of the interpretation of that verse, not of the inference drawn from it for the legitimacy of marriage with a deceased wife's sister, which was as uniformly rejected by Christian divines. By failing to distinguish between the two questions, Professor Onciuls of Czernowitz, is led to say that 'St. Basil the Great, in his letter to Diodorus, Bishop of Tarsus, . . . has inveighed probably only from the standpoint of Christian morals against the above simple and natural version of the passage in question, in order to combat such marriages amongst the Christians' (p. 20). Now, the fact is, that St. Basil in that letter does not dispute but accepts the interpretation in question, and contends that it does not permit marriage with a deceased wife's sister, which he holds to be forbidden in Leviticus xviii. 6. This further illustrates the importance of distinguishing the general question, What is the Levitical law on this point? from the smaller and subordinate one, What is the meaning of Leviticus xviii. 18?

The opinions of the professors of Greek are given under the heading 'The Christian Law,' a title more grossly disproportionate to their contents than even that of the entire collection; for, as before stated, they are only on the question whether from the single verse, Eph. v. 31, ' it can be reasonably inferred that all the relatives of a wife become by her marriage, and so remain after her death, one flesh with the husband.' Does Lord Dalhousie or the Marriage

Law Reform Association think that the Christian law is to be learned simply from the grammatical criticism of a single text? Must not the Christian law be determined by the careful discussion of such questions as these: Is the Levitical law of forbidden degrees repealed by Christ? Is that law moral or merely ceremonial? Are its provisions specially adapted to the Jews, or suited to all men? Is it agreeable to the general principles and spirit of Christ's and His apostles' teaching about marriage? What does the spirit of Christianity suggest as an appropriate law on this subject? Such inquiries used to be thought necessary; but now it seems *nous avons changé tout cela*, and there is a short and easy method of discovering whether marriage with a deceased wife's sister is allowed by the Christian law, just to see whether mere Greek scholarship can deduce a prohibition from one particular verse by itself. No one maintains, or ever has maintained, that Eph. v. 31 by itself proves the unlawfulness of such marriages; and therefore opinions on the negative side of the question proposed by Lord Dalhousie are utterly irrelevant.

Lord Dalhousie says, that some of the opponents of his Bill seek to justify their hostility on the assumption that such marriages are prohibited in the New Testament passage, 'They two shall be one flesh' (Eph. v. 31); but this shows an entire misapprehension of the use they make of this text. For one thing, they do not rely on Eph. v. 31 alone, but observe that it is a quotation from Gen. ii. 24, and that the same words are also quoted by our Lord in Matt. xix. 5 and Mark x. 8, and by Paul in 1 Cor. vi. 16. Thus it is not merely a single verse, but a weighty saying that is thrice over quoted in the New Testament, and treated as a principle, from which conclusions are drawn as to the law of marriage that were not perceived by the Scribes who clung to the letter of the law.

Again, they do not argue from these passages by themselves, but observe the bearing that the principle enunciated in them has on the law of prohibited degrees in Leviticus. The general rule of that law is, 'None of you shall approach to any that is near of kin to him [literally flesh of his flesh] to uncover their nakedness' (Lev. xviii. 6). That, taken by itself, might be understood to mean only relatives by blood;

and so it is interpreted by some. But it is certain that the law here given prohibited marriage with those related by affinity; v. 8, 'The nakedness of thy father's wife . . . is thy father's nakedness'; v. 14, 'Thy father's brother's wife is thine aunt'; v. 16, 'The nakedness of thy brother's wife is thy brother's nakedness'; and in v. 17, marriage with a wife's daughter or granddaughter is forbidden, because 'they are her flesh,' and being hers, are as little to be approached as thine own. Obviously, the principle that underlies these laws is, that husband and wife are one flesh, as declared in Gen. ii. 24. Now, are these laws obsolete? Were they merely Judaic ordinances, such as have no force for Christians? So it has sometimes been held. But when we find that the principle on which they rest is thrice over repeated in the New Testament, and declared by our Lord Himself to be the fundamental principle of the marriage law, must we not conclude that that principle should still rule the law of prohibited degrees?

This is the use that the opponents of legalising marriage with a deceased wife's sister make of these New Testament passages. It is true the wife's relations are not specially in view in any of them, but they all assert the principle on which affinity is to be regarded as interposing a bar to marriage to the same extent as consanguinity. This is, as Professor Blackie says, not a question of Greek, but of common sense ; and though he thinks that is a quality with which commentators and theologians are not specially dowered, the replies of some of the professors of Greek show that the same remark might be made about them. Thus Professor Pellicioni of Bologna says :

'If it be granted that the relatives of the wife are one sole flesh with the husband, it would follow that after her death the husband might exercise the same marital rights on her relations, (who are flesh of his flesh), that he had exercised upon his defunct consort' (p. 91).

On the other hand, Professor Nicole of Geneva, argues :

'That if a man may not marry his sister-in-law because she has become part of his own flesh, it follows *à fortiori* that he may have no intercourse with his wife when once the marriage has been solemnised' (p. 100).

If this is not unseemly trifling with a grave subject, it shows utter ignorance and incapacity to give an intelligent opinion on the question at issue. Hardly less lacking in understanding of the subject is the argument of Professors Campbell of St. Andrews, and Herwerden of Utrecht, that if the assumption of Lord Dalhousie's opponents were true, no second marriage at all would be morally possible (pp. 119, 120). There is no means of scriptural proof by which that conclusion can be drawn from the general principle; whereas it is certain that in the Old Testament the principle was the ground of the prohibition of marriage between those nearly related by affinity. Must it not infer such a prohibition in the New Testament also?

It is to be observed that the argument from the New Testament, which the opinions of the professors of Greek entirely fail to touch, applies equally to whatever view be taken of the Levitical law. If the view of the Karaites and of most Christian divines be true, then that law consistently carries out the general principle so frequently repeated in the New Testament, save in the strictly limited exception of the Levirate law, which is universally admitted to be · now obsolete. The New Testament principle therefore requires no other change in the Levitical law, but confirms and sanctions it as so interpreted. If, on the other hand, the interpretation of the Levitical law preferred by the Talmudists and most modern Hebrew scholars be correct, then, though it undoubtedly recognises the principle that the union of husband and wife makes affinity a bar to marriage, it does not carry it out consistently. This is possible, for the Mosaic law, as our Lord testified, failed to do so also in regard to divorce. But in that case does not the emphatic assertion of the principle in the New Testament, and its application to the law of divorce, indicate that in Christian legislation it should be carried out fully and consistently?

The Levitical law in some particulars left women in a position of less rights and liberty than men. This was the case in polygamy itself; for a man might have many wives, but the woman was restricted to one husband. It was so in the law of divorce; for the husband might for some causes put away his wife, while the wife had no corresponding right to divorce her husband. But in Christian legislation this has disappeared, and, where divorce is permitted at all, both sexes are put on the same level. A like inequality appears in the law of vows (Num. xxx.).

Now, on that construction of the Levitical law of prohibited degrees which modern scholars generally prefer, and which permits marriage with a deceased wife's sister, it is closely bound up with the toleration of polygamy, and is an instance of that unequal treatment of the sexes which occurs in other parts of the law. The husband is to be at liberty to marry certain relatives of his wife ; while the wife is not at liberty to marry the same relatives of her husband. The husband is guarded against the possibility of his brother being his rival and successor ; but the wife has no such protection in relation to her sister. It is possible that such a law was given by God to Israel, an Oriental nation, in an uncultivated age, when polygamy and arbitrary divorce were tolerated ; but is it conceivable that that is the law which God's revelation in Christ teaches to be proper for the state of enlightenment and humanity that we have now reached?

If the spirit of Christianity is to be attended to, we shall take the Levitical law as indicating the extent to which the bar of relationship should be carried, since in this respect there is no indication in the New Testament that it was accommodated to a stage of imperfect moral progress ; but we must free it from that anomaly which mars its symmetry, and was due probably to the inferior position of women in a polygamous society.

Even, therefore, though it be held that the modern interpretation of the Levitical law is correct, and that the proposed alteration of our law would bring it more into accordance with that of the Pentateuch, we still maintain that the teaching of Scripture, as a whole, and the principles and spirit of Christianity, strongly condemn such legislation.

This is confirmed by the opinions of some of the most distinguished of the Hebrew professors who have responded to Lord Dalhousie's inquiry. Thus Lagarde says : ' It is impossible to consider Lev. xviii. 18 as being in force in Christian times because polygamy is by this verse supposed to be in general use ' (p. 35). So also Merx of Heidelberg writes : ' All prescriptions regarding marriage in the Mosaic writings must be viewed in the light of the constant validity of polygamy' (p. 39), and limits his decision as to the meaning of the Jewish law thus : ' Whoever will transfer this Jewish limitation of the permission to have more than one wife at the same time to a Christian state of society, can draw but one conclusion—that is, the Mosaic law clearly allows marriage with the deceased wife's sister ' (p. 45).

Further, Professor Watkins of Durham, and Wellhausen of Greifswald, while holding that the Levitical law did not prohibit the marriage in question, yet believe on other grounds that it ought not to be legalised.

It appears, then, from a careful examination of these opinions—

(1) That nearly all the professors of Hebrew have given their opinion that Lev. xviii. 18 prohibits marriage with a wife's sister only during the wife's lifetime. On this their opinion is entitled to great weight, but it is only a subordinate part of the Scriptural argument.

(2) That the majority of them have only given an opinion on the meaning of that verse, and have not considered, and therefore given no deliberate judgment on, the grounds on which it is held that the Levitical law as a whole forbids marriage with a deceased wife's sister.

(3) That the comparatively few who have considered the law as a whole, differ widely among themselves in the interpretation of it ; and that as many maintain the old Christian view as agree explicitly in any other interpretation.

(4) That the professors of Greek have all given their opinion, not on what is the Christian law as taught in the New Testament generally, but only whether one single text affords a reasonable inference against the marriage in question.

(5) That some of the professors, whose opinions are not the least valuable, indicate that had the question been what ought to be the Christian law, their opinions would be different from what they are as to the Levitical law or the text Eph. v. 31.

It is therefore not presumptuous to say that the opinions here collected have not invalidated the Scriptural argument against marriage with a deceased wife's sister.

May be had at the Offices of the Union, or of E. W. ALLEN, 4 *Ave Maria Lane, E.C.*

Price One Penny.

Spottiswoode & Co., Printers, New-street Square, London.

Marriage Law Defence Union Tracts.
No. XXVI.

OFFICE: 1 KING STREET, WESTMINSTER, S.W.

Speech of the late Bishop (Wilberforce) of Oxford,

At a Meeting of the Marriage Law Defence Association, February 1, 1860.

THE BISHOP OF OXFORD,—My lord duke, ladies, and gentlemen—I can only say that it is a perfectly frightful thing for any man to have to second, at such a meeting as this, a resolution which has been moved in such a speech as that we have just heard. If we could but here, as we do in another place, where we, my lord duke, often happily agree together—if we could but find any person weak enough or foolish enough to get up and attempt to answer such a speech, I should have the greatest possible pleasure in dealing with that answer ; but when a resolution has been moved in a speech which has exhausted every argument and touched every string of feeling, what remains for the unhappy seconder to say? The learned Vice-Chancellor * says that he hopes, when the question comes next before Parliament, a larger number of episcopal votes will be registered against the passing of the Bill. I can venture to assure him that if God gives me life and strength, he will at least see my vote registered against it. (Cheers.) For me it seems to be a ruled question even before I go

* Vice-Chancellor Page Wood.

into the sacred presence of God's revealed Word ; because the Church of which I am a sworn minister has declared it to be contrary to God's Word ; and if I thought her wrong in that, I could but conscientiously take one of two courses —either seek to alter her law, or else leave her community. As one sworn in the most solemn hour of my life to take her interpretation of the Word of God and to act upon it, I, for one, as an honest man, could not stand up in the senate of my country, and say, 'Alter the law of the nation,' when the law of the Church precludes such alteration. Perhaps you will allow me to stamp this conclusion again upon my own mind, and upon the minds of all present—for it is all-important—that we should have ready at every moment, as an answer to every assailant, the complete Scripture argument to their objections. The objections appear to me to resolve themselves in these separate heads. In the first place, when we quote to the objector the written Word of God as contained in the Old Testament, he says, 'Yes, but you must draw no inference from it, but take it as it stands.' What is the simple answer to that? That he proves too much upon his own showing ; for if we take it as it stands, and draw no inference from it, we charge the Most High with allowing to His own people the marriage of the father with his daughter ; and as no one of these gentlemen has yet gone so far as that, we have a complete answer to the argument which forbids our drawing an inference by analogy. The second argument we have to meet is this : 'Yes, but supposing you may argue by inference and analogy, and by inference and analogy you condemn these marriages, yet there is another text which seems by one interpretation to contradict that position.' The answer lies in a nutshell. It is this : That no law, human or divine, could bind anyone, if you may interpret the plain by the obscure, instead of the

3

obscure by the plain. We need not lose our time in proving the great obscurity of the second verse. The Vice-Chancellor just glanced at the high probability that what it intended to forbid was polygamy. But there is another view—a construction which has lately come over from America—namely, that that verse is really intended to be a limitation of that particular law of the Jewish ritual which, under certain circumstances, bade the brother marry the widow of his deceased brother ; that it was the limitation of the Levirate law, and that it meant to declare that the law should not apply where such brother had already a wife living. It has been actually argued out in the document that has reached me from America, that in the case of Boaz and Ruth, where the nearer kinsman was challenged to perform the kinsman's duty and refused, he was not, as the law of Moses required, struck upon the cheek and branded as refusing to build up his brother's house, but his refusal was accepted, and the duty passed on to Boaz. And it is said he was not allowed to marry his brother's widow because he was already married. This may be the true interpretation, or it may not ; but if the case is capable of such exceeding doubt of every kind, does it not come under the category in which the law meets those faltering consciences which seek, by some miserable subterfuge, to set dark things against plain, doubtful things against certain, in order to allow them the liberty they seek of gratifying their sensual appetites, as the rock of adamant meets the surges of the sea? (Cheers.) The argument next assumes this form : 'Given, that it is forbidden in this chapter of Leviticus ; I take my stand upon this position, that it is the law given to the Jews, and I have nothing to do with it.' I wish they would hold to that opinion throughout. I shall have a word to say upon that presently, but let me clear the way as we go on. I say

4

be ready at once with this answer to every such objector—
'I grant your position, and I do not say that it is forbidden
to us because it was forbidden to the Jews, or because it was
in the law given to the Jews ; but I say it is forbidden to us.
The All-wise Legislator has Himself revealed that there was
a prohibition not grounded on anything peculiar to the Jews,
but on the law of universal purity and of universal right. It
was a prohibition not for the Jews only. It was a part of
that wonderful prescience which, as we scan God's Word,
meets us in fresh developments in every page. It is
written for us, the Christian men of this day, who have to
wrestle with the enemy upon this accursed question. It was
written for us that these things God hated in the Canaanite
and Egyptian, as well as in the man who was under the
ceremonial law of Moses. This is the distinction—It is
not forbidden to the Christian because it was forbidden to
the Jew ; but it is forbidden to the Christian as well as to
the Jew, because it was an abomination in His sight as to
any man. If we go a little further with the religious argument, I come to that code of the Gospel which is binding
on every man who admits the truth of revelation. Is it in
vain, think you—when you consider the way in which God's
Word teaches—that there should be recorded in one of the
Epistles one strong and distinct censure, written, remember,
under the direct guidance of the Holy Ghost, as to one of
these unclean mixtures, and that that one selected instance
should be an instance of affinity and not of consanguinity—
setting at rest for ever that other miserable argument
that, after all, the law of nature is what we ought to come
to, and that that law of nature teaches us the evils of those
consanguineous unions, but has nothing to with unions of
affinity ? The law of nature ! Whenever that argument is
used I should like to ask the person who uses it—'What

5

do you mean by the law of nature ?—do you mean the law written by the finger of God on our common nature ?' because, if you do, if you are going to quote that, you must prove that it agrees with His written law, for no two laws of the Almighty Legislator can thwart one another ; and if I can show you that the written law says there was an abomination in all men, then the law of nature written by God in man's heart must say the same. But what is it that people commonly mean when they talk of the law of nature ? I have uniformly found that it means their own predispositions—that the conclusion to which they have come is right. It means nothing more. Men are always this way arguing—always selecting parts of God's law which go against their own particular inclinations and temptations, and endeavouring to wear that law down until it suits their own case, by introducing licenses and private dispensations. This is the meaning of the ' law of nature.' It must be God's rule written in the heart of man if it is to mean anything of truth. And then I say of this law that, in the words of the resolution, ' it is dangerous to religion to alter the law of marriage,' as abundantly confirmed by every argument that can be used. But there is another argument which I consider most important. One special ground which I have for wholly detesting the nature of the argument by which the advocates for a change of the law seek to maintain their opinion is this, that it is continually slipping back from the Christian standing-place into the old Jewish bondage. That is a grave charge to bring, but I can establish it in a single word. Amongst the newest arguments advanced by the most able, learned, and I believe religious, advocates of the change, stands this, in monstrous prominence —' Yes, this is all very well, but you are not to deal with the two sexes as upon an equality ; you must deal with the man in one way, and the woman in another. I say that that whole argument is a detestable piece of miserable sophistry. What! stand up in a Christian community—amongst men whom Christ has made free—amongst those who have been taught the perfect equality of man and woman in the regenerate Church of Christ—and whisper to us that we are to go back to those miserable, half-heathen, half-Jewish fables, all of which are based in truth if you search it out— to tell us that woman is created for man's use and pleasure and not as a sharer with him of regeneration and of eternal salvation. I can hardly conceive any set of arguments more fatal in truth to all all real religion, in its power and in its purity, amongst us, than those which have been introduced, not by accident, but of necessity, in order to support this despicable question. Then I may take the ground that this is fraught with the greatest danger to our religion, and I agree with the Vice-Chancellor in thinking that it is fraught with the greatest danger to our morals also. And for this plain reason—that I know nothing more certain to sap the morals of any country than to lower down the requirements of law to the invitations of appetite. It is a universal principle—once admit that your law is to forbid not what God has forbidden, but what man is able to observe, and you sap the very foundation of all moral power. And in this case indubitably what has been said already is perfectly true. Even if you grant this wretched relaxation, could you stop there? Does any man believe you could? Do the advocates of the change themselves even tell you so? This is the deceit commonly used in almost every question which involves downhill progress. You are told 'Concede this one thing, and all will be peace.' But surely in vain the net is spread. It is openly stated by the men who want you to take this step,

7

that instead of being the final step, it is only the beginning
of a series. Why, only in the last debate in the House of
Commons on the subject, a great statesman stood up and
openly declared that if the alteration of the law which he advocated took place, it would be impossible to stop short, and
that the change must go on to a still greater extent. Oh !
what a lamentable utterance for a British statesman ! How
deplorable an exhibition of a man floating upon the placid
edge of the mighty cataract which in a moment is going to
whirl him into depths which he cannot fathom ! What an
instance of human weakness is the man who gives up the
moral principle for an external cry, and then tells you
he does not know how far it may carry him ! And he is
right. This is no theory, it is a certainty. It is the result
of existing fact. It is a frightful fact that at this moment, in
this highly favoured land, there might be found advocates
for legalising unions in the very closest blood relationship,
even more in number, if the violation of the law is to be
received as an argument for its alteration. I was rejoiced
to hear the argument of the Vice-Chancellor. I was
rejoiced to hear him say that when the advocates for the
change contend that this is a poor man's question, they
simply tell as great an untruth as could be stated. He tells
us that he has made an investigation in a certain district
with which he is acquainted in this metropolis. I felt it my
duty to make an inquiry in my diocese through the paro-
chial clergy of three large counties, and I foun l that there
was scarcely throughout the whole of those three counties
a poor man's case, but that the people who desired the
change were the lazy, the wealthy, and the somewhat sensual
middle class. The result of the inquiry was that in no
sense was it a poor man's question. But I also found one
person after another saying, ‘ We lament that the breaches

of the moral law, which it is pretended would be prevented by this alteration, are more in number in cases of near blood relationship, than they are in the marriage of the sister to a deceased wife.' Look at what you are to come to. The law of the Church, based upon the unchanged word of God, is to be tempered down until it meets the appetites of a degraded sensuality. The British law, based in this case upon that law of the Church, is to be lowered down professedly because people require it, and will marry illegally if you do not make it lawful so to marry. I say that this will sap the very foundation of national morality. One thing more the resolution says—that any alteration of the law of marriage which should permit marriage with a wife's sister or any other person within the degrees now prohibited, would be fraught with grave danger and injury to religion, morality, and family life. Does any man deny that statement? Does any man, after hearing the admirable way in which the Vice-Chancellor impressed it upon you, doubt that there are certain things (for the most part the deepest laws of our nature) which it is not safe to erect in the face of fallen man in the shape of a bare and simple prohibition, but which you must fence round with the feelings which are generated in the mind by education, by religious impressions, and by the whole tone of decent society protesting against them as an abomination. And not this only. I beseech you to consider this—are such prohibitions as this part of an unkind denial by God of what, if granted, would be for man's happiness ; or are they a merciful hedge, to include a greater amount of happiness than could in any other way be secured, and therefore given where strength is most required to maintain it and fence it round? That is the whole point of the question. Is the saying that blood relations shall not inter-

9

marry—putting everything else aside—is the forbidding of blood relations to marry a cause of personal happiness or unhappiness in society? Does not all the sanctity of family life depend upon this prohibition? Does not the fact of its being impossible for a brother and sister-in-law to marry, spread the blessed law of holiness, like some dew from heaven, around every tenderly shooting plant in every English house and home? If all this depends upon the prohibition, is not the issuing of that prohibition a mark of love? When it is extended to the near of kin through the wife, is it a prohibition causing unhappiness or happiness? Does not every man know that it is just the foundation of the blessedness of family life in England that these reserved cases are so strictly enforced, and that therefore the liberty within them may be so perfect and so unsuspected? Is not this the climax of all? Is it not the teaching of our blessed Lord, that marriage, however debased by the ignorance of man's heart, however lifted up again to its true level—even under the dispensation which God himself gave to the Jews, because the Spirit was not to them given, and because then Christ had not given to those who believe on Him the marvellous gifts it has bestowed on them—yet, from the beginning, marriage in God's institution was the union of the one man with the one woman, so that they twain might become one flesh. Is not that the principle of marriage as published by our blessed Lord? And if so, how can any man dare to say that my wife's near blood is not my near kin, without going altogether astray from the first notion of what holy matrimony is? Now see the puerility of the argument of those who advocate this change of the law. We have proved to you that God's Word prohibits these unions—we have shown that the Church, from the beginning, has prohibited them. I will add one thing, and the only thing the Vice-Chancellor omitted saying on this point. How can any man possibly account for the Emperor Constantine, in the year 355, having prohibited these marriages by the Roman law, except through the influence of the Church? They were allowed by the Roman law; but, within thirty years of the Empire becoming Christian, the law was altered in that respect. The Roman Empire at that time was increasing in corruption. The people were becoming so decayed in morals that it needed the irruption of the northern hordes to restore them to that manhood on which morality can alone be grafted; yet in their decomposing state of morality they issued this rescript changing the marriage law, declaring that those marriages which had hitherto been allowed were henceforth unlawful; and I challenge any man to a solution of that circumstance except on the principle that the Church had introduced those restraints and had published them through the Imperial law. Then, I say that Scripture condemns these marriages; that the Church has condemned them from the beginning; that they are contrary to religion and dangerous to morality. I ask you to look at the cumulative force of these two arguments as to their effect on family life. What does it depend on for its blessedness? Does it not depend upon the blessing of God on that union, which is an appointed instrument of His goodness to man, of His presence being with the wedded couple in the trials, in the sorrows, in the distresses, and in the manifold crosses and troubles of married life? And if you are now asked to introduce into your marriage law a principle which is contrary to religion and to morals, what are you doing? Bidding God's presence withdraw itself from the then unhallowed fane. What are you doing but, so far as you can, banishing that which makes Christian matrimony blessed? And if, as I believe, it is to the purity of England's family life, above all God's other blessings, secured to us in the unfathomable reservoir of His goodness by that holy institution, that we owe that moral and religious character upon which the position and prosperity of this nation depends, I do beseech you to set a front that no man can mistake against the proposition to alter it. Yes, when we have done with arguments we may venture to address your feelings. It is the apathy of those who believe this to be contrary to God's law that makes the danger. If there was half the zeal amongst those who believe the change to be contrary to the mind of God to prevent its enactment, which has been manifested by those who, to suit their own private ends, are trying to effect the change, their puny voice would be unheard amidst the universal condemnation. Scotland, to a man, is against it. England in its moral instincts, in its religious convictions, in its family life, is almost to a man, united against the measure. It is but the old story—a band of a few, thoroughly in earnest for private ends, using, money, means, voices, public political influence, bringing them to bear on men whose seat is trembling in the balance in certain boroughs, and to whom the question is put— ' Will you have my support and give up the wife's sister, or will you protect the wife's sister and lose my vote?' Then, I say, let every man of us be in earnest—let every woman be in earnest—let us show in our demeanour, in our language, and in our conduct, that this is one of those questions which we will not suffer to be stirred without marking our disapprobation of the stirrer. The mischief is half done when the question is stirred at all. In those deep interests affecting morality and family life the very declaration by that respectable carriage keeper—(laughter)—that it is lawful to do it--the very publication of that opinion has done harni somewhere.   It is like those states of the atmosphere predisposing countries to some diseases.   Let the seeds of that disease fall where they may, they are sure to find some one predisposed to receive them.   Depend upon it, on this great moral question, a strong moral disapprobation of the troublers of moral law is never misplaced.   In that which God has from time to time signally honoured and specially rewarded, go, I pray you, forth, one and all, determin in ed that so far as your influence goes, the very debating of this question shall be put down, and, God helping us, England is safe.

Price One Halfpenny.

Spottiswoole & Co., Printers, New-street Square, London.

𝕸arriage 𝕷aw 𝕯efence 𝖀nion 𝕿racts.
No. XXIX.
OFFICE: 1 KING STREET, WESTMINSTER, S.W.

Inclination bowing to Scripture and Conscience;

*Or, Dr. Berriman's Advice upon Marrying a Deceased Wife's Sister, and how it was followed in 1734.**

REVEREND SIR,—'Tis not without the utmost reason that I have the greatest opinion of your judgment, and therefore beg you would indulge me with as full an answer as your leisure will admit of, to the following case of conscience : *Whether it be lawful to marry a wife's sister?* If not, I desire the strongest reasons against it. I resolve to be governed by Scripture, but am far from thinking that there is anything in Scripture against it—I am sure nothing in reason. The only thing which seems to make against it in Scripture is *St. John's* condemning *Herod*, about which case I earnestly beg to have your opinion ; and whether 'tis not highly probable, from the known custom of frequent divorces in those days, that *Herodias's* husband was then living. The occasion, Sir, of my begging your opinion is this : Some time since I lost an excellent wife, and since

---

* In July, 1734, Dr. Berriman was consulted upon the case of marrying two sisters, and his resolution of it had the good effect of saving the person who consulted him from engaging in that unlawful connection.

William Berriman, D.D. (1688–1749), a celebrated scholar in Greek, Hebrew, Chaldee, Arabic, and Syriac, Fellow of Eton, and Lady Moyer and Boyle Lecturer.

that have almost been under an obligation to live in the same house with her sister. Were it not unlawful, everything in the world, I believe, would conspire to make us mutually happy, both here and hereafter. To say no more, Sir, tho' I should gain the whole world in having her, yet, if you judge it might in the least endanger my soul, I should absolutely determine against it. Further advice from your superior judgment will be esteemed an infinite obligation by,

Reverend Sir,

Your most obedient humble servant.

July 30.

P.S.—I think 'tis proper to acquaint you that our circumstances are such that any possible inconveniences from the Ecclesiastical Courts will avail nothing.

Sir,—Though in a matter of real difficulty. I should willingly refer you to some able person for advice and satisfaction, yet, in the case which you propose, I think the matter is so clear, and so generally agreed on by the best Casuists, that I make no scruple to deliver my opinion that *the marrying of two sisters is utterly unlawful.* You will allow me (I suppose) that the prohibitions in *Leviticus* are part of the moral law obliging all nations, since the neglect of them is charged among the abominations of those nations that were cast out before the *Israelites.* And then, in applying those prohibitions to our purpose, there are two rules to be observed, which, being clear and rational, will put the matter out of dispute: (1) That, as the man and his wife are become one flesh by marriage, whatever degree of *consanguinity* makes it unlawful for him to marry with his *own* relations, the same degree of *affinity* makes it unlawful to marry with his *wife's* relations. So that, if he is expressly forbidden to marry his *own* sister (*Levit.* xviii. 9), he is implicitly forbidden to marry his *wife's* sister.

3

(2) That whatever is forbidden to *one* sex is in the same degree unlawful to the *other* sex ; so that, if a woman is not allowed to marry two brothers, neither may a man, by parity of reason, marry two sisters. But that a woman cannot marry two brothers, or, which is the same thing, that a man may not marry his brother's wife, is plain from *Levit.* xviii. 16,* and upon that law, I make no doubt, *St. John Baptist* grounded his reproof to *Herod.* Pray read over that 18th chapter of *Leviticus,* and see if you can fairly acquit the marriage you propose from the charge of incest, and from being one of those abominations which God had so severely punished in time of greater ignorance, and cannot be expected to approve in times of clearer light. As you seem to put this matter wholly on the foot of conscience, I beseech you to weigh it very seriously, and to refrain from such freedoms as may be the means of drawing you into further snares and temptations, and I pray God preserve you from sinning against Him.

W. B.

July 31, 1734.

SIR,—Since I sent you my opinion against the marrying of two sisters (which I hope you received by the penny post), I have more fully considered the case of *Herod;* and upon comparing the history of the Gospel with *Josephus's* Antiquities (L. 18, c. 6), I see reason to admit that *Herodias* had left her husband *Philip* in his lifetime, and probably was then received by *Herod.* But yet *Grotius* concludes from the form of *Josephus's* expression, that *Philip* did not live long after, and observes that *that* historian blames *Herodias* as well for marrying a husband's brother against the law of *Leviticus* (which must be the law I mentioned) as for

* N.B.—The law concerning the marrying of the elder brother's wife *to raise up seed unto the brother,* was special and peculiar; a *temporary* dispensation appointed by the Supreme Lawgiver in a *particular* case, which did not weaken but confirm the *general* law, in cases not excepted.

leaving her husband whilst he lived. 'Tis certain the *Baptist's* reproof of *Herod* was not pointed at his first taking her, but his continuing then to have her ; nor grounded upon her being the wife of another man in general, but his *brother's* wife. There is a like instance in the case of *Archelaus*, who married the wife of his brother *Alexander*, which *Josephus* (Antiq. L. 17, c. 15) mentions as an abominable thing, and contrary to law.

W. B.

August 3, 1734.

REVEREND SIR,—As you were so good as to lay before me those scriptural arguments that might be urged against the lawfulness of marrying a wife's sister, I doubt not but it must be some satisfaction to you to be assured that they have had the desired effect. Though to discard all thoughts of it is like plucking out a right eye, or cutting off a right hand, yet *the parties concerned are*, by God's grace assisting us, absolutely and irreversibly *determined never to think of it more.*

Be pleased, Sir, to accept of my grateful acknowledgments for your goodness to me, and believe me to be, with the utmost respect,

Reverend Sir,

Your most obliged and obedient humble servant.

September 14.

Spottiswoode & Co., Printers, New-street Square, London.

𝔐arriage 𝔏aw 𝔇efence 𝔘nion 𝔗racts.
No. XXXI.
OFFICE: 1 KING STREET, WESTMINSTER, S.W.

Speech of Henry, Bishop of Exeter,

In the House of Lords, February 25, 1851.

(FROM 'HANSARD'S PARLIAMENTARY DEBATES,' SLIGHTLY ABRIDGED.)

MY LORDS : It is my intention to state, in some detail, the reasons for which I shall presume to urge your lordships not to give your sanction to the principle of this Bill by allowing it to be now read a second time.

But, before I proceed further, there is one particular to which I feel it necessary to address myself in the very outset. The noble earl (St. Germans) has remarked, seemingly with some censure, on an expression which I used last night in presenting some petitions to your lordships against the Bill. I called it the 'Incestuous Marriages' Bill ; and of this the noble earl complains, as prejudging the question now before the House. My lords, I cannot but rejoice that the noble earl ascribed so much importance to that phrase—for, if the use of it be to prejudge the question, it is plain that he considers that, supposing the marriages which the Bill would legalise to be incestuous, your lordships ought not to pass it into an Act. Now, my lords, in using the phrase, I had no wish to prejudge the question; I simply used it as the only expression by which I could, consistently, not only with my own convictions, but also with my own sense of my duty as a bishop, characterise such marriages. It is very true that the heading of this Bill is simply 'Marriages.' But as the Bill is not concerned with marriages in general, but only with a particular class of marriages, I could not satisfy myself, without specifying that class by the title which is given to them by the Church in which I am a bishop. My lords, the Church, in its 99th canon, expressly requires that these marriages be adjudged incestuous. Was a bishop, therefore, wrong in so denominating them, when the Church in which he bears his high office expressly requires that they be so adjudged, and when the petitioners, whose earnest prayer he was presenting, did on that account implore your lordships not to inflict so deep an injury on the religion and morality of the nation as would, in their judgment, be inflicted by the passing of this Bill? I am sure that the noble earl will not, on reflection, think there is any real ground of complaint against me for thus acting and speaking in conformity with the express judgment of the Church.

But, my lords, after all, the noble earl does not appear to have thought that I did any harm to his cause by thus prematurely calling these marriages incestuous. It gave him an opportunity of urging a taunt against me, which I think that, holding his opinion, he was quite right in urging. 'If the right rev. prelate,' says he, 'does indeed consider these marriages incestuous, how can he reconcile that principle with the support, or at least the assent, which he gave to passing the Act of 5 and 6 William IV., commonly called "Lord Lyndhurst's Act," "An Act to render valid certain Marriages," which marriages he now declares to have been incestuous?' My lords, I have no difficulty whatever in answering the noble earl's inquiry, and in show-

ing that my concurrence in passing that Act was not only
entirely consistent with my considering the marriages
in question incestuous, but was actually prompted and
strengthened by that very consideration. It is very true
that the title of the Act is 'To render valid certain Marriages'; but is it the effect of the Act itself to do this?
Look into the Act, and see whether there is a single provision, or a single word in it, which has any bearing on such
a point. My lords, it is with all deference to the noble and
learned lords whom I see near me that I venture to say
that, in construing an Act of Parliament, the first and main
thing is to ascertain whether the words of the enacting parts
be plain, intelligible, and consistent. If they be, it is a
matter of perfect indifference what may be the language
even of the preamble, much more of the title. I hope that
the noble and learned lords will correct me if I am wrong.
[Lords Brougham and Campbell : Hear, hear !] I thank
the noble and learned lords for thus sanctioning the rule
which I have ventured to cite. Well, then, my lords, if this
be the rule of construing an Act of Parliament, let the noble
earl look into the statute in question, and see, I repeat,
whether there be anything whatever in it which justifies its
title, or the representation which the noble earl has given of
its import.

My lords, before I assented to the passing of this Act,
or rather warmly concurred in passing it, I deemed it my
duty to ascertain that, if it passed, it would not have that
effect which the noble earl ascribes to it. On examination,
I found that it did no more than protect the innocent issue
of these marriages from suffering for the guilt of their parents.
It effected this, which there is no man who could consider
otherwise than a most satisfactory and gratifying result, by
putting them in the same position as they would be placed
in under the law as it before stood, if one of their parents
were dead. This, I repeat, was the full effect of Lord

4

Lyndhurst's Act : it enacted that marriages already contracted within the prohibited degrees of affinity should not be annulled by any sentence of the Ecclesiastical Courts, even during the lifetime of the parties ; just as under the previously existing law no such marriage could be annulled after the death of either of the parties to it. Such, my lords, I repeat, was the full effect of this much misrepresented statute. (Lord Brougham : Hear !)

But it will be said—it has been said by the noble earl—that I thus assisted in binding together, by an indissoluble bond, the parties in every one of those marriages, which yet I avow that I consider as incestuous, and, if incestuous, as highly sinful. But here, too, I must again tell the noble earl that he wholly misconceives the effect of this statute. True, it forbade the Ecclesiastical Courts to pronounce any sentence annulling such marriages ; but did it impose, did it recognise the duty of such parties to live together in a state of sinful and incestuous intercourse? So far from it, that the highest Ecclesiastical Court in England, having occasion to comment on the effect of that statute in the case of Sherwood v. Ray, declared that there was nothing in it which interfered with the existing law further than I have already stated ; and the great judge who presides in that Court intimated pretty plainly and strongly that if any such parties were proceeded against for incest, even though the statute forbade any sentence to annul the marriage, the Court would, nevertheless, admit the libel, and award ecclesiastical censures, if the incestuous intercourse were proved. My lords, you will find in one of the legal opinions given in the Appendix (App. No. 13, Dr. Phillimore) to the Report of the Commission on the Law of Marriage, that the learned counsel who had been consulted gave it as his decided opinion that, if any such case were brought before Sir Herbert Jenner, he would act on the opinion which he had already declared—that it is competent to the Ecclesiastical

5

Court to punish parties who had contracted such a marriage with ecclesiastical censures, though the marriage itself could not be declared void. In Lord Chief Justice Vaughan's Reports, and in the very case specially cited by the noble earl, the case of Hill *v.* Good (Vaughan, 322), there is express authority to show that a previous sentence, declaring an incestuous marriage null and void, is not necessary in order to sustain a libel against the parties for incest. Chief Justice Vaughan said :

In Lord Hobart's *Reports* I find that one Rennington was questioned by the High Commissioners for marrying his wife's niece, and was sentenced to penance, and bound to abstain from her company ; but they were not divorced *a vinculo matrimonii*, though there was cause, saith the book, and therefore the wife had her dower, nor was there any prohibition in the case.

My lords, there is another leading case, the case of Harris *v.* Hicks (Salkeld, 548), in which the suit was against the plaintiff for incest, in marrying his first wife's sister. Pending the suit, the second wife died, and the husband moved for prohibition, on the ground established by all the judges in James First's time, that, for the protection of the children, no marriage within the Levitical degrees should be declared null after the death of either of the parents. But what did the Court of King's Bench ? Did it issue prohibition in that case, a case of incest? No, my lords ; it decided, that while 'prohibition should go as to annulling the marriage or bastardising the issue, the Ecclesiastical Court might proceed to punish the incest.'

Well, then, my lords, when this had before been the law, as declared by the highest and the most unquestionable authorities, and when there was nothing in the Statute of 5 and 6 William IV.—except the blundering title—which bore even the semblance of interfering with this law, what is there which needs excuse or explanation from one who, like myself, holding, as the laws both Ecclesiastical and temporal

6

held and hold, these marriages to be incestuous, did yet concur, for a very grave consideration, in forbidding the passing of any judicial sentence of the nullity of certain of those marriages which had been already contracted, but leaving untouched their sinful and incestuous character, and still leaving it open to the proper court to proceed against the guilty parties who had contracted them, to sentence them to live apart, and, if they persisted in their sinful intercourse, to punish them, even with excommunication? My lords, in the thing itself no principle was violated, no sin was protected. But, on the other hand, a great benefit was gained—a very great boon to the cause of religion and morality—by putting an end for ever (as we hoped, ay, and will still confidently hope) to that anomalous and most pernicious state of law which tempted parties to the most unhallowed unions by holding forth the assured prospect of security, so long as none were found to undertake the invidious and costly course of proceeding judicially to annul them. Instead of this, Lord Lyndhurst's Act (so, to his lasting honour, it is named) made all such marriages to be in future, without any sentence of any court, absolutely null and void to all intents and purposes.

My lords, if in meeting the noble earl's taunt against me I have dwelt on this matter at greater length than would have become me in vindicating merely my own consistency, I yet offer no apology for so doing ; for I feel that I have thus been the humble instrument of bringing your lordships' minds, and, it may be, the minds of others, to a consideration of the real character of an Act which has been made the subject of more misconstruction and misrepresentation than almost any legislative Act which can be named. That misrepresentation has, in truth, been one of the most favourite and most successful expedients of the agitation out of doors on this very remarkable occasion.

7

My lords, I turn to other matters. The noble earl claims as a high authority on his side a prelate of great eminence, the Archbishop of Dublin. In the absence of the most rev. prelate, I will not make any remarks on the general tone and principle of his Grace's argument—tempting, I frankly own, as I feel such a subject to be. And from this I abstain altogether. The only passage on which I will observe is one which I cannot but feel as an unjust, and not very liberal, insinuation against all who hold, as I do, that 'the allegations from the Levitical law '—so the most rev. prelate writes—in other words, the prohibitions in the 18th chapter of Leviticus—are binding upon Christians. His Grace is pleased pretty plainly to imply that he does not believe we are sincere in holding this opinion; and he is further pleased to impose upon us what he considers the duty of adhering to the Levitical law in all points alike. Among others, in what is in a certain case commanded in the Book of Deuteronomy, namely, ' the marriage of a brother with his deceased brother's widow.'

My lords, I hold, and I will not do myself the injustice of saying I hold sincerely, that the prohibitions of marriages in the 18th chapter of Leviticus are still binding upon Christians. I also hold that the compulsory marriage specified in Deuteronomy is not binding upon Christians. I will, with your lordships' permission, proceed to say why I hold both particulars.

It has been customary, among all who have treated the matter, to divide the Jewish law under three heads—the ceremonial, the civil, and the moral. Now the ceremonial and the civil laws of the Jews were binding only for a time, and only on the nation to whom they were immediately delivered. But the moral law is of perpetual and universal obligation.

That the 18th chapter of Leviticus, containing the prohibited degrees of marriage, is part of the moral law, however certain, may yet seem to require some proof; your lordships, therefore, will pardon me, if I briefly state one or two considerations for that purpose. First, these prohibitions are declared by the mouth of God Himself. Six times in the course of this one chapter He says, in solemn confirmation of His words, 'I am the Lord.' But this, it may be said, proves only that this is God's law; it would be so if it related to the Jews only. Let me, then, next call your lordships' attention to the manner in which He speaks of His law. He commanded Moses to speak to the people, saying, that they should keep His laws and His ordinances, and not do after the abominations of the Egyptians and the Canaanites, who had thereby drawn down the vengeance of God on their guilty heads. Now, what were these abominations? They are solemnly recounted; and among them are those marriages which the Bill now before the House would legalise in England. At the end of the enumeration it is said :

'Defile not ye yourselves in any of these things; for in all these the nations are defiled which I have cast out before you. And the land is defiled : therefore do I visit the iniquity thereof upon it, and the land itself vomiteth out her inhabitants.'

My lords, is it possible to doubt that this is part of the moral law? Could such awful denunciations of wrath be uttered against a people who had only not done according to some ceremonial, or civil law, which had never been delivered to them? Well, then, if this be the moral law, and if we avow that we believe it to be, as such, binding on us and the whole race of man, must we on that account—as the Archbishop of Dublin says we must—assert that every part of the Mosaic law is equally binding in all times and in all nations? In particular, as is specified by his Grace, must we say this of the compulsory marriage of a brother with his deceased brother's widow? My lords, that precept

9

is found in the 25th chapter of Deuteronomy, in the midst of a series of civil and peculiar practices enjoined on the Jews, as a people to be kept separate by their customs and polity from the other nations of the earth. The very reason given for the precept proves this to be the case ; it is, to keep up the family of the deceased brother, 'that his name be not put out of Israel,' and that the land allotted to him pass not into the hands of strangers.

My lords, is not this then manifestly, and in the face of it, a part merely of the civil law of the Jews ? But if this be so, I would ask the most rev. prelate, if he were here present, not whether he is sincere in holding (for I am sure he is sincere in holding whatever he professes to hold), but whether he does indeed hold that this precept or commandment in Deuteronomy is equally binding, or equally free, to all nations, Jew and Gentile, Christian and heathen? If he does, how will he reconcile such a tenet with his repeated subscription to the seventh Article, which declares that —

Although the ceremonial parts of the law given by God to the Jews do not bind Christians, nor ought the civil precepts to be necessarily imposed on any other nation, yet, notwithstanding, no Christian man is free from the obedience of the Commandments which are called moral.

My lords, I hope that this question may meet either the ear or the eye of that most rev. prelate, and that he will feel himself bound to state how he reconciles his taunt on us with—I will not imitate that taunt by saying his sincerity, but—his consistency in subscribing the seventh Article, while yet he thus makes the civil and the moral law of the Jews equally binding or equally free to all mankind.

My lords, this matter brings me to what is the main question to be decided by your vote on this night—whether to admit or reject the principle of the Bill. Now, if the marriages which the Bill would legalise be contrary to the moral law of God—as they are, if they be included in the prohibitions of the 18th chapter of Leviticus—then this House, as a body of Christian legislators, must refuse to give a second reading to the Bill on our table. I will, with your lordships' permission, proceed to consider this question, and I venture to assure your lordships that I shall be able to bring my argument within a very moderate compass.

The 6th verse states the general principle, 'None of you shall approach to any that is near of kin to him, to uncover their nakedness.' Now, what is 'near of kin'? They are manifestly words which, if they stood alone, would hardly admit any satisfactory—at least, any definite solution. The Divine Lawgiver was, therefore, pleased to give us a rule of interpretation. In doing this, He does not enumerate all the cases which fall under the rule, but He lays down certain specified degrees of propinquity; and leaves it to us to examine by them every particular case, and in such examination to decide for ourselves, whether it be within any of the specified degrees. If it be, such marriage must be considered as forbidden by the law of God as unlawful and incestuous.

Now, as respects the marriages which are the objects of the present Bill—marriage with a deceased wife's sister, and marriage with the daughter of a deceased wife's brother or sister—the 16th and the 14th verses are those which are to be specially considered. The 16th says, 'Thou shalt not uncover the nakedness of thy brother's wife.' This is the degree of propinquity which is here forbidden, and every case which falls within this degree must be considered as equally forbidden. Now, it is manifest at once, that a wife's sister is in the same degree of nearness as a brother's wife, therefore, in the prohibition of marriage with a brother's wife, marriage with a wife's sister is included.

Again, the 14th verse, 'Thou shalt not uncover the nakedness of thy father's brother; thou shalt not approach

I I

to his wife, she is thine aunt,' equally applies to the marriage of the daughter of a deceased 'wife's brother or sister,' for the degree of propinquity is the same; and it might equally be said to the wife of such a husband, ' He is thine uncle.'

Now this last-mentioned degree is especially worthy of our attention ; for it is a distinct declaration by God himself, that degrees of affinity are not less regarded in His law as impediments to holy matrimony than similar degrees of consanguinity. It is, indeed, remarkable (and the words may have been used for this very purpose—that is, to point the sameness of affinity and consanguinity) that it is in the case of affinity only those words are added, 'She is thine aunt.'

The truth is, that this great principle is throughout enforced in the Divine law in the strongest manner. The first positive commandment delivered by God to man, after his creation, was that man and wife shall be one flesh. It was again promulgated by our Lord himself—' They twain shall be one flesh.' His apostle declared the union of holy matrimony to be so complete, that it is a type of the mystical union of Christ with His Church. It becomes us, therefore, to be specially cautious not to admit any construction of God's words which shall interfere with this great primal law. Thus much I have deemed it necessary to say of the absolute sameness of affinity and consanguinity, as they affect the lawfulness of marriage.

The noble earl has remarked (and he indicated some surprise that I should assent to the remark) that the phrase to ' uncover nakedness' does not apply to the conjugal union, but always includes the notion of turpitude and pollution. I fully agree in this criticism. It is sustained by the uniform use of the expression in all the places in Holy Scripture in which it occurs —upwards of twenty in number; and from this I draw a confident conclusion, that the union with a wife's sister, spoken of in those reproachful terms, is incestuous, and cannot partake of the innocence, much less of the sanctity, of holy matrimony.

But there is another main branch of the subject on which the noble lord has made it necessary that I should detain your lordships with a few observations. My lords, the noble earl refuses to admit that all the degrees enumerated in the 18th chapter of Leviticus are such degrees of nearness of kin as render marriages of persons within them unlawfuL He denies that they are to be regarded *pari ratione*, and maintains that those only which are specially mentioned are to be considered by us as binding ; and yet, if this notion be sound, it will follow that marriage of a man with his daughter is not forbidden, for such marriage is not there specified, though it is included, *pari ratione*, under the prohibition of marriage with a mother, and, *a fortiori*, of marriage with a daughter-in-law. The noble earl was conscious of the weight of this objection ; but, to do him justice, he has devised a very convenient method of meeting it. He says that the nearness of kin of a daughter, though not specified in the 18th chapter, is expressly declared in the 21st ; and that nearness of kin is there limited to a man's father and mother, his son and his daughter, his brother and his sister. Therefore, says he, the absence of all specification of the nearness of kin of father and daughter in the 18th chapter affords no argument for the necessity of estimating nearness of kin *pari ratione*. Now, however the noble earl may triumph in this discovery respecting father and daughter, what will he say of the case of uncle and niece? There is, I repeat, no express prohibition of marriage between persons so related ; but there is an express prohibition of marriage of nephew-in-law with his aunt-in-law. Therefore, *pari ratione*, we conclude that the marriage of uncle and niece is unlawful.

My lords, it is with unfeigned reluctance that I occupy

your attention with a detailed argument on such a subject, but it is forced upon us by the Bill which is before you. I must therefore crave your indulgence while I deal with another portion of the noble earl's argument—his interpretation of the 18th verse of this chapter of Leviticus. This, indeed, forms the whole strength of the cause of which he is the advocate. He says, as has been repeatedly said by others, that in this verse there is a plainly implied permission of marriage of a wife's sister after the death of the first wife : ' Neither shalt thou take a wife to her sister, to vex her, to uncover her nakedness, beside the other, in her lifetime.'

The noble earl repudiates the version given in the margin of our English Bible, which would make this to be only a prohibition of polygamy. My lords, on this point, and in accordance with the judgment of the ablest Hebrew scholars, I agree with the noble earl; I willingly concur with him in not setting any value on the version in the margin. In truth, I understand both this verse and the verse which immediately precedes it, as recognising the permission of polygamy to the Jews ; but regulating it by a prohibition against having two wives who are in certain degrees of propinquity of kin to each other. The 17th verse is manifestly of this kind. It forbids the taking of a woman and her daughter, or her son's daughter, or her daughter's daughter ; and the reason given is, ' for they are her near kinswoman ; it is wickedness.'

Now, I contend that the 18th verse must receive a similar construction. Can it indeed, be gravely said, that if a wife's son's daughter, or daughter's daughter, 'are her near kinswomen,' her sister is not her near kinswoman too?

My lords, not content to rest such a matter on my own very slender authority, I wrote to the Regius Professors of Hebrew in the two universities of Oxford and Cambridge, requesting them separately to give me their literal version of this controverted text. These learned persons complied with my request ; and I was not surprised to find that their versions were substantially, and indeed almost verbatim, the same. I will read it, as given to me by Dr. Mill, the Hebrew Professor at Cambridge : ' And a woman unto her sister thou shalt not take ' (here is a stop equivalent to our colon, thus making the prohibition to be absolute), it proceeds, 'to annoyance'—without any pronoun (as is indicated in our version, where 'her,' after 'to annoy,' is printed in italics), 'to uncover her nakedness upon her in her life'! Now, much stress is ordinarily laid on these last words, ' in her life,' as if they necessarily apply to the wife, whereas there is nothing whatsoever in the original so to fix them ; and there is much to make it most probable that they really apply to the super-induced wife—for so the preceding pronouns manifestly do—and then the phrase would only mark an emphatic prohibition of such an union at any time—even during the whole life of the sister, whether she survive the other or not.

Such, according to these high authorities, is the real import of the 18th verse of the 18th chapter of Leviticus— the text on which, above all others, the advocates of the present measure rely.

It is a positive and absolute prohibition of this special case of polygamy—'a wife to her sister thou shalt not take ' ; and two reasons are given : first, that it would cause domestic misery ; the second, that by nearness of kin, it would be a defilement. Now, this second reason, I need hardly say, is equally strong against taking such a party, whether during the life or after the death of the other.

With this statement of the real import of this much con- troverted text, given out of the highest living authorities, I rejoice to relieve your lordships from the tedium of listening any longer to what must have been a very tiresome portion of our discussion.

But the noble earl has stated—and he has ascribed much

15

importance to the statement—that throughout the New Testament there is nothing whatever like an approach to a prohibition of these marriages. I am well aware that this is very commonly said, but it is quite astonishing that such a notion should ever have obtained currency. Why, marriage within that degree of propinquity of kin, which *pari ratione* includes the wife's sister—I mean the marriage of a deceased brother's wife—is denounced in the New Testament in the very strongest terms. What was it for which John the Baptist lost his head? For telling the tyrant Herod that it was 'not lawful for him to have his brother Phillip's wife.' My lords, I am not ignorant that Roman commentators are anxious to make it appear that Herod's was a case of adultery, not of incest. This is a point of great importance to that Church, for since the serious embarrassment which was caused by Clement VII.'s decision, that the dispensation for the marriage of Henry VIII. with his brother's wife was valid, it has been deemed necessary to hold that the Levitical prohibitions are no longer a part of the law of God, but owe their force altogether to the authority of the Church ; and yet it is plain, that if Herod's sin, for which John the Baptist so openly condemned him, was the sin of marrying his deceased brother's wife, then the binding force of the Levitical prohibitions is recognised under the new dispensation ; but all the three Evangelists who record this matter leave a main stress on Herodias's being Herod's brother Philip's wife. One of them, indeed, St. Mark, especially says, 'For he had married her.' It should seem, therefore, on all plain rules of construction, that the sin was in marrying his brother's wife ; but Roman commentators will not allow this. They say, and they adduce the authority of Josephus for the assertion, that Herod's brother Philip, whose wife Herodias was, still lived ; and therefore, that Herod's sin was his adulterous cohabitation with her. Now, my lords, I feel that this is not a place, nor an occasion, on which it would be fitting to enter into a disquisition on such a matter ; but I venture to tell the noble lords whom I now see near me (Lord Beaumont and one or two other Roman Catholic lords), and I say it with great respect, that I am ready to establish my assertion, by proofs drawn from Josephus himself, that Herod's brother Philip, whose wife Herodias had been, was dead ; he left a daughter ; consequently, therefore, Herod's marriage with her thus denounced by John as sinful, was sinful simply by reason of her being 'near of kin' to him.

Thus we find that John the Baptist died a martyr to the great principle of the incestuousness of these marriages ; and our Church requires us to pray God 'to make us, after his example, boldly rebuke vice,' especially that vice against which he faithfully contended, even unto death—the vice of contracting marriages which the present Bill would legalise.

But, my lords, this is not the only part of the New Testament in which these marriages are condemned. The 'fornication' (Acts xv. 29) named in the Acts of the Apostles as one of the 'necessary things' from which the Gentile converts were commanded 'to abstain,' is regarded by the best commentators as referring to the Levitical prohibitions of marriage : and the word is plainly used in a sense connected with this in reference to the incestuous Corinthian (1 Cor. v. 1) who had married his father's wife. In saying this I am sure I shall have the assent of my right reverend brethren near me.

My lords, I again feel it necessary to apologise for dwelling so much at length on matters which I am well aware are not only unusual in this House, but can hardly fail to be distasteful. Let me, however, again plead in my excuse the nature of the Bill itself, the course of the noble earl's argument (I am far from blaming him for it), and, above all, the immense importance of the interests, the spiritual interests, involved in this discussion.

But do you, I may be asked—do you call on this House to decide on a matter of so much moment and so much delicacy, for reasons depending mainly on questions of Biblical criticism? My lords, this is the very thing which I wish you not to do ; it is the very thing which I think you ought not to do. I would submit to you, rather, that your votes this night ought to be decided by deference to that authority which both the constitutional law of England and the law of that Church of which you are members require you to submit to—the interpretation of the Church. But the noble earl tells us that 'the Church is not infallible.' Very true ; but neither is the Court of Queen's Bench infallible; nor even this House itself when it exercises its highest attribute as the Supreme Court of Appeal and pronounces a sentence which is absolutely irreversible. But is the fallibility of every human tribunal a sufficient reason for questioning the sentence which it pronounces? Has such sentence no authority because it has not the authority which God's judgment only can have?

My lords, the laws of both our Church and State have declared that the Church hath authority in controversies of faith ; and the application of the law of God to the great question involved in this Bill is such a controversy. Now the Church, from the very earliest time to which we can look back, even from the second century, when the knowledge of the Gospel was first vouchsafed to our forefathers, has always held these marriages to be contrary to the law of God. The noble earl has spoken with some disparagement of the *Apostolic Canon*, which marks the Church's reprobation of such marriages by excluding those who may have contracted them from the episcopate, and even from the clergy ; and again, of the Council of Elvira, which awards sentence of excommunication for five years on the same account ; and he adds, with an air of triumph, that neither the one nor the other attempted to annul those marriages.

The noble earl is quite correct in saying this; but it is possible that he has forgotten that in those days the Church had no power to do what he thinks it must have done, if it judged of such marriages as the Church now judges of them? My lords, St. Paul, in censuring that incestuous union, of which he says that it was too foul to be so much as named among the Gentiles, ' that a man should have his father's wife,' even St. Paul did not pronounce a sentence of nullity, he was content to sever the guilty pair by the terrors of excommunication.

My lords, during no less a period than the first 1,500 years, the whole Church persisted in holding that these marriages are contrary to the law of God, and as such admit not of being made lawful by any human authority whatsoever.

At length, a Pope was found hardy enough to grant a dispensation to marry the sister of a deceased wife; it was in the case of Emanuel, king of Portugal, who had married a daughter of Ferdinand of Spain, and, after her death, wished to marry her sister. Now, my lords, who was this Pope who ventured on so unheard-of an assumption of spiritual authority? It was Alexander VI., Alexander Borgia—it was that man—I recall the words, I beg pardon of our common humanity for so applying it—it was that monster in human shape, himself stained with incest of the deepest dye, as well as by every other vice which can pollute and degrade our nature. It was Alexander Borgia who first granted a dispensation for one of those marriages which the present Bill would legalise in the gross. Yes, my lords, Alexander Borgia it is whose principle your lord-ships are invited to make your own; whose legislation in a single case you are now called upon to extend to the whole compass of similar relations. Are your lordships prepared to follow such a guide?—to choose such a guardian of the sanctity of our English hearths and homes? My lords, I may answer my own question—You will not.

19

The next instance of a dispensation, in a similar case, was that granted by Julius II., a Pontiff scarcely less regardless of spiritual considerations than Alexander; in short, the most turbulent spirit of the very turbulent age in which he lived. It was granted on the death of Arthur, Prince of Wales, the elder brother of King Henry VIII., to enable a marriage to be contracted between him (I need not say a mere child at the time) and Katherine of Arragon, the widow of his deceased brother. My lords, it is gratifying to know that this marriage was opposed in council by Warham, Archbishop of Canterbury, as contrary to the law of God, and therefore not admitting of a dispensation by the Pope. And this proves the accuracy of what I just now said, that until it was rendered necessary by the refusal of Clement VII. to decide against this dispensation, the Church of Rome never pretended to deny that the Levitical prohibitions of marriage are still binding as a part of the moral law of God.

My lords, the noble earl has cited, with high commendation, a sentence of the report made to her Majesty by the Commissioners of Inquiry into the laws of marriage. That sentence, I must take leave to say, notwithstanding his commendation, is in my judgment most contrary to sound principle, most mischievous, most corrupting. 'These marriages,' says the report, and the noble lord applauds the saying—

These marriages will take place—will take place when a concurrence of circumstances gives rise to mutual attachment; they are not dependent on legislation. It is not the state of the law, prohibiting or permissive, which has governed, or, as we think, ever will effectually govern them.

Why, my lords, what is the meaning of this, but to give up the reins to the sexual passions altogether, to say that they are beyond the reach and control of any moral restraint? And this is the well-weighed counsel of grave and honourable men—the summary of their judgment, after serious and extensive research—delivered to their sovereign as the principle by which her Majesty and Parliament are to direct their legislation on the most important of all the relations of social life ! My lords, it is some little relief to read a contradiction of this polluting doctrine in the very page of the report which immediately precedes it. There the Commissioners tell us, that, although in some cases these connections will take place, 'because no natural repugnance to them exists,' yet

They are prevented more or less by two considerations, namely, when a belief exists that such an union is opposed to divine law, and where there is a strong conviction that it is against the opinion of friends and of society, and a great desire to retain their good opinion.

So, then, we see by the authority of these Commissioners that moral restraint does operate to prevent these marriages—restraint, however, which it is the practical tendency of this report altogether to remove.

But we have not merely the authority of the Commissioners for the efficacy of moral restraint in these cases, but an authority which we have sometimes found to be still better—that of their witnesses. I am unwilling to weary your lordships with a detail of these cases of individuals ; but there is one case, in this part of our subject, which I read myself with so much respect, and, I must say, so much pity for the parties, that I scruple not to refer to it in some detail. It is the case of an officer in the service of the East India Company, who tells us that he became warmly attached to his deceased wife's sister ; and yet, my lords, he was not so much the slave of his passion as not to inquire, anxiously inquire, whether he could innocently, conscientiously, marry the object of his affections. My lords, I grieve to read the answer of this gentleman to one of the questions put to him—

Of all the clerical opinions you obtained, there was none against the marriage upon Scriptural grounds?—None whatever. I think a decidedly clerical opinion against it, from competent authority, would have deterred me, if backed by other compe'ent authority. What I mean is, that were the Church—(he shows the importance he ascribes to the authority of the Church by printing the words in Roman capitals)—were the Church unanimous in declaring such a marriage contrary to God's law, both my wife and I would have bowed to such a decision.

My lords, I am sorry to find that this Christian gentleman had recourse to so very bad spiritual advisers. A faithful minister would have told him that the very authority which he sought, the Church in national Synod, the Church of England by representation, had solemnly pronounced the marriage which he meditated unlawful and incestuous. Had such faithful advice been given, in one instance, at least, incest would have been prevented.

My lords, I will not trouble you with other cases of individuals. But I will show from the evidence appended to the report, that even in whole nations the restraints of religious and moral considerations, when honestly suffered to have their due weight, are effectual. My lords, in Ireland such considerations have produced a strong abhorrence of the marriages which this Bill would legalise ; in Scotland a still stronger. If we look to the vast empire of Russia, and to its enormous population, we see the abhorrence still growing in intensity ; ay, and throughout the whole extent of the Greek Church, and of the communions which have branched from it—a reach of country scarcely less extensive than the whole of the rest of Christendom—the feeling is the same. My lords, the noble earl has spoken disparagingly of the Greek Church. I cannot partake of his sentiment in this respect. I regard that Church not only as a very large, but as a most venerable portion of the Church Catholic, infected indeed with errors, but with errors by no means fatal —a Church worthy of our special attention, as conveying and attesting to us the traditional judgments formed by the whole Church of Christ on this subject before the unhappy schism which rent Christendom in twain.

My lords, one single word more of this report. In it the Commissioners tell us that there is 'no natural repugnance to such connexions.' Now what are we to understand by 'natural'? Do they mean by the word, that which is a necessary part of the nature of man, as he is man? If so, I fully assent to their proposition. For, in this sense, I know not whether any or what connexion is contrary to man's nature. I may indeed hope, and I do hope, that the union of parent and child is so : but certainly I cannot go a step further. The union of brothers and sisters cannot be contrary to the nature of man, as man : for we know that the world was peopled originally through such unions. My lords, I hold that the true and sound way of speaking of our nature, in connection with such matters, is to consider it as that moral sense by which the Divine Author of nature has made man capable of having his practical convictions moulded by the working of sound law, virtuous education, and, above all, pure religion. This second nature it is that we are bound to mean when we talk with these Commissioners of natural repugnance to certain connexions, and this second nature ought to be formed by those very conditions which their premises affirm and their conclusion denies.

My lords, before I conclude, I must take some notice—it shall be but brief—of the structure and provisions of the Bill itself. That Bill is, I believe, the most extraordinary specimen of legislation ever offered to Parliament. Its object, its principle, its effect, is to make marriages with a wife's sister or niece lawful, because they are not forbidden by the law of God. I say this, for I do not suppose it possible that if the noble earl really thought them contrary to the Divine law he would attempt to legalise them. In truth, the main argument of the noble earl this night has been to convince you that they are not contrary to that law. Well, then, what shall we say to the 3rd Clause? It runs thus :—

That nothing in this Act contained shall be deemed or construed to alter or affect any doctrine, canon, or law ecclesiastical of the Church of England, &c.

What doctrine of the Church is there on the matter? The doctrine contained in the 99th Canon, that these marriages are 'prohibited by the laws of God,' are 'incestuous and unlawful'; and this doctrine, it seems, is not to be in any wise affected by the Bill, which would make them lawful; we are still to hold as true that these marriages are contrary to the law of God, even while we refuse to suffer them any longer to be contrary to the law of England.

So much for doctrine. Now let us look at the canon. It enjoins that all such marriages 'shall be adjudged incestuous, and, consequently, shall be dissolved as void from the beginning.' The Bill, when it shall become an Act, is to be deemed and construed not in anywise to alter or affect this canon; and yet the very principle of the Bill, its one sole proclaimed end and purpose, is that no such marriage shall 'hereafter be annulled or pronounced void.'

So much for 'canon.' Now, for 'law ecclesiastical.' The law ecclesiastical is, that no minister shall, under the gravest spiritual censures, solemnise any of these marriages. Nothing in this Bill is to be construed in anywise to affect this law; and yet it is provided, that, if there be any liberal clergyman bold enough to set it at defiance, he shall not be subject for so doing to any censure or punishment whatever.

But I will waste no more of your lordships' time in dealing with such a tissue of crudities, absurdities, and contradictions.

My lord, in conclusion, permit me to say something on the last part of the noble earl's speech. He called on your lordships, with great gravity and great eloquence, to ponder the considerations which he brought before you—to pause before you give your votes this night—to weigh well the awful responsibility of maintaining the present law—and, if any of you have a doubt, to give him the benefit of that doubt.

My lords, I assent from the bottom of my soul to what the noble earl has said of the awful responsibility which must attach to the vote of this night; and to those who doubt what vote to give, I, too, would venture to submit a very few words. With this view, permit me briefly to remind the House what it can do, and what it cannot do.

My lords, this House may pass the Bill; it may prevail with the other House to join in passing it—it may procure the royal assent to its becoming part of the law of the land. This, my lords, this House may do, and something more ; it may draw down the wrath of God upon ourselves, upon our country, and upon our Queen—by daring to do what, if the Church, of which most of your lordships profess to be members, tells us truly, we shall do : for we shall set at nought the express law of God. Now, my lords, while this House can do all this, there remains one thing which it cannot do—it cannot make sin to be not sin—incest to be not incest.

Refrain, therefore, I implore you, from going further with this ill-judged measure ; touch not these prohibitions, which the Bill before us would remove : ' if they be,' as all Christendom before the Council of Trent believed them to be—as our own reformed Church, I again say, still believes them to be—' of God,' ye cannot overthrow them—lest haply ye be found even to fight against God.

Spottiswoode & Co , Printers, New-street Square, London.

𝕸arriage 𝕷aw 𝕯efence 𝖀nion 𝕿racts.
No. **XXXIV.**
OFFICE: I KING STREET, WESTMINSTER, S.W.

The Report of the Upper House of the Convocation of Canterbury, agreed to at its Session, July 6, 1883.

THE BISHOP OF GLOUCESTER AND BRISTOL presented to the House a report which had been drawn up by a committee, in obedience to a resolution of the House, on the subject of marriage with a deceased wife's sister. He said that the terms of the report would be better understood if he shortly stated the substance of the request of the Lower House which had led to the Report. The communication from the Lower House represented that there was a fear in the minds of those who made the representation that there would be an immediate renewal of the agitation upon the question, and it was possible that many might think that such fears were not altogether ill-founded. They also represented that there was a widespread ignorance of the principles of Christian marriage. In that representation, again, the House, he thought, would probably concur, because most people would feel at the present time that a large proportion of the Christian laity were quite ignorant of the gravity of the subject, and the number of sound arguments that could be used against any change in the marriage laws, especially in regard to the table of prohibited degrees. The prayer was that the Bishops should take steps to induce the clergy from time to time to set forth the true principles of Christian marriage. The answer to this representation was contained in a report which had been drawn up as follows :

" The Committee of the Upper House of Convocation appointed to draw up an answer to the representation and request of the Lower House, recommend the Upper House to adopt the following resolution : 'Resolved that this House concurs with the Lower House in their earnest desire for the maintenance in its integrity of the table of prohibited degrees, set forth in the year of our Lord 1563, and ordered to be publicly set up in the churches by the 99th canon. They deem the following considerations amongst others to be of great moment—*First*, that the proposal to legalise marriage with a deceased wife's sister is contrary to the just inferences drawn from prohibition in Holy Scripture on the subject of unlawful marriages ; that in the book of Leviticus a marriage between a widow and a deceased husband's kindred within the third degree is especially prohibited ; that our Lord and the Apostle St. Paul, having declared that in regard to holy matrimony husband and wife are on an equality, a widower is by necessary inference forbidden to marry his deceased wife's kindred within the same limits, and whatsoever rule or concession to the contrary may have been made in the Mosaic law is, by our Lord's authority, thus formally abolished. The formal declaration in Holy Scripture thus repeated by our blessed Lord only

3

receives in the table of prohibited degrees its fuller and more detailed exposition. *Secondly*, that the Church had so understood and interpreted the declarations of Holy Scripture from the beginning ; and that there is no trace whatever of any such marriage having been recognised as permissible in the Church of Christ until, fourteen centuries after Christ, dispensations were first granted by Papal authority. The mind of the Church of England on this subject has been clearly declared in her table of prohibited degrees, her canons, and in the decisions of her ecclesiastical courts. In Scotland and on the Continent the Reformers, both Calvinistic and Lutheran, were equally clear in interpreting the Word of God as condemnatory of these marriages. *Thirdly*, that if the rule thus derived from God's Word be set aside, no other rule or principle can be found to take its place. No distinction between the wife's sister and the rest of the wife's kindred has ever been made out. If relationship by affinity is no bar in one case, it is no bar in any case. All stand or fall together. A code of laws which should allow one, and only one relation, would be on the face of it self-condemned ; nor is there any example in Europe, of a country in which the law has been so altered as to permit marriage with a deceased wife's sister without further relaxation. *Fourthly*, that the proposed relaxation of the marriage laws would tend to impair the reverence felt for the sanctity of Christian marriage, and to produce a more widely-spreading social corruption. In countries which have allowed union between persons near of kin, divorce has been

4

more and more freely permitted, with the inevitable effect of effacing the true signifiance of our Lord's solemn repetition of the words " They twain shall be one flesh." *Fifthly*, that it is the plain duty of the Church to guard and maintain the purity of domestic life, and to teach that the members of a Christian family are bound together by common interests and mutual affection growing out of the marriage tie between the parents. That the aunt or other near kinswoman of the children should stand in no relation to their father, and be regarded by him as a stranger, would be inconsistent with the very idea of the family, and subversive both of its happiness and of its moral welfare. *Lastly*, that if the law of the land which in regard to marriages of this nature has from the very first been identical with the Divine law, should be changed, grave scandal and perplexity would unavoidably ensue. The clergy, bound to obey the law as contained in the Bible, and referred to in the Book of Common Prayer, would be brought into frequent collision with the claims of those who might have availed themselves of the relaxation that would thus have been granted for the first time. It is of the utmost importance that the clergy should thoroughly inform themselves on these points, and on others which bear on this grave question, and that they should, on proper occasions, explain clearly and firmly, with all charity to opponents, its true character and bearing.' "

Price Twopence per dozen.

N.B.—The Reports on the Marriage Law adopted by the Lower Houses of Convocation may be had at the Office of THE MARRIAGE LAW DEFENCE UNION. *Price Twopence.*

Spottiswoode & Co., Printers, New-street Square, London.

Marriage Law Defence Union Tracts.

No. XXXVI.

OFFICE: 1 KING STREET, WESTMINSTER, S.W.

What a Joint Committee of the American Church says; in its Report on Marriage with Relatives,

Presented to the General Convention of the Church, U.S.A., at its Session in New York, October, 1880.

MAJORITY REPORT.

THE Committee appointed in 1877 to consider the subject of 'the Marriage with Relatives,' that is, in the degrees heretofore prohibited by the old 'Table of Kindred and Affinity,' have adopted the following Report :

The only degrees of relationship, as enumerated in the old table, which have been named to your Committee as suggesting any question of Scriptural obligation, are three, with their correlative degrees for the other sex ; to wit, in the case of a man :

1. Wife's sister.
2. Wife's brother's daughter.
3. Wife's sister's daughter.

It will be observed that, if these prohibitions be removed, a man will hereafter be at liberty, by the judgment of this Church, to marry :

1. His sister-in-law.
2. His niece on his brother-in-law's side.
3. His niece on his sister-in-law's side.

And it will also be observed that the principle affected by the proposed changes is the old Canonical law, that affinity creates the same relationship as consanguinity ; a law supposed to be based on the divine precept, ' they twain shall be one flesh,' and on the inspired comment, ' this is a great mystery '—something that is not to be dissected by cold human reason, but rather accepted by faith as a sacramental verity.

Your Committee, first of all, viewed the proposed changes in the practical light of the inquiry,. How would they operate on existing and time-honoured institutions? We find that in ultimate analysis they touch the whole fabric of society, and introduce a radical change into the constitution of the Christian family. This change, by parity of reason, must lead to a system of innovations of the same grave character, but such as would now be tolerated by no body among Christians.

In the next place, your Committee find that the laws which must be remodelled, in order to legalise the marriages proposed, are laws which rest, by no means, upon the legislation of any single Church ; they are, on the contrary, laws which have been for ages universally respected by all Christians from the beginning, and handed down to us, not merely as the dictate of human prudence, but as a principle most sacred and fundamental, resting on the sure warrant of God's Holy Word.   :

Two principles of sound Churchmanship are thus brought prominently to mind and conscience, as bearing on the subject. First of all, this Church professes to receive whatever comes to us by unanimous consent, provided it be not contrary to God's Word ; and we are sure that what is contrary to that Holy Word has never been universally consented to in the Church of Christ. But this principle becomes more potent when affirmatively stated in behalf of laws which rest on unanimous consent as to what God's

3

Word positively enjoins. Now, the unbroken testimony of ancient authors as to the requirements of Holy Scripture in respect to holy matrimony is faithfully presented us in the old table aforesaid, and this consent of antiquity is justly respected in the voice of our Mother Church, which asserts that the prohibitions in question rest not on laws merely ecclesiastical, but are essentially divine.

But, again, this Church professes herself 'far from intending to depart from the Church of England in any essential point of doctrine, discipline, or worship'; and surely, if words mean anything, the *doctrine* and *discipline* of the Church of England as to marriage and the constitution of the family are here reaffirmed; for what can be more *essential* than these to the preservation of Christian morals and civilisation? Now, ever since her blessed reformation, and even before, the Church of England has published constantly, and has set up in her churches to be read by all men, a 'Table of Kindred and Affinity, wherein whosoever are related are forbidden in Scripture (and our laws) to marry together.'

Unless the Church of England and all the ancient Churches of Christendom have erred from the beginning as to the requirements of Holy Scripture in the fundamental doctrine and morals of holy matrimony, the questions now raised have in view nothing less than a relaxation of the law of God as revealed in His Holy Word.

And here, in our opinion, two practical considerations must be examined. First, even supposing it lawful, is it wise to accept a novel interpretation of Scripture against such overwhelming testimony? What that we hold sacred is not endangered if we begin to prefer new and private opinions to the grand system of Catholic interpretation, as it has been accepted alike by Protestants and Romanists amid all their differences upon other matters, some of them unspeakably less important? And, secondly, is any injury done to society or to Christian morals by the operation of the law which our House of Bishops, in 1808, regarded as obligatory in this Church? If so, is the evil complained of so great as to call for a remedy which many will regard as worse than the disease itself? So we must regard any abrogation of laws which the vast majority of Christians have always regarded as enacted by the Spirit of God.

In the consideration of these inquiries we have reached our practical conclusions. And here we might naturally introduce the testimony of a great cloud of witnesses who have always been regarded as authorities in this Church, and in the light of whose learning and wisdom we have been forced to our convictions. Such citations, however, seem to us unnecessary, because no qualified opponent disputes the fact that such authorities may be quoted in our favour to an almost unlimited extent. It will be said, however, that eminent critics disallow their expositions and contradict their conclusions. This is true; and we are not disposed to under estimate their just influence, nor to deny the respectability of their names. Starting from their premises, their conclusions may be honestly, though not necessarily, reached; and we are glad to recognise the fact that some who have accepted their ingenious argumentation, in all honesty and purity, as a practical rule, have a claim to our respect, in view of the good and great men whose opinions have overcome their scruples. But we cannot admit that the Scriptural argument is to be settled on their principles. Even where two expositions are admissible on grounds of mere criticism, we hold that the novel exposition must perish before that of the whole Church for fifteen hundred years. We do not see how this canon of interpretation is to be gainsaid; but, unless it can be refuted, the law we are now considering is the Law of God. And now, as to any evils which are supposed to arise from the prohibitions before us. Nothing in the old

5

table is even imagined to work a social wrong except the point touching a deceased wife's sister. This is thought to bear with painful severity on some who have contracted the prohibited relations ; and also, it is urged, that it prevents marriages which would greatly benefit a widower looking for a second mother to his children.

But if these prohibitions, as we have argued, are divine, no such views of mere expediency are of any weight in our inquiry. And even should we be constrained to admit the lawfulness of the marriages in question, we suppose a very grave doubt would still remain as to the expediency of giving privileges *to the few* at the cost of *enormous disadvantages to the many.* This consideration merits a few words to explain the importance with which it is invested in our minds.

The severity with which the present state of the laws bears on a few individuals who have been united in wedlock in defiance of them, entitles them to our sympathy if they have innocently encumbered themselves in this way. But it is a great duty of the Church to warn her children against even questionable conduct in matters so serious. To mitigate the penalties of indiscretion, by removing all obstacles to conduct which has always been censured by Christian moralists, is to stimulate the multiplication of cases which can never be wholly freed from a taint of illegitimacy. ' Whatsoever is not of faith is sin '; but how can it be a matter of *faith*, even if it be a tolerated opinion, that something is right which from the beginning has been severely censured by the whole Church? No tender conscience can be quite easy in defying such considerations. Legislate as you may, the marriage of a deceased wife's sister will remain unlawful and scandalous in the convictions of a large portion of the Christian community. Is it expedient to encourage such marriages? ' Whatsoever is of good report, wherein there is virtue and wherein there is praise,' is commended to us as practical duty.

6

Such marriages are of *evil report* almost everywhere. They are not commonly the subject of *praise*, and the Fathers of the Church often censure them as by no means the fruit of virtuous and continent living. If made lawful we shall find the clergy, and, possibly, even bishops involved in them, and so becoming a scandal to thousands of conscientious souls in the communion of the Church. Nor will changing the law change the fact that all Christians who reverence Holy Scripture as interpreted by ancient authors, must always be conscientiously opposed to such marriages. It follows that the peace of families will be sacrificed wherever a daughter is induced to make such relations against the convictions of parental love. To shake the established order of Christian society in behalf of a few exceptional cases, at the expense of those who are content with the time-honoured constitution of the family, is largely to increase the sources of domestic unhappiness, and seems to us the reverse of wisdom.

As to the other point. For one, here and there, who seeks a sister-in-law to wife, there are hundreds who prefer to find in such a relation a sister only. But if you make her the candidate for a possible succession to her sister as her brother-in-law's second wife, a sister she can be no longer. She can no longer render a sister's services during a long illness to her dying sister, the married wife ; and delicacy must lead her to quit the home of her brother-in-law as soon as the wife dies—that is, at the very moment when her services are ordinarily most required. She cannot continue to show a particular and tender interest in her young nephews and nieces without incurring painful suspicion. In such circumstances, as *things now are*, a sister-in-law becomes the natural and pure source of aid and comfort to children, and this is specially true in *the homes of the poor*. It is said she is therefore the rather eligible as a successor to the deceased. But this idea is founded

7

on the sisterly relation created by the law *as it now exists.*
Change this law : there will be no more sisters-in-law ; the
wife's sister will be turned out of the family organisation, or,
in violation of feminine propriety, she will remain in it in a
very equivocal position, such as compromises a woman in
the estimation of her own sex. Among the poor, as we
have said, the relation of a sister-in-law to her sister's
husband is often practically that of an own sister ; and,
while she is so regarded, she is a most important and
useful member of the household. Admit the thought of
future marriage : this honourable position is changed, and
becomes one of great peril. In a long illness of the wife,
relations are formed and pledges are prematurely inter-
changed as to prospective marriage, and guilt too commonly
ensues. Imagine the condition of a dying woman who sees
such a state of things around her as she declines into the
grave. We are informed that in England the agitation for
a change of law has already produced such bitter fruits in
the lower walks of social life.

These considerations lead us to believe that this Church
can perform no higher duty to the American people than to
guard them by her testimony against any change, even in
popular opinion, as to the laws of God governing the institution and relation of marriage.

They respectfully propose the passing by both Houses
of the General Convention of the declaration made by the
House of Bishops in 1808, in the form of a resolution, as
follows :

Resolved—That '*the old Table of Affinity and Kindred,
wherein whosoever are related are forbidden in Scripture to
marry together,* is now obligatory on this Church, and must
remain so unless there should hereafter appear cause to
alter it without departing from the Word of God, or en-
dangering the peace and good order of this Church.'

But while reporting this resolution it is the unanimous

8

opinion of the Committee that it should lie over for consideration at the next Convention, it being obviously too late to give it adequate attention at this time.

A. CLEVELAND COXE,
Bishop of Western New York.

A. N. LITTLEJOHN,
Bishop of Long Island.

HENRY A. COIT,
PHILANDER K. CADY, } *Priests.*

BENJ. STARK,
ORLANDO MEADS, } *Laymen.*

October, 1880

*** The Minority Report was signed by only two members out of the whole number (8) constituting the Committee. So far as those appointed from the Lower House are concerned, the Report, as reprinted above, was unanimous.

RECENTLY PUBLISHED.

TRACT XXXIV. REPORT OF THE UPPER HOUSE OF CONVOCATION OF CANTERBURY, JULY 1883, ON THE MARRIAGE LAWS. Price One Halfpenny.

MAY ALSO BE HAD.

REPORT OF THE LOWER HOUSE OF CONVOCATION. Price Twopence.

Price One Halfpenny.

Spottiswoode & Co. Printers, New-street Square, London.

Marriage Law Defence Union Tracts.

No. XXXVIII.

OFFICE : 1 KING STREET, WESTMINSTER, S.W.

The Church of England

*In its Diocesan Conferences in 1883 on Marriage
with a Wife's Sister.*

THE opinion of the whole Church of England (when
it can be certainly reached) is of great importance to
the whole country. Churchmen will naturally defer to
it, and nonconformists cannot deny that if they differ
from it they will have to reckon with a great power
in England.

The new machinery of Diocesan Conferences, in
which the laity join the clergy on equal terms in
deliberating on the Church's concerns, gives means for
reaching that opinion, which on the question of
marriage with a wife's sister has spoken with no
uncertain sound.

Diocesan Conferences were held, with very few
exceptions, in the various dioceses of England
during the last year ; the question of legalising marriage with a wife's sister came before nineteen of
them, and, as will be seen, in no single case was the
innovation approved.

2

BATH AND WELLS.

Sir A. A. Hood moved the following resolution :

'That this Conference desires to express its best thanks to the Bishops for their united and determined opposition to the Marriage with a Deceased Wife's Sister Bill ; and would respectfully urge upon them continued resistance to any change in the law which shall violate the Table of Kindred and Affinity, contained in the Prayer Book.'

Major Paget, M.P., seconded.

The motion was carried with but one dissentient vote.

CANTERBURY.

Mr. J. G. Talbot, M.P., moved the following resolution, which was adopted by a large majority of the Conference :

'The diocesan Conference of the clergy and laity of the diocese of Canterbury expresses its thankfulness for the action of the bishops in the matter of the Bill for legalising marriage with the sister of a deceased wife, and records its distinct opinion that the proposed measure is (1) in contravention of the teaching of Holy Scripture ; (2) in subversion of the continuous practice of the Christian Church ; and (3) would, if it became law, be injurious to the peace of the family and to general morals.'

CARLISLE.

The Rev. W. Jones moved :

'That whilst this Conference rejoices at the rejection by the House of Lords, on June 28, 1883, of the Bill for legalising marriage with a deceased wife's sister, it has reason to apprehend a renewal of the agitation upon this question, and believing that there is much ignorance of the principles of Christian marriage, it would urge the clergy of the diocese to give more instruction in the doctrine of holy

3

matrimony, its sanctity, and the limits which are its safe-guards.'

The motion was seconded by the Rev. R. H. KIRBY, and carried with one or two dissentients.

CHICHESTER.

Dr. SANDERSON moved :

'That this Conference is resolutely opposed to all attempts to alter the existing law of England which prohibits marriage with a deceased wife's sister, because such mar-riages (1) are plainly repugnant to Holy Scripture ; (2) would be gravely injurious to the purity and happiness of married life; and (3) if sanctioned by the Legislature, would place the law of the land in conflict with the law of the Church.'

The Dean of CHICHESTER seconded the motion, which was carried *nem. con.*

DURHAM.

Two papers were read condemning any relaxation of the law prohibiting marriage with a deceased wife's sister.

ELY.

Canon LOWE moved:

'That this Conference respectfully requests his lordship the President to use every influence at his command, both in his place in Parliament and elsewhere, to prevent the introduction of any change in the Deceased Wife's Sister Bill which shall permit the ceremony of marriage to be performed in our churches over persons who wish to avail themselves of the Act, or which shall permit the clergy to read the marriage service in church after such persons have been married at the registrar's office.'

The Chancellor (Dr. I. BRUNEL) seconded, and the motion was carried unanimously.

4

EXETER.

Mr. SHELLY (Mayor of Plymouth), seconded by Prebendary KEMPE, moved:

'That the attempt to legalise marriage with a deceased wife's sister should be resisted to the utmost, and that every possible effort should be made to diffuse information on the true principles of the law of marriage.'

The motion was agreed to, with only three dissentients.

LICHFIELD.

Mr. STANLEY LEIGHTON, M.P., moved :

'That the best thanks of the Conference be given to the House of Lords for their brave, wise, and so far successful opposition to the Bill for legalising marriage with a deceased wife's sister.'

The motion was seconded by Canon LONSDALE, and carried, only two dissentients.

LIVERPOOL.

Canon E. H. McNEILE moved:

'That this Conference holds the Table of Prohibited Degrees set forth by authority and commonly printed in our Prayer-books, to be in accordance with the Word of God, and is therefore opposed to any legalisation of unions therein forbidden.'

Canon CLARKE (of Southport) seconded the motion.

The Rev. R. G. MATTHEW (Wigan) moved, and the Rev. H. MITCHELL seconded, the following amendment:

'It is inexpedient to disturb the present marriage law as it is based upon clear principle, which cannot be said of any proposed emendation.'

Which was carried unanimously.

5

LONDON.

Mr. BERESFORD HOPE, M.P., moved :

'That this Conference is of opinion that any alteration of the existing law which would legalise the union of a man with the sister of his deceased wife is to be strenuously resisted.'

Cannon GREGORY seconded the motion, which was supported by Earl CAIRNS, and carried, with two or three 'Noes' to it.

MANCHESTER.

Moved by Lord EGERTON of TATTON, seconded by the DEAN of MANCHESTER, carried with acclamation :

'That this Conference heartily thanks the Bishop for his vote in the House of Lords last Session against the Bill to legalise marriage with a deceased wife's sister, and expresses its earnest protest against any such alteration of the marriage law.'

NEWCASTLE.

Two papers were read and discussed on 'The Marriage Laws,' 'Marriage with a Deceased Wife's Sister.'

NORWICH.

Canon FRERE (Finningham, Suffolk) moved and Chancellor BLOFELD seconded :

'That this Conference disapproves any attempt to disturb the principle of the Table of Prohibited Degrees by legalising marriage with a deceased wife's sister.'

The Rev. V. J. STANTON moved an amendment.

The amendment was rejected by 63 clerical and 27 lay votes against 8 clerical and 12 lay. The resolution was then put and carried.

6

RIPON.

Canon Temple moved and Mr. Collins, M.P., seconded :

'That the proposal to permit marriage between a man and the sister of his deceased wife rests on no sound principle, is opposed to the teaching of Holy Scripture, and if adopted is likely to be fraught with great social danger to our country.'

Mr. Collins then moved, and the Dean of Ripon seconded, as an amendment, the insertion after the words ' Holy Scripture ' of the following words, ' as understood by the Church, and expressed in the 99th Canon.' Canon Temple having accepted the amendment, it was carried, amid loud cheers, with only four dissentients.

ROCHESTER.

The Rev. E. J. Beck (Rotherhithe) moved :

'That this Conference, desiring to preserve the ancient marriage laws of the realm intact, and viewing with serious alarm the proposed relaxation by Parliament of the restriction which at present prohibits a widower marrying his deceased wife's sister, resolves to memorialise the Houses of Parliament and Convocation to this effect.'

Mr. W. H. Heaton (Reigate), as a Liberal, not to say a Radical, seconded.

The motion was carried by 60 to 9.

S. ALBANS.

Mr. Menet, seconded by Mr. H. H. Gibbs, moved:

'That this Conference considers it to be of the utmost importance that the most strenuous opposition should be offered to the Bill for legalising marriage with a deceased wife's sister, if it should again be brought forward ; and that every effort be made to inform and influence public opinion in order that the evils of any such legislation may be better understood.'

Only seven voted against the motion, which was adopted with practical unanimity.

SALISBURY.

Archdeacon LEAR, seconded by Admiral FULFORD moved a petition against this measure.

Mr. C. H. BASKETT moved as an amendment a petition in favour of the future legalisation of marriages with a deceased wife's sister.

The amendment was rejected by 112 votes to 13.

TRURO.

The Rev. Canon HOCKIN moved :

'That this Conference adheres to the law prohibiting marriage with a deceased wife's sister, as held from early times, and reaffirmed by the Reformers of the sixteenth century.'

The Rev. Canon THORNTON seconded the motion, which was carried unanimously.

WINCHESTER.

Moved by the Bishop of WINCHESTER, seconded by Lord H. SCOTT, M P., carried unanimously:

'(1) That a Committee be appointed for the purpose of establishing throughout the diocese an organisation for the purpose of spreading information as to the true position of the marriage laws of the Church and country, with special reference to the serious nature of the attack made upon them by the Deceased Wife's Sister's Bill. (2) To take such means as might appear desirable to prevent that Bill passing into law.'

Marriage Law Defence Union Tracts.

No. XLI.

OFFICE : 1 KING STREET, WESTMINSTER, S.W.

The Bishop of Liverpool (Dr. J. C. Ryle) on Marriage with a Deceased Wife's Sister.

[Extracted from his Address to the Liverpool Diocesan Conference in 1884.]

LET me here take occasion to say that the whole subject of a high standard of purity in the relation between the sexes, and the other kindred subject of maintaining inviolate and unaltered our present marriage laws, appear to me to demand the most serious and vigilant attention of all Christians, and of all British patriots, in these days. There is a most painful tendency at the present time to think lightly of the obligations of the Seventh Commandment, to trifle with sins which God has solemnly declared that He " will judge " at the last day, to set up two different standards of purity for men and for women, and to regard conduct in one sex as venial and pardonable, which is not regarded as venial and pardonable in the other. There is besides an avowed anxiety in some quarters to allow people to contract marriages which have long been forbidden in this country both by law and the general feeling of society. I will not trouble you with further details on this point, or bring forward arguments

2

with which you are all familiar. I will only remark that the permission to marry a deceased wife's sister, which some persons are seeking to have sanctioned by law, would certainly break up the happy family circle of very many, and would only gratify a very few. I believe, myself, that the number of men who want to marry a deceased wife's sister is extremely small. And worst of all, if the law were once altered in this direction, the alteration would certainly not stop there. No logical reason could be shown why men should not marry their deceased wife's aunt or niece, and why a woman should not marry her deceased husband's brother, uncle, or nephew. From such a consummation, good Lord, deliver us !

I make no apology for dwelling on this matter, for I am satisfied it is a subject for the times, and I can find no words to express my sense of the duty of resisting in every possible way the tendencies to which I have referred. Facility of divorce, and a general low view of the sanctity of the marriage bond, were among the leading sins which our Lord Jesus Christ denounced and condemned among the Jews. Besides this, I need hardly remind every reading man who hears me that impurity, facility of divorce, and a disgustingly low view of the relation between the sexes were leading characteristics of the days of the decline and fall of the Roman Empire. Even a heathen poet like Juvenal gives a fearful picture of the state of things in his time. Nor can I refrain from saying that at this moment the condition of society in the United States of America,—notwithstanding the marvellous progress of that great Republic in temporal matters,—is most unsatisfactory on the subject about which I am speaking. The triennial Charge of Bishop

3

Littlejohn, Bishop of the Diocese of Long Island, delivered this very year, contains statements of a very horrible kind about the growing frequency of divorce. I wish that Charge could be read by every one that hears me. I see it there stated that in the records of the County Clerk's Office of King's County, New York, no less than 300 fraudulent cases of divorce had been found in one year. I see it stated, in the same Charge, in the report of a speech delivered by Senator Brown of Georgia in the United States Senate this very year, that within the last twenty years 27,000 divorces have been granted in the State of New England alone. He further states, that in Massachusetts, within the last twenty years, population increased 44 per cent., and marriages 62 per cent., while divorces had increased 147 per cent. I do hope that all who hear me will ponder these facts, and not refer us to America or the Colonies for precedents to justify any alteration in our marriage laws. And I repeat the expression of my earnest hope that throughout this Diocese, at any rate, there will be an unceasing effort to uphold the cause of purity, and to maintain unaltered our marriage laws. We must remember that a nation is made up of families, and that any movement which tends to diminish family purity, and to facilitate divorce between husbands and wives, after the manner of France and America, is likely to do unmixed harm.

Marriage Law Defence Union Tracts

No. XLII

Questions as to the Purpose and Outcome of the proposed Changes in the Marriage Laws

BY THE

REV. R. C. MOBERLY, M.A.

VICAR OF GREAT BUDWORTH
EXAMINING CHAPLAIN TO THE LORD BISHOP OF CHESTER

LONDON

THE MARRIAGE LAW DEFENCE UNION

1 KING STREET, WESTMINSTER, S.W.

1885

Price One Halfpenny

Questions

&c. &c.

THESE questions are not addressed to everyone. They are not addressed to avowed enemies of the Church. There is even one section of Churchmen supporting the proposed alterations whom they would not touch. These are those who already recognise and intend all the ecclesiastical consequences here foreshadowed, but maintain neverthe-less the change of law on some such ground as that the people desire it, and that the people, being free to be Mahommedans or infidels, have a right also (if they so will by a majority) to Mahommedan or infidel practices. You have no right, such men would say, because you are Church-men yourselves, to enforce therefore penally upon all, the limitations which properly belong to the Church of Christ.

However faulty such a position may be, the present questions make no attempt to touch it. But if anyone is inclined to support the proposed changes, neither with a view to all these consequences, nor yet as an enemy to the Church, these questions are addressed to him. Their object is to make such an one gauge more accurately the real purport and outcome of his action. Their success would be that they should compel such an one to choose between

3

supporting the Bill on the line here indicated only, or changing his support to opposition.

For hitherto, of all the arguments currently used on either side of the question—*against* the Bill not less than *for* it—an extraordinary proportion appear to be based upon the tacit and unexamined assumption that what is proposed is really a change of Church law as well as State law ; so that if the present agitation should be successful, the new marriages (instead of setting Church and State in sharp antithesis) would themselves be allowed by Church as well as by State ; that they would be to English Churchmen, as well as to outsiders, 'lawful' ; misliked, perhaps, by some Church authorities ; even repudiated, perhaps, by some individuals ; but none the less freely accepted, and to be accepted, in ordinary, well-conducted, Christian, English society.   Let anyone consider for himself how many of the current arguments, whether 'pro' or 'contra,' would cease at once to be relevant, if this assumption were once unequivocally withdrawn.

---

(1) You think it desirable that the marriage law should be altered.   Which law? the law of the State, or the law of the Church ?

If the latter ; then

(2) By what means could such an alteration be brought about ?

(3) What steps are you taking with a view to the proposed alteration ?

(4) Upon what line of argument do you rely ?

If the former ; then

(5) What will be the condition of things reached in the event of your success ?

(6) Do you suppose that by the alteration of English

4

Statute law, the belief and rule of the Church will be *ipso facto* altered?

(7) If you think so, do you expect acquiescence in this position, and its resulting consequences, on the part of the Church?

(8) Or, if not, then are you prepared, in the teeth of the Church herself, to maintain (by penal legislation or otherwise) that the rule of the Church is changed?

(9) If you do not maintain this, then do you contemplate, on the other hand, creating a gulf between State law and Church rule on this subject?

(10) Do you contemplate legalising marriages which are nevertheless to be stigmatised by the Church as incestuous?

(11) If so, what effect do you anticipate upon the action of the Church herself?

(12) Is it not probable that, if that be declared to the English people to be lawful which she holds to be incestuous, she will find it necessary to restate with fresh emphasis, for the information of her own children, and for her own internal discipline, the lines of her own rule?

(13) Considering that individual questions (perhaps about marrying, certainly about receiving to Communion) must presently arise, and, having arisen, must presently be pressed to authoritative decision; do you think it even a possibility that the Church should long continue without being compelled, *either* expressly to sanction *or else* unmistakably, with whatever consequences, to ban the new alliances.

(14) Much reference has been made to the example of the Colonies. Have the Colonies any experience on this point? *

(15) Do you rely upon the difficulty which the Church

* See the Note.

5

may experience in England in giving adequate effect to her own mind?

(16) Do you propose to include in the new law any provisoes as to the action of the Church, or of individual Church officers?

(17) If such marriages are legalized, is it contemplated that the Church shall have complete freedom secured to her to pronounce and enforce, as she may deem necessary, the excommunication of those who avail themselves of the law?

(18) If, in point of fact, all such persons as may be relieved by the change of law, or take advantage of it, should find themselves hereafter rejected from Communion, would this accord with what you expect and desire?

(19) Do you contemplate attempting to compel clergymen, by force of law, either to perform such marriages, or to allow them to be performed?

(20) If an individual clergyman should agree with the law, and perform a marriage in accordance with it, is it contemplated that he should be defended, by force of law, against effective ecclesiastical punishment?

(21) Or do you contemplate, on the contrary, the necessity of securing to the Church adequate facility for punishing him, in accordance with her own view of what he has done?

(22) If the feeling throughout the Church be very strong, not only as to the policy or impolicy, but as to the right and wrong of these matters; is it not probable that the demand for freedom in whatever is necessary for pronouncing and enforcing her own rule within her own borders, will become increasingly general and increasingly urgent?

(23) As a politician, do you not feel bound to give full force to such a probability?

(24) As a politician, do you not consider that the cir-

6

cumstances which you will create by altering the law, make the demand in itself a fair, and even necessary, one?

(25) As a Churchman, do you not feel that by taking part in any such alteration, you will yourself be pledged—not merely to accept or allow, but to strain every nerve to secure to the Church such power to declare her own rule, and exercise her own discipline, as the new circumstances will cause her to demand?

(26) Do you desire the Disestablishment of the Church in England?

(27) Do you not consider that the danger created to the Establishment by so sharp an antagonism between Church and State on a vital matter, as the change of law would produce, will be even acuter, and more immediate, than any other with which it is threatened?

(28) Do you think that that danger could anyhow be averted, otherwise than by securing to the Church, simultaneously with the change of law, such freedom as has been indicated?

(29) And if not; then is it not true to say that the proposed change of law would affect Church and State so deeply, that it must, of necessity, lead either to a remarkable modification of the existing terms of the Establishment, or to Disestablishment; or, in other words, that Disestablishment itself could only be averted by such a modification of Establishment, as has had hitherto, in England, no precedent?

NOTE.—As a contribution towards the answer to this question, the following extracts, taken from the charge (1880) of the venerable Metropolitan of Canada, are very noteworthy.

'If, then, persons married "otherwise than God's word

7

doth allow are not joined together by God, neither is their matrimony lawful," and what God's word doth not allow is assured us by our Church in the Table of Degrees, and in the 99th Canon ; if we as Canadian clergy and laity have acknowledged the Book of Common Prayer (which contains the Table of Degrees) to be "a true and faithful declaration of the doctrines contained in Holy Scripture"; if, moreover, a resolution of both houses of our Provincial Synod declares, that no clergyman of this ecclesiastical province shall knowingly solemnise a marriage forbidden by the 99th Canon of 1603, how can we deny the force of such solemn obligations ? I do not hesitate to say that if a clergyman of our Church do not consider himself bound by them, I cannot conceive any oaths that would bind his conscience, and I should distrust his declarations on any subject whatever.

   .   .   .   .

You may now ask of me, perhaps, what are we, the clergy, to do? I answer plainly, you are to decline to solemnise such marriages. If the State relax its obligations and pronounces marriage a civil contract only, the Divine law of the Church is still binding upon you. You are to be guardians, not betrayers, of public morals. Nor ought persons who live in incest to be admitted to Holy Communion.'

Compare also the whole ground and argument of the remarkable 'Pastoral Letter' of the Bishop of Bombay, July, 1882.

Perhaps the time is hardly yet ripe for more than indications of an answer, which will be formulated more definitely by-and-by. But there are words adopted by the 100 Bishops assembled at Lambeth in 1878, which in this reference begin to be of the very gravest importance, and may be said to have laid down already for the Anglican Church in and out of England, with something approaching to Synodal authority, the ruling principle of future formal action. The Lambeth Pastoral Letter incorporates the following : 'With regard to those questions in connection with the Laws of Marriage, which have been submitted to them, your Committee, while fully recognising the difficulties in which various branches of the Church have been placed by the action of local Legislatures, are of opinion that steps should be taken by each branch of the Church, according to its own discretion, to maintain the sanctity of marriage, agreeably to the principles set forth in the Word of God, as the Church of Christ hath hitherto received the same.'

By the same Author.

CHURCH MEMBERSHIP AND LAWS OF MARRIAGE.

Published by

Messrs. PHILLIPSON & GOLDER, Chester.

Spottiswoode & Co., Printers, New-street Square, London.

𝔐**arriage** 𝔏**aw** 𝔇**efence** 𝔘**nion** 𝔗**racts.**

No. XLIII.

OFFICE: 1 KING STREET, WESTMINSTER, S.W.

Six Grand Objections to Marrying with a Deceased Wife's Sister;

Being the substance of a Paper on the objections to altering the existing Law of Marriage, so far as to permit a Man to contract a union with the Sister of his Deceased Wife, prepared for, and, in part, read at the Church Congress at Reading, October 1883, *by* JAMES AUGUSTUS HESSEY, D.C.L., *Archdeacon of Middlesex.*

MY LORD BISHOP OF OXFORD,

You have desired me to read a Paper on the objections which cluster about the proposal to alter the existing Law of Marriage, so far as to permit a Man to contract a union with the Sister of his Deceased Wife.

I obey you without preface or introduction.

The objections to such an alteration may be classed roughly as (1) *à priori* and (2) *à posteriori* objections.

The former will include arguments against it,

1.—On *Scriptural grounds, i.e.,* because it contravenes the spirit, if not the exact letter of Scripture.

2.—On *Logical grounds, i.e.,* because the admission of it must, in strictness of reasoning, involve a great deal more than is contemplated, or, at least, than is generally avowed, by the promoters of it at present.

3.—On *Historical grounds, i.e.,* because it would go counter to the custom or enactment, or both, of the Church Universal down to the beginning of the fifteenth century, and of the Church of England both before and after the Reformation.

The latter, or *à posteriori,* will include arguments against it,

4.—On *Political grounds, i.e.,* because the success of a measure, pressed forwards by the means and with the motives which have in this case been brought into action, will weaken the obligation of Law generally.

5.—On *Social grounds, i.e.,* because it will produce an utter breaking up of the particular relationship invaded.

6.—On *Ecclesiastical grounds, i.e.,* because it will greatly disturb, if not fatally endanger, the existing connection of Church and State.

I proceed to treat of each of these, severally,* as briefly as I can. But the subject is a large one. It is one which has been agitated, more or less, for nearly half a century. A vast amount of literature has been bestowed upon it. And, dry and technical as it appears to be, it is connected most intimately and delicately with our collective and individual life.

I. Among the positions that are 'either read in Holy Scripture, or may be proved thereby' is most certainly to be included the prohibition to marry a Wife's Sister. The Chapter, Leviticus xviii., on which it is founded, does not form part either of the Ceremonial Law of the Jews, or of their Political Law, but of the Moral Law. This is self-evident, because its precepts are, as appears both from the beginning and from the end of the Chapter, a warning against transgressions which the Canaanites and other Gentiles committed, and for the commission of which,

---

* The First and Second Classes of Objections were, for want of time, not treated of before the Congress, and, for the same reason, certain other passages were somewhat abbreviated.

3

because they might have known them, they deserved rebuke. They could not, having been left to the light of nature, have known any precepts except those of the Moral Law. Therefore, the precepts contained therein, whatever they be, must be such as 'from obedience to which no Christian man is free.'

It may be said, however, that this particular connection with which we are concerned is not mentioned there *totidem verbis*. True. But then this is the case also as to a man's marrying his own daughter or his own niece. Specimens only of relationships are mentioned, but, these specimens granted, the law of proof by analogy and of converse comes in. It is said that a man may not marry his mother—analogously, a woman may not marry her father—and, conversely, a man may not marry his daughter. It is said that a man may not marry his aunt—conversely, a woman may not marry her nephew—and, analogously, a man may not marry his niece. So, it is said, a man may not marry his brother's wife—conversely, a woman may not marry her husband's brother—and, analogously, a man may not marry his wife's sister.

Unless, then, we allow these methods of inference in all the cases thus cited, and in others which might be cited, we ought, if we were consistent, to allow them in none. And if we allow them in one case, we ought, if we were consistent, to allow them in all. To do their penetration justice, the original promoters of the proposed relaxation perceived this. The first draft of Lord Lyndhurst's Bill, in 1835, specified by name the connection not merely of a man with his wife's sister, but of a man with his niece. Afterwards, to avoid the appearance of a *privilegium*, the Bill was recast in more general terms. And nearly the latest manifesto of the 'Marriage Law Reform Association' says that 'if the Bishop of Oxford, and those who think with him, would vote for the second reading of the Deceased Wife's Sister's Bill, and in Committee move an amendment including the niece, it is believed that none of the supporters of that Bill would be found opposing him.'

In 1882, in the House of Lords, Lord Dalhousie

4

candidly confessed that, 'in theory, no doubt, the cases for legislation of a woman's marriage with her deceased husband's brother, and of a man's marriage with his niece, were as strong as that which is dealt with in the Bill.' And, with similar candour, the Marquis of Waterford said that he thought that 'it was quite clear that in legislation we should stop with blood relations.'

This admission on the part of the Marquis reminds me that two methods have been tried in vain, in order to escape the difficulty above alluded to. One is to assert that there is a difference between consanguinity and affinity. Granted. But how can this be urged compatibly with any reference to the chapter in Leviticus, and any retention of the Table? For, *first*, the marriage of a woman and her husband's brother appears in both those documents—and this is a relationship of affinity, as certainly as that of a man and his wife's sister. It is to be remembered also that a union which is mentioned in the New Testament with great abhorrence, namely, that of a man with his father's wife, is a transgression of the laws not of consanguinity, but of affinity. And, *secondly*, the Table is founded on the view that, to the third degree, a wife's relations are considered to be as nearly connected with a man as his own. A man and his wife are, by God's ordinance, one flesh, and a circle is formed around them of those in near intercourse with whom they are necessarily thrown. Within the limits of this circle, as the Bishop of Exeter beautifully said, 'there is to be neither marrying nor giving in marriage.' The area contained therein is to be, as it were, a sacred precinct, the purity of whose air is to resemble that of heaven.

Driven from this method, which you will see is perfectly untenable, the next pretext is to assert that the list of prohibitions is part of the Jewish Political Law, not part of the Moral Law. This falls to the ground at once, for the reason I have before mentioned to you—and for another reason, which I have never seen confuted, that one of the prohibitions contained in it (to which I alluded just now, the marriage of a man with his father's wife), is noticed in the New Testament, and in remarkable terms of repro-

5

bation. Inconsistently, however, enough, the assailants of the existing Law can allege the example of the Jews when it suits them to do so. They say the Jews marry their wives' sisters. No doubt some do. But they are the Traditionists, the successors of those who, even in our Lord's day, made the Law of God of none effect by their Traditions. The Karaites, or strict abiders by the letter of the Old Testament, do not do so. But, supposing the Jews to have universally violated the Law, is it not possible that their isolated condition in the dispersion, their tribal feelings, and the location, in many instances, of only one or. a few families in one place, may have given birth to the violation? Be the case, however, as it may, the Altera-tionists—for thus we may designate them—can scarcely be allowed to repudiate the prohibition as Judaical, and with the same breath to cite the example of the Jews for transgressing it.

But I am reminded that the 18th verse of Leviticus xviii. says, 'Neither shalt thou take a wife to her sister to vex her, to uncover her nakedness, beside the other in her lifetime.' And I am told that the Septuagint version translates this literally. Hence it is argued, granting that such an alliance is wrong during one sister's lifetime, it is permissible afterwards. Now to pass over the considerations that it is at least curious that a case already provided for by implication should be mentioned over again—and that it is strange that a permission should occur in a chapter which is otherwise wholly concerned with prohibitions—it is worth noticing—1st, that the phrase, 'a woman to her sister,' and a parallel phrase, 'a man to his brother,' are, as every student of Hebrew knows, metaphorical expres-sions, and are employed in the Bible to denote two of the same kind or designation. It would, therefore, be an exception to common usage to interpret one of them literally here. As for the Septuagint translation, we know perfectly well that it was not made by one author, or by one set of authors, but by different men, at different times, and of very unequal knowledge of Hebrew. And it is more than possible that, this being a difficult expression, the translator merely, as in many other instances, rendered

6

the original word for word.   Its difficulty, and the example
of the Septuagint, were a double snare to the framers of our
Authorised Version.   But though, out of deference to the
Septuagint, to which they were in other places much
indebted, they gave this rendering in the text, they placed
an alternative rendering in the margin, which no doubt
is the true one : 'Neither shalt thou take one wife to
another, to vex her, to uncover her nakedness, beside the
other, in her lifetime'—*i.e.*, during the lifetime of an
existing wife.   Thus the precept is made to forbid Polygamy, which was just as much a breach of the Moral Law
as were marriages within certain degrees, and various
unnatural offences, mentioned later on, and just as much
practised by the heathen, whose example is emphatically
forbidden to the Israelites.   It should be added that, unless
this passage thus refers to it, Polygamy does not appear to
be forbidden in the Pentateuch.   Yet it is a violation of the
original Law of Marriage.

I need not detain you by discussing at much length
another interpretation of the verse, namely, that it indicates
a limitation of the institution of the Levirate.*   By that
institution, which was connected with Jewish inheritance
of land, if a man died without heirs, one of his kin, who
might be, but was not necessarily, his brother, was to
marry his widow.   And the issue of this marriage was to
be accounted not his own heir, but the heir of the deceased.
It has been supposed that the verse before us forbade him
to do this, if the wife of the deceased brother happened
to be the sister of his own wife, until his own wife should
have died.   Understood in this way, the precept would
imply some restriction upon Polygamy.   But is it likely
that a modified Polygamy would find place in a Chapter
otherwise wholly prohibitory, Polygamy pure and simple
being only forbidden by inference?   I reject this interpretation, both as strained and unnecessary, in the presence
of that given in the margin of the Bible, and as not hinted
at elsewhere.   There is also another reason against it.   If

---

* So called from the Latin word, *Levir* (Greek, ΔΑΗΡ), a husband's
brother, who, of course, is brother-in-law to his brother's wife.

7

admitted, it would introduce something connected with the Jewish Political Law, about which the heathen could not have known, into a section connected purely with the Moral Law. Besides, it is not urged by our opponents, but, I think, erroneously and too curiously, by some on our own side. I only mention it at all because the Law of the Levirate, *i.e.*, the allowal of a man's marriage with the widow of his brother under certain circumstances, has been made an argument for the lawfulness of a woman's marriage with her sister's widower. It is said, ' the latter prohibition could not be Divine, or the Author of Law would not under any circumstances have dispensed with the former.' Surely, we may reply, He who is the Fountain of Law may dispense with this ordinance at His good pleasure—just as, for the ends of justice, He dispenses with the prohibition of taking away life. We may summarily dismiss the objection. It could not be maintained for a moment, except at the expense of ignoring the Table. But even if it were maintainable, one does not see how it would serve the purpose of the opponents of the existing Law. Because a *widow without children* might, in that exceptional case, marry with her deceased husband's brother, does it follow that a *widower with children* (for that is an argument largely employed) may marry his deceased wife's sister?

A legal friend of considerable eminence has supplied me with some additional remarks under this head. I venture to quote them to you. He writes thus: ' The verses 6 to 17 make up a Statute-law, and a Statute most logically arranged. Verse 6 contains the general prohibitive enactment, "None of you shall approach to any that is near of kin to him, to uncover their nakedness : I am the Lord." Verses 7 to 17 contain specimens of the classes which come within that enactment under the words " near of kin." They show the scope of the prohibition.

' The advocates of the Bill found their chief argument upon the presumed negative pregnant contained in the 18th verse. They draw from it an inference which they set against the Statute-law expressed in the preceding verses. Were Counsel to argue upon any other subject before Lord

Bramwell by using an inference of this kind against a distinct enactment, what would he not say against it?

'The opponents of the Bill in both Houses of Parliament seem to me to be abandoning ground that cannot be shaken, when they are silent upon the authority of Leviticus. Should they not rather say, Here is the law laid down in the Bible. Will you vote against it? If the majority of either House were satisfied upon this point, they would, I think, resist it. Lord Bramwell himself said in the House of Lords, June 20, 1883, strongly as he was in favour of the Bill on other grounds, "If there were a Divine prohibition of these marriages, then there was an end to the matter, and they need not consider what might happen afterwards. They ought to say at once, No, it shall not be done."'

The truth is, that selfishness, and a determination to effect an object *quocunque modo*, in this as in the other specimens of arguments employed by them, have blinded those who are the real agents in the matter, to the unsoundness of what they adduce against Scripture, and the Scripturally-based inferences found in the Table. I do not of course imply that the many who have supported them are all actuated by selfishness—a large proportion see in the proposal something which is distasteful to the Church, and so join in the cry. But a vast number of persons are simply easy-going, and good-natured, and too indolent to examine the subject. I fear that among them are even a few Churchmen. And for their sake it is that the whole matter should be carefully examined.

II. I have trespassed somewhat on the second point: That the proposed alteration of the Law is objectionable on Logical grounds. I could not help doing so, for logic is simply common-sense formulated.

Something, however, may be added to what has been brought forward already. The Table is founded on principle. Break in upon that principle, and the whole collapses. If a man may marry his wife's sister because she is not connected with him by blood, and because that particular alliance is not expressly put down in the Table,

9

then a woman may marry with her husband's brother, because he is not connected with her by blood ; but that alliance is expressly put down in the Table.

If a woman may marry her uncle because that alliance is not set down in the Table, then a man may marry his aunt, which he is expressly forbidden in the Table to do.

The assumption which allows the one set of cases, must inevitably allow the other.

This has been already perceived. It suits the more cautious of the promoters to assert that they only ask for one relaxation. Though, as we have seen already, they allow that others must follow. The more candid, and the bolder, speak out. I may add just two instances to those already given. The late Lord John Russell, in 1859, said : 'The law would be utterly imperfect, unless it was further altered so as to make it applicable to both sexes, and to all the degrees of relationship which have been mentioned.' A meeting of two hundred persons at Leeds was held only a short time ago, at which a Resolution in favour of Lord Dalhousie's Bill was carried. A second Resolution was afterwards proposed—I am ashamed to say, by a woman— 'That a woman should be allowed to marry her deceased husband's brother.' This was carried also, six hands only being held up against it. There can, in fact, be no doubt that the whole Table must go, if one infringement is permitted. And this was the meaning of the indignant exclamation of a Member of the House of Commons, when he said, 'Why does not the honorable proposer marry his grandmother like a man?' In other words, why does he not confess that the removal of one restriction destroys the principle on which the whole Table is founded?

Until, then, we are ready to adopt what has now become, practically, the Code of Western Europe, which makes the only forbidden alliances those of parent and child in their several descents, and those of uterine brothers and sisters, we must abide by our Table. People have smiled at that anecdote which was current lately. It stated that a man married two sisters successively—that his son by his first marriage desired . to marry his daughter by the second. The father expressed his disapproval by saying, 'She is your sister.' The son grounded his demand by asserting, 'She is my cousin.' The case is, at any rate, a supposable one—when regard to Scripture, and to the Table founded on it, is swept away.

III. But I come now to the third ground on which the movement for the alteration of the existing Law of Marriage is objectionable. It would set at nought the best evidence by which a correct interpretation of Scripture is in this, as in other cases, ascertainable. This evidence is the historical practice of the whole Church down to the fifteenth century, and that of our own Church and nation since the Reformation. I have heard it urged, with some pertinacity, that in the very earliest ages of the Church these marriages were not prohibited. The fact is that we have no sufficient proof that they occurred. The first notice that we find of them is in the Apostolic Canons—a somewhat doubtful document, but probably in parts at least ante-Nicene. There, in Canon 19, one who had married a wife's sister is for ever excluded from the Clergy. And what was so absolutely condemned in the Clergy, could hardly have been creditable in the Laity. But, waiving this, it is an undoubted fact that St. Basil, living in the fourth century, spoke of marriage with a wife's sister with extreme horror, and as opposed to the practice among Christians delivered down to his day by holy men. This means that the Common Law of the Church was against it. After and about his time, such a marriage, and others prohibited, expressly, or by inference, in Leviticus, were condemned by Councils, and generally disallowed as contrary to the Law of God. Laboured efforts, indeed, have been made to prove that this was not so. But the statements brought forward are found, when carefully examined, to be quite beside the point. Putting aside Jewish interpretations, not a single authority has been produced which bears upon our question before Nicholas de Lyra of the fourteenth, and Alphonsus Tostatus of the fifteenth century. No doubt a great many additional restrictions as to marriage with cousins of various degrees, and even with persons of spiritual or sponsorial affinity, were introduced as time went ·on. But there is documentary evidence that the Church of Rome, which, from time to time, added so much to the Table, and now, for her own purposes, considers all the prohibitions to be merely of Ecclesiastical ruling, and so dispensable, did not venture to dispense with this particular prohibition, or others contained or implied in Leviticus, until the fifteenth century. Then began a series of dispensations to Kings and Princes chiefly, culminating in that to our Henry VIII. to marry his deceased brother's widow. Mr. Froude says that this dispensation was reluctantly granted by the Pope, and reluctantly accepted by the English Ministry. It was not, however, till 1563 that the Council of Trent formally asserted the power of the Church to dispense ' in *some* of the degrees named in Leviticus,' but without specifying which. A decree passed in the same session of the Council forbade any dispensation to be granted in the second degree, except to crowned heads, and for some cause of grave public interest ; thereby implying that in the first degree they could never be allowed at all. Cardinal Manning has said recently, that the Holy See can alone dispense in such cases, and that it never dispenses in such cases, except (1) rarely ; (2) with reluctance ; and (3) for grave reasons, and to avoid greater evils. That permission is not refused was manifested in the instance of Don Carlos, the Spanish Pretender, who troubled Queen Isabella. He had two wives, sisters to each other, and both of them nieces to himself. In Roman Catholic countries dispensations are more or less frequent, while in Protestant countries, possibly as a reaction from the super-additions of Rome, extreme laxity as to relationship prevails. And coincidently with this infringement on the original prohibitions, great facilities of divorce are supplied.

And now for England itself. No statutable prohibition even of the unions mentioned actually in, or inferentially gathered from, Leviticus, and formulated in the Table, existed until the Reformation began. But why? Because, when Christianity came to England, it brought the Common Law, as I have called it, of the Church with it, and

'Christianity became (as Mr. Dodd has well put it), and is still reputed to be, part of the Common Law of England. And so it became part of the Common Law of the land that marriage with a deceased wife's sister was unlawful. The prohibition was part of the law of England before any Act of Parliament was ever passed, or, indeed, any English Parliament existed.' No wonder, then, that, as we have said, the English Ministers accepted the dispensation to Henry VIII. of the collateral prohibition with reluctance. It was an innovation which shocked the moral sense. And probably this consideration, combined with one quite in the opposite direction—that of impatience at the vexatiousness of Rome's superadded restrictions—rendered the Parliament the more ready to pass the 32nd of Henry VIII. c. 38. By this it was laid down that 'no reservation or prohibition, God's law except, shall trouble or impeach any marriage without (*i.e.* outside of) the Levitical degrees.' The effect of it was, not to enact those prohibitions as of force for the first time, but, leaving them as they were, to assert the unlawfulness of any other prohibitions. It simply continued what lawfully existed on the definite and intelligible ground of God's (not the Pope's) ordaining, and of the Levitical degrees. Shortly afterwards, in Elizabeth's reign, the Table was formulated by Archbishop Parker, and has been printed at the end of our Prayer Books.

Of course the limit which the Table propounds may be called an arbitrary one. Granted that it is. But, by universal consent, a limit must be made somewhere. And the particular limit which has been made, namely, at the third degree, is, if there is anything in what has been urged hitherto, of Divine appointing. It is a *limes* DIVINO ARBITRIO *impositus*. Beyond the third degree of consanguinity and affinity, by Divine regulation a line is drawn ; and no one may presume to lay down another line :

'Sunt certi denique fines
Quos ultrà citràque nequit consistere rectum.'

Well, the Common Law of England and of the Church, as cleared from all accretions, and set forth in its simplicity by Statute, prevailed without interruption to 1835. Marriages within the degrees were, in the language of our 99th Canon, void from the beginning, in the sense that no woman could claim alimony, or restitution of conjugal rights, as a married person, from her pretended husband, if she had contracted such a union. Again and again they were declared void in the Ecclesiastical Courts—if impeached during the lifetime of both parties. Before the reign of James I. they were declared void, even after the death of one of the parties. But as suits in the Ecclesiastical Courts were nominally for the prevention of sin, by the breaking off of cohabitation, and as this was unnecessary after the death of one of them, the Civil Courts limited declaration by the Ecclesiastical Courts of the void character of the unions, and consequently of the illegitimacy of the issue of them, to the lifetime of both. Practically, therefore, they were only voidable, though intrinsically void from the beginning. And this technicality having given something like an excuse for their having been contracted, and some plausibility to the plea that the children were kept in undue suspense as to their position, Lord Lyndhurst's Act, to remove all ambiguity, and to remove all shadow of doubt or pretence of ignorance, set forth that henceforward, without any waiting for a declaration on the part of the Ecclesiastical Courts, they were to be considered void from the beginning.

One would fain believe, had it been possible to do so in the presence of the more than rumours of 1835, that this Act was passed solely from the motives which are set forth in its preamble. But it is impossible to do so. For, though the relief was expressed in general terms, there is little doubt that, as the Church of Rome commenced its system of dispensations to meet the exigencies of Princes, so the Statute in question was carried through in order to meet the purposes of a certain noble family.

I have now completed all that I have time to say of what I called *à priori* objections to any change in the law. But my treatment will not be exhaustive, without a consideration of what I have called *à posteriori* objections, viz., the disastrous effects which will follow, setting aside for a moment the inherent iniquity of the alteration itself.

IV. The obligation of law generally will be weakened, if this measure passes. The alteration cannot now be said to be called for by any mistake on the part of the real promoters of it. They have been well aware what they were about. The pleas they have alleged, like those which have been mentioned already, are not to be depended upon. It has been proved that the poor do not call for any alteration, and that, in fact, their feeling is strongly against it. But, even were this not so, would it be right to legalise sin ?

It has been proved also that no general and genuine cry for relief has been raised. But, even if it had, the Legislature would still be bound to pause, in a case relating to the Law of God.

And so with two other pleas, of which abundant use has been made :

It has been shown over and over again that though a few important names of Judges and Peers and Bishops have been quoted in favour of altering the law, such Judges as the late Lords Campbell and Hatherley, the late Mr. Justice Coleridge, the late Lord Chief Justice Whiteside, the late Sir Herbert Jenner Fust, with Lord Cairns, Lord Coleridge, and Lord Selborne, have invariably opposed it. That such lay Peers as Lords Shaftesbury and Salisbury, the late Duke of Marlborough, and the Duke of Argyll, are found on the same side of the question. And that in the recent Divisions in the House of Lords, twenty-four out of the twenty-six Bishops having seats there either voted or paired against the measure. That the late Premier, Lord Beaconsfield, disliked it and voted against it in 1879 and in 1880, and that one of the best speeches ever delivered against it was by the present Premier, Mr. Gladstone. If authority and intelligence are any counterpoise to mere numbers, they may have a place here.

It is urged that children are visited for the sins of their parents in this particular case. But, as I have observed elsewhere, if they are to be considered in this instance, what is to be said of the children of other incestuous unions, with or without the form of marriage, or of illegitimate children generally, or of children who, through their parents' extravagance and vice, have a miserable inheritance of poverty or diseased constitutions? It is not man but God who has ordained the relation of the sin or of the righteousness of parents to the condition of their children. 'I, the Lord thy God, am a jealous God, and visit the sins of the fathers upon the children unto the third and fourth generation of them that hate Me, and show mercy unto thousands in them that love Me and keep My Commandments.'

The fact is, that certain persons have broken or desire to break the law. And an agitation, now extending through almost fifty years, has been carried on by a profuse expenditure of money, with the view of obtaining a legalisation of their acts or intentions. And in order to gain their end, they have first exaggerated by hundreds the number of instances in which the law has been broken, and then urged that it must be a bad law because it has been broken. It is obvious to remark that such a plea proves much more than they want or profess to want. The laws of kindred and affinity have been transgressed in many points besides that in which they are interested. And it would tell against other laws than those which relate to marriage, in fact against every law in the statute book, for the 'Law is because of transgressions.'

The Preamble, then, of a Bill on the subject should be, '*Whereas it is expedient that whenever a law has been broken, or confidently alleged to have been broken, it should be repealed: And whereas certain parties have, at great cost, raised a cry that the law forbidding marriage of a man with his wife's sister has been broken: And whereas it is expedient that a particular alleged grievance should be redressed, without reference to any considerations how far such relief may bear inconveniently on the general law involved: And whereas it is expedient that no man's liberty should be restrained for the general good: And whereas all such checks on the power of Parliament as were contained in old Statutes, such as in the sixteenth century, in 25 Henry VIII. c. 22— " Albeit they be plainly prohibited and detested by the laws of God," and the like, are out of date in this nineteenth century : And whereas divers foreign nations have got rid of such reference to the laws of God, and it is expedient that their example should be followed : And whereas it is expedient that any legislation which has occurred in the Colonies should not be merely sanctioned there, but be adopted as a law of the Empire : And whereas permission of marriage with a deceased wife's sister is part of the legislation which has occurred in the Colonies : Be it therefore enacted by the Queen's Most Excellent Majesty, by and with, &c., that from the date of the passing of this Act, a man shall be permitted to marry his deceased wife's sister, any prohibition in the law of the Bible, or in the Table of Archbishop Parker, and any ordinance or custom of the Church Universal, or of this particular Church of England, or in the Canon or Common or Statute Law notwithstanding.'*

Now this is hardly a caricature ; but even if it is, would an Act which may so be caricatured weaken or strengthen general respect for Law ? What, with such an example before us, might we not expect in the future ?

It is bad enough when misrepresentation and money and perseverance combined bring their influence on Parliament and destroy some merely human institutions. It will be most miserable, and augur sadly for the State and Church which endure it, that such efforts should succeed in impairing a Divine law.

V. But what will be the effect of this alteration of the law, Socially ?

It has been already intimated that if the law is weakened by one invasion of principle, other invasions of principle must necessarily follow. Instances have been adduced which show that the supporters of the Bill not merely look forward with expectation but with hope that a woman's marriage with two brothers, and a man's marriage with his niece,* and certainly all marriages of affinity, will follow in the wake of the concession to a man that he may marry two sisters. But I will not dwell upon these more remote effects. I will just mention one that is immediate.

At present a wife's sister is in most cases thrown into such intimate connection with a man's family that she is regarded as his own sister. She is in his household as freely as his own sister, in his wife's illnesses or troubles. She is a most confidential friend of both parties, and at his wife's death she may live under his roof without suspicion, and become, during his widowhood, the kind educator of his children. No matter whether she is young or old, no reproach can attach to her. As the wife, when alive, is unable to look upon her as a possible successor in wifehood, so, after the wife's death, the world has not a word to say against her assuming an office which might, in any other young woman's case, lead to wifehood or unlawful connection, and might therefore be regarded as dangerous. The poor especially enjoy such adopted sisterhood, and the prospect of such motherly care being bestowed upon her children has frequently consoled a wife's dying bed. But not the poor only but those of the middle class, and even the opulent. Are they to be deprived of this comfort? I remember that a distinguished Member of Parliament, being then a widower, said to me many years ago with great indignation: 'Since my wife's death, I have enjoyed the greatest consolation in securing a most kind aunt's care for my children, and a most kind sister's ever-present attention for myself. Am I to be deprived of this because a few selfish persons have determined, *coûte qui coûte*, to abolish sisters-in-law, to prevent my having my children's aunt in my house, unless I am prepared to make her my wife? Granting for a moment that a sister-

* The Bishop of London said in the House of Lords, May, 1879, 'An advertisement had recently appeared in a newspaper calling upon those who desired to marry their nieces to support Sir Thomas Chambers' Bill' (to the same effect as Lord Dalhousie's) 'as a Bill to legalise such marriages would be sure to be introduced and carried soon after the present Bill became law.'

in-law or aunt is one of the best guardians for my orphaned children, why divert her affection from them to children of her own ? Why convert her into a possible step-mother? Even if the law of God were not against this union as incestuous, the dictates of the most ordinary rules of prudence would set us against legalising it as inexpedient.'*

Let me add that it is notorious that the feelings of the great mass of women are even stronger if possible against the measure than those of right-thinking men. And, moreover, that it is very hard that a maiden sister-in-law, perhaps without any home but her brother-in-law's house, should be unable, after her sister's death, to enjoy that protection any longer. If one were to compare the two relationships—that of wife's sister and that of a husband's brother, it would almost seem that the former, which is not expressly mentioned in Leviticus, requires hallowing by a Divine sanction, more than the latter which is expressly mentioned. A sister is more frequently, from the circumstances of the wife and from her own unmarried position probably, brought into contact with her brother-in-law—than a brother into contact with his sister-in-law. Of this, however, by the way. I only pause to ask, Are we willing to abolish sisters-in-law ?

VI. Lastly, what will be the effect of this alteration of the law on the discipline of the Church, especially in reference to one of its holiest ordinances, the Holy Communion, the consciences of those who partake of it, the position of Priests who celebrate it, and eventually of the Church itself, if this measure is passed? I will endeavour, as my last point, to show you this.

. You are aware of course that the 99th Canon of our Church speaks on the subject of Marriage in the following terms : 'No person shall marry within the degrees prohibited by the Laws of God, and expressed in a Table set forth by authority in the year of our Lord God,

---

* The Bishop of London said in the House of Lords, May, 1879, ' Very recently the painful case had been brought under his notice of a man who had married his deceased son's widow, and who defended the fact on the ground that he was the natural guardian of his son's children.'

1563. And all marriages so made and contracted shall be judged incestuous and unlawful, and consequently shall be dissolved as void from the beginning, and the parties so married shall by course of law be separated. And the aforesaid Table shall be in every Church publicly set up and fixed at the charge of the Parish.'

The Canon thus sets forth that persons related within the degrees expressed in the Table are forbidden by the Laws of God to marry, and as we have seen, the Common and Statute Law of the Land agree with the Laws of God. The Canon also speaks of such cohabitation as incestuous. In like manner the Prayer Book itself, in the form for publication of Banns, appeals to the Congregation whether they 'know of any cause or just impediment why the persons whose Banns are asked may not be joined together in Holy Matrimony, and if so, they are to declare it.' Before the marriage is celebrated, the parties themselves are solemnly admonished that if 'either of them know any impediment why they may not be lawfully joined together in matrimony, they are then and there to confess it.' For they are warned that 'so many as are coupled together otherwise than God's word doth allow are not joined together by God: neither is their matrimony lawful.' And the Rubric goes on to say besides this, that if any man do allege and declare any impediment why the parties may not be coupled together in matrimony, by God's Law or the Laws of this Realm, &c., the marriage must be deferred.

It is evident then that so far as our own Prayer Book is concerned, the Law of God and the Law of the land, as to Marriage, are at present regarded as coincident. It is further evident that persons related as a man and his deceased wife's sister presenting themselves to be married, could (for the Prayer Book is part of the Law of the land) be repelled as desirous of entering into an unlawful and incestuous engagement; and that if they have, by fraud or evasion, gone through the marriage ceremony, it is yet further evident that if they present themselves for Holy Communion the Priest may lawfully repel them as open and notorious evil livers (cohabiting in incest) until they have repented. And when this is reported to the Bishop, the Priest must be supported by the Bishop, and the offending persons must be proceeded against according to the Canon. These latter points appear from the Rubrics at the commencement of the Communion Service.

At present, then, there is no difficulty in these matters. But what if the State-law contradicts the Church? It is evident that then every one of the sentences quoted from the Rubrics about the banns and the celebration of marriage becomes nugatory and a mockery. That the Priest cannot celebrate marriage between a man and his wife's sister. But an alternative may be suggested—the State may have pronounced it lawful for them to be married before a Registrar, they are thus no longer in the eye of the Law of the land notorious evil livers. And it may be, it will be, that they present themselves for Holy Communion. Then how is the Priest to repel them without incurring grave danger? And how is the Bishop, without accepting the danger himself, to sanction the Priest's act? Yet both Bishop and Priest must resist if they feel that it is better to obey God than to obey man. They must pronounce the marriage to be void in the sight of God. The matter goes into the Courts; and the Church being an Established Church, and admission to the Holy Communion being asserted to be a Common Law right, and it being shown that the marriage is not forbidden by the Laws of the land, and it being assumed that the State could not in its wisdom have ordained anything contrary to God's law, the Bishop or the Priest, it may be, is sent to prison, and a conflict begins between Church and State, which may issue in the consummation of the wildest wishes of the Liberation Society.

It is not to be supposed for a moment that this is an imaginary danger. The Divorce Act may warn us of this. A Clergyman is not compelled to marry divorced persons, but he is not allowed to refuse permission to any other person, if he objects to perform the ceremony himself, to marry them. He probably tells his parishioners that he does not consider them married at all. They present themselves for Holy Communion. He refuses to admit them—what then? He must either admit them, or he must evade doing so. A case of this nature actually occurred. The parties consulted the late Dr. Stephens. He advised that they had a right to be admitted, and could maintain that right in the Courts. The conflict ended, in a manner no one could wish it to end, by the Clergyman absenting himself, and by another Clergyman officiating for him.

It is clear, then, that though a measure for permitting marriage with a deceased wife's sister may contain some clause like that contained in the Divorce Act, which may appear to relieve a Clergyman's conscience by giving him permission to refuse to officiate, or by relegating the office to a Registrar, such relief must very soon be found inadequate. No clause will meet the ultimate difficulty except one which shall expressly say, 'No Clergyman shall be permitted to receive to the Holy Communion any parties who have contracted matrimony within the prohibited degrees.' It will not be enough to say no Clergyman shall be *compelled*, for if any Clergyman were at liberty to receive such parties, the Church would be compromised and the congregation offended. ' No Clergyman shall be *permitted*,' must be the form. Whether it is likely that such a clause will be acceptable to, or passed by, the Legislature of the present day, I leave you to judge.* If the Bill does not contain it, then, I say, comes that last conflict between Church and State of which I have been speaking.

Such, which may God avert, would be the consequences to the Church of making what designing persons denominate, and easy-going but ill-informed persons passively or actively join in denominating, the small concession of legalising Marriage with a Deceased Wife's Sister.

It was not a small concession, but a grave national sin, in 1835, to validate retrospectively marriages of such a description, and others against the Prohibited Degrees, out

---

* I am told that a Society is in course of formation which is to contend that the Clergy shall be allowed to perform such marriages. This point gained, admission to Holy Communion would soon follow.

of respect to persons—though it was veiled under specious pretences of charity to children, and warning for the future.

> ' Fecunda culpae saecula nuptias
> Primum inquinavere et genus et domos.'

The Divine Law of Marriage was to a certain extent impaired. And

> ' Hoc fonte derivata clades,
> In patriam populumque fluxit.'

We are called upon to validate prospectively and perhaps retrospectively one phase of incestuous marriages—for ever. Let us pause, for a few months' time is allowed us, before we make up our minds to admit anything of the sort, out of respect to mere money.

If this miserable Bill of Lord Dalhousie's or anything like it becomes Law, see what will take place.

Holy Scripture, the virtual interpretation of Holy Scripture by the Church from the beginning, Canonical Law, the 99th Canon of our own Church, the religious feelings of the best disposed in our community, will all be set at nought. The authoritative Table of Prohibited Degrees, hitherto considered to be founded on the Moral Law, and to represent God's will, and thoroughly consistent with itself, will be maimed, and its remaining prohibitions reduced to a collection of dislocated human enactments. And many of these may be, as mere human enactments, and will be, repealed by-and-by. Consistency and cohesion will have disappeared ; nay, I can discover no reason, on the supposition that nothing is forbidden that is not forbidden *totidem verbis* in Scripture, why, even if some respect for Leviticus remains, a man should not be allowed to marry his own daughter. Thus there will be all sorts of complications, utterly breaking up the sacredness of family life. Then there may be even the dreadful spectacle of Clergymen contracting such incestuous connections as the law will then allow, or possibly, persons in very high station. Then there will be the situation of the Crown, and of the House of Lords, of whose all-but sanction of the measure, and of

23

the character of the influence almost successfully brought to bear upon it recently, I will not now speak particularly ; and of the House of Commons, in its tone, so far as this measure is concerned, ready to promote the views of the Liberation Society. And then there will be the position of the Clergy. Can it be supposed that if some of them would go to prison rather than be coerced into abandoning a Eucharistic vestment, which they believe to be legal, a vast number will not suffer great hardships rather than admit to the Holy Communion those whom they believe to be not really married, according to the Divine Law? Before these days of ours, Priests and Bishops also have endured such things for the Truth's sake. It is true of Ecclesiastics as well as of Soldiers, that

> ' Not once or twice, in our rough Island's story,
> The path of duty was the way to glory.'

And then will not the relations of Church and State, already strained, be strained to the uttermost? And then— but I will not further anticipate.

Shall we not imitate our adversaries, and be lavish of our means? Shall we not use our best efforts to diffuse sound information on the subject in order to avert all this? And shall we not employ another weapon, which cannot be really theirs, namely prayer, that 'God's continual pity may cleanse and defend His Church?'

We will do so, and find the words of that noble hymn come true,

> ' O God, our help in ages past,
> Our hope for years to come !'

Marriage Law Defence Union Tracts.
No. XLIV.
OFFICE: 1 KING STREET, WESTMINSTER, S.W.

Thirteen Objections to the Deceased Wife's Sister Bill.

BY THE

REV. A. M. WILCOX, M.A., Vicar of Spelsbury.

1. It is *contrary to the law of the Church.*

2. In the opinion of the vast majority of leading Church-men, it is *contrary to the Bible;* or, in other words, the Church law can be satisfactorily defended by Scripture warrant, viz., by the *general* and solemn prohibition in Lev. xviii. 6. Of the *particular* prohibitions which follow, as instances of the general law, the majority are marriages of *affinity*; and if the wife's sister is not expressly named, neither is a man's own daughter or niece.

3 It is *inconsistent*, selecting the wife's sister, but *not* the husband's brother, a corresponding connection, nor the wife's niece, an even more distant one.

4. It is utterly *selfish*, being promoted by a few *men, for their own gratification* and that of their friends, without regard to the widespread unhappiness it would undoubtedly cause to others ; and it proposes to *sacrifice women*, distinctly, and for the first time in our history, deliberately placing them in a position of marked inferiority and disability as regards the marriage tie.

5. It is *retrospective*, and therefore flagrantly unrighteous, proposing to declare that those who have already broken the law shall be held to have *not* broken it This is much as if a law were to be passed declaring murder legal, not merely in the future, but also in the past.

6. *Its origin is extremely discreditable.* It is notorious

that its first promoters were men who had broken the law and wished to escape the inconvenience of the illegitimacy of their children.

7. *It would create a breach between Church and State.* For all clergymen would still be bound to regard and treat such ' marriages ' as ' incestuous,' and yet the law would cease to protect them in so doing.

8. *It would be very cruel to hundreds of thousands of wives,* who would for obvious reasons fear to have their younger sisters staying with them, as they can freely do at present. In the case of a dying wife, afraid to have her young sister to nurse her and see after the children, the cruelty of the proposed law would be extreme.

9. *It would be very cruel to hundreds of thousands of young unmarried women,* who would be debarred from staying with their married sisters.

10. *It would be very cruel to many children,* viz., those who, having just been bereaved of their mothers, would be deprived also of the care which a maternal aunt can now extend without scandal.

11. *It is highly unnecessary,* because the number of men who want to marry a sister-in-law must always be an exceedingly small percentage : and of them there must also be a proportion whose sisters-in-law are unwilling to marry them. And here it may be noted that widowers are less numerous than widows, since the husband is usually older than the wife, and a man's life is not likely to last so long as a woman's.

12. *It would undoubtedly lead the way to still more odious licence.* In no country where these unions have been legalised has the relaxation of the Marriage Law stopped there. The wife's niece, and even the niece by blood, would soon follow the wife's sister as possible ' wives.'

13 Lastly, *it is a Bill for the rich, and not for the poor.* It is rich men's money which has *bought* the agitation in its favour ; and without that money the Bill would have had no chance at all, and probably would not have been heard of.

PRICE ONE PENNY PER DOZEN.

Spottiswoode & Co., Printers, New-street Square, London.

Marriage Law Defence Union Tracts.

No. XLV.

OFFICE: 1 KING STREET, WESTMINSTER, S.W.

The True Meaning of Leviticus xviii. 18, as translated in the Revised Old Testament.

The old translation of this verse, in the Authorised Version, is this :—

'Neither shalt thou take a wife to her sister [Margin, or, one *wife to another*], to vex her . . . . beside the other in her life time.'

The opponents of the ancient marriage-law of the Church and the State have tried to found on this verse, so translated, a direct argument—the only direct argument which they can even pretend to find in Holy Scripture—for the permission of marriage with a wife's sister after the wife is dead. On the other hand, it has always been contended that the true meaning of this verse was expressed by the marginal reading, 'one wife to another,' and that it had no reference whatever to marriages of consanguinity or affinity, but only condemned *polygamy*, which is an infraction of the moral law and was a sin of the heathen, against whose abominations the Israelites were warned both at the beginning and at the end of this chapter.

That this is the true meaning of this verse is now established by the consent of the learned Revisers of the Old Testament. Their translation runs thus :—

'And thou shalt not take a woman to her sister, to be a rival to her . . . . beside the other in her life time.'

Upon this it is to be observed, (i.) that, by giving no alternative reading in the margin, they show their conviction that the only possible literal meaning of the proverbial or figurative phrase אִשָּׁה אֶל־אֲחֹתָהּ has no reference whatever to consanguinity or affinity between the parties, but only to similarity. The expression means—as could be shown by its use in other parts of the Bible—'one to another'—'a man to his brother'—'a woman to her sister.' The Revisers exclude the idea that a wife's natural sister is intended, and extend the precept so as to imply the universal sisterhood of women, and to refer to any woman besides the actual wife. In other places the Revisers have translated this idiomatic phrase 'one to another.' If they have not done so in this verse they were probably deterred by their determination to be translators only and not commentators.

(ii.) The new rendering thus makes it plain that the verse is intended to prohibit polygamy, or the marrying more than one woman at the same time. And this relieves the whole chapter in which it occurs from two most serious difficulties. The first is that this verse, if it did sanction the marriage with a deceased wife's sister, would be inconsistent with the prohibition, by analogy and implication, of such a marriage contained in verse 16. The second is that this verse, so explained, would not only give an incidental permission to a certain marriage out of a prohibition—an affirmative out of a negative—but would be the only permission contained in the whole chapter.

Spottiswoode & Co., Printers, New-street Square, London.

𝕸arriage 𝕷aw 𝕯efence 𝖀nion 𝕿racts.

No. LIII.

OFFICE: 1 KING STREET, WESTMINSTER, S.W.

Why Abolish Sisters-in-Law ?

THE Scotch Bill for legalising marriage with a deceased wife's sister, which has appeared in the House of Commons, and is similar to the contemplated English measure which is down for its second reading in June, is more truly described as a Bill for the Abolition of Sisters-in-Law. And for the rightfulness or even the expediency of such abolition no case has yet been shown, no case can conceivably be shown. The pleas put forward by the ' Marriage Law Reform Association,' which is the machinery employed by the advocates of the measure, are of such a character that it is impossible to credit their authors and propagators with belief in their validity or their honesty, so misleading and irrelevant are they, taken at their best.

Of course that which is brought forward most constantly is the social and domestic argument : that when a widower is left with young children, no one is likely to make them so kind a step-mother as their mother's sister, not only their near kinswoman by blood, but so familiar with them already in most cases as to be much more favourably situated for dealing wisely and tenderly with them than any other possible wife could be, even if free from unworthy jealousy of a stranger's children. And this is more especially represented as ' a poor man's question,' it is constantly urged that his deceased wife's sister is his sole possible refuge in such a contingency.

But what are the real facts of the case when compared with this ideal picture ? Simply that, whereas wives' sisters must needs be reckoned by hundreds of thousands, on the other hand the number of men at any given time who want to marry into this particular class cannot amount to more than a few hundreds, taking an outside calculation. And the result of altering the law to meet the desires of this extremely small section of society is virtually to abolish the whole teeming class of unmarried sisters-in-law, to destroy the maiden aunts. For it is precisely because it is impossible in the present healthy state of the law for a woman in this position to be her sister's rival or successor, that she can live in the same house with her, and on the frankest terms of intimacy with the husband ; nay, that she can continue such residence after her sister's death without incurring blame or suspicion. Once make it possible for her to be her sister's competitor for the husband's affections, and she is straightway placed on the footing of any outsider. If she happens to be younger and more attractive than her sister, she cannot even be very frequently a visitor at the house; and it is quite impracticable for her to reside in it after her sister's death. The disadvantage thus wantonly created cannot be estimated at less than five-hundredfold greater than any convenience which could result from the proposed change, even if we were to accept the statistics of the Marriage Law Reform Association as genuine.

The refutation of the plea, so far as poor men are concerned, is simple : the wage-earning class is exactly that which is sure not to be advantaged by any such measure. And that because if a man wants to marry his sister-in-law, she must be there at her home for him to marry. But that is exactly what she is not in modern working England. The girls of poor families do not stay at home, they go out to work, to domestic service, or get married themselves, and home is just the one place where they are not. And, besides, while in the upper and middle classes childhood lasts long ; contrariwise, the children of the poor mature with notable swiftness, and begin keeping house for a widowed father at an incredibly early age, a fact which did not escape the acute vision of Thackeray; while, in addition to this, there is much more publicity and co-operation amongst the poorer classes than in those more prosperous. The neighbour of a poor man with small children and no wife will come in and 'do for him' as would be impossible with richer folks ; will light his fire and sweep up his room, and get his dinner ready for cooking, thus lightening much of his burden ; while very rich people can get rid of their burdens in other ways. The wife's sister question thus becomes mainly a middle-class question, and so the point to emphasize is that it is precisely the middle-class which must produce what we may call the raw material of sisters-in-law in the largest quantity. To enact the proposed change would at once, we repeat, destroy the unmarried sister-in-law for the whole of this class, and injure thereby unnumbered children, forcibly and needlessly deprived of their aunts, in virtue of a statute which would set up a diversity, instead of a community, of interests between husband and wife ; which would degrade the status of women by necessarily denying their equality of dignity with men, the equality of their union with men ; would bring chaos and anarchy into the place of a simple and intelligible principle ; and all this for no better end and motive than to give licence to the evil passions of a few wealthy reprobates of both sexes, who have either broken the laws of God and man already, or wish to do so. We do not alter our laws to facilitate burglary, arson, homicide ; though the number of persons who would be sensibly relieved by such indulgent legislation is much greater than of those who suffer restraint under the present law of marriage. Why should we make a difference in favour of the last ?

4

The stock answer is, that there is no express condemnation or prohibition in Scripture of the union in question, and that it is consequently open to Christians to contract it. Now, the honesty of this special plea may be judged at once from the simple fact that there is no explicit mention in Leviticus of a man's own daughter, nor any mention of his niece, amongst those of his kindred whom he is forbidden to marry (though a nephew is forbidden to marry his aunt) ; and from the other fact that all the prohibitions, such as they are, are directed to men only, so that it might be argued thence that, though men would sin by contracting the forbidden unions, women would be quite innocent in the matter, as not expressly addressed.

The truth is that the whole principle is governed by the one broad maxim laid down in Leviticus xviii. 6 : 'None of you shall approach to any that is near of kin to him'; while examination of the degrees actually enumerated shows that six of them are blood-relationships and seven marriage-relationships, and of these seven, more than half (four out of the seven) are concerned with the wife's kindred. As to verse 18, 'Thou shalt not take a wife to her sister, to vex her . . . beside the other in her lifetime,' there are two arguments against its being interpreted as a permission to marry a deceased wife's sister, which are singly of great weight, and jointly conclusive. On the one hand, to explain the verse as permitting the marriage in question is to throw it into contradiction to the rest of the code, to make it an unintelligible exception, with no assignable ground, so that there is a strong antecedent presumption against such a gloss.

On the other hand, the phrase 'a wife to her sister' is a peculiar Hebrew idiom, which need not imply any tie of kindred at all, but only plurality of number ; 'a sister,' in this collocation, meaning only 'another woman,' or even 'another thing.' This is no specious cavil, trumped up for

the occasion ; the fact is that the turn of wording in question occurs forty-two times in the Hebrew Bible, and in
forty-one of the forty-two it means only two persons or two
things of the same kind, that is, 'fellows,' and has no reference whatsoever to blood-relationship.   One example will
suffice in illustration, Exodus xxvi. 3 runs thus in the
Authorised Version : 'Five curtains shall be coupled one
to another ; and the other five curtains shall be coupled
one to another;' while the literal Hebrew here is : 'The
curtains shall be joined, *woman to her sister*,' so that a
literal translation makes sheer nonsense.

Consequently, the only sense which can be put on Levit.
xviii. 18 which will agree with all the facts is, that it is a
prohibition of polygamy, and at the same time a permission
for successive marriages of widowers ; or, to word it technically, it forbids bigamy, but permits digamy.   One very
important bearing, nevertheless, this verse has upon the
point in debate ; it destroys that appeal to the example
of Jacob which is one of the stalking-horses of the Marriage Law Reform Association ; since, if Jacob can be cited,
as he is constantly cited, in proof that Divine favour was
bestowed on one who contracted the particular union under
discussion, it is plain that the special circumstances of his
case are not only excluded from approval, but are specifically
condemned, so that it is not permissible to import his name
into the discussion.   Indeed, it may just be said here, once
for all, that any appeal to the earlier portions of the Old
Testament is disingenuous and misleading which does not
boldly face the question : 'Whom did Adam's immediate
progeny marry?' If Jacob may be quoted for marrying
two sisters, Seth must be equally quotable for marrying his
sister by full blood ; and even the Marriage Law Reform
Association is not prepared to go that length as yet.

That the Levitical prohibitions are not a mere clause of
the Mosaic code, no longer any more binding on Christians

6

than circumcision or the Jewish Sabbath, is clearly proved by the mere fact that the prevalence of the class of unions condemned in Leviticus xviii. is charged against the Canaanites as one of the especial sins which drew down the Divine judgments upon them, although they had never so much as heard of the Mosaic Law, and therefore could in no wise be treated as bound thereby, nor regarded as sinners for disregarding its precepts. Such marriages, therefore, are sins against natural law.

Another point needs to be noted here: that the relationship created by marriage is not terminated by the death of one of the married couple; for the prohibition of union with a step-mother, an uncle's wife, and a daughter-in-law, is absolute, though the affinity caused by these unions is bound up with the fact of previous marriage with a blood-relation, and with that only, but yet survives death.

As regards the precedents alleged in favour of the practice, they are reducible to four: the Jewish usage, the usage of pagan Greece and Rome, the usage of the post-mediæval Roman Church, and the usage of modern Continental Protestants, chiefly in Germany and Switzerland.

As regards the Jews, they are inconsistent in the matter. The Karaite Jews, who set Scripture above tradition, forbid unions of the kind altogether; and even the Talmudical Jews will not permit such a marriage in the case of divorce creating the vacancy. Moreover, it is to be remembered that we Christians cannot take the Jews as our guides in the matter of Scripture interpretation, seeing that Our Lord expressly condemned them for making it void by their tradition; and yet more forcibly, that if we follow them, we must accept their rejection of Him as the Messiah, and must acknowledge that He was most justly put to death as a religious impostor of the worst kind.

As regards ancient classical Paganism, its morals are

7

certainly not such as to offer them for our imitation, and the real use of bringing it into the discussion at all is that the fact comes out that speedily after Christianity became the religion of the Roman Empire, a law was enacted by the Emperors Constantius and Constans in A.D. 355, prohibiting all such marriages thenceforward ; while St. Basil the Great, writing about the same time, states clearly that they had been disallowed from the first by the Christian Church.

As regards the post-mediæval Roman Church, there are four facts of the utmost importance in the debate : (1) such marriages have never been permitted save by special dispensation, wherein some grave necessity must be alleged as the ground for its issue, thereby asserting the general obligation of the law dispensed ; (2) the actual ground for the issue of such dispensations has been almost always a money payment (thus not only giving a simoniacal colour to every such transaction, but making an unjust class-distinction between rich and poor) ; (3) the first grant of a dispensation of the particular kind in debate was made in the year 1500 to Manuel, King of Portugal, by the most infamous monster in ecclesiastical history, Roderic Borgia, Pope Alexander VI. (described truly by George Eliot as 'a greedy, lustful, and murderous old man') ; (4) the range which the dispensing system speedily assumed went far beyond anything claimed now, for the Act 25 Henry VIII. c. 22 (the first English statute bearing on the question) states : 'Many inconveniences have fallen as well within this realm as in others, by reason of marrying within the degrees of marriage prohibited by God's laws, that is to say, the son to marry the mother or the step-mother, the brother the sister, the father his son's daughter or his daughter's daughter, or the son to marry the daughter of his father, procreate and born by his step-mother, or the son to marry his aunt, being his father's or mother's

8

sister, or to marry his uncle's wife, or the father to marry his son's wife, or the brother to marry his brother's wife, or any man to marry his wife's daughter, or his wife's son's daughter, or his wife's daughter's daughter, or his wife's sister, which marriages, although they be plainly prohibited and detested by the laws of God, yet nevertheless at some times they have proceeded under colour of dispensation by man's power, which of right ought not to be granted.'

As regards the practice of modern Protestantism abroad, there are these points to be borne in mind: The marriages in question were expressly condemned by Luther and Melanchthon on the one hand, and by the Westminster Divines on the other, so that the existing usage cannot cite the leading Reformers in its favour, but merely exemplifies the 'down-grade' now prevalent all over Continental Protestantism (charged by Mr. Spurgeon against English Nonconformity also), which makes its claim to be so much as called Christian a matter of grave doubt, even if the fact be overlooked that the whole status of marriage has been weakened and degraded under its influence, not only by permitting unions implicitly forbidden in Scripture, as that between uncles and nieces, but by flagitious laxity and facility of divorce, making marriage virtually terminable at pleasure, and setting up a form of polygamy in its stead, to the unspeakable injury of society and the serious dissolution of morals. This remark applies also to the United States, where 328,716 divorces, often for the most trivial pretexts, have been pronounced within the last twenty years; a total compared with which the English record of 7,321 divorces in thirty years is almost a clean one.

Our law, so far as the Church of England is concerned, has remained unaltered ever since St. Theodore of Tarsus, Archbishop of Canterbury, published his Penitential in A.D. 668, and any apparent conflict between the secular laws and this prohibition vanishes upon inquiry. For the civil law viewed marriage solely in its aspect as a civil contract, and dealt with no cases save those where the parties were civilly incapable of entering into the contract at all. These were bigamy, impuberty (*i.e.* where the boy was under fourteen or the girl under twelve), lack of consent to minors from their parents or guardians, and insanity of either party at the time of marriage (of course because consent could not then be established). These, accordingly, were all cases of original nullity of marriage on civil grounds, and in no way touched the religious side of the matter, or raised any question as to impediments to marriage from that point of view.

All such cases, however grave, were left to the operation of the Ecclesiastical Courts. But one part of the procedure of these courts really opened up the way to the modern innovators. A distinction was drawn between marriages which were inherently void from the beginning, and such as were ' voidable ' if made matter of formal investigation in the lifetime of the contracting parties, but connived at if no such investigation took place, and allowed to stand after the death of the parties ; amongst which that with a deceased wife's sister was no doubt included. But no assumption favourable to this connexion can be drawn thence, since the actual scope of the matter is far wider, insomuch that Lord Coke, laying down what the law was in his day, says : ' If a man take his sister to wife, they are *baron* and *feme* ' (*i.e.* husband and wife), 'and the issue are not bastards until a divorce.' This startling pronouncement serves admirably to illustrate a most important distinction which is studiously confused by the innovating party : that between what is *legal* and what is *lawful*. For all things which the civil laws of any country enjoin or even permit are *legal* within the operation of those laws, and yet may be *unlawful* in the highest degree by the Divine laws or by the common rules of morality. Two contemporary examples will suffice : atheism and adultery are neither of them offences against the existing civil laws of Great Britain, they are legally open to anyone to commit if he pleases, and no penalty will follow. And if marriage with a deceased wife's sister were legalised to-morrow, it would still remain a sin.

Lord Lyndhurst's Act in 1835, by which the practice of the civil courts is now governed, has been carefully misrepresented by the innovators. What it enacted was that all 'voidable' marriages of affinity which had been neglected by the Church courts up to that time, so that they were all either those of deceased persons, or of living persons whose irregular unions had been connived at, were to stand good, but that all future unions of the sort should be not voidable only, but absolutely void from the beginning. It is pretended that this was the first prohibition of these unions, and that they were legal till then. This is knowingly false : the facts are that such unions were always illegal, only it was necessary to establish their illegality in one particular way, that is, by a suit instituted during the lifetime of the parties, failing which they were tacitly connived at ; but if any such case came into court, the judge had no option in the matter, he must have pronounced the marriage void. The object of Lord Lyndhurst's Act, so far as its retrospective clause is concerned, was not to establish the legality of such marriages in the past, but to protect the interests of children born from them, who would be most unjustly treated if bastardised in consequence of a marriage which no one had taken the trouble to prevent or break. But the Act did one piece of mischief. By the wording of one clause, it drew for the first time that distinction between ties of consanguinity and those of affinity which is now traded on, but which is unknown to the Bible and to old Christian legislation.

The Scotch Bill is drawn in such very wide terms that it

makes the marriage of a father-in-law with his daughter-in-law, or of a son-in-law with his mother-in-law, feasible, if a father and son happen to have married two sisters, and deaths occur, leaving a widower and a widow surviving, for in that case the widow is the widower's deceased wife's sister, and he may marry her, the Bill says: 'Any law or custom, or any canonical or other objection or impediment to the contrary notwithstanding'—words which amply bear out our contention as to their scope and force. The mere fact of such a draft having proved possible is enough to warn the public that even the wife's sister may not prove the single subtraction to be made from the list of prohibited degrees. The same lawless passions and the same unscrupulous agitation may just as easily be then brought to bear upon other parts of the table, and their erasure will be demanded on grounds of which it can be at any rate truly said, that if they are no better than those alleged in favour of marriage with a deceased wife's sister, they are at least no worse.

MARRIAGE LAW DEFENCE UNION TRACTS.

Nos. 1 *to* 43, *in one vol. cloth,* 2s. 6d. *; post free,* 3s.

TO BE HAD OF THE SECRETARY

AT THE OFFICE OF THE UNION,

1 KING STREET, WESTMINSTER.

𝔐arriage 𝔏aw 𝔇efence 𝔘nion 𝔗racts.

No LV.

OFFICE: 1 KING STREET, WESTMINSTER, S.W.

Is a Wife's Sister near of Kin to the Husband?

'BUT a wife's sister is no real relation to the husband.'

This is frequently said in reply to those who protest against the proposal to give Parliamentary sanction to marriage with a deceased wife's sister ; and it is said even by those who accept the Bible as the Revelation of the Law and Will of God.

Such people ought to be convinced if it can be shown that God's Word, reasonably understood, includes a wife's sister among those who are 'near of kin' to the husband.

The xviiith chapter of Leviticus contains the law prohibiting marriage between those that are 'near of kin.'

The xxth chapter prescribes *penalties* of death, &c., to be inflicted *on Israelites* for breaches of this law.

But the prohibitory law in chapter xviii. is evidently the Divine Law for all nations, and not simply a national law for Israel, as the Egyptians and Canaanites are condemned for violating it.   See xviii. 3, and 24 to 30 ; xx, 22, 23.

In the prohibitory law for mankind (xviii. 6), marriage is forbidden between any that are 'near of kin.'

This general rule forbids the marriage of those that are reckoned by the Divine Law as 'near of kin,' even if they be not mentioned by name in the list that follows.

For example, a man is forbidden to marry his granddaughter, so of course he may not marry his daughter, who is a nearer relation, although she is not mentioned by name.

As a man is forbidden to marry his granddaughter, so also he is forbidden to marry his wife's granddaughter, on the express reason that the wife's granddaughter is a '*near kinswoman*' *of the wife* (verse 17).

He is also forbidden to marry his father's sister, because she is his 'father's near kinswoman' (verse 12) ; and his mother's sister, because she is his 'mother's near kinswoman' (verse 13).

Putting these together we see

1. A man is forbidden to marry those that are 'near of kin' to him.

2. A sister is reckoned to be 'near of kin,' as indeed no one doubts.

3. A man is forbidden to marry those that are '*near of kin' to his wife*, as expressly stated in verse 17, and as implied in several other verses that assert the unity of man and wife as the reason why a man may not marry his father's wife (verse 8), his son's wife (verse 15), or his brother's wife (verse 16). This unity is the basis of the whole Marriage Law for all nations and through all time. (*See* Genesis ii. 24 ; St. Matthew xix. 3 to 9 ; Ephesians v. 28 to 31.)

So it is evident that God reckons a wife's sister as 'near of kin' to both the wife and to her husband.

And, therefore, if a man marries his deceased wife's sister, 'it is wickedness' (verse 17), and an 'abomination' before God (verses 26, 29, and 30).

Thus the general rules of the law prohibiting incest forbid marriage with a sister-in-law. ·

Yet some people suppose that verse 18 permits it ! !

If so, it makes a breach in an otherwise consistent scale of relationships, which includes all within three degrees of either husband or wife ! That verse is difficult to translate from the Hebrew into English, and difficult to explain positively, but it is almost certain for many reasons that its real meaning and purpose, at the time the law was given, was to guard a wife from being 'vexed' by other wives, and thus to check polygamy, and prepare a way for its abolition and the restoration of the original law—one for one. The Revised Version of the Bible makes this more evident, as we there read, 'Thou shalt not take a woman to her sister to be a rival to her.' 'A woman to her sister' is a Hebrew idiom usually translated 'one to another,' and is used in speaking of things as well as of persons ; for example, the curtains of the Tabernacle, in Exodus xxvi. 3.

Another common difficulty must be noticed. It is often said, 'A man was permitted to marry his brother's wife.' This is a mistake. In the *national law for Israel*, if a man died *childless*, leaving a widow, his next of kin was *commanded* by a special enactment to take the widow and 'build up his brother's house' (Deut. xxv. 5–10). Except in obedience to this rule, such a marriage was *forbidden* to Israel, under the penalty, 'They shall be childless' (Lev. xx. 21). It was also *emphatically forbidden* in the prohibitory law for *mankind.* (Lev. xviii. 16.)

It should be recognised that Parliament has no authority to change the law of God.

Sin will continue to be sin, whether Parliament condemns or sanctions it.

Spottiswoode & Co. Printers, New-street Square, London.

INDEX TO VOL. I.

ii

iv